DESTINY'S HEROES

CONAIRE MOR—The bastard son of Ireland's high-king, he was fated to be her greatest leader and know her deepest sorrow.

MEAVE—A daughter of the Sidhe and wife to a king, she was now disgraced and outcast, but the future of Ireland still held her spirit as no man ever could.

CONCHOBAR—The willful king of Ulster, he put nothing before his reign over the isle's strongest province.

CALATIN—An exiled high-druid, he served the high-king faithfully as long as it furthered his own dark plans.

SENTANTA—The youngest warrior of the Red Branch, he could not escape from the prophecy of the Sidhe.

CATHBAD—Bound to serve Conchobar, he was the only man with the power to protect Ireland from Calatin's evil enchantments.

ISLE OF DESTINY:

A Novel of Ancient Ireland

by
Kenneth C. Flint

BANTAM BOOKS

TORONTO • NEW YORK • LONDON • SYDNEY • AUCKLAND

ISLE OF DESTINY
A Bantam Spectra Book / November 1988

ISBN 0-553-27544-5

Published simultaneously in the United States and Canada

Bantam Books are published by Bantam Books, a division of Bantam Doubleday
Dell Publishing Group, Inc. Its trademark, consisting of the words ''Bantam Books''
and the portrayal of a rooster, is Registered in U.S. Patent and Trademark Office
and in other countries. Marca Registrada. Bantam Books, 666 Fifth Avenue, New
York, New York 10103.

PRINTED IN THE UNITED STATES OF AMERICA

KR   0 9 8 7 6 5 4 3 2 1

Inisfail, translated from the Celtic, means "Isle of Destiny." It is one of the ancient names for Ireland.

And lo, where afar o'er ocean shines
A sparkle of radiant green,
As though in that deep lay emerald mines
Whose light through the wave was seen,
'Tis Inisfail—'tis Inisfail!
Rings o'er the echoing sea;
While, bending to heaven, the warriors hail
That home of the brave and free.

"The Coming of the Milesians"
—Thomas Moore

Prologue

Long before the rest of it, in the swirling, sea-bred mists of the uncertain past, it began.

In a forest shrouded in a death cloak of white snow, six chariots halted. The clearing in which they drew up was very small, only a tiny patch in the gray weave of the surrounding woods. It forced the chariots into a tight ring. The drivers held back their teams, anxious to keep moving against the cold and snorting their impatience in white, short-lived blossoms of warm breath.

Beside the drivers, cloaked riders looked about uneasily at the unfamiliar pattern of the trees which rose above them like the walls of some high dun.

They were lost.

Across the whole of Ulster, across Slieve Fuad and Magh Grossa, between Fir Rois and Fir Ardae they had come that day, following a flight of birds.

A marvelous flight it had been, with nine flocks of graceful, gleaming birds like none ever seen before, linked two-and-two by silver chains, each flock led by a pair of multicolored birds linked by a chain of gold. Their appearance had drawn the

men from the fortress called Emain Macha at the insistence of
Cathbad, the ard-druid.

The hunters had pursued the birds until, quite suddenly,
the flocks had disappeared, leaving the men alone, without a
trail. And now the sun was setting. Across the gleaming snow,
long shadows flowed like black streams that multiplied and
spread, joining into one great pool of darkness that would soon
fill the clearing and engulf them all.

In the lead chariot, the rider shrugged back the hood of his
heavy cloak with an angry gesture. The revealed face was young,
lean, and sharp-featured, drawn by a tension that cut deep
furrows between the dark eyes and around the thin, tight mouth.
He held himself stiffly erect and fixed a burning look upon the
trees which barred their way.

In the group at his back, a rider in a druid's cloak of many
hues leaned toward the rider in the chariot close beside him.

"Just look at how the man glares about," he murmured. "As
if his will alone could command the trees to open a way for
him!"

The one addressed looked toward the speaker in astonishment. He was a giant man, hoodless in the cold, the curling
red hair and beard which framed his massive head flickering
like flames against the cold background.

"Go gently, Cathbad," he warned quietly. "Conchobar isn't
likely to find your barbed wit so amusing now that you've lost
us here."

"Is that so?" the other replied, a sardonic smile animating
the long, placid face. The ard-druid was not in the least concerned. He knew that the powers which had led them there
would show them where and when they should go now. He
could feel that they were already near their goal.

The tall man in the lead chariot must have sensed these
powers too. He stirred uneasily and swept his gaze over the
men who waited behind him. It came to rest upon the druid.

"Well, Cathbad," he called, "we've followed your lead, and
it has brought us here. The path is gone, the light is gone.
Now, would it be too great a trouble for you to be telling us
where we are?"

The tone of his voice was irritated, with a ragged edge. But
Cathbad's reply was calm, warmed by the faint touch of amusement that still lit his expression.

"I think we are where we should be."

The tall man eyed him sharply, his tone growing impatient now. "And . . . just where, by the blessed Dagda, is that?"

"We simply go on as we're pointed," the druid said easily. "The signs say that we will find your sister. That's all we need to know. I can feel the forces about us now, moving in the depths of the woods like the shadows of the birds we followed here."

At these words, the rest of the party looked around them once again, more uneasily. All of them could feel something too. There was a most peculiar silence in this place, a silence compounded by the chill air and the muffling blanket of snow. Something was waiting out there for them.

"Ah, I've no faith in the signs!" the red-haired man said abruptly, his clear, booming voice breaking the spell. "Conchobar's sister has been gone nearly a year. It'll take more than magic to find her." He looked at the druid. "Unless you can show us some signpost which can't take to its wings and fly away?"

"I've nothing like that to give you," Cathbad replied frankly.

"Then so much for your druidical lore," sneered the tall one called Conchobar, "and for foolish hunts begun on winter afternoons."

He turned his gaze once more on the forest about him but found no new inspiration there. He shook his head sharply, forced to a resignation he clearly did not like.

"Well, there's little else to do now but to keep on driving deeper into this and hope to find some shelter for the night." He turned to the red-haired man and spoke brusquely: "Fergus, ride ahead and lead us along the easiest path you can."

Fergus accepted the order without comment, only nodding his head. He touched the shoulder of his driver once, and the chariot moved forward, leading the party into the confusing shadows of the trees.

They forced their way ahead for a time, moving as rapidly as they could through the dense wood, feeling the pressure of the darkness fully upon them now. The night was overcast, but the moon was full, and the sky and forest glowed a pale gray. They saw nothing and heard nothing in the tangled growth surrounding them, and each man, save Cathbad, tried to ignore the watchful presence he felt there.

Then, like a first star in a clear evening sky, a light winked into being among the trees ahead. They moved toward it, coming abruptly upon another small clearing.

In its center sat a round timber house, smoke rising from the roof hole at its peak.

Cautious, the party pulled in at the forest's edge and peered curiously at the solitary structure. It seemed an ordinary home, unfortified. A modest liss, its log walls unadorned, its roof weathered gray thatch. It looked quite lonely there, in the heart of that vast, *sheoguey* wilderness.

The flame-haired Fergus, always careful, signaled his driver forward. The others waited, hidden by the trees, watching as he rode boldly to the liss.

The driver pulled the car up to the door, and Fergus leaned over the chariot's wicker bulwark to knock loudly. The door opened at once, revealing the lean silhouette of a man against the brightly lit interior. Warm air carrying the scent of cooking food welled out in a sensuous blast, taunting the chilled men in the chariot.

"Who is it who comes here in the darkness?" the figure challenged in a soft but firm voice.

"It's Fergus MacRogh I am, a chieftain of the Clanna Rury. I've a party seeking shelter from this night."

"And who is in your party?" came the gentle inquiry.

Fergus grew more wary. He didn't wish to make it known who it was that traveled abroad with only six companions.

"What difference is there?" his great voice boomed in the stillness. "We're warriors of the province asking shelter. You're bound to let us in."

"It's said that Laegaire Budthatch, the Battle Winner, rides with you, along with other Red Branch champions, and that you accompany Conchobar MacNessa, Ard-Rie of all Ulster."

"And how could you know that?" Fergus demanded.

"A noble party surely to be visiting my humble liss," the man went on graciously, ignoring Fergus's question. "Let no fears trouble you, MacRogh. Take shelter here, and welcome."

At those words, the doubts of Fergus were dispelled. Somehow, he only felt now that he could trust this man. He hesitated no longer, ordering the driver back, and the chariot moved away from the liss, returning to the party in the woods.

Soon he was leading the others back to the liss. There the riders dismounted, leaving the chariots in their drivers' care. As before, Fergus approached the door and knocked.

This time there was no answer.

Carefully, he pushed open the door and the men followed him inside. The main room of the liss was well lit by torches, pleasantly warmed by a central fire where broth bubbled in a pot and venison roasted on a spit. But the room was deserted.

Once more growing wary, Fergus drew back his cloak. The others did so as well. Beneath the heavy wool were revealed the richly embroidered tunics of nobility, the jeweled trappings and weapons of the warrior class. Fergus pulled out his slender longsword, and the polished black iron blade of it flashed red fire in the light.

Cathbad smiled at his companion's move. "That's not to be needed here, Fergus, I'm certain."

As he spoke the ard-druid looked around him at the liss, so richly adorned for such a humble dwelling. The outer walls of the room were fitted with plates of softly glowing bronze, and the timber roof pillars were finely carved with interlaced designs. He especially noted the tapestries, wrought with delicate care, and the fresh, fragrant rushes strewn upon the earthen floor, a miracle in winter.

"There is more here than a normal home," he said. "I feel it's what we have been looking for."

As if in answer to his words, a strange, high wail lifted in the quiet. As one, the other warriors drew their swords, the blades a sweep of light.

"Behind that wall," Fergus said softly, pointing to a partition which closed off a section of the liss across the fire from them.

The men spread apart and moved around the fire toward the wall. It was of movable wickerwork, a screen to give that portion of the room some privacy. At Conchobar's direction, two men seized it while the rest stood ready.

The wail had stopped now, but small, odd squeaks and gurgles could be heard. Cathbad listened, a look of wonder filling his usually placid face.

At a signal, the wall was pulled away. The men moved forward, then stopped in surprise. On a thick pile of furs lay a woman cradling a baby in her arms.

The baby, thickly swaddled in soft blankets, was newborn. It moved fitfully and made its first, small noises in the world. The woman, exhausted by her labor, seemed to be sleeping.

Even with the recent pain and effort marking her face, it was clear how beautiful she was, fair-skinned to glowing whiteness, pale blond hair flowing about her shoulders. She slept the sleep of total surrender, her face relaxed, looking so young, so smooth, so soft, her features seemed blurred in the fire's shifting light.

The men stood motionless, staring in wonder at the pair. Cathbad, at first awed, now seemed seized by a great joy. But Conchobar, face clouded by stormy doubts, moved toward her.

"Dechtire!" he said. "Are you all right?"

She stirred restlessly but seemed not to wake.

"Sister!" he said more sharply. "Where have you been? What are you doing here?"

She spoke, but still from sleep, and the words came as if bundled in the thick soft blanket of it.

"It's on the wings of the wind I've been, and in the arms of the sea. And the warm, clinging sea drew me in. It swirled about me and caressed me with its waves and filled me with its warmth and comfort until I sank into the depths of the sea and drowned . . . and . . . drowned. . . ."

The sensual images teased at the men's minds, and Conchobar, shocked by her words, leaned forward to shake her roughly.

"Dechtire, wake up!"

Her eyes snapped open, showing a brilliant green. They filled with alarm, and she pushed the man's hand away. "Your hand is cold," she told him.

He leaned closer, his words coming tersely. "Dechtire, this is your brother! It has been a year since you vanished from Emain Macha. You are found."

She focused her uncertain gaze upon him for the first time. Understanding flooded the open features, and reality came to her in a chilling wave of pain.

"Conchobar!" she breathed in astonishment. Then, in agony, her face twisted tight. "No! Oh . . . no! It isn't over! Why?"

"What is over?" Conchobar demanded. "What kinds of fools have you made of us all?"

"I . . . I've had a long dream," she said softly. "A dream of a fair man, gentle as spring. It's an ache I feel in my heart at losing that. But there's fear, too, in knowing where I've been."

"What are you saying, Dechtire?" her brother asked angrily. "Your husband waits for you in your own dun. Who is the man who fathered this child?"

The harshness of his words brought a sudden hardness to her gentle face. Her gaze was icy as it met Conchobar's, her voice as frozen iron.

"Brother, understand me now! You will never ask me that again! You will never have an answer. The child is mine. That is enough."

"A child without a father's name?" the tall man asked.

"My child. The child of Dechtire, daughter of kings, sister of the High-King of Ulster. And, as he is, I claim for him my rights. You cannot deny them."

"Sualtim will never accept it."

"That has nothing to do with you. But somehow I will see that my son never knows of this."

The others had moved in around the woman now, forming a crimson wall with their woolen cloaks. The young warriors who were Eire's greatest fighters, the deadly weapons of their king, ruthless and hardened already by their lives, stood gazing with wonder like the children they had been not so many years before. And the tiny bit of new humanity ignored their stares, settling himself more snugly into his mother's warmth.

Fergus MacRogh, drawn by a fascination for the child, moved closer to the bed. Carefully he extended a hand, then paused as his eyes met Dechtire's. But she knew and trusted this giant warrior, and she smiled.

Gently he moved a finger to lift a tiny hand. Immediately the hand grasped his thick finger in a tight grip, and Fergus looked up at his fellows, his marvel at the infant lighting his broad face.

"It's a fine grip he has," he told them admiringly. "A warrior's grip surely."

The smile faded from Dechtire's face. She looked around her at the circle of stolid young faces and at the glinting weapons of their work still clutched in their hands. Fear seized her, and she pulled the baby closer, away from Fergus, in a gesture of defense.

"It's not a warrior he is!" she said with force.

"Then what is he?" Conchobar asked. "Sister, one day he will be old enough, and then, like other lads, he'll wish to take his place in the world. What then?"

"When it is time," said Cathbad, "the boy must come to Emain Macha to be trained with the rest of Ulster's noble sons."

"No bastard child who can never carry a name in truth will ever come in fosterage to me!" Conchobar stormed. "Even his own mother is ashamed."

"Not ashamed," she retorted. "Afraid. Afraid for him. He is a part of me and a part of something you don't understand and never will."

Deep within her mind she knew that some fate awaited this

infant in the tangled skein of future events. But she also knew that fate was meant only for a warrior.

Cathbad too had sensed the destiny that lay with this tiny, helpless child. To him it meant a great many other things.

"It's not for us to be denying his right," Cathbad told her in uncompromising tones. "It is the Others, the hidden Sidhe, who have had a part in this. The child must be accepted. I will give my own bond to protect him and teach him in the way of *filidh* and druid, to play upon the harp and sing the songs and know the wisdom of all Ireland."

Fergus had stood looking down at the small face, held by its frailty and its immense calm in the torrent of emotions surging around it. Now he looked up and spoke decisively.

"And I'll accept the fosterage of this boy when it's time." He fixed his glowering king with a defiant eye. "I'll gladly give my bond to be his teacher in the arts of war if Conchobar will not. I'll show him the warrior's ways, the battle, the chariot pole, and the weight of a true sword."

With the words of Cathbad, Dechtire was content. But at the words of Fergus, she grew solemn again. She knew that if the choice were hers, the time when her son must learn the warrior's skills would never come.

Yet, as she looked down on the tiny, smooth, innocent face, now so peacefully slumbering, a voice spoke within her, saying that she would fail.

"He will know great pain and great unhappiness, beyond that of any man," it said. "But he will know a greater glory too. And with that, Dechtire, you must be content."

Chapter One

The Choosing

The white face of the dead man stared up into the blue-white sky. The eyes squinting, the face was pinched tight, as if it were grimacing at the unnatural brightness of the day.

A lonely figure the man looked, lying upon his simple bier of wood, dwarfed by the great burial mound which loomed above it. And lonely he was, with no one there to keep him final company save for a tiny flock of bright-cloaked druids huddled at the entrance to the ancient tomb.

The keening of these few fluttered up sadly, thinly, like starved crows struggling and complaining their way toward the scattered clouds above.

The dismal scene contrasted sharply with the brilliance of the surrounding countryside. It was especially bright by the river just below the high-rounded hill of earth. The clear, hard rays of the sun fell and shattered against the surface of the Boinne's flowing waters, the bright shards drifting upon its waves, multiplying and intensifying the light to painful sharpness.

Everything about seemed to shine from it—everything save for the black square beyond the carved stones framing the tomb's entrance. Soon that blackness would receive the ashes of the man, to mix them with those of other ages, to lose them as if they had never been.

More fitting might a day of mist and cold have been. Instead, this fair and glowing day seemed to mock him, as his whole life had.

For this lonely figure was a high-king of all Ireland. The rich cloak, finely jeweled brooch, and weapons of war laid with him there announced that. But the lack of warriors to host about his bier gave evidence of something else. And the thin face, unmarked by war but scarred by the deep lines of fear, said much more.

The chanting died, its last notes drifting away. From the gathering of druids one man stepped forward. The golden torque about his neck marked him as the highest of their rank. He stepped up beside the bier, pausing to look across it, over the wide Boinne to the land beyond. It spread away in a ragged patchwork of gold and yellow that shifted with the moving shadows of the few, high clouds.

"It's truly a fitting place for high-kings to lie," he murmured thoughtfully. Then he glanced down at the still figure, adding with regret, "Maybe too fine for the likes of such as you, my poor Eterscel." He shook his head. "Ah well," he said resignedly, "go now. Join with the ashes of the rest."

From a small fire set before the bier, the ard-druid lifted a flaming brand. With a quick intonation of the proper words of reverence to his watching gods, he laid it against the pile of yew and ash wood piled beneath the corpse. As the fire caught, grew, and rose about it, the man turned to the others who watched silently.

"It's time now," he told them, his tone becoming brisk. "The preparations for the Bull Feast must be made."

Behind him, the fire leaped up higher around the bier. The wavering flames obscured the image of the lonely figure with a final screen of brightness.

Flames from the sacred wood of the fire licked up around the base of a great caldron suspended over it on heavy chains.

The fire colored the long enclosure of the druids with shuddering yellow light, throwing the shadows of the cloaked, moving men in intertwining serpents of blackness upon the rough timber walls.

A white, writhing column of thick steam rose from the roiling waters of the black iron vat, whispering up into the night sky above the open yard.

An unnatural child this steam-wraith was, born of the marriage of earth's most potent elements, forced to a mating by man's cleverness, dying and reborn continuously. A fusing of two sworn foes, like the soul of man himself—each life and death, love and hatred, beauty and horror all at once.

Into the enclosure a white bull was herded then, eyes bulging, massive body moving reluctantly. It was frightened by this strangeness, by these robed men, and by the scent of death that drifted with the steam in the still night.

The druids moved in around the animal, holding it with the press of their numbers. It stood, lock-kneed and tensed, staring suspiciously as the ard-druid approached it.

But he spoke gently to it while the others chanted softly, creating a soothing sound that lulled the animal. Finally reassured, it watched the ard-druid move closer, coming up against its side just behind its head.

It did not see the knife he held down within the cloak's folds, or the red-black gleam of the polished blade as it swept up and gently stroked across its neck. And it didn't feel the pain from the neat cut until its blood had already begun a hot gush into the bronze vat two other druids held.

With the skill of years of practice, the druids swiftly drained the carcass and butchered it. They fed its raw meat, still hot with its life, into the steaming caldron.

Soon the scent of the cooking meat billowed up with the white steam to savor the night air. While it cooked, a new ceremony began, another part of the complex ritual.

The table was prepared, the chosen druid conducted to his place and charged with his sacred task. His failure in it meant his instant death. The cooked meat, swimming in broth crimson-laced with the fresh blood, was brought to him in a finely worked bowl of gleaming gold.

And he began to eat.

Bowl upon bowl he consumed, gulping down the parboiled meat, draining the hot broth, beginning each full bowl that immediately replaced the emptied one.

Around him the others gathered, their faces glistening in the humid air of the enclosure. They watched the Devourer, who shone too from the sweat and from the grease that filmed the surface of the broth and now covered his face, ran down his neck, dripped from his working jaws.

He ate and he drank on, filling himself, forcing himself further with a massive effort of will until, stomach distended, bloated to his limits by the gorging, he signed away the next cup.

With help he rose and made his painful way to the bed readied for him beside a second fire. He laid himself heavily among its furs while the voices of the gathered druids began a new chant. Their softly rising and falling voices raised a spell of sleep about the chosen one, sending him at last into a trancelike slumber.

It was a fitful, agonizing sleep that tormented him with sounds and images. The druids circled him in constant vigil, their still, rigid bodies a sharp contrast to the convulsions of his tortured frame. Their voices continued the soft chant in rhythmic phrases punctuated unevenly by his moans.

Four ard-druids led the ritual, standing at the four corners of the bed, at the four corners of the winds that now rose and whirled above them in the darkness, drawing off the still rising steam from the caldron in a twisting pillar of white.

They sent their chant up into the wailing air, fashioning the charm that would bring the dreams to him. Their magic spun the separate strands of voice into one knotted rope of sound. Through his heavy sleep it wound its way, into the heated chaos choked with shadows, lights, and images. It threaded these together like glass beads, drawing them into a single pattern. Like the design of some ornately fashioned jewelry it formed against the dark fabric of his entranced mind. Slowly the image resolved itself, sharpened itself into a vivid scene.

He jerked upright suddenly, staring ahead, asleep and awake at once. In the smoky air before him the image hung, still bright and sharp.

The chanting died.

One of the four ard-druids leaned forward. His voice was urgent in the hanging silence as he asked, "What is it that you see? Tell us the dream!"

"It is a young man I see," the speaker intoned, laboring to speak. "A young man . . . naked . . . a stone in the sling he swings in his hand. He comes . . . he comes along the road to Tara."

"When does he come? When?"

The man shook himself—a great shudder that tightened his whole body—and his burning gaze shifted upward to meet that of the druid leaning over him, holding it with a power far beyond his own.

"Soon!" he breathed. "He will be coming soon!"

A hand sprayed water into the young lad's face. He laughed and dived forward, grasping the middle of the other boy with one long arm, lifting him to throw him down into the rushing stream.

Around them, other boys played boisterously, churning the waters to a foaming white. Meantime, from the bank, a slender, dark-haired girl enthusiastically cheered them on.

Then, abruptly, her smile vanished. She jumped up and stood stiffly, her eyes fixed on the meadow across the stream.

Lomna Druth—the rotund, good-natured boy affectionately called The Fool by his comrades—noted her move. He followed her gaze and saw the two men striding purposefully across the meadow toward them.

"Conaire!" he called out to another lad. "They're coming to speak to you again!"

The young man he addressed was then engaged in playfully holding the head of a younger comrade named Ferogain beneath the water. But at these words he instantly released the red-haired boy, who shot to the surface spluttering.

Ferogain wiped his eyes and prepared to continue the struggle, then realized that the rest had ceased their play to watch the two men who approached the stream.

As the pair, dressed in the plain, rough wool tunics and trousers of herdsmen, reached the low bank, the lad named Conaire called to them in a stubborn tone, "There's no use your coming to me again. You'll not convince me to go."

"Conaire, you must!" one of them pleaded. "We've had word that the Bull Feast has been held. Soon they'll be choosing a new ard-rie. You must be there."

"There's little point to that," the young man answered flatly.

"You refused to go when he was laid to rest. You must go now. You are his son."

"He was nothing to me," was the short, harsh reply.

"He was the High-King of all Ireland!"

"And he did no more for her than for myself," Conaire told them. "It was you who raised me. You and my mother's people. You are the only fathers I've known."

"It was the choice of your mother that you live with us, not the king," the second herdsman reasoned. "She meant for you to know all the people of Ireland."

"And it's with those people that I'm wishing to stay," he replied. "My mother may have chosen to have me live here, but it was my father who chose to let her, and to cut himself off from me. He did me the only good turn of his life. I've no ambitions for power, only for enjoying my life. I've no interest at all in what takes place in Tara. It's a fine day, and I'm free to spend it here, with my friends."

"Conaire," the first herdsman said in exasperation, "you're bound by blood and duty to attend the ceremonies. If you won't go at all, you'll be bringing disgrace on us, your mother's family, and her blessed memory. If you've no care about yourself, then think of us."

The young man gave a heavy sigh. "All right, then," he told them. "I'll do it if you wish. I'll ride to Tara."

"We'll go with you," said Ferogain at once, throwing an arm around an eagerly grinning Lomna Druth.

Conaire grinned in return. "Thank you, my friends," he said, putting a hand on the shoulder of each. "But stay here and enjoy the day. No one else should be made to go on this foolish errand."

He started to wade out of the stream, the others following. But as he climbed onto the bank, a voice stopped him.

"Conaire, wait!"

He turned to see the girl leap from the bank on the far side of the stream. Like a colt she ran, her mane of black hair flying behind her, slender legs flashing through the shallow water. Without slowing she ran up to the lad and flung herself against him, clutching him tightly, her head pressed against his chest.

"Oh, Conaire! You can't be leaving us!" she cried out.

"Fionualla, what's wrong?" he asked in a puzzled voice.

"A great fear took me when I saw you going away," she said brokenly, "that you'd be gone from us forever, taken away and never even saying a word of farewell to me."

"But it's only for a short while I'll be gone," he assured her. "And I'd never leave without a farewell."

She lifted her head to look up at him. "Are you certain?" she asked.

He smiled and brushed the tangle of dark hair back gently, revealing a pale child's face dominated by bright brown eyes now wide and filled with tears.

"I'd never leave my foster-brothers," he said. "It's all one that we are." He cupped the small chin, looking into the troubled eyes. "And I'd surely never leave you. How could any man?"

He released her and she stepped back reluctantly. With the gathered boys, she watched silently as he joined the two men and started back across the meadows.

As he walked, Conaire's attention was caught by a great silver bird. It appeared from nowhere and swung down to soar low over them.

There were more birds above him now. He watched them as he guided his light, one-passenger chariot along the North Tara Road.

He couldn't decide what kind of birds they were. He'd never seen any of their likes before. Such strange, bright colors they were—golds, scarlets, blues, and greens—and so large!

They stayed near him as he rode along, one or another of them dropping low at times, until the lad was sorely tempted to use the new sling he carried with him.

He lifted it and swung it in his hand as they wheeled over him, considering. But he shook his head resignedly and let it fall back. He needed to reach Tara an Rie by dark, and he was already late. He urged his horses on.

He reached a place along the coastal road, near by the village known as Ath Cliath. It was then that the birds began to swoop lower upon him. They soared up and back in great arcs, whooping past him, teasing him with jeering rasps like rusty wheel rims grating upon stones. They really were the strangest birds he'd ever seen, he thought. A bit like swans, only much larger.

And the temptation grew in him to have a try at them.

At last, when one swept past him, snatching at the long hair gathered behind his head, he could stand no more of it. He fitted a round stone into the sling, swung it up, and made a cast at the birds when the flock curved down again.

They scattered at the throw, breaking away, shooting up sharply, easily dodging the stone, then gathering once more above him, daring him to try again.

It was a dare the boy could not ignore.

Then began a long and ludicrous contest. The boy, more determined with each miss, began to follow them. They left the road and sailed off, but turning often to tease him on. He went after them, across the countryside, always toward the sea. His frustration grew as they evaded every cast.

Finally, the horses topped a rise and the ocean gleamed ahead. A broad beach of white sand separated him from the water's edge.

He pulled up there, watching the birds. They soared back over him once more, then out over the sea, drifting down like fall leaves to settle lightly upon the gentle surf. They drifted in the water lazily, barely a long stone's cast from shore, taunting him.

The thwarted boy was now muttering dark oaths that he would not be beaten by these arrogant birds. He'd have one of them flying or sitting on the waves.

He left his chariot and made his way carefully to the shore. There he threw off his cloak, unbuckled his harness and sword, and pulled off his linen tunic. Naked and unarmed, save for the sling, he slipped into the water and began to swim out slowly toward the birds, hoping to get close enough for a sure throw before they took alarm.

They waited, floating quietly, making no moves to escape, seeming oblivious to him. He grew nearer, nearer to them, until he could see them clearly. But then something began to change.

The birds' outlines seemed to become somehow hazy to him, as if a curtain of mist had lifted about them. The shadowy figures within this mist then began to move. They seemed to be rising, and he feared they were flying up as they reared higher from the water's surface and stretched out their great wings.

He leaped upright in the shallow water, sling ready for a cast. But then the mist fell away, revealing them clearly again.

The lad moved back, amazed, letting drop his sling. For it wasn't birds he now faced, but men clad in bright, shimmering cloaks. Tall, slender men they were, their faces long and smooth and elegant of feature, their eyes bright-shining, silver-blue jewels.

With slim, silver-pointed spears they advanced upon him. "I am Nemglan," said one at their front. "And it's not casting at birds you should be doing if they have such a strange appearance as ourselves."

"I see now that it's of the Sidhe you are," Conaire replied, awed by these men of Ireland's Hidden Ones, but showing no fear, for he was afraid of nothing he could see.

"Conaire Mor, you will be the next high-king of Ireland," Nemglan told him bluntly.

"High-king?" Conaire said, astonished. "But . . . I've no wish for that!"

"It's of little matter what you feel now. The power is in you. Under you, Ireland can know a peace and richness it has never had."

The young man shook his head in disbelief. "It can't be!" he protested. "The kings and chieftains of the five provinces will never accept me."

"The Devourer at the Bull Feast of the druids has already seen who the next ard-rie will be. He will come naked and carrying a sling, as you are now, walking along the road to Tara. That man will be you, Conaire Mor. You must accept the kingship."

"No," he retorted, still struggling against this nearly over-whelming notion. "I needn't do it. I can don my clothes and ride on. I can defy your will."

The man smiled in a sly amusement.

"You will find your clothes have vanished, as we will do ourselves." He shook his head in mock regret. "And I'm afraid your horses have wandered away with your chariot as well. No, my lad, you must face it—the fates and ourselves have blessed you with kingship."

"Cursed me with it, you mean," Mor answered bitterly.

"And is it really the truth you're speaking now?" Nemglan asked, his voice taking on a soft, cajoling tone. "And haven't you had a long grievance yourself with the way your father ruled? Haven't you your own dream, muttered to the skies late in the night, or cast to the winds when you're alone upon the hills?"

Conaire met the man's shining gaze for a moment. Then he nodded.

"Yes," he admitted. "I would wish to bring a real peace to Ireland, to see her strong and prosperous and well. A place where children could always play in safety. My father failed in that."

"Then the chance to do so is yours," the other assured him. "And if you rule well, our power will be with you, and your reign will be a great one."

"I've still the power to refuse this," the young man said defiantly. "You can't force me to it, no matter what tricks you play. Steal my clothes and my chariot you may, but I can still just turn north again, go back homeward afoot, naked as I am."

"So you might," Nemglan agreed. "And we'd want no other way for it. When it comes to the all and all, the real choice must be your own." He paused, fixing the young man with a searching eye before going on, his voice growing more intense. "But listen to me now, Conaire Mor, and think of this too before you decide: there will be *gessas* upon you from the time that you accept the kingship—bonds you must not break.

"Do not hunt the evil beasts of Cerna or seek to settle the quarrel of two warring chiefs. Do not sleep in a house where you see firelight after sunset, or let a man and woman enter the same house, or let three Reds go before you to the house of Red."

The man of the Sidhe stepped forward, placing a hand upon the shoulder of the mortal.

"Most of all, Conaire Mor," he added emphatically, "let no robbery be done in your reign, and always build your rule upon justice."

With these final words, Nemglan and the figures of the men behind him rose from the waves together. Their forms changed as they rose, and it was as great birds again that they soared into the sky.

The young man watched them until they had vanished from sight. Then he waded out of the waves and made his way back up to the road. It was as the birdman had said. His clothes were gone, his chariot vanished. He stood naked and alone in the empty countryside, on the brown ribbon of road that vanished away in either direction.

He looked toward the north, back along the way he had traveled, back toward home. A dreadful longing came into his face as the images of his friends and of Fionualla came into his mind. He felt the pull of them, of her, as if it were a physical thing, as if their hands gripped him, drew him back to their safety, to their innocence.

Then, with an effort of will, he turned his gaze southward. He looked along that road to where it swept over a hill's crest and out of sight, now visualizing the great fortress of Tara that lay beyond. A sense of new purpose rose in him, too strong to ignore. For a moment the longing struggled against it, but was swiftly overwhelmed. There was a sense of mingled elation and regret, a quick, wrenching sense of something lost and never to be regained. Then there was only the new, warm rush of resolution, the tingle of a new excitement.

He drew himself up and with a decisive first step started toward the south, striding on to cover the last distance to Tara.

Chapter Two

The Acceptance

The three white-robed druids stood beside Slighe Midluachra, the North Tara Road. Their bodies were taut with anxiety, their eyes fixed intently, searchingly on the point where the long, curving road vanished in a last graceful sweep behind a distant soft swell of green hill.

Not far from them, three chariots were drawn up. Their horses were hobbled and grazing nearby. Their trousered drivers sat about a small fire within the triangle of the cars, playing at *brandub*, using curved bits of wood as the black raven pieces, moving them across a crude board scratched in a patch of bare earth.

"Ah, the Bloody Morrigan take it!" one driver cursed, disgustedly throwing down the carved bone dice. "I've no luck at all today."

He stood and stretched and glanced over the bulwark of a car toward the three druids.

"Still at it, are they?" another driver inquired.

"Aye. Still like three pillars of white stone they are, still staring down the road. Not moved an eyelash's worth since the dawn, I'd say."

The third man rose far enough to glance toward the druids, then dropped back, shaking his head in disbelief.

"And I'd swear by the gods of my fathers they've not blinked once in that time. Their eyeballs will be drying up and dropping from their heads with it. How long can they stand there that way?"

"There's nothing even saying this is the right place," said the first. "I heard that druids would be watching on each of the five great Tara roads. One in five. That's poor odds in my mind to be getting them so excited."

"Waiting for a naked man to just come striding along," the third said, snorting derisively. "Madness I call that. All this faith put in that druid-foreseeing business. Well, a thing like this makes you wonder how much to believe."

"I . . . I believe it," said the first man.

The other two realized he had suddenly gone quite stiff and was staring off with an intent that matched the druids', his mouth hanging open in astonishment.

"What is it?" the second man asked, as he and the third stood up.

The first man, too astonished to speak more, simply raised a hand and pointed.

There, moving up the road with a long, easy stride, came the naked form of Conaire Mor, the sling swinging in his hand.

"So, there he is," the third man said in awe. "The druids were right after all!"

"But he's just a lad!" said the second. "Can he really be our new high-king?"

The three druids, at first beaming in triumph at being the ones blessed with finding the promised one, now took on more disconcerted looks as Mor approached and they too saw how young he seemed.

Still, theirs was not to question the powers at work. They did as their ard-druid commanded. While the drivers hurried to reharness the horses to the cars, they went forward to meet the naked man. They wrapped him in a warm cloak of the finest green wool trimmed with gold fringe and led him to the chariots. In moments they were speeding toward the fortress called Tara.

There, within the long timber-walled rectangle of the sacred enclosure, the druids had gathered once again. But this time they had been joined by many bards and champions and chieftains of all Ireland who had come to Tara to witness the fulfillment of this prophecy. Many scores of them jammed the enclosure, filling the space along the timber walls several deep, leaving only a narrow avenue open down the middle. The different and brightly hued cloaks of the various groups created a colorful pattern that ruffled constantly, uneasily, with the breeze of the crowd's impatience.

When the three druids with the green-cloaked figure entered the sacred place, all eyes turned toward them; those closest to them widened with surprise. As the druids began to lead Mor up the narrow passage through the crowd, the sound of astonished muttering surged ahead of them, sweeping the length of the gathering. Men exchanged glances that were confused or troubled, sometimes irritated or dismayed.

The young man looked around him, seeing the expressions, trying to keep up a determined front despite his anxiety. He had tried to envision this reception on his way here. It was much as he'd expected. In fact, too much. For what he had envisioned was the worst.

After what seemed to him an endless march up that strange alleyway of staring eyes, he and his escorts reached the far end. There the feather-cloaked figures of several of the highest-ranking druids awaited. They were flanked by others of tremendous power in Ireland: great chieftains, renowned champions, and the most senior ollavs.

As Mor had approached this group, the expression of the highest ard-druid—usually one of great calm and self-possession—had slipped a bit. But it had been only momentary. Now he had regained his composure, putting on an impassive look. This, however, was not true of those around him, who made no attempt to hide their astonishment as they looked over the youthful figure.

"And whom have you brought to us?" the highest ard-druid intoned, determined that his only course was to rigidly follow through with the ritual.

"It is the One Who Was Foreseen," the three druids with Mor replied.

"And how do you know this is the One?"

"He came as he was seen by the Devourer," was the reply, "naked but for his sling, striding afoot along the high North Road to Tara."

The ard-druid looked at the young man once more. There was a certain question in his eye. There was a faint hesitation in his manner. So young! But then he steeled himself again.

"And who is it who has come so to us?" he asked Mor.

Now it was Mor's turn to steel himself. He met the man's eye squarely and said with determination, "It is Conaire I am, son of the cowherd's foster-child, son of Eterscel, who was high-king, grandson of Eochaid, who was high-king before him."

That was all right, the ard-druid thought. At least it was not some vagabond who had come to him, but a son and grandson of kings. He nodded with more animation.

"And why do you come thus across the roads of Ireland to Tara?"

"I come as I was sent by the great powers of the Men of Dea, to fulfill my destiny."

This was even better, thought the ard-druid. The Others were taking a part in this. That surely put the sanction of the truth upon things. He nodded again, relief relaxing his taut expression, making him speak with greater energy.

"And do you then willingly accept the seat of the high-kingship of all Ireland?" he asked.

Mor drew himself up and replied in clear and certain tones, "I do!"

There was a general uproar in the crowd. One of the chieftains pushed forward from the rest, crying out, "You can't mean this!"

The ard-druid turned to him in surprise. "What are you saying, Aodh?"

"That this is complete madness!" the other stormed.

He was a brawny, squarely built chieftain with a great bush of curling red hair, flaring eyebrows, and mustaches. His manner was as boisterous and inflammatory as his look. His voice was like thunder rolling along a rocky vale.

"Because one of your charlatan magicians had a nightmare while in a drunken daze, do you really mean to just hand the rulership of all of us to this stripling? If so, you've surely lost whatever little sense you ever had!"

There were many low mutterings and growlings of agreement with these bold words from others around the enclosure, largely from others of the warrior class.

The ard-druid, shocked by this insulting attack, drew himself up haughtily.

"I follow the laws and beliefs of our people, declared by our gods and our forefathers, sworn to by every chieftain and king of Ireland. They are the laws that we all obey."

"The laws that *you* obey," Aodh shot back, advancing on the ard-druid in a clearly aggressive way. "Any warrior of Ireland must see now what foolishness they are." He cast his gaze challengingly about him at the crowd, calling to them, "Don't you all see what fool sheep we would be to blindly follow their bell when they've gone so far astray?" He looked back to the ard-druid, fixing him with a fiercely glittering eye. "It's too powerful your kind has become, druid. Far too powerful."

"You have no right at all to be disputing this," the chief druid returned, standing his ground and putting on a brave show, but one that couldn't fully hide his tremor of fear at the chieftain's threat. "This Conaire Mor has an honest claim to the high-king's seat. As the son of Eterscel, the blood of our rulers flows in him. And that his coming was foretold to us proves the great powers of the Tuatha de Danann favor him."

"It proves only that you and this 'promised one' of yours have leagued in some dark chicanery to place the druids' own puppet on the throne of Ireland," was the burly chieftain's uncompromising reply. He eyed Mor scornfully. "And this is no man. It's a boy, barely past his beardless years. He's not fit to rule."

"It's true what Aodh's saying now," another chieftain called out, accompanied by other noises of support from the warriors. "Your Bull Feast and your Charm of Truth aren't worth much to us when this is all they bring us."

"No!" the ard-druid cried out in horror. "What Aodh is saying is not truth. It's blasphemy. He's bringing the wrath of the gods upon us surely. The great winds of the Sidhe will blast across this dun of Tara and sweep us away like the dried leaves of fall."

Aodh laughed derisively. "And where is that wind?" he challenged. "I've seen no signs of your great Sidhe in all my life. I've no fear of their powers. Now we've listened to enough, old man." He looked around him at the crowd again. "I say we end this here. Do away with the foolish rules these feathered enchanters have tried to bind us with. Once all it needed to prove a king was a strong arm and a good sword, not chants and visions."

There were more mutterings of agreement at that, while even among the ard-druid's own people there were looks of doubt and few voices of support for him.

Conaire Mor, who had stood motionless, watching through all of this, now spoke up, his voice calm and quiet, but still carrying clearly across the enclosure.

"It's not an unarmed druid such a brave warrior as yourself should be threatening. It's me."

"Are you giving me an insult, boy?" Aodh snarled, wheeling on the young man. "You don't really mean to face me, naked and unarmed. Run away now, and give up your game here."

"I know you," Mor said coldly, standing his ground. "I've seen your kind too often before. You are a bully, Aodh. You know about nothing but swords and raids and killing. You don't care about Ireland or anyone besides yourself. It was the threat of men like you that made my poor father a weak and useless king. It's men like you who keep Ireland torn apart, bleeding, and poor."

"Careful, boy," Aodh said in a low and deadly voice. His hand dropped to grip tightly the hilt of his sword. "It is truly madness that you're speaking to me now."

"You say I'm mad and that the druids are mad," Conaire replied, hitting each word sharply, like hammer strokes driving spikes home. "Well, it's only yourself who brought the madness here."

Driven to violence by Mor's attack, the chieftain drew his sword. "I'll finish this myself!" he bellowed in rage, and charged upon the young man.

Mor showed no sign of fear, made no move to retreat. As the man plunged toward him, his arm shot out from the folds of the heavy cloak, revealing the loaded sling that he still held.

In a quick move, Mor swung back the weapon and snapped it forward. The stone pellet in the sling, expertly aimed, whizzed to its mark, striking the center of Aodh's forehead just above the flaring brows.

There was the sharp *crack* of smashed bone. The man was stopped dead as his head snapped back. He swayed and then tumbled backward, crashing heavily to the ground, the ball of stone imbedded deeply in his skull.

For a moment there was a stunned silence, then shouts of anger from the chieftain's warrior comrades.

A dozen of them surged forward at once, hot for revenge, drawing swords as they advanced on the lone and now completely unarmed young man.

He stood unflinchingly before the attack while the druids and bards around him cowered back. Though some few screamed in protest, more cried out in fear. None moved to defend their promised one.

The warriors were nearly upon Conaire Mor when another figure leaped suddenly from the crowd and moved before him.

A great shield came up, slamming back the lead attacker. The swift flashing of a sword parried another's blade and sent a third man staggering back with a cut across the cheek. The rest of the warriors collided together in their attempt to come up short before this unexpected barrier.

It was a tall and lean and stalwart man who had moved before Mor. His body was sinewy, and his long-featured face, though still youthful, was marked by the hardness of one who had seen much fighting. Now his pale blue eyes gleamed icily, and his wide mouth was drawn in a grim line.

"What do you mean, to come before us?" one of the attacking warriors demanded. "He's just killed Aodh with that bloody sling!"

"He defended himself from an unfair attack in the only way he could, and with great skill," the other countered. "Aodh would have deserved death at my own hand, or that of any other true warrior of Ireland, for such an attack. And you have brought a great shame upon your own selves as well."

"How can you defend him?" another man demanded.

"It's the honor of Ireland that I'm defending here," he answered, "and the oaths to her laws that we've all sworn to obey." He gave the young man a look. "I may not like this, but I'll not be the one to break the law or see it broken and bring a dishonor upon myself. If what the druids and this Conaire Mor say is true, he is our new high-king."

"Warrior, I do thank you," Mor said with great earnestness. He eyed the crimson cloak about the man's shoulders. "Is it of the Clanna Rury, the Red Branch of Ulster, that you come?"

"It is," he said. "My name is Conal Carna, sent by King Conchobar to witness this choosing."

"Well, Conal Carna, I ask only one thing from you: that you give me a chance to prove myself." Mor turned to address the crowd, raising his voice. That strange, hot flood of new energy was surging within him again, filling him up. His clear, simple words carried to all the gathering. The sudden, commanding power of his speech, amazing to them from such a slender young man, brought all to listen.

"I ask each of you only to give that chance to me. I never sought to become your high-king. I don't understand the ways of this, or why I was chosen. But it's come, and I mean to try my best at it. I thought that I accepted it to make amends for my father's wrongs to Ireland. Now I know there's more in it than that. Now I know that I mean to bring a new justice and a new peace."

He stepped forward to stand over the body of Aodh, pointing down at it.

"Haven't you grown weary of the violence of men like this? It was to contain such men that our laws were meant, and to fairly serve the good of all. Don't you want that? Or will you go on letting a few like him keep tearing Ireland apart?"

He leaned forward and picked up the chieftain's sword. In a short, hard move, he bent the iron blade over his knee, then flung the twisted metal back down to the packed earth.

"Well, I mean to do something," he told them fiercely. "It will be hard, and I may not succeed, but I will listen and I will learn and I will labor, and if I do succeed, I may bring a peace, a richness, and a happiness to Ireland that it has never known. Just let me try. And if I fail you, no man will have to challenge me again, for it's by my choice that I'll leave the high-king's seat. That I vow to you, here in this sacred place, before all the high druids and the chiefs and warriors and the gods of Ireland. Will you accept me?"

The power in him held them, and the truth in his words touched them. They looked at one another, But none spoke. Druids and bards were still eyeing the warriors in an uncertain way. And the warriors, though many were clearly moved, were still hesitating.

"I'll accept you, and I will defend you, Conaire Mor," said Conal Carna, stepping up before him. There was a strange, bright look in his eye, and he spoke with both graveness and great urgency. "I've been no more than a warrior all my life. A hard man and a ruthless man and a man of great violence, like Aodh. But accept me as your champion, and I promise you, so long as you try to do honestly what you have promised, you'll have no more loyal man." He turned and swept his gaze across the warriors. "And what of you?" he challenged. "Will we all agree and see if we can help Ireland, or will we here, today, plunge her into more bloody wars?"

The other warriors, many still reluctant but all understanding the logic of Conal's words, agreed. The comrades of Aodh sheathed their blades and nodded their consent.

A sudden gust of wind blew down across them then, fluttering their cloaks and robes. A great, glad, sighing sound it made, as if nature herself were joining in the relief and joy over the young high-king's acceptance.

"It is the Sidhe," the ard-druid whispered in awe, gazing upward.

And Conaire Mor lifted his face to the skies, into the sighing wind. He felt its soft fingers caress his face and ruffle his long hair.

Chapter Three

Dun Dalgan

The boy sat astride a wave-smoothed boulder, gazing out at the glistening sea.

He had gone there quite often in the last months. It was the only place he could feel any freedom.

It was a dangerous place to go, but that only added a kind of excitement to it. Above him a narrow, ragged scar twisted down the smooth cheek of the cliffs. He looked up at the broken trail and experienced that flare of satisfying victory at having found some challenge in spite of his mother's obsessive care.

Perhaps it was unfair, his sense told him, but at the age of twelve, the world pressed in suffocatingly, especially on one whose life had been sheltered behind a timber palisade.

His eyes followed the trail up to where Dun Dalgan sat upon the jutting clifftop. From so far below, the high walls seemed harmless, soft, like a gray cloth draped across the rocks. They held no power over him here. Only the sea did.

From within the fortress even the sea was kept at a safe distance. The immense power of the crashing waves was far below, and the outstretching fingers of the spray couldn't reach him. But here—here he could feel it, smell it, wade in its cold, gripping waters. He was aware of the life, the violence, that lay always ready in it. Often he felt it was the only thing he had to himself. And more than once he had experienced the impulse to lie down in the waves that tugged at him, to let them lift him, carry him away.

But today the sun was setting, dropping behind the cliffs, sending a wall of shadow out to trap him between it and the lapping sea. He knew he had to start the long trip back while he could see the trail.

He rose from the rock and turned, then stiffened with surprise. A girl stood near him, beneath the rocky cliff by the trail's base.

At least, she seemed a girl at first, barely older than himself. Her slender body was outlined by a light tunic of gray shimmering cloth, which the sea wind pressed against her. Her face was smooth and pale, and her hair, a white-gold flow, glowed even in the shadow of the cliff. But as he searched the face, he found that in the glistening, blue-silver eyes was something that went far beyond physical youth.

There was eternity glowing in the bright circles of light, and its power held him.

Then his surprise was overwhelmed by anger and disappointment. Someone had found his hiding place!

"Who are you?" he challenged.

"Faythleen I am," she answered in a gentle, soothing voice. "Don't worry, Sentanta. I'll not be telling anyone about your coming here."

He was startled by her reading of his thoughts, but for some reason he had no doubt at all that she spoke the truth.

"Where are you from?" he asked. "I've not seen you about here before."

That seemed to amuse her.

"And just how much do you know of things beyond your circling timber walls?" she asked, smiling.

He frowned and dropped his eyes. "Almost nothing," he admitted grudgingly.

"And why do you come here?" she asked.

"What else is there to do?" he answered. "When the winter is upon us, I've no arguments with staying by the fire in our hall. But on these summer days . . ."

"I know," she said, nodding. "It's hard not to have the freedom to get about."

Something about her inspired his confidence. He moved toward her.

"You're not from the dun," he said. "Tell me, are all lads

my age trapped like this? Does everyone go through this agony? It doesn't seem right for Mother to keep me so close to home."

"And what does your father say?"

"My father?" A sadness filled the boy's eyes.

"Is he dead, then?" she asked gently.

"He's alive. But they say the Fool-of-the-Forth has touched him."

"Fool-of-the-Forth?" she repeated.

"You must surely be a stranger here if you've not heard of that!" he said with amazement. "He is one of the Sidhe —the Hidden Ones. His touch brings madness. Ah, he must be a terrible, powerful, monstrous being, like all the rest of Them."

"Oh, I see," she said, another hint of amusement brightening her silver eyes.

"My father has been that way since before I was old enough to know him. For a time he wandered the dun like a gray wraith stalking and frightening people. Now my mother has made rooms for him, and there he keeps himself."

"And do you think he's mad?"

The lad considered this thoughtfully before replying, "No. To me it seems that he's in hiding, as I often hid in my childhood when there was something awful I wanted to avoid."

She nodded. She seemed quite pleased with his perceptions, but she did not speak.

"And so my mother rules the dun," he went on, a note of chagrin apparent in the words.

"And you as well," the girl added.

"Until I decide to go," he told her, more decisively. "I do know something of the world outside the dun. Someday I'll be old enough to enter it."

"Sentanta, I think the time for that decision is coming very soon."

"What do you mean?" he asked, confused.

"Listen to me now, Sentanta."

She moved close to him. He felt her closeness in the sense of warmth that enveloped him, smelled it in a fragrance of spring fields. She laid a fine, slim hand upon his arm and spoke with earnestness, meeting his gaze.

"Today, now, while we are talking here, things are changing in that world you know so little of. Events are beginning to form. It's time that you became a part of them."

A surge of excitement, like the rush of a chill sea wave, rose in him at these words. But it receded as reality returned.

"But I can't leave my mother now. And I've no place to go."

"Your mother may not be wishing you to go, but she knows you will. Yes, she knows. Where and when is coming in its time."

The natural wariness of his age brought him to step back suddenly, eyeing her. "And just what matter is all of this to you?" he demanded.

She smiled disarmingly. "I've an interest in those who love the sea," she said in a genial way.

He wasn't satisfied, but the sun had dropped beyond the clifftop, and an early nightfall was coming to the sheltered beach. He would have to begin the climb while he could still see.

"Could we talk again?" he asked her. "It's time to be going up now."

"We'll talk again," she promised.

"Good. Now come with me. I'll help you along the path."

He started toward the path, but stopped when he didn't hear her following. He turned back; she was gone. There was nothing behind him but the empty beach and the sea.

A sense of strangeness seized him, and he scrambled up the trail.

Sentanta reached the clifftop easily and circled the timber palisade to Dun Dalgan's front gates. When he reached them, he found the fortress in commotion. Troops of the household company and people from the village below the dun were in the inner yard, milling excitedly. As they shifted about, he caught a glimpse of what was within the circle of the crowd, and his interest soared. The late sun glinted on the brass and iron fittings of several massive chariots of war.

He ran forward to see more, but as he passed the gateway he collided with a figure just inside.

He found himself facing a tall, lean-bodied man. A warrior he was, his red cloak clasped by a brooch of enameled bronze, his tunic richly embroidered with gold, his sword and short sword ornately fitted.

The boy stared in astonishment until a voice said to him, "Boy, what's wrong? Is it stunned by the blow you are?"

He looked up to a face nearly half a head above his own.

Quiet, light blue eyes regarded him curiously, and a faint smile played around the wide, thin mouth.

Sentanta realized that the man had found his clumsiness amusing, and he would have felt foolish if he had not been so much in awe.

"You're a warrior of the Red Branch!" he managed to get out haltingly.

"Aye, lad." The amusement turned to puzzlement. "And haven't you seen such as myself before?"

"No. No, sir. I've not been much beyond these walls."

The look of puzzlement deepened. "Why not, boy? You look old enough."

"I'm twelve, sir."

"Twelve? Then you're surely a tall and strong-appearing lad for your age. And you're not in trousers, so you must have some rank. Who are you?"

"I'm called Sentanta, son of Sualtim."

A shadow crossed the tall man's face. Sentanta noted it without understanding the reason for it.

"You're nephew to Conchobar then, lad?"

"I am," he answered proudly, glad of this connection with the famed Red Branch champions.

The man sounded suddenly angry, but his words seemed directed to someone else. "So, it is true! That such a lad, a high-king's nephew, is hidden away here!"

He looked searchingly at Sentanta as if he would speak more, but then he shook his head, turning to another matter more pressing to him at the moment.

"Look here, Sentanta, I've brought news for those of the dun. Could you take me in to see your mother now?"

"I will, certainly," the boy answered with eagerness.

The warrior turned to pick up his shield, and Sentanta saw that the circle of iron-bound leather was painted red and fitted with plates of enameled brass in a pattern like that of his brooch. The design was a familiar one to the boy.

"Why, you are Conal Carna!" he exclaimed, with even greater exuberance than before.

The man seemed flattered and smiled again. "How do you know about me so isolated here?"

"Though I've not been much outside the dun, I've learned about Ulster's champions listening to the bards. Mother won't allow them within the great hall, but I've managed to make my way to the warriors' quarters a time or two and hear them sing their lays before the warriors' fires." He smiled slyly at his cleverness.

While he had expected the man to laugh at this, Conal Carna only looked at the boy in a pitying way. But in the excitement of meeting such a renowned warrior, Sentanta took little note of it. He made haste to lead the visitor toward the tec.

The tec was the main building of the dun—a round, timber-sided building roofed with thatch. As they approached its main doors, Sentanta gathered the courage to ask a question:

"Why are you here, champion? It must be some great news to bring you. They say no warriors of note have come here since my uncle took the throne of Ulster."

"It's great news, right enough," Conal said emphatically. "I've ridden hard and long to bring it to all of Ulster's duns."

It was then that Sentanta saw something he hadn't noticed in the excitement. Conal was moving stiffly, and his rich tunic and cloak were spotted with mud thrown up by galloping teams.

As they passed by the chariots surrounded by the crowd, he saw that the cars and wheels were also black with the rich mud of Ireland's roads. The horses stood with heads hung forward in fatigue, while drivers as weary as they moved sluggishly to unhitch them. For even the greatest weariness and the pain of wounds would never stop a charioteer from seeing first to his team and his vehicle.

Near the doorway of the tec was a group of other warriors, drooping in attitudes of fatigue. They were more of the crimson-cloaked Red Branch warriors of the heroic songs, the boy noted, but also men who tired like other men. And though the bardic tales lost a bit of their heroic gleam, they yet became more real to him too.

Conal paused and told the men to wait. Then he and the boy strode on into the hall.

Though Dun Dalgan hadn't the grandness of a high-king's dun, it was the principal fortress of a rich tuath, and its hall was a fair rival for most in Ireland. The great ceiling timbers and the bronze-paneled walls of the circular room had been decorated by the finest artisans in the province.

The room was empty when they first entered. But as they started across the broad floor, Sentanta's mother appeared from a chamber on the far side. She moved out through the rows of dining tables to meet them by the central fire pit, where a low fire burned.

As they neared her, the warrior saw that Dechtire was yet a beautiful woman, honey-haired, slim, unmarked by age. But Sentanta could see that she was disturbed, for lines of worry deepened about her eyes and mouth as she watched her son approaching with the Ulster champion.

Still, she greeted Conal Carna politely.

"We welcome you to Dun Dalgan," she said. "It is some years since I have seen you."

"You have stayed away from Emain Macha too long, Dechtire," he responded graciously. "Your beauty is missed there."

Sentanta looked at his mother with new eyes. He had not thought of her in that way before. After all, she was nearly thirty years of age.

Dechtire did not find pleasure in Conal's words. She only answered flatly, "I can't leave the dun. I've my son and my husband to think of here."

"Ah, yes," he replied slowly. "And where is Sualtim? Is he better?"

"He is the same," she said tonelessly. "He has his own rooms nearby, and we keep him within them most of the day. No one goes near him. They're afraid that they'll be touched by the same madness that has reached him."

"I'm sorry for that," said Conal, looking a bit startled by her candor.

"So, you can see why I must stay with him," she said. "Now, what of you? What's driven you abroad in this wet time?"

"I've brought word that I think means well for all of Ireland," he said, his face brightening and an enthusiasm entering his voice. "I've come from Tara. Conaire Mor has taken the throne of the ard-rie."

"A new high-king for Ireland?" the boy gasped. "How?"

"Quiet, Sentanta," his mother said, eyeing him sharply.

She noted the rising color in his face, the tenseness of excitement in his limbs, and she felt a prickling of fear. He should have been sent away from here.

But Conal grinned at the boy's excitement, for it further rekindled his own, despite his weariness.

"The Bull Feast has found him to be the rightful king," he went on. "And by all the gods my people swear by, I can feel it's the truth. He's a man of justice and of strength; a young man, not even twenty years of age. He means to unite Ireland and bring it peace, and I've come to find support for him through all the tuaths of Ulster."

"Why is it I've heard nothing before of this Conaire Mor?" she asked.

"The story is that his mother was an orphan," Carna supplied, "fostered by a family of herding men of Eterscel, but a woman of great beauty. The king saw her one day and ordered his warriors to bring her to him, asking no leave of the cowherds. It seems his druids had prophesied that it was only a woman of an unknown race who could bear him a son, and he was certain this was the woman who had been foretold.

"But she was a brave and a proud one, and she boldly told the king she'd not wed him or bear his child unless she was given freedom after it, and the child with her.

"Eterscel, being a weak and a frightened man, agreed. She wed him, and bore him a boy child, and named him Conaire, son of Mes Buachall—that is, son of the cowherd's foster-child. But she brought the child away with her, back to the household where she was raised, where she said he would have a better rearing and come to know more of the common people of Ireland and the truths of life.

"They say the king had little heart to see the boy after that, and he was beset with his own trials till his end. He saw that the household of the cowherds was treated well. He ordered that other young nobles—five orphaned boys of the house of Donn Dessa, a champion of the clans from Muclesi—be reared with the boy for company, and that his own champions and druids should give help in the boy's proper bringing up. But he never visited young Conaire himself.

"Though the lad had no love for his father, still he came to Tara after the king's death. He came as the druids foresaw and he proved his courage. To me he also proved his honesty. I don't know why or how, but I believe he can do as he says."

Even the bare sketch of events Conal had given was enough to inflame Sentanta's imagination. The boy fleshed it out with fantasy and bardic tales, envisioning great battles, racing chariots, flashing swords and spears.

But his mother seemed unmoved by the momentous event

that had taken place. Her manner remained distant and very
cool.

"This man must be unusual indeed to have billowed to life
a new spark in so burned down a cinder as yourself, Conal,"
she said bluntly. "But what is it you're wanting of me?"

"Only your acceptance of this new high-king, and that of the
other tuath chieftains, to take to Conchobar."

At this a faint touch of amusement lit her face, lifting away
some of the years which her solemness gave her.

"I know nothing about this Conaire Mor," she said, "but I
do know that my brother will never accept the authority of
any other."

"Conchobar is a fair man," Conal answered in a careful way.
"He'll see what this unity can do for Ireland."

"Fair," she repeated thoughtfully. Then she shrugged. "Well,
if this new king can truly bring a peace, you'll certainly have
my own support."

"Good!" Conal said delightedly. "Then, my Queen, I've only
to request food and lodging for my men tonight."

"Tonight?" That brought a look of concern into her face once
more. Quickly she said, "But if your mission is an urgent one,
you must be wishing to go on."

"My Queen," Conal said in surprise and puzzlement, "it's
nearly dark! My men are exhausted and none has eaten in a
full day."

"There's a bruidhean at the next road crossing," she answered shortly.

The boy couldn't understand her reluctance. Brehon Law
demanded that she give shelter to warriors, especially ones of
such rank as Conal Carna. Conal himself seemed scarcely able
to credit her denial.

"But, my Queen, this is a service you would grant to any
wandering *filidh* or traveling herdsman," he protested.

"Mother, you must let them stay. . . ." Sentanta broke in
impulsively.

"Wait!" she told the warrior and turned sharply upon her
son. "Sentanta, it is getting late. Go to the kitchens and have
the cook feed you. Then go to bed!"

"But, Mother . . ." he began in agony. Missing even a moment with the champion was unthinkable to him.

She cut off his protest. "Go now! I'll see to this."

He knew from her tone that she was not to be defied. Angrily he left them and went out through the back of the hall to the kitchens. But it was only a moment's work for him to exit the building there, run around the outside of the tec, and sneak in through the front doors again, slipping into the room's peripheral shadows where he could hear their talk echoing in the large, empty space.

"And for what real reason would you be wishing to keep us away from here?" Conal was saying angrily. "What is it that makes you so afraid?"

"I've no need for the boy's head to be filled with warrior tales or further excited with visions of Tara or Emain Macha," she replied sternly.

"Why? So you can keep him here?" The warrior's vexation was causing him to throw aside the deference he would normally have paid in speaking to ranking nobility. "I can see what you've done. The lad wants only to know the world as others do. He's soaked up every bit of it he can, despite your efforts to keep him locked away here."

"He is happy," she said with force.

"He will leave you, Lady," Conal shot back. "And your own strangling hold on him may be the cause of it."

"I will keep him," she said stubbornly.

"Is that the reason Sualtim's locked away?" he accused. "So he'll not tell the boy truths you don't want him to know?"

"Careful, Carna," she said icily. "A champion of the Red Branch you may be, but it's a queen you're addressing now, and a sister to your high-king!"

"All right, my Queen," he said, but not contritely. "I'll take my men out of this sacred dun of yours. But I'll tell you now that you'll not be keeping that boy here once he knows he's of an age to enter the training school at Emain Macha!"

Stiffly Conal turned and marched from the hall. He gathered his warriors and rode out of the dun, proudly disdaining the comforts of the nearby hostel. Instead they drove on, heading west, into fading light of the fallen sun, toward some tuath more hospitable.

It was early the next morning, long before the fortress had begun to wake, that a slim figure lithely swung himself over the parapet and, with a length of rope, lowered himself down on the outside.

At the bottom, Sentanta stopped, surveying the countryside with grim determination. The main highway led north, and he would take it, somehow finding his way to fabled Emain Macha.

He knew what he had to do now. The events of the past day had shown him, and the need burned in him, allowing him no rest.

It was a pain within him to be leaving his mother so, but now he understood that she had kept him there unfairly, all but a prisoner, and that she would never willingly let him go.

But he had to go.

He had to know if the warrior he had met was the image of what he must become. And Conal had pointed the way for him: to enter the training school at his uncle's court.

He had with him his only real possessions, his hurley stick and ball. Briskly he started off along the road, driving the ball ahead of him with smooth, sure strokes that sent it flying far before him, along the path that he would follow into a new world.

Chapter Four

Emain Macha

From the high sunroom of Emain Macha's main hall, Meave watched the boys playing at hurley in the *faithchte* below.

It was a glorious day. One of those rare, cloudless days that come to Ireland in early summer. The long, narrow room was warm, and all the shutters were open to admit the fragrant breezes.

Behind her, the other women of the dun sat, chatting amiably, working at their weaving or at embroidering fine designs into the light wool summer cloaks. Several small children, little interested in such tedious labor, sat on the plank floor amid the women, playing with a tiny household of carved wooden figures.

Meave's attention was fully absorbed by the hurley game. There was nothing else to stimulate her interest, ebbed like a sea at lowest tide by the soft summer afternoon. No violent waves, no spreading ripples stirred within Meave. There was only the ennui of the captive wolf, the boredom of the tethered hawk. A strange, unnatural-seeming state for one who radiated such an aura of active life.

Her looks were youthful, bold, her features clean of line, with a strong chin, a wide, firm mouth, and widely spaced eyes of blue that flickered light and dark with her changing moods. And the hair which fell about her shoulders was a thick, undulating flow of molten bronze.

Yet, although she seemed a girl in looks and in the slim, pliant body she now stretched to ease the ache of inactivity, at twenty years of age Meave had already been five years a queen.

She stretched further, pulling herself taut, trying to draw tingling pain into her limbs to convince herself that they were still alive. She looked around at the other women docilely doing their work in the quiet room and longed for escape. Oh, some escape!

Meave envied the freedom of the small children, and even more that of the boys playing below. She turned back to watch their hurley game again. She found at least a certain exhilaration in the savage, fast-moving sport.

Next to war, it was the most demanding activity in its need for skill and strength. The wooden ball flew back and forth across the green, impelled by the flailing sticks of fifty determined players. The sounds of their cheers, like the screams and rattles of a flock of angry crows, filled the otherwise somnolent afternoon.

Vaguely, above the players' din, Meave was also aware of voices drifting up from just below her. They belonged to her husband, Conchobar, and his chieftain, Fergus MacRogh, who sat playing *fidchell* and talking near the main doors of the hall. She paid them little mind until she heard the name of Conaire Mor.

Curious, she craned out over the windowsill and looked down toward the men. She felt some interest in hearing about her young nephew, the new ard-rie of all Ireland.

Fergus and Conchobar were facing each other across the square wooden playing board. Both contemplated the finely wrought set of gold and silver men, but it was clear that their minds were on a more serious game—a political one.

"Why is it we're expected to support this whelp?" Conchobar

was saying in the elaborately casual voice which so often masked a cutting edge. Behind his thick brows, dark eyes glittered like the sun on a deep pond. "High-kings of Ireland have come and gone like the seasons, and with as little effect on the way of things. Only Ulster has remained strong."

How like her husband to place Ulster first, Meave thought. Even though what he said was true.

"Conal feels that this is a man who can unite all Ireland strongly at last," Fergus answered carefully. The red-haired giant was a deceptive man. While outwardly seeming fit for only the physical arts of war, he had a keen mind as well, and a patience and practical sense that aided him in dealing with his intractable king.

"No man can unite Ireland," Conchobar said derisively, shaking his head. "Why, that goes against the very spirit that makes her strong! I'll never live to see it done, nor do I hope to."

"Yet Conal's saying the other provinces are ready to support him. If he's strong enough to bring this unity and peace, we'll look the fools surely for not joining in."

"Maybe," Conchobar growled, like some wolfhound prodded from its food, "but we'll wait till we know his power won't just fade away in the sunlight like a dusting of new snow. If he can pull together a ruling power, and if the other province kings truly let him rule, then maybe we'll think of sending hostages and giving a bond to him. Maybe!"

"Conal says he needs our support now," Fergus persisted, "to show the others that unity will come. He's already urged most of our clan chieftains to agree."

"Bloody Raven!" Conchobar swore. "Can that sword bender be so in love with him? I sent Conal to Tara to see what had happened there, not to involve us in their little intrigues. He can't think past the point of his own spear. He's a man-killer, Fergus, not a druid! By the Dagda, we're talking about our independence here!"

Anger flared in Fergus a bit at that. Conal was a friend, and a bright and dedicated warrior as well. What he proposed made sense, and only Conchobar's cursed arrogance kept the Ulster ruler from accepting it.

"Take off that blind boar's head and think clearly, my friend," Fergus said boldly. "There's much Ireland can gain from real unity. Your chieftains have agreed to that, and so have I."

Conchobar, son of Nessa, did not take such a tone with good

grace, even from his closest friend and greatest chieftain. He drew his head up slowly to glare at Fergus with the shiny black marbles of his eyes.

"I will not give my support before another Tailteen Fair has come," he said slowly, coldly, finally.

"But we've more than two years until that time," Fergus protested.

"True enough," the king agreed. "By then we should know how much this Mor can do."

As their argument continued, Meave's interest flagged. She neither understood nor cared about such things. But then a sharp remark from Conchobar reclaimed her attention.

"What's happening out there?"

Meave lifted her gaze toward the playing field. The game had stopped, and the boys had gathered in a large circle around a lad she had never seen before. She noted that Cormac Conlingas, the arrogant product of Conchobar's first marriage, confronted the stranger while the rest watched uneasily.

"Who is that boy?" asked Conchobar.

"I'm not certain," Fergus replied. "He came into the game from nowhere. I saw him take the ball and play it around the field as if he were alone. They couldn't stop him. Now Cormac has challenged him."

He said this last without approval. He knew Cormac to be a bully with the other lads, using his father's position like a club. He didn't like the way Cormac was taking advantage of the new boy.

"It looks as if there may be trouble there," he said to Conchobar. "Should we go down?"

The high-king was watching the confrontation with interest. "No," he answered. "Let them work it out themselves."

On the field, the newcomer was facing his opposition with tremendous calm. He was a handsome lad, tall and sinewy of build. And his skill at hurley made him a threat that Cormac could not ignore.

"Be out of it now," Cormac said. A strongly built fifteen-year-old, he moved forward aggressively, his stick clasped tightly in both hands. "You're not of our school here. You weren't asked to play."

"I've come as a stranger here, and I'm only asking a stranger's welcome from you," the other replied reasonably.

"You've no right to come into our game without asking leave or putting your life under our protection."

The boy appeared to find that amusing. "I've little need of protection from the likes of you."

"What is it you're saying?" cried Cormac, moving closer and lifting his stick higher. "Who are you to deny it?" He looked around at his friends and added derisively, "It's certain that he's no more than a common warrior's son."

He didn't note the glint that entered the new boy's eyes at that, or see the muscles tighten in the smooth, innocent-seeming face.

"There's no reason why we can't be letting him play," put in a dark-haired youth who stepped out from the group, two others at his back.

"Keep out of this, Naoise," Cormac snapped. "And your brothers too. I'm the one to make the decision here, and I say that our teams are chosen and we've no need for new players."

"And just who are you?" asked the new boy.

"I'm Cormac Conlingas," he said proudly, affronted that this intruder would not know.

"Are you the king's son, then?" the stranger said, his face brightening with an amiable smile. "Why, we've no cause at all to be fighting. You and I—"

"You and I will be going different ways right now!" Cormac broke in.

That hurt the new boy. The smile was wiped away. Anger touched his voice as he said, "Your being the king's son doesn't make you the captain here. Only the best playing does."

Some sounds of amusement, though quickly stifled, rose from the group of boys at that. More than a few disliked Cormac.

"Would you be saying that I'm not the best one here?" Cormac replied, reddening with indignation.

"From the little play I've seen, I'd not call you the best, or even one as good as myself. If you would care to play instead of talk, we might find out."

This challenge from a stripling pushed Cormac's outrage to the brink. He took another step forward, shoving the boy back with the curved end of his stick. "Boy, I'll tell you again: get out of this!"

The intruder stepped back defensively. His own stick still hung beside him in one hand. "I've not come here seeking a fight with you," he said tightly.

"Come on, lads!" Cormac called to his friends. "Let's drive him away from here!"

Some dozen of the boys started forward, sticks up in attack. And, as they did, the lone boy's stick swung up in a swift, sweeping, one-handed blow that caught Cormac unprepared, knocking him unceremoniously to the hard-packed earth.

There were a muddled few moments after that as the boy descended in fury upon the other attackers in the group. Cormac's supporters tried to surround their foe, but he seemed to move in all directions at once, parrying, swinging, thrusting with the stick. His heavy instrument struck home with accuracy and force, while all their blows seemed wasted.

"Stop! Stop this!" Naoise cried, he and his two brothers moving into the embattled group. "This is no fair fight!"

The fighting did abruptly stop, but not because of the efforts of the three. There were simply no combatants left.

Some had staggered away, bruised by the heavy stick. Others stood dazed or lay upon the ground, nursing damaged limbs or bleeding heads. Only the new boy stood unmarked, his stick still raised, glaring about him for signs of a new attack.

"I didn't realize I meant unfair to them," Naoise said with a grin.

This sign of friendliness reached through the victor's rage. He lowered his stick and somewhat sheepishly smiled back. Then, as he gazed around him again, more lucidly, he looked a bit disconcerted by the devastation he had caused.

Conchobar and Fergus, who had started for the group when the fight began, now arrived to find it ended. As they walked up, the other youths fell back, leaving the newcomer facing two imposing figures, one bearlike in girth, the other lean and stiff like a tall pine.

Conchobar looked the boy over intently. The king's grim mouth was straight and firm with displeasure, but behind the heavy brows the dark eyes smiled, as if he approved of what the boy had done but could not show it while his own son lay bleeding on the ground.

"Come here," the ard-rie commanded.

The boy stepped closer, without a sign of fear. "I meant only to play," he said boldly, unashamed by what he'd done.

"You're handy enough with that stick in many ways, lad," Conchobar replied. "Cormac, get up!"

"He came at us without warning or cause," his son whined as he climbed unsteadily to his feet, one hand pressed tightly against a bleeding head.

Conchobar turned a cold eye on him. "Quiet! It seems to

me you've gotten what you were seeking. Perhaps you'll be gauging your opponent a bit more carefully next time. Now go clean your wounds, and take the rest of your sorry pack with you!"

For a moment Cormac stared in shock, unused to such lack of support. Then he turned and charged blindly away, followed by the rest of his wounded comrades. The others of the group stayed close about, eager to find out more of the new boy.

"You've quite an arm, lad," Conchobar remarked. "And even with your height, you seem too slender of build to have such a surprising power. What age are you—fourteen?"

"Twelve, my King."

"Twelve! You are a tall lad for your age! And have you had training in arms before?"

"None, my King."

"You've a born talent for the fighting then, that's certain enough." He smiled openly now. "But tell me, lad, you seem to know me, while I don't know you. Who is it sent you into fosterage to me at such an age?"

"No one, my King," the boy answered honestly. "I've come here myself to join the training school and become a Red Branch warrior." He drew himself up proudly. "I am Sentanta, son of your own sister Dechtire."

The warmth died from the king's face instantly, extinguished like a candle snuffed out by a sudden gust. The eyes became fixed, the lids dropping to become slits through which the dark glitter came, hard and chill as ice. But the smile remained, though now set with the hardness of a graven stone.

It was Fergus who spoke next, swooping forward to clasp the boy in a two-handed grip, bellowing his greeting with joy. "Sentanta! It's glad I am to be seeing you after these long years!"

"What are you doing here?" Conchobar asked in a voice as cold as his look. "Your mother vowed to keep you at Dun Dalgan."

"It's time he was in school here," Fergus said.

"He is too young," the king shot back.

Fergus turned from the lad to face his ruler squarely, not prepared to lose this argument. "I say that by the virtue of the skill he's shown today, and by his great gallantry in seeking to avoid the fight, he's proven to us that he *is* old enough."

Conchobar confronted Fergus in return, alarming the boys

with the sudden rage that filled his voice. "It'll take more than a cat-and-dog fight with a gang of boys to prove to *me* that this . . ." he seemed to force a word back, "this MacDechtire is worthy of our bond. It's in your hands, Fergus, as once agreed. Do what you wish. I'll take no part in it!"

With that the king turned and stalked away, leaving Sentanta bewildered by his sudden change in attitude. Fergus also stared after Conchobar, puzzled himself and a bit irritated. Then he shrugged and looked back at the boy.

"Don't be worrying about that," he said dismissingly. "Conchobar's a man of temper, and he's troubled now. He'll take to you—in time."

"My mother's told me of him," the boy said, trying to smile, though something else still troubled him.

Fergus clapped a giant paw on the lad's shoulder, his own broad smile of elation returning.

"So, Sentanta, you've finally escaped your mother to join us here!" He shook his head in amazement. "You know, Cathbad told me not a day ago that you'd be coming soon. Maybe there is some truth in that druidic lore."

The boy looked up at the giant warrior in curiosity. "Cathbad?" he said. "You mean the ard-druid?"

"Aye, lad. And I've a feeling he'll be wanting to see you once he knows you're here."

"The ard-druid of all Ulster!" the boy said in an awed voice. "And, are you really Fergus MacRogh?"

"You know me too, then?"

"Who wouldn't know the fiery look of Ireland's great champion!" the boy said, his buoyant spirits restored. "The bards sing their finest lays of you!"

Fergus laughed boomingly and said, "With a tongue of silver to accompany your strong arm, you'll have no trouble making friends here." He nodded toward the three lads who had given Sentanta their support. "You've some good ones already, by the look of it."

"And I thank them," the boy said graciously.

"It's ourselves who're thanking you for blunting the sharp point of Cormac's spear," the tallest of them said. "We are the sons of Usna. I'm Naoise. These two are Ainnle and Ardan. We're glad to welcome you to our company, Sentanta."

Fergus looked around him at the remaining group of youths. "Well then, lads, now that we've settled things, let's have the game continue with your new player." To Sentanta he added, "After the game, I'll see you're properly settled. For now, let's see you use those skills of yours—on the ball!"

From her sunroom, Meave had watched the confrontation closely, tensely, her body stretched far out over the windowsill. The new boy's victory had surprised her, filled her with excitement and a sense of tingling satisfaction she hadn't felt in a long while. It was as if he'd struck for her a blow against her years of enforced enslavement here. The tyranny of Conchobar, as represented in his son, had been challenged at last.

Now, as Conchobar reached the hall, stalking in through the great doors just below, she moved away to the stairway that opened into the vast central chamber. She leaned over the balcony and called out to her husband as he crossed the floor.

He stopped and looked up toward her. "My Queen?" he asked impatiently.

She smiled slightly, not able to hide the strange, exhilarating sense that this had been a victory over him.

"I think you made a misjudgment to allow that fight," she said almost tauntingly. "Your son seems incapable of carrying through his bullying alone."

The face below grew sharper as its muscles tensed. "And what do you know of training a warrior, Meave? He must be prepared to fight all the time!"

"Must he also learn how to intimidate a boy?"

"That boy proved himself quite well enough," the king admitted grudgingly.

"And if he hadn't?"

"We all have things we have to prove, my Queen," he said in measured tones.

"What does that mean?" she demanded.

"It means that I at least do have a son."

With that he turned and strode on, leaving her to glare after him silently.

Behind her the sunroom was hushed, all conversation having suddenly stopped. She turned to find the ladies of the dun busily at their work. None of them looked up at her, but she knew that they had heard the exchange.

Well, let them hear! she thought rebelliously. It was no secret that she and Conchobar shared little love.

She recrossed the plank floor to the windows and looked out

again. Out in the yard, the boys were back at their play, and the new lad had joined them—apparently accepted now—though under the watchful eye of Fergus. The lad played beautifully, with the practiced grace of the maturer boys and with a natural speed and skill even the oldest of them couldn't match.

Strange how he attracted her interest. He was an intriguing blend of contrasts: that fresh, boyish, almost pretty face and the skills and physique of maturity; that pleasant manner and that potential for violence.

Yet it wasn't his physical appearance or his manner that drew her. She wondered if it was simply his being there alone and defying that taunting crowd. It was much the same situation as her own had been when, at fourteen, she had been brought alone from her sweet Connacht to be Conchobar's bride. And it was much the same as the situation she still lived with after all these years—still an alien here, still trapped and useless.

She turned to glare back at the women again, catching an eye or two that quickly looked away. She knew they thought her a curse to Conchobar, as did the king himself.

She wished she had the courage that boy had, to face them and make them accept her as she was. But Conchobar always had her great, unforgivable failure to throw up to her.

The game below was ending. The boys scattered, heading off on different missions of their own. Fergus called the new boy to him, and together they walked up toward the main hall.

They were heading around the tec toward the quarters of the boys in the training school. As they passed near the sunroom, Meave called out to Fergus.

He stopped and looked up at her, his face lighting with a great smile. "Meave!" he boomed jovially. "You're a fair sight on a fine day. Fresh as the air itself!"

The hearty, friendly voice cheered her, as always. Kind Fergus. The only one here who had always been a comfort, a support.

"Where are you taking our new arrival?" she asked.

"To see him settled in quarters so he'll have some chance to wash and rest himself."

"Please see also that he has his supper with us in the hall tonight," she requested. "We must show him some better welcome than he's had this far."

"Aye, Meave, I will do that," he agreed, but wondering why she was taking this unusual interest in one of the boys.

She realized then that Sentanta was staring rather fixedly up at her. She met his eye and felt a sudden, startling surge of energy, a sense like recognition, as if somehow she knew him. Some strange power there was that met between them, locking them together, holding them.

She was in that instant aware that what had drawn her to the boy was something greater, something deeper, which she didn't really understand. It was just a flicker, like a lightning stroke illuminating and then gone, leaving the darkness to close in again. The contact was broken. Fergus gave her a farewell wave and started off. The boy gave her a boy's broad grin in parting and fell in behind him.

Her face drawn in a thoughtful frown, she watched them round the side of the tec and pass from sight.

Chapter Five

Family

The train of four-wheeled carts and two-wheeled chariots rolled in through the wide gateway in Tara's outer palisade.

As it pulled up before the long stable sheds set against the curved wall of logs, a beaming Conaire Mor rushed across the yard to it. With great hugs and laughter and exclamations of joy he greeted the passengers as they descended from the cars.

This open display of such warmth and elation was viewed by those going about their business in the bustling fortress yard—warriors and workers and serving folk—with amusement. But the faces of a small group of druids and bards who watched from the yard's far side showed no slightest trace of humor, expressing their disapproval for such improperly frivolous behavior in their high-king.

Mor gave no heed to them in his welcoming, putting arms

out to encompass all five of the young men who moved in around him to clasp him in return.

"My brothers!" he said in a most emphatic way, wrestling the lot of them playfully for a moment. "You don't know how good it is to have you in this lonely place!"

Then he saw the dark-haired young woman who had descended from her own car and now moved toward him, beaming happily.

"Fionualla!" he cried, and rushed forward, sweeping up the slender form of the girl and whirling her around.

Delighted, she began to laugh, her fair cheeks taking on a rosy flush. He dropped her then and seized both her hands, looking down into her bright eyes.

"Fionualla, it was you I most feared wouldn't come," he told her.

"Well, I nearly didn't, Conaire," she said frankly. "My father and my uncle felt it wasn't my place, that I . . ." she became suddenly shy, dropping her eyes, her voice growing uncertain, "well, that you shouldn't be bothered by the likes of any of my family here."

"How could they think that?" Conaire said in shock. "It's like my own blood they are. They know that."

"They do, Conaire," said Fergel, the eldest of the five young men. "But you know them, too. They're only herdsmen, simple folk, and feel a bit strange about the grand ways of kings and such."

"Aye, that's true enough," Ferogain, the youngest, red-haired brother, said with a laugh. "They've even fears that we'll be corrupted by the rich, wild life here."

"Here's hoping that they're right!" enthusiastically added the rotund brother named Lomna Druth.

"Hush, Fool!" Fergel said sharply. "Yes, I suppose they do fear that a little, Conaire. But they'll come around to it in time, I know. And then we'll have them here."

"I'm certain that we will," Mor told his foster-brother, grinning. "And I do thank you for persuading them to let Fionualla come."

He put up a hand to her chin and gently lifted her gaze back to meet his.

"The only thing that would be a bother to me from you would be your absence," he told her.

She saw the truth of his words glowing in his eyes and her smile returned.

"Better," he declared. Then, keeping a hold on one of her hands, he turned to the others. "And now I want you to come along with me. I want to show all of Tara to you. It really is a most wonderful place!"

He gave orders to the drivers and the stable grooms to tend to the vehicles. After that, with Fionualla beside him, he led the way across the fortress yard.

As they went, he pointed out the features of the great dun. The herdsman's daughter and his foster-brothers, who, like Mor, had been raised in the country and away from such sights as this, stared about them in open wonder.

The *faithchte* of Tara an Rie was an immense space. The circular area enclosed by the ringing defensive bank and palisade was over a thousand feet across. This yard contained several large structures. There were lean-to sheds for the stables and for the dun's many craftsmen. There were oval, thatch-roofed buildings for storage and for quartering the servants and soldiers of the household. But two other structures were particularly prominent.

This pair of buildings was near the center of the yard, each one perched upon its own low, rounded mound, each surrounded by a secondary defensive ditch and earth rampart. Both were circular, their curving, wood-shingled walls rising some three stories, and their high peaked roofs of shake rising nearly two more above that. Like twins the two were, save that one was a third greater in girth.

"That building closest to us, the larger one," said Conaire, "that's the Tec Mi-Cuarta, the great banqueting hall. We'll go in there first. Behind it are my own quarters, called the Royal Seat."

As they moved toward the main hall, those about them in the yard or passing by greeted them most congenially, even the serving folk treating their young high-king in a familiar, easy way, though never with disrespect.

"They seem a good-hearted people here," commented Fionualla.

"They are that," Conaire agreed. "And they seem to like me well enough."

"Except that lot, it seems," remarked Lomna Druth. He nodded toward the group of robed men who stood soberly watching them from before a smaller round building at the south side of the yard.

"Well, that is one group I've not gotten quite as close to

as I'd like," Mor admitted thoughtfully. "They've supported me loyally enough. They can't do much else. Still, they're not really sure of me yet. Right now they are a tight and separate little band, like a herd of nervous cows in a lightning storm. That place behind them is their meeting house. The Star of the Bards, it's called. All the Files and the physicians and the Brehons and the druids can go there and plot. It's very private." He shook his head as if to throw off his concern and smiled again. "Ah well. Never mind them. Let's go in."

They had reached the outer rampart of the main hall's defensive ring. He led his company up a ramp and across an earthen causeway to the main doors. As they passed inside the building, there were exclamations of wonder from his friends.

The interior of the huge structure was largely one vast space. Wooden partitions fixed by copper rivets divided the area around the outer wall like wheel spokes, creating fourteen wedge-shaped spaces separate from one another, but still open to the central portion of the hall. Between these rooms and the circle of stones that formed the hearth of the central fire pit, low tables filled the open floor, providing places for several hundred to dine.

All the wood was red yew, the huge panels dividing the outer compartments faced with softly glowing bronze sheets. Each one of the inner ring of wooden pillars supporting the heavy roof beams was thicker than a man and soared up nearly five times a man's height. All were carved from top to bottom with the sinuous, smooth line of some artist of great skill. The curiously distorted birds and beasts who intertwined in chase and play formed a single, complex, continuous design that at once both confused and delighted the eye.

"Conaire," said Ferogain in the breathless voice of an awed child, "this *is* a marvelous place! I could never even have dreamed of something as grand as this. It glows! Like a jewel it is! Like a great, golden brooch!"

"Don't be too much awed by the look of it, my lad," Conaire said lightly, giving Ferogain's hair a playful tousling. "It's still just a place to live, like any other."

"To live," said Lomna Druth, looking around him at the scores of dining tables with great avidity. "And to eat! Where is the food?"

"I warned you, Fool," Fergel scolded in sharp tones. "Don't

be demanding here. Remember, it's the high-king you're speaking to now."

"Now, don't be thinking that way," Mor admonished quickly. "I'm still your brother and your friend. I'll always be that first to you. And I want you to think of this place as your own. Your home as well as mine."

"Well, it's most kind of you to say that," the eldest brother said, but still in a careful, almost deferential manner, not really accepting Mor's declaration. "And it's kind of you to be bothering yourself with bringing us here and showing us about, as busy as you must be now."

"You still don't understand, do you?" Conaire said with a laugh. "This is no bother to me. It's important. And I didn't bring you here to show off my grand fortress. I brought you here to live!"

"Oh, no!" protested Fergel. "Conaire, you can't mean that. We're folk of the country, not of the court. This . . ." he waved his hands around, "this isn't meant for the likes of us!"

"I'm one of you," Mor said. "What's meant for me is meant for you as well."

"I wouldn't mind it," Lomna Druth said frankly, smiling greedily. "There must be lots to eat."

"I wouldn't mind either," added Ferogain, still staring around him in awe.

"Quiet, both of you," the elder brother said sternly. "You'll be shaming us."

"No, they will not," Conaire said. "You are my family. My only family now. I will have you with me. Look here, don't fight me in this. Stay on, at least awhile. I promise you that you'll accept this place. Please!"

"Well . . ." the eldest brother looked doubtful. But he exchanged glances with the others, seeing the eager looks in all their eyes. "All right, Conaire," he agreed. Then he grinned and let his own excitement show. "I can't say I would mind trying it myself."

A man had appeared from the rear of the hall during this discussion and approached them. He was tall, spare, sharp-featured, and severe of look, with graying hair and the leather apron of a household servant. His rigid, spear-pole stance, imperious manner, and long staff of oak also announced that his role was one of command.

"Ah, Chief Steward," Conaire said, turning now to this man. "Let me introduce my family to you." He put an arm around the dark-haired girl's waist. "This is Fionualla, daughter of my foster-father," he began. He raised his other hand to point out his foster-brothers as he announced their names beginning with the eldest: "These are Fergel, Ferger, and Ferobain. This jolly one is Lomna Druth—don't let him in the larder or he'll empty it. And this dazed lad is Ferogain."

The red-haired boy, recalled from his rapt gazing by his name, started and looked around sheepishly.

The steward seemed vastly unimpressed. He looked along his long, sharp beak of nose at them with a supercilious eye, taking in their simple manner and their coarse clothing as if viewing some vagrants who had come begging at the door.

"Yes, my King," was his terse reply.

"I want you to make quarters for them in my own Royal Seat," Conaire told him.

The man's lean, hard, impassive face registered the tiniest twitch of surprise, indicating how massive the shock of this was to him.

"What, these people, my King?" he said. The disbelief in Mor's wishing to do, to him, such an extraordinary thing was clear in his voice.

Conaire noted it, and his own voice took on an uncharacteristically commanding tone. "They are my family. You'll do as I ask. See that all their needs are provided for. Well provided for!"

The rebuke caused the man to raise an entire eyebrow in reaction. But when he spoke again, his voice was more carefully neutral.

"I'll do as you ask, my King," he said. Still, the look he cast upon the visitors made it clear that he felt it beneath his dignity to deal with the likes of such country louts as these.

As he turned and strode grandly off to make the arrangements, Conaire looked after him with a smile.

"Don't mind the old man too much. He's been steward here since my grandfather's time. He does tend to put on some airs."

"And we are a pretty coarse lot as well, Conaire," said Fergel, lifting the edge of his rough wool cloak.

"Well, that's easily remedied," the young king assured them, "and he'll soon grow used to you." He clapped a hand to the shoulders of Fergel and Ferogain. "Now, my good lads, would you mind my leaving you for a while? I've something else I want to show Fionualla."

"What, me?" she said, surprised.

"Yes," he said, turning to her. "It's something especially for you. Would you come with me?"

"Of course," she happily agreed.

"We'll just look about the dun, then, if it's all right," said Fergel.

"Aye. I'd like to see the great armory," said Ferger.

"And I the trophy house," Ferogain put in.

"Anything you like," Conaire said. "I told you my home is now also yours as well, and that I meant."

"Good!" cried a beaming Lomna Druth. "Then it's the larder that I most want to see."

He bustled away in search of it. The others headed toward the main doors to continue their excursions of the wonders of the fortress. Conaire took Fionualla's hand and led her away, across the acres of floor to a wooden staircase at the rear of the vast room.

Curious, she followed him up to a narrow balcony room that rimmed the outer wall on the upper level. Windows here let in the sunlight. He followed the walkway around to a door, which he opened to reveal a small bridge connecting the hall to the companion structure so close by.

"This crosses to my own quarters," he explained. "It's there that I've the surprise for you."

He led her across the bridge and through another door. Here they found themselves in an upper chamber, a sunroom for the high-king's royal house.

It was a wide room, lined along the south with large windows. The shutters of all were thrown fully open now, allowing the warm afternoon sun to flood in and wash the room in a molten gold glow.

The room was appointed sumptuously. Cushions in rich brocades covered the low pallets and seats. The surfaces of oaken tables were polished to a dark, rich sheen. Plush rugs of wool dyed in deep greens covered the plank floor, and tapestries with elaborately worked designs hung on the walls.

"Conaire!" she said softly, staring about with wide eyes.

"Do you like it?" he asked anxiously, peering closely to gauge her reaction.

"It's the most beautiful room I've seen," she replied with great earnestness.

He gave a deep sigh of relief. "It's glad I am to hear that! And the servants will be too. I've had them working for these last days to have this *granian* ready when you came. Look here." He drew her over to the windows. "Look. From here you can see out over the whole countryside. Clear to the Boinne, almost."

It was a most spectacular panorama that lay before them. From the upper floor of the high building atop the great hill of Tara, they could see across a wide expanse of the rolling countryside, the green hills glowing like a golden sea in the sun, rippling in the soft summer wind. They flowed off to the rim of the world, it seemed, where a few white clouds scudded slowly, lazily, across a brilliant blue sky.

"Conaire, I am surprised," she said. "It is all most lovely. But why did you go to such trouble for me?"

"Because I want it to be your room. A place that pleases you."

"My room? But these are your quarters. I . . ." She paused, seeing a sudden and quite unnatural shyness come into his face. And her own expression brightened with hope and with excitement as she grasped the implication.

"Oh, no, Conaire. You can't mean . . ."

"I do, Fionualla," he said quickly, taking up both her hands, grasping them tightly. But then he hesitated, his face twisting in the agony of his awkwardness in this. "I . . . I'm not awfully good at this kind of thing."

"That you certainly are not," she said in an amused way. But then, seeing his distress, she quickly softened. "Oh, my dear Conaire, I'm sorry. I understand."

"Do you?" he said with great relief, his taut face relaxing. "Ah, that's good. I don't see why it should be so difficult. We've known each other all our lives."

"But that was as children. As friends," she said. "This is something else."

"Then you do feel that way, too?" he asked. "Love, I mean?"

"Of course," she said, leaning forward. "And could I feel any way else for you?"

She put her lips up to his and for a long moment the two kissed. Then they clung together, her head on his shoulder, each content with feeling the other's closeness and warmth.

"I'm a happy man to hear that," he said after a time. "I was afraid . . ." He stopped, leaving that unpleasant thought unfinished. Instead he said, "Then, that means you will be my wife?"

She pulled back, meeting his eyes searchingly. "Are you certain that you really wish it?" she asked in a practical way. "You know I'm just a simple girl, without any of the court's ways. I've worn no grand clothes, nor dyed my nails, nor even curled my hair. My family are herdsmen. . . ."

"Ah, you know that means nothing to me."

"I know it didn't once," she corrected. "But now, with you here, with all this about you, with all the beautiful young women of the nobility of Ireland fawning about you . . ."

"There's not a one can come close to yourself," he said with great sincerity.

"Of course not," she said with jesting immodesty. Then she laughed. "But you are a bit of a fool, you know. And easily led astray."

He laughed too.

"Never with you about to protect me," he said, and hugged her close again.

"Fionualla," he went on yet more earnestly, "just say that you'll do it—that you'll become my wife. I've got Tara and all of Ireland now, for good or ill. More than anything else now, I'd like you with me. If you don't think that to be a curse, then accept me. I don't think I could stand doing what I'll have to do with no one beside me. And there's no other person I'd want to share my life with."

"I would never disappoint you, Conaire," she said. She lifted her face to his, and once more he joined her in a kiss, this time a much longer and much more ardent one.

With their attention so taken up, it was no surprise that neither noted through the window that other visitors were just arriving at Tara.

Dark and piercing eyes scanned the yard of the fortress as their owner, followed by two other figures, came through the main gates.

"Hold on there," challenged one of the gates' armed guardians. "Who are you?"

He eyed the group narrowly, suspiciously, and there seemed good reason for his wariness in the look of them. They were a decidedly peculiar-appearing lot, all dressed in long robes of brown wool, much worn and grayed with dust. And all three had their large hoods pulled up, totally masking their features. Even so, the yards of heavy cloth could not disguise that the pair who followed were most unnaturally thin and lank of form, while the leader was of a much broader, stockier build.

Confronted by this protector of the dun, the three men stopped. The leader, with an unhurried move, lifted a wide, thick-fingered hand to tug back his hood.

The face revealed was a quite foreign one. He was very swarthy of skin and coarse of looks, not unhandsome, but rough in features. They seemed as if a master sculptor had quickly chiseled them, but never smoothed or polished—somehow giving them the effect of even greater strength. His nose was broad, his eyes wide set behind thick brows, his mouth wide and mobile. Thick, shining black hair was swept straight back from a high forehead over a massive skull.

The man's look, so vastly different from that of the fair, lean, long-featured men of Ireland, did nothing to ease the suspicions of the guard.

"And just what are the likes of you doing here?" he said more brusquely. "Be off, back to wherever you came from. We want no beggars about here!"

The dark man fixed him with a hard gaze. The eyes glinted like polished iron spheres. It was a chilling and an ominous look, and the guard felt suddenly unsure.

"My name is Calatin," the stranger said in a deep, slow rasp. "I am a high-druid of Espan. We have traveled a hard and very long way to come to this place."

"Oh, so it's a high-druid you are?" the guard said skeptically. "We'll, I've never seen one the likes of you."

"Is this the so famous Irish hospitality I've heard about?" Calatin replied, now irritably. He stepped forward, lifting a hand toward the guard, his eye still holding the other's gaze. "Let us pass!" he said sharply. "Don't be fool enough to make me prove my powers to you."

In the mind of the guard, a dark bouquet of bizarre images suddenly blossomed. Each image was equally clear, their scenes graphic, unpleasant, and always involving him. The combined effect was mind-numbing.

With no other protest, the guard simply stepped aside, watching the three in wide-eyed horror as they glided by.

They moved across the yard, the dark-haired leader scrutinizing everything about. They stopped at a small crowd of idlers watching servants unload the carts and chariots which had recently arrived.

"And what is this?" Calatin asked a young warrior.

"What do you mean?" the man replied in surprise. "Don't you know—" He looked toward Calatin as he spoke, his voice cutting off abruptly as he saw the strange face.

"I have just arrived here," Calatin said in a softly purring, friendly voice, giving a broad smile. "I am a stranger to your land."

"I can see that you are," the warrior said, not certain how to react. But the smile seemed to assure him, for he shrugged and went on congenially, "Well, all this lot here belongs to some of the high-king's family. They've just come to Tara as well. Those are their goods the lads are unloading."

"This king," said Calatin, "is it the young man, the one called Conaire Mor, who I have heard just came to the rule?"

"It is he."

"It's been said that he is a man of miracles," prompted the dark one.

"Well, I don't know about miracles," the warrior said. He considered and went on thoughtfully, "Though maybe it is true. He's promised to bring a new peace to Ireland, and in these past days he's done more to bring together the chieftains than any king I've heard the bards speak of. He does seem to have a skill in it that some would call magical."

"Does he?" Calatin said, his eyes flaring with interest. "Thank you, my friend."

He moved away from the crowd and spoke conspiratorially to his two companions.

"My sons, it is better than I could have hoped. It seems this man, this Conaire Mor, might have the will to do as I have wished. I can feel it! And we will be part of it! Yes, yes. We will! But we must act quickly. Let us return to your brothers now. We must find quarters, settle ourselves, and learn more about this high-king and his court. Then we will consider how to act. Then . . ." he looked around the fortress yard and smiled, "then we will find a way to give our services to this man."

Chapter Six

Cathbad

The great hall of Emain Macha was a glowing tapestry of sensations, woven of the sounds and smells, the colors and textures that drew their separate strands about the awestruck Sentanta. His supper lay unheeded before him as he stared around, striving to hear, see, smell, and feel them all at once.

He seized upon the familiar first, comparing the tec to that of his own dun. In shape they were the same: the circular wall of timbers typical of the Irish structures.

But there the sameness ended. For the space that this tec enclosed was twice as great as that of his hall and many times more grand. In size and beauty it was a rival to the great Tec Mi-Cuarta of Tara itself, which had awed Mor's foster-brothers as this now awed Sentanta. Conchobar, with his arrogance and sense of superiority, would have accepted nothing less. That hall, however, had then been empty. This one was filled with life.

In the ring of compartments, brightly garbed champions, chieftains, druids, and ollavs—the legendary folk who peopled the glittering world Sentanta had learned about from the bardic lays—sat with their families and friends. Laegaire Buadthatch, the Battle Winner, was there, and so was Dubthatch Doel Uladh, the Beetle of Ulster. He saw Cethern, Eoghan, Morann who could give no wrong judgment, Feceirtne the Learned, and Athairne, chief poet of Ulster. All of them sat eating and laughing and enjoying the activities in the hall just like any other ordinary men.

The place was so alive with varied sensations that it was almost overwhelming, especially to a boy whose own home tec had been silent and nearly empty all his life. Jugglers and acrobats moved among the tables. Near the fire, a group of musicians played, filling the air with their fast, merry tune. Pipes and *tiompan* and harp created their own tapestry in sound, the drummer tapping out a vigorous rhythm on the skin, the pipers and harper spinning their light air about it, high and shining, like silver and gold threads woven into the design.

Around the warriors' tables the men drank and ate, indulging in their most loved sport, the talk. And, like almost everything else in their lives, it was a form of competition. They tried to exceed one another with the grandness of their tales, or sought the greatest laughter with their joking lies. They argued horses or the best new swords or what deed in hunting or fighting had been the best. And none of them came armed into the hall, a cautionary measure to reduce the number of possibly fatal brawls.

Nearest the outer doors (and the winter drafts) were the tables of the lowest ranks, including the boys who were training in the school. Across the hall from them, on a raised dais within his somewhat larger partitioned space, sat Conchobar. At his left sat the chieftain Fergus MacRogh, never disputed in his right to the champion's portion of the feast. On the other side of the king, Meave sat placidly by her husband, her red hair unbound and falling to her shoulders in a stream of flame that burned brilliantly against her white silk gown.

Sentanta tried not to stare at her, but found himself drawn by a fascination that he had felt since first seeing her. Fergus had told him she was the queen, though he had never heard her spoken of by the bards. Surely she was little older than himself, he thought.

He watched her movements, trying to focus on the distant figure, on the slim face and the bright gray eyes.

Then he realized with a sudden jump of his heart that those eyes had met his! She was looking at him fixedly, as if she'd picked him out of the large crowd of men. He felt the touch of her gaze and, embarrassed, tried to look away. But he could not.

The brilliant, blue-gray eyes seemed very close. They smiled at him, and in their clear shining he saw something brighter yet. He felt as if he should know the vision hidden there, that it was something they shared which made them separate from the rest. He felt as if it were drawing him toward her, into her.

Then one of the sons of Usna spoke to him and he looked away. The feeling faded and his interest was reclaimed by the activity around him.

On the dais, Meave continued watching him, intrigued by the odd attraction she felt for him. What was the force in him that claimed her so?

"Who is that new lad?" she asked Conchobar in a casual voice.

The king looked searchingly at her, his penetrating gaze noting the intensity she tried to shield behind a barrier of carelessness.

"He is my sister's son, Sentanta," he told her irritably. "A child she promised to hide away forever. I'd hoped she would succeed."

"Why are you so against his being here?" Fergus asked him, overhearing his remark. "He's a bright lad, gentle as his mother, but with the streak of hardness a warrior needs. I've never seen a finer natural ability to handle weapons. You noted that yourself. He used that stick as if he were born with a longsword in his hand."

"Perhaps it's the way that stick was used which has angered Conchobar," Meave put in tauntingly. "He wants to avoid more damage to his son's body and pride."

"I told you, Lady, what I thought of that!" the king shot back. "Cormac must learn to handle himself." He looked to Fergus. "There are other reasons why this boy troubles me."

Fergus already suspected what those reasons were. Now he leaned closer to his king and spoke quietly, masked from eavesdroppers by the surrounded noise. "Is it his birth that's still disturbing you?"

"More than his birth," the king replied darkly.

"What then? That fantasy of Cathbad?" Fergus said scoffingly. "And what if it is true and the blood of the Others flows with the mortal in his veins? It can only make the boy stronger."

"But to what purpose, MacRogh?"

"Why, to help the king he seems so loyal to!" Fergus answered, a bit astonished by his ruler's concern.

"Do you believe that's true?" Conchobar returned with a tone of doubt. "Somehow I feel a shadow is rising, and I'll be lost in it."

For a long moment Fergus looked searchingly at the tall man who sat so tensely staring out over the crowd.

"Conchobar, are you afraid of him?" he ventured at last.

The king's head jerked around toward him. He glared, and then he smiled, shaking his head slowly. "Afraid? No, no, Fergus," he said with great casualness. "It's only a fantasy, as you've said. He's only a boy whose mother wished to keep him hidden away. That's all."

Meave had been attempting to overhear their little talk, but only this last remark carried to her.

"Why should his mother hide the boy?" she asked.

Conchobar hesitated. Though he had never accepted his sister's bastard child, yet he had agreed to keep the secret she had successfully guarded all these years. There was nothing to gain by revealing it now.

"She feared his becoming a warrior," was all the king said. "He doesn't belong among us here."

"Well, my feelings lie with those of Fergus," she replied boldly. "The boy is fit and courageous and finer in looks than any other in the school. He should be allowed to stay, and welcome!"

Conchobar eyed his wife again, more sharply than before. His thin mouth curled upward in a sardonic smile. "Are you so concerned about him, then?" he asked. "I'm pleased to see you taking so much interest in this boy you don't know instead of in your duties as a wife!"

"And when is it that you've ever been denied?" she asked him coldly.

"Oh, never, my Queen," he admitted, but in words with a biting edge. "And it is always such a great pleasure for us both!"

"Excuse me, Conchobar," Fergus said, abruptly rising to his feet. "My meal is finished and I've some things I must be seeing to."

He withdrew rather swiftly, leaving Conchobar to look after him in amusement.

"Poor, simple Fergus," the king said pityingly. "He can face a score of warriors without fear, but he flies in embarrassment before our little quarrel."

"His feelings are my own," Meave told him tersely, rising too. "Good night, my King. I'll be retiring now."

She ran from him, as he knew she would. She'd learned to escape him rather than stay to fight. He merely shrugged, not even turning to watch her go. His gaze was fixed again on the boy whose mere presence here had begun the argument.

Then he noted that Fergus had reappeared at that far end of the great hall. He watched sharply, interest aroused, as the chieftain moved to Sentanta's table and touched the boy's shoulder. The boy looked up and Fergus spoke briefly to him.

Sentanta rose at once and followed the giant warrior obediently.

With narrowed eyes, the king gazed after the two as they
moved to the main doors and left the hall.

Outside, the night was cool, refreshing in contrast to the
closeness of the tec. The drifting music followed Fergus and
the boy, flavoring the stillness of the night with the clear tang
of the harp and pipes.

Fergus led the boy across the dun's enclosure toward the
outer wall. Curious, Sentanta was moved to question him.

"Where are we going, Fergus? Where is it you're taking
me?"

"Cathbad's wishing to speak with you," Fergus said in a
sharp, disgruntled tone. "Though why it must be done tonight,
and in this way, I can't understand."

So, the boy thought, he was to see the ard-druid himself,
the man whose power in Ulster was second only to the king's,
and not even to his in some things.

They crossed the yard to a structure of upright timbers set
close against the enclosure's outer wall. It was of peculiar
shape—a long, narrow rectangle—and devoid of openings save
at one end, where a small door allowed entrance. As they
passed through it and into the structure, Sentanta saw that it
was open to the sky.

The interior was nearly empty. Before them lay two rows of
man-high stakes, each topped by a polished white human skull.
The rows formed a macabre avenue leading to a small hut at
the far end. A man stood there, the red flames of a small fire
burnishing the smooth linen of his long robe, glowing in many
shades against the multicolored cloth.

Sentanta approached him with some feelings of trepidation.
He had never met an ard-druid before. It was not a human
being that he would face, he felt sure. A druid of such exalted
rank was master of vast and unnatural powers. He could command the seen and unseen and was the subject of many astonishing bardic tales. Certainly he must be a creature as much
of the sky as of the earth!

As he and Fergus slowly walked the length of that shadowed
yard toward the glowing light, the boy's impression grew ever
stronger. Beyond the fire he could see the robed figure moving,
first blending with the darkness, then flickering with the flames,
growing to a towering shape and fading away in an instant.

They came nearer, and his heart beat like a *tiompan*, louder at every step, until he thought that surely Fergus must hear. The figure loomed larger, an undefined shape in the draped robe, the face unseen within the masking hood.

Sentanta stopped before the ard-druid and waited nervously. A long, slim hand appeared from the folds of the robe, rose to the hood, and flicked it back.

A lean, cheerful face smiled at him. A soft and comfortable voice enveloped him with its warmth as it greeted him.

"How are you, lad? Sit here and have a bit of roasted salmon with me."

The other hand lifted into view, offering up a filleted strip of fish neatly skewered on a long stick. The boy took it a little uncertainly and then watched as the robed figure dropped unceremoniously onto the ground and crossed his legs.

"Sit down, sit down!" Cathbad said expansively. "The night's grown chill. Be comfortable while we talk."

The boy sat, still bewildered. Fergus crouched next to him, clearly puzzled himself at what was happening, but keeping his own counsel as usual.

"To answer the first question in your mind," the man went on, "I am Cathbad. Yes, my lad, I am." He picked up another stick and a strip of fish from a nearby tray and carefully skewered the fillet as he talked. "And I'm indeed capable of many things, though likely not as many as your bard's tales have said." He shook the stick at Sentanta emphatically. "But power and pride should be two different things. And it's best never to forget to be a human being, don't you think?" He held the boy's eyes appraisingly.

Feeling he was meant to answer, Sentanta squirmed in discomfort. "Ah, it's not something I've thought much about," he said truthfully.

"Of course not," Cathbad said with an affable grin, handing the skewered salmon to the boy. "At your age it's only the thought of your own adventures that moves you."

He held his fish out over the low fire, turning it slowly.

After a moment's hesitation, Sentanta did the same.

"Tell me, has Fergus seen you well settled?" Cathbad asked in a conversational way.

"Yes, Ard-Druid."

"Fergus tells me you brought no baggage with you."

"None but my hurley stick and ball."

"Both very useful in your hands, I understand." The face was impassive at this remark, but the eyes still smiled at him. "And what about your chariot and driver?"

"I have neither. I walked from Dun Dalgan these past days."

"Walked?" The usually far-seeing druid sounded amazed. "And alone? Why would Dechtire allow such a thing?"

"My mother doesn't know," Sentanta began, then added uncomfortably, "or, she didn't. She's likely guessed by now."

Cathbad threw Fergus a sharp look and said, "Well, then it's likely we'll be hearing from her on this matter soon."

Fergus nodded agreement, his face grave.

"But you wouldn't send me back?" the boy cried in alarm. "Fergus said I should be here. He said I was ready!"

"Are you, Sentanta?" Cathbad asked in a soft but sober, earnest voice. "Just why was it you felt you had to come here now? What are you seeking?"

The fish was done. Gingerly the boy peeled the crisp fillet from the stick as he pondered the ard-druid's question.

What was it that he wanted here? He wasn't certain he knew. To become a warrior, surely that! And to know, maybe. To know what it was he really meant in the world.

He looked up at the druid and said with an intensity that welled out from deep inside him, "I knew it was my time to come here now. My mother, my home, none of that had any value to me. I don't even know if I was meant to ask why, only to come."

This answer seemed to satisfy the druid. He smiled gently and nodded approval.

"What you're meant for is what you've wished for, lad. You will stay here and become a warrior of the Red Branch, with all the skill in arms and fighting sense, and all the wisdom and lore Fergus and I can give you. It will be hard work for you, and maybe dangerous as well. Are you prepared for that?"

Sentanta didn't hesitate. "I am, Ard-Druid," he said in a stalwart way.

"Good!" Cathbad sat back, at ease, and lifted his fish out of the flames. He blew on the steaming salmon to cool it, took an experimental bite, and pronounced it properly done.

"Eat now," he told the boy, "and tell me more about your life at Dun Dalgan."

The boy did so, prompted by questions from the druid. The more they talked, the more Sentanta warmed to this placid, amiable man. When he was done, he felt that they were friends and that, in the druid, as in Fergus, he had found someone to trust, even with his life.

"Enough now, boy," Cathbad said at last. "The night is going fast. You've had a long, wearying day. Get on to bed. Tomorrow your training will begin."

Sentanta rose with the other two, then hesitated, looking to Fergus. The druid understood.

"Fergus will be staying with me awhile so we can talk. Will you be able to find your quarters alone?"

"I will," the boy assured him. "Good night to you."

Cathbad stood watching him until the boy's slender figure had passed down the grim avenue of skulls and disappeared into the darkness beyond the doors. Then he looked at Fergus, the easy manner replaced by a grim one.

"Be careful, Fergus," he said pointedly. "Repeat none of this to Conchobar. There's a force in that boy which will bring him to something great."

"But it's not disciplined," the chieftain replied. "He's quiet, modest, wishing only to become a warrior and prove himself."

"But he knows, or he will when it's time, just as he knew to come here now. Something's begun, Fergus, and we're to play our parts in it."

"Visions again, Cathbad?" said Fergus, half-amused, half-awed by his friend's mystical air.

"I've known since he was born that he'd return," the druid said gravely. "There is some need for him. I feel it, my old friend. He'll overshadow the rest of us one day, including Conchobar."

"For the Dagda's sake, Cathbad, quiet now! Even the ard-druid might be called a traitor."

Cathbad gave his friend a reproving glance. "Fergus, you're a fool. A clever man, a hard man, one of the most honest I've ever met. But you've a blind spot. You trust too much. Look at the man who used his own mother to trick the kingship from you. Look at the arrogant man who uses all around him to his own ends."

"You're going too far now, Cathbad," Fergus said warningly. "He's a great warrior! A great king!"

"All right, I'll grant those to you. He's led Ulster to becoming the greatest power in Ireland. He's feared by all the provinces. But, as a man, Fergus? Why, look at his treatment of Meave!"

Fergus was touched by that, but he shook his great head, stubbornly refusing to be convinced.

"All of us may have problems within our own households," he argued. "It says nothing about him as someone of honor or loyalty. In my mind, we've nothing to fear from him, and you've no need for this secrecy of yours."

"Just let me be humored in this," the ard-druid pleaded. "Conchobar is against the lad's being here and may look for any excuse to be rid of him. Until Sentanta becomes a warrior of Ireland, his fate is in our hands. We can't let anything interfere."

Reluctantly Fergus agreed with his friend. "Although I think you'll soon be seeing that this boy needs no one to look after him," he added. "Good night to you, Cathbad. Don't be dreaming of *sheoguey* beasts hidden in every thicket, now."

He left the druid, walking back the length of the enclosure and out its door into the night.

As he strode back across the yard toward the lighted doorway of the main hall, a tall figure slid forward from the darkness near the outer wall and stood looking after him with black, glittering eyes.

Chapter Seven

The Training

Conchobar's sharp gaze stayed fixed on the form of young Sentanta, watching his movements as he parried his attacker's cuts with his blade and shield.

The king of Ulster stood at one side of the wide training ground of hard-packed earth that lay just below the dun of Emain Macha. Before him, more than a hundred men—seasoned warriors and the youths of the training school—were engaged in practicing the brutal arts of war. The shouts and clatter of arms filled the early-morning air.

Varied fighting skills were being taught and sharpened here. At one side of the field, a score of the young warriors-to-be hurled short, sleek, barb-pointed casting spears at wooden posts close before them, then yanked back on leather thongs attached to their hafts to tear the weapons free again for another strike. Far across the wide grounds, chariots wheeled and raced and intertwined as drivers and warriors practiced the graceful but deadly choreography needed to fight effectively from the moving cars.

In the area just before Conchobar, some two dozen of the students of warfare practiced their sword-fighting skills. Coupled with seasoned veterans who tried, sometimes with great frustration, to pass on their expertise, the young men learned from often painful experience.

They were far from gentle in this. To be gentle in teaching the art of defense and of killing would help no one learn to stay alive. So real swords were used, and the evidence of mistakes and clumsiness on the part of the students was clearly and indelibly scored in the bleeding cuts that marked nearly all of them.

But the son of Sualtim, one of the youngest and least experienced there, was still untouched.

He parried the attack of his opponent with incredible speed and skill, under the watchful eye of his trainer, Fergus MacRogh, who stood nearby. Often he returned thrusts and swings so well aimed that the sweating warrior he faced was hard pressed to fend them off.

The warrior, trying harsher tactics, dived in suddenly, trying to force down the lad's sword with his shield. But Sentanta was faster, wheeling around, blocking sword and shield with his own, throwing his body forward to slam the man away. The warrior staggered back and recovered, but looked all the more warily at his deceptively boyish and slender adversary.

"A fine move, lad!" declared Fergus heartily, moving in to clap a hand to Sentanta's shoulder. Then he noted the king watching from the field's side. "Keep up your work," he told the two. "I'll be back."

As Fergus moved away, the warrior, clearly unhappy with the chieftain's order to go on, sighed, lifted weapons, and closed in again.

Fergus strode off the field and approached Conchobar. "Come down for a little practice, my King?" the red-headed chieftain asked with a smile.

"Just come to see the boys' progress," the king answered in a neutral way. "How are they doing?"

"Well, your nephew's doing quite well, if that's what you mean," Fergus shrewdly replied. "In fact, miraculous, I'd call it. Never seen a lad like him. Learned the handling of a blade as if he'd had one in his hand since birth."

Conchobar gave Fergus a searching look, as if wondering whether his old comrade was purposely teasing him.

"I suppose he does seem suited to the skills," he finally admitted grudgingly. Then he added darkly, "Maybe too well."

"And what does that mean?"

"He seems to me almost too miraculous a boy," the king said slowly, carefully. "There has been that sense of something wrong about him since his birth. Some power that I don't like. This incredible skill only proves it's in him. Worse, he traffics with Cathbad. That sly druid has always been a barbed point, pricking at me. And what about you? You treat him as if he were a . . . well, a king himself."

"I don't understand you, Conchobar," said Fergus in puzzlement. "You keep sounding as if you think of this lad as some kind of threat!"

"No, no," Conchobar said quickly, realizing he had spoken too much of his true mind. "It's only that he's so skilled. Don't you agree that there must be something . . . well . . . something magical behind it?"

"It may be he does have some gift beyond the natural," Fergus said thoughtfully, gazing out toward Sentanta. "Cathbad surely thinks it's there. Of course I doubted it myself. Even laughed at him. But now . . ."

Any further comments Fergus was about to make were cut short. Sentanta had parried another attack by his opponent and then struck back in a sharp, swift move that laid open the other's cheek. The hapless man staggered back, blood streaming down his chin. A sudden light shone in the boy's face at the sight of it. His features seemed to contort in a sort of wild ecstasy; his youthful prettiness vanished in a wild, animal snarl, as if the drawing of blood had inflamed him, possessed him with a battle fervor. He leaped forward, giving a high, shrill, piercing cry of triumph, sword sweeping up to strike again.

But Fergus was there first, using his own shield to knock down the weapon and his massive body to butt the boy away.

Sentanta recovered, and looked at his trainer with a face still aglow with the light of violence. He kept his weapons up, ready to fight on.

"Boy! Boy!" Fergus said sharply. "It's all right! It's over!"

At these words, the lad seemed to recover his sense, shaking

his head. He appeared momentarily confused, as if awakening
from a dream. He straightened, lowering his weapons.

"Fergus!" he said in amazement. "I . . . I'm sorry. I don't
know what happened. The blade . . . it seemed to have it's
own life. I only meant . . . to kill. . . ."

He looked to his opponent warrior, who had lowered his
own weapons to clutch his wound. "Angus, I'm sorry!" Sentanta
said contritely. "I didn't mean . . ."

"You needn't apologize," Fergus told the boy sternly. "If
a warrior draws sword, he must mean to heat its iron in his
opponent's blood. Any other thought would be fatal. And
Angus's own mistakes brought this to him. However," he
added, considering the still flushed and panting youth, "I
think we've had enough of this today. Angus, see to your
wound. Sentanta, why don't you work awhile now with the
chariots?"

He led his charge off across the training grounds. From the
side, Conchobar watched them go with a narrowed, searching
gaze. This sudden show of bloodlust in the boy—this glow of
battle light about him like a glimpse of some Other spirit—
disturbed the king greatly.

He watched Fergus and the boy cross to the chariots, then
he moved out across the field to where his son Cormac and
his comrades were at the spear practice. He drew Cormac
aside and spoke quietly to him.

"I see you've been avoiding your cousin."

Cormac seemed abashed. "I . . . I've just not been grouped
with him so far. That's all."

"I see," his father said, a hint of sarcasm in his tone. "I
thought you might not wish to be put against him again."

"Of course not!" his son protested quickly.

"Well, it seems to me that boy could use a bit of humbling,"
said Conchobar. "He's been doing far too well."

"That I've seen," said Cormac ruefully.

"But if he becomes too proud, it will be bad for him. It's
our task, as his family, to look out for him."

"Yes?" said Cormac, confused by this suddenly solicitous
tone from his father.

"He's good with a sword. Maybe too good for you," the king
taunted cruelly. "But he's had less training in fighting from
the cars. It might be your only chance to best him and redeem
yourself at the same time."

"I could do it," said Cormac. "But Fergus wouldn't like it. He's warned us again about fighting among ourselves. And he is the chief trainer."

"And I am the king and your father," Conchobar said harshly. "Whom do you obey first?"

"Yes, Father," he said meekly.

"I think you should spare nothing in doing this," the king went on. "If the boy eats some sod, and feels a bruise or two after, it will be so much the better lesson."

"But I could do more than hurt him, Father," Cormac said, not yet fully grasping what his father implied. "He might be killed!"

Conchobar met his son's eye. His gaze was cold, his face expressionless. "That would be a great pity," he said flatly, "but it is a risk you all take."

"Not when we've had as little practice as he has!" his son argued. "I—"

"Are you really telling me you're afraid?" Conchobar demanded.

"No. No, Father!" Cormac hastily replied.

"Then I can't understand your reluctance to regain your pride. Your beating at his hands was a humiliation to you and to myself as well."

"I know, Father," Cormac said, coloring with shame. Then he drew himself up. "All right," he promised with great bravado. "I'll see that whelp has his backside soundly whipped."

He turned away from the king and called to his companions, "Come on, you lot. I want to take a turn at the chariots now."

Conchobar watched his son and his friends cross the field toward the chariot track. He smiled faintly and with a satisfied air. Then he moved back across the training field, away from them, as if he wanted to divorce himself from what would happen now.

Cormac and his band approached Sentanta where he and the sons of Usna stood by a chariot. Fergus was within the car, standing behind the driver, a casting spear in hand, instructing the young men.

"You must time your throw to the speed and rhythm of the chariot," he was telling them. "You must practice it until you can throw without thinking, until the feel and action of it becomes as natural to you as the act of love."

The boys exchanged quizzical glances at this, and Fergus, noting them, amended his allusion.

"Sorry, lads," he said, grinning. "For you, I'll say 'natural as eating.' You all do that well enough."

"Can we try it now, Fergus?" Naoise, eldest of the sons of Usna, asked eagerly.

"Aye, that you can. Let me find drivers for each of you, and you can have a time round the course."

Seeing Fergus move off to find the charioteers, Cormac chose that moment to approach Sentanta.

"Well, the child wishes to try himself with the warrior's tools," he said to his cousin.

"Watch your tongue, Cormac," returned Naoise. "Sentanta's already a match for you in fighting from the cars . . . after no more than a dozen rides!"

"Is he now?" said Cormac with mock astonishment. "Well, well!" He strutted up before the boy. "And would you then want to try your skills against my own, little cousin?"

Sentanta bridled at the demeaning name, but held himself back from a sharp reply. "It's not for me to decide. Fergus . . ."

"I see," said Cormac nastily. "You've got to wait for Fergus to come back and protect you."

That was too much. Sentanta's face reddened and he drew stiffly erect, shooting back indignantly, "I've no need of protecting. If you mean to do this, then I will ride against you."

Realizing what was happening, an aghast Naoise quickly tried to intervene.

"No, Sentanta! Don't let him force you into anything. Wait for Fergus."

"Too late, MacUsna," Cormac told him tersely. "The boy's made his choice." He gave a little, gloating smile. "So, get yourself a chariot, cousin. We're racing now!"

He strode off with a haughty swagger, his comrades following, but looking back often at Sentanta with broad grins and derisive laughter.

"That was a mistake," declared Ainnle, second of Usna's sons. "There's no one in the training school who has so fine a chariot and driver as Cormac."

"Aye," agreed his younger brother, Ardan, in disgust. "His father saw to that."

"And he has a greater skill in the fighting from the car than all of us," Naoise added unhappily.

"But you just said that my skill was a match for his!" Sentanta said, dismayed by this sudden lack of confidence.

"I may have been telling tales just a bit," Naoise admitted sheepishly. "Sorry. But I couldn't stand Cormac's thinking himself better than you."

"Well, I thank you for that," Sentanta told him sardonically. "And now that you've helped me into this foolish race, why don't you help me find a chariot and driver?"

"It won't be an easy task," said Ainnle. "Few drivers will be willing to risk themselves or their cars against the likes of Cormac."

"Please, don't be giving me any more such cheering news. Just help me look."

"There's no need to look," came a voice from behind them.

They turned to see a figure in the simple wool tunic and trousers of a charioteer jump from his car. He was a young man, little older than Sentanta. He had a similar, boyish handsomeness, but with a darker complexion and a great, curling mass of glowing black hair caught up loosely at his neck. He moved toward them with an easy, sure, athletic stride, swinging a long whip in one hand.

"I heard you talkin' with that *son of the king*," he said, making the name sound like an insult. "I'll drive for you myself, so I will!"

"You will?" Sentanta said, not certain how to respond to this gracious offer. "Why?"

"Well, I don't usually waste my time drivin' for the pups in the training school," he replied insolently. "But I've no more liking for that struttin' jay than yourselves, and I've always wanted to try myself against his driver." He gave the son of Sualtim a long, slow, calculating look. "You don't seem as if you'd be much as a fighter, but at least I can give you a fair chance against him."

"Oh, can you?" said an indignant Sentanta. "And what is it that makes you take on such grand airs? You're no older than I am."

"Careful, my friend," cautioned Naoise. "Don't be angering this one. It may just be that he can save your life."

"What do you mean?" Sentanta asked.

"This is Laeg, son of Laegaire, who was the greatest driver in all of Ulster, some say all Ireland. And nothing he says to you is putting on airs. No one will deny he is the finest driver here, young or old."

Laeg smiled smugly.

"Well, you're surely a brash enough one," Sentanta said. "But I'd be more the fool not to accept your offer."

"That you would," Laeg agreed. "Get yourself ready now. I see Cormac has found his own chariot."

He moved off to give his car, harness, and horses a final inspection. Sentanta and his friends looked to the weapons he would need. While they were thus engaged, Fergus reappeared, stalking up to them, his expression one of anger.

"What are you doing?" he demanded. "The word is running like a stag through the men that Sentanta is to race against Cormac!"

"It was Cormac challenged Sentanta to a race," Ardan told him by way of defense.

"Oh, did he now?" Fergus bellowed, his face darkening with anger. "Well, I'll see to that. I warned him against his private rivalries."

"But you can't," Sentanta told him earnestly. "I've accepted him, Fergus. I have to do this."

Fergus sighed heavily, knowing it was true. "Of course," he said. "But, my lad, your brashness may just be your death someday, for all that I can do."

Cormac's chariot now pulled up beside them. The son of Conchobar leaned down over the side of the car to smile triumphantly at his opponent.

"Ready for your lesson, little cousin?" he asked.

"You know what I think of this, Cormac," Fergus growled.

"You're not the king," was the curt reply. And, to Sentanta: "I'll meet you on the course, cousin. Don't delay."

He tapped his driver, and the chariot moved off.

"I'm ready," Laeg called to Sentanta. "Climb on, boy."

"You have Laeg driving for you?" Fergus said with some faint measure of relief. "Well, that's some help anyway."

"I'm happy to see that everyone is so confident about my skills," said the boy.

He went to the car and climbed up behind the charioteer. Naoise handed him three long, slender casting spears, which he settled into sockets against the car's bulwark.

"Good fortune ride with you," Fergus told him. "Remember, feel the rhythm of the horses. Become one with the car. And trust your driver."

"And at least try not to do anything to make me look the fool along with you," advised Laeg.

"Even if I die in the trying," Sentanta promised in a sarcastic tone.

Laeg shook the reins and the chariot moved off behind its team of stocky, powerful chestnut steeds. It came out of the press of cars and men onto the verge of the racing course and pulled up beside Cormac's.

The course was a long, narrow oval of beaten earth with tight curves at either end. The straight stretches were unevenly spotted with tall posts of wood that the chariots had to negotiate at full speed. The curves were rimmed with life-size plank targets which had to be transfixed by spears thrown from the racing, jouncing cars.

Word of the impending race had spread through the gathering, and a hundred men now lined the course, watching avidly. And, of course, many bets were being laid.

"Ready?" Cormac asked.

"If you are," Sentanta replied.

Cormac nodded to a warrior standing just before and between the cars. The man pulled out his sword, raised it, paused, then plunged it to the ground.

The horses charged ahead, jerking the cars forward. Side by side they sped up the straightway, toward the first posts.

Both chariots negotiated them brilliantly, their drivers weaving through at full speed with an almost careless ease. Laeg grinned and hooted with the exhilaration of it, the wind blowing back his long mane of hair, as it did Sentanta's.

The first turn was coming up very quickly.

"Now!" Laeg told his passenger.

Sentanta moved at once, taking up one of the spears, clambering out the front of the car and onto the thin pole of the vehicle, edging his way forward between the straining animals until he was near the bronze-shod point, the plunging heads of the steeds at either hand.

Beside him, Cormac had made a similar move. Both young men were now poised with what seemed great precariousness on the poles, swaying with the movement of the cars. A slip could send either down to be trampled by flying hooves or rolled over by the huge, iron-rimmed wheels.

Cormac cast a glance sideways to note his rival prepared as he was. He gave a sneer and then turned his attention to the row of man-shaped wooden poles edging the curve, shooting toward them with breathtaking speed. He crouched, taking one of the spears in his right hand and lifting it in readiness.

Sentanta prepared himself likewise. He remembered the advice of Fergus. He tried to relax, to move with the racing steeds, swaying with them, meeting their rhythm, letting go . . . letting go.

The first target was before him. His arm shot back and fired the spear forward. His judgment was exact. The head of his spear sank home in the heart of the wooden chest. But close beside it, another spear thunked into the figure, and Cormac turned to meet Sentanta's gaze with a defiant glare.

They swept around the curve, drivers fighting to hold the cars on the track as they skidded sideways from the speed. They came into the second straight, and Laeg urged his team full out. Slowly they began to draw ahead.

Cormac angrily gestured to his driver. The man nodded and grinned maliciously as he pulled his reins hard over. The car shifted sideways, the massive wheel smashing into that of Sentanta's chariot, slamming the car away.

Laeg was surprised and nearly lost control, the chariot shimmying wildly. Sentanta wobbled on the pole, slipping down. Desperately he grabbed one of the horse's long manes as his feet slid from the smooth, rounded pole and he was hanging, being dragged along, feet scraping along the ground, feeling himself being pulled down into the churning chaos of hooves and spinning wheels.

The next field of obstacle posts came up. Laeg battled to regain control with his rider dragging and hauling on one steed's mane. Cormac grinned in triumph.

They swept between the posts, Laeg using the reins masterfully to guide the horses along the staggered course. They rocked dangerously, skimming past the wood posts within a hair's breadth at times. Sentanta, thrown violently back and forth, unable to find purchase for his feet, could only hang on as post after post flew past.

Then they were out on the straight again. With an effort he hauled himself up, feeling for the pole. His feet were bleeding and scraped, the light leather boots nearly torn away, but he got a firm hold at last and pulled himself upright, releasing the mane.

Cormac had drawn ahead, and Laeg now urged his horses on at their fullest speed. The sleek animals stretched out, powerful muscles pumping as they strained to catch their opponents.

"Second turn!" Laeg shouted. He yanked the last two spears from their sockets and tossed them to Sentanta.

The boy edged out to the point of the chariot pole again. He crouched, readying himself. His hardest trial would come now, hitting the two targets that they would pass in rapid succession. Ahead, Cormac was already prepared to throw, his spear up, his own car nearly to the curve.

As they swept into the turn, he released his first spear, striking home in the wooden figure's chest. The second target came up, and he had only a moment to raise the second spear and cast again. The spear went high and wide, catching only the figure's shoulder.

And then, suddenly, two more spears slammed home in the targets, so near together that they came almost as one, both striking their targets at the heart. Startled, Cormac looked back to see Sentanta rising from his throws, meeting Cormac's gaze with an impudent grin.

His chariot was now less than a spear's length behind Cormac's. As they came into the final straightway, the king's son screamed to his driver, "Full speed! Full speed! Keep them back!" With the botched throw, his only chance of victory now was to reach the finish ahead of his cousin.

But Laeg was not going to allow that. As they came into the straight, he used voice and reins to coax his horses to an even greater effort. They pulled nearly level with the other car.

"Stop them!" Cormac screamed in desperation.

Again his driver tried to use his car to knock the other aside. This time Laeg was ready, pulling his own car sideways in a counterblow. The two slammed together and stayed locked there, hub to hub, speeding down the course.

"Now we'll see what real courage that driver has!" Laeg called to Sentanta, grinning with delight.

Ahead were the final set of upright logs they must negotiate to reach the finish line. They were careening toward them at full attack speed. Each driver was intent on keeping his car against his rival's, both seemingly oblivious to the posts ahead—against which they would surely crash if they didn't separate.

They swept toward the obstacles. The posts loomed up, solid and black and threatening. The inside horses shouldered into one another as they galloped ahead. The cars creaked and bounced together, staying side by side. In a moment they would strike.

The nerve of Cormac's driver broke. With a cry of anguish and anger he jerked the reins aside to turn his chariot. His move was made too hastily, too recklessly. As the horses turned, the car swerved around sharply, tipped up on one wheel, and crashed down. The car's woven bulwarks disintegrated in an explosion of splinters. The driver was cast free. The pole twisted, shattered, pulled away, releasing the still racing steeds, and Cormac toppled backward, slamming heavily onto the packed earth of the track.

Freed of his opponent, Laeg, with an almost arrogant ease, guided his chariot through the last obstacles, rolled up to the finish line, and reined in to a stop. There was wild cheering from all save the disgruntled bettors on Cormac. Men rushed in around them, Fergus and the sons of Usna at the front, to give congratulations.

"Well, you may not be quite so bad at that," Laeg grudgingly admitted to Sentanta over the cheering.

"I'm most honored by your overwhelming praise," Sentanta told him with a smile, clapping a hand to his shoulder.

Back on the course, Cormac was rising painfully to his feet, ignored even by his own comrades in the excitement. Grimacing with the agony of his many bruises, he looked ruefully toward the victors. Then his eyes lifted to the hillside above, where a familiar tall figure stood watching.

Even at that distance, Cormac could read the anger and humiliation in his father's eyes.

"Somehow," the young man muttered darkly, glowering toward his cousin, "somehow I will yet have my revenge on you!"

Chapter Eight

Calatin

The half-tumbled tower of weathered gray stone squatted on the very rim of the point of high cliffs and frowned out upon the sea like some grim, ancient, monstrous creature.

Around its landward side, as if it had once been imprisoned there, two curving lines of broken wall separated it and the point from the rest of Ireland.

A single chariot rolled up the faint line of the neglected and nearly vanished track which led across the waves of inland hills to the old fortress. It pulled up before the outer wall, before a wide, ragged gap that once had been a gateway. Through it the brooding tower was framed. The car's inhabitants, a white-robed druid and his driver, stared at the ominous-looking structure—the driver with simple curiosity, the druid with concern.

"You're certain this is the place?" the druid asked, as if hoping that it was not.

"It's the only abandoned stone fortress within a day's ride of Tara an Rie," the driver assured him, sounding indignant that his skill should be questioned. "Of course I'm sure."

The driver was short, lean, and sinewy, with a brusque manner and no sign of being in the least intimidated by his prestigious passenger. The druid was a man of once long, finely chiseled looks, but they were blurred now by the fat of too much good living, which had also given his pale skin a florid glow and his form a certain plushness.

"It's certainly an unpleasant-looking place," he said with distaste.

"It is that, Ard-Druid," the other agreed. "It was a home for one of the most powerful clans on the eastern shore once, long long ago. No one really knows what happened to them. Some say a sickness brought on them for their arrogance by the curse of Manannan. Terrible, they say. Made them bloat up, their skin turn black, great oozing sores appear on their . . ."

"Enough, Kinkaeth!" the druid interrupted sharply, grimacing in disgust.

The driver fell silent, but smiled to himself, revealing a wide gap between his two large front teeth.

The druid turned to contemplating the ruined tower thoughtfully again. "A dreadful place," he said, half to himself. "I don't know what it is that would make me come here."

"Don't you, Ard-Druid?" the driver asked slyly. "And why was it no one was to know of your coming but myself?"

"And what's that to you?" the druid asked suspiciously. "What do you know about this?"

"I hear the talk," the man said in a superior way. "And maybe more than you. I know something of this Calatin who's said to be inhabiting that old tower now. A great ard-druid of Espan he was, before the others of his own kind chased him out. Very powerful. And it's great magic he's said to have. Black powers that make men fear. But . . ." he added with a meaningful glance at the druid, "could also make a man greater than others, or make him rich."

"You know too much," the druid told him curtly. "This is merely a call of courtesy, from one ard-druid to another. Still," he looked again at the uninviting pile of stone, "he had some gall indeed, expecting me to travel here to him."

"You came," the driver said, flashing his gap-toothed smile.

"Yes . . . well . . ." the druid said uncomfortably, harrumphing loudly and leaving his reply unfinished. "Just take me up to the tower, driver," he ordered brusquely.

The driver urged his horses ahead. The car jolted over the rubble in the gateway of the first wall, then through the shattered gateway of the second, into a dank, weed-infested yard littered with debris. He carefully steered a path through the maze of rubble and ruined, roofless hulks of outbuildings scattered about the broad yard. Finally, he pulled up before a large opening into the tower, a black, gaping, ragged hole that looked like an open maw.

The druid stared into the blackness beyond it with clear loathing at the notion of entering.

"It looks deserted. Likely filled with birds and who knows what," he said, shivering with horror.

"You've come this far," the driver urged. "You'll gain nothing standing here."

"You go and have a look," the druid ordered.

"I'm your driver, not your servant," the little man replied insolently. "Go see yourself."

The druid shot the driver a most outraged and venomous look, which made no impression at all on the defiant one. He looked again at the black and ominous doorway, still hesitant. But another force, a much more powerful one than fear, decided him.

With a sigh he climbed down from the car and walked to the doorway. A chill, sharp sea wind scouring across the stark clifftop yanked at his white robes. He shivered again.

There was an ancient, tarnished, weather-worn bell of bronze hanging from an iron hook beside the opening. This he rang, at first tentatively, then with more force, the sound echoing hollowly in the enclosure.

It died away and there was again silence, save for the sound of waves breaking below the cliffs and the snuffling of the standing horses.

"No one here," he said in a tone of mixed disappointment and relief.

But, as he began to turn, he heard a soft, scraping noise within the darkness of the tower. As he looked back, his eyes widened in dismay.

A wretched creature—limbs withered and gray as weathered twigs, face like a corpse, dressed in a ragged tunic a beggar would have scorned—had crept like a slug into his view. It stopped, regarding him with impassive face and dull, sunken eyes. As it said nothing, the druid was forced to speak, his voice a trifle hoarse.

"I . . . is this the place where the druid Calatin lives?"

The creature still did not speak. Its response was to nod, moving the head upon the stalky neck slowly, as if it were a great weight, then to turn and start back into the recesses of the tower.

The druid cast a most reluctant gaze toward his driver, then steeled himself and followed. They passed through a musty, filthy entry hall and then entered a large room in the tower's heart.

It was circular, windowless, lit fitfully and eerily by a score of thick, guttering candles and a central fire. The ruddy and lurid rays cast wavering shadows and left the outer margins of the wide room in darkness. The firelight glowed red on a stream of smoke that coiled sinuously toward a ceiling hidden in blackness far above.

The druid stopped to peer around him in uncertainty, worry narrowing his eyes and tightening his mouth. It was impossible to discern details in the room, furniture or decorations or inhabitants. But there were a number of bizarre and somehow disquieting forms looming around him, and it seemed as if all of them were moving, moving in the shifting glow.

Directly before him was the only part of the eerie scene that he could clearly identify. The figure of a robed man stood leaning over a large caldron suspended by heavy chains above the fire. His swarthy complexion was cast in the yellow light of the flames, throwing long arching shadows up across his rough-hewn face and making his eyes glitter like molten gold. It was toward him that the creature who had led the druid now scuffled.

The man at the caldron seemed not to notice their entrance until the wasted being reached him and muttered something in a ghastly whisper. Then the man lifted his head and turned, fixing upon the druid a gaze that seemed still to glow with a bright red-gold light.

"My friend!" came the soft, rich, slowly rolling voice of Calatin. "So you have decided to come to me after all! Welcome." A hand lifted, beckoning. "Come closer!"

The druid hesitated, his face a shifting mask of mixed emotions. Again the desire won out over the caution. He moved across the room toward the dark man.

As he drew closer, he realized that by the caldron was pulled up a long table of rough planks, its surface crowded with objects whose many shapes and textures reflected and multiplied the lights. There were metal implements—tools and instruments of a type he could not guess, but whose terrible barbs and points and glinting edges invoked images of pain. And there were containers of glass and pottery holding powders, liquids, and bits of things that looked organic but were unrecognizable. But one object was: a severed human head, still pink with the freshness of life, which stared at him with dead eyes. Its scalp had been peeled aside and hung grotesquely over one ear. The skull had been neatly cut all around the crown and the cap removed. The shining whorls of the brain were exposed.

Shocked by this sight, he stopped again, near the center of the room.

"Ah, I am sorry," said the ard-druid of Espan. He took a bloodstained scrap of cloth and tossed it casually across the head. "I forgot. You know there are secrets to be pulled from the depths of a human brain, even after death."

"What do you want, Calatin?" the druid demanded, unable to hide the quaver of nervousness in his voice.

"I think the question is: what do *you* want, Ard-Druid?" Calatin countered, smiling.

"Your great . . . ah . . . renown precedes you," the other replied. "It's said that you bring immense powers from Espan. Powers the druids of Ireland do not know."

"And that they fear. Yes. And you, of all I offered, of all I invited, only you had the courage and wisdom to come."

"Well, when you offered to show some of your knowledge to me, I . . . I just couldn't resist," the visitor admitted. "As a druid, such powers could be used to benefit Ireland. . . ."

"And perhaps yourself as well?" Calatin smiled in a knowing, conspiratorial way. "I knew you were a man who appreciated the value of such things." His eyes shone with pleasure that the man's greed had brought him.

"Ha, humph," said the druid uncomfortably.

"Ah, think nothing of that," Calatin said assuringly. "I understand. In my country, the power is everything. That's why I have devoted my life to learning such dark things as others fear."

"Of course such powers which are considered evil or dishonorable would be shunned by any druid of Ireland," the other said hastily.

"Of course," Calatin agreed. He came closer, his voice cajoling, promising, luring. "Still, you asked yourself, just to see such powers, to understand them, what harm could that do? And you came."

"That may be," the druid said slowly, cautiously. "But why would you do this for me? What would you gain?"

"Why, only what you want," Calatin said jovially, clapping a broad hand to the other's shoulder. "Only to help Ireland. I've come here from Espan because of that. I've heard of this new king of yours, of his wish to unite this land, to bring it rule by laws and by justice and by force of the mind instead of bloody iron. I want to help him."

"How would you do that?"

"I would use my powers for his ends." He slipped his arm about the druid's shoulders, and, while he held the man engrossed by his hypnotic speech, he slowly walked him closer to the fire. "You must understand, my friend, your high-king's dream is as my own. I wish peace. I wish the mindless violence of the warrior classes tethered like a raging wolf. I wish to make the wisdom of the druids supreme. This I tried to do in Espan, but those fools didn't understand."

His face grew hard, his voice harsher, his glinting gaze fixed on a hated vision from the past.

"No. Those fools didn't understand. They were jealous of my powers. Afraid! Their warriors rose against me and cast me out. But this time . . . this time I have a king who will do my bidding. This time I will succeed."

"Your bidding?" the druid said, these words breaking Calatin's spell over him. He looked at the dark man, confused and a little alarmed by his intensity. "But it's the high-king who rules. We are only his advisers."

"And so will I be, within his own circle of high-druids at Tara."

The druid shook his head. "That is impossible. The circle is filled. No other druid, no matter of what rank or powers, can join it now."

"But that is why I invited you here," said Calatin, smiling.

"I cannot help you in this," said the other, pushing off the encircling arm and stepping away. "No matter what magic you offer me. No new wealth or rank that you can promise me will buy my help in finding a place for you."

"There will be a place," the soft, insinuating purr of voice came in reply. "Yes. There will be an empty seat in the circle of druids. Very, very soon."

"What?" the druid said, now fully alarmed, backing away as Calatin moved forward. "What seat?"

"Why, your own," Calatin said with a malicious grin. "Surely even a fool such as yourself must realize that now."

Panic seized the druid. His head swiveled frantically back and forth as he sought a way to flee. But now from the shadows about the room figures moved forward, detaching themselves from the monstrous jumble and gliding forward into the light. Some two dozen figures moved in to form a ring, a cordon, hemming him in.

They were a ghastly-looking band, all cadaverously thin, so long and bony of limb that even their ragged and heavy cloaks of dark wool could not disguise it. With their knobbed joints and dull, gray-white skin, they looked more like weathered bundles of twigs than men. Their heads, high-domed, were nearly bald, save for some curling wisps. Their lips were thin, their cheeks sunken, giving them a decidedly skeletal look. That they were not walking corpses was attested only by their large and luminous eyes, which glowed in their sockets like the waters of a bottomless tarn beneath a full moon.

"These twenty-six around you are my sons," Calatin said, waving his arms out over them. "Sorry creatures, the product of my unions with their mothers, weak women whom I hoped to find strong enough to match my will. Still, they are part of me, part of my power. Each a little by himself, but together a great force, multiplying the effect of my magic. They will help me to achieve my dream, to control your druids, your king, and finally your Ireland."

"You . . . you can't do this!" the druid said tremulously, looking at Calatin.

"Oh, but I can," he softly intoned as he moved forward, forward, his gaze burning into the gaze of the other. "I will join the king's advisers, and with my powers I will become his most loyal, most valuable friend. I will make his peace and justice work. I will make the rule of the druids supreme. Soon after, it's my own power that will be in control. And then . . . finally . . . the rule of warriors, of war and brutality, will end forever!"

The hapless druid tried to tear his gaze away, but he could not. He was frozen, staring, trapped by the eyes, trembling as the ring tightened. He was like a hare in a trap, paralyzed with fear.

The sons of Calatin closed in about him. Long, bony hands reached out to seize him. He opened his mouth, but not even a scream came out. They moved forward, forcing him back toward the caldron.

He was pushed to its edge. Two of them, powerful for their scrawny look, bent him forward, his head over the brew. It was a stinking, noxious mass of gray-green bubbling bile with strange, soft, shining objects roiling in it.

"Your greed is your undoing, my druid," Calatin said, moving up behind him. "Now you will serve me. You will give me what I want, and you will add to my own powers with your living body."

He put out a hand. One of the sons slapped something into the open palm. Calatin held it up. It glinted in the light: a long dagger with a needle point and a sharpened edge. He smiled in satisfaction.

"Nothing will be wasted," he said. "Your own blood will seal my charm. You wanted to know of my magic?" He gave a laugh. "Well, now you'll be a part of it."

He nodded to the two holding the man. One grasped the druid's hair, pulling his head back to stretch his neck. Calatin leaned forward and swung his arm around the man, bringing the weapon up in a sweep of light toward the unprotected throat.

Outside, the driver jerked around from his bored contemplation of the seascape to stare at the tower. The faint, shrill sound still hung, echoing, in the air. Was it a scream?

He climbed from the car and went to the door. He smiled his gap-toothed smile. Likely the poor, skittish druid was needing help. Seen a cat, or his own shadow maybe.

He went through the ruined doorway into the blackness. Once inside he felt less assured. He didn't like the place. It was too dark. It seemed deserted. It smelled of mustiness and of something else—something unpleasant.

Entering the inner room, he saw the light of the fire beneath the caldron. There seemed no one around. He moved slowly toward the fire, peering around him into the clumps of sinister shadows.

"Ard-Druid?" he called.

The words rang hollowly. There was no response.

He moved forward, puzzled and growing steadily more alarmed. He approached the caldron. He could see now the table beside it, the objects upon it. His eyes strayed over them. Then he stopped, frozen in horror.

It was the head of his own ard-druid that now sat there upon a block, staring at him with liquid eyes that still held the shock of death.

"By all the gods!" the man cried. He turned to run. But suddenly there were figures all around him, sweeping like a flock of starved crows upon carrion, flapping in, covering him, blocking him, stifling his cries. The last echoed hollowly, forlornly, hopelessly, in the room.

* * *

Joyous people surged close about the dais in the great hall of Tara. A glittering, richly gowned crowd it was that had just witnessed the marriage of Conaire Mor and Fionualla.

Musicians had struck up a bright tune. Ale was flowing in golden streams from scores of silver ewers. Food of all kinds was heaped upon the tables, awaiting the onslaught of a gloating Lomna Druth. Everything glowed or sparkled from the light of a thousand tapers.

The king's closest company—chiefs, champions, druids, Brehons, and ollavs—stood close about, giving him best wishes. The warriors did so with great gusto and joy, the learned men more aloofly, one or two even casting surreptitious and doubt-filled glances on the bride, so beautiful but still the daughter of a herdsman.

"We all give the full blessings of ourselves and of the great Others to you, High-King," said the gray-haired chief of the ard-druids. "May the good goddess Danu herself guide and make you happy."

"I thank you, as I thank all your fellows," Mor said, looking around. "But where is Ard-Druid Dolan? I've not seen him today."

"I don't know, my King," said the chief druid, clearly troubled and dismayed. "There's nothing that should keep him from such an occasion. It is most shaming for the rest of us."

"Think no more about it," Mor said lightly.

"I must, as I am his chief. But there is something else. If you would, my King, a most high druid, a visitor to our land, has come to see your wedding and to offer his services to you. Would you greet him?"

He moved back, revealing the figure that had stood hidden behind him. The man was in a most elegant robe, gilt and fringed with gold. His head was bowed. But then he lifted it, smiling, his dark eyes alight.

"Good fortune to you, my most gracious High-King," Calatin said.

Chapter Nine

Meeting

"And so, the great Lugh of the Long Arm struck down Balor One-eye, and the people of the Tuatha de Danann took power in Ireland!" Cathbad concluded with a flourish.

Sentanta sat cross-legged on the grassy hillside just below the ard-druid, listening raptly.

"They ruled, as the Firbolgs before them and the sons of Mileus since, from that same hill of Tara, that was called the Beautiful Ridge. And there, atop it, just beside the high-king's Royal Seat, is the mound of hostages, built by the people of Danu so long ago."

"It's one of my greatest wishes to see Tara," Sentanta said dreamily, staring off into a vision of that golden past.

"That you will, boy," Cathbad assured him. "I know it. But, enough of this for today." He clambered to his feet, and Sentanta did likewise, with a bit more agility.

"My boy, you are learning fast," he went on. "Your mind is as nimble as I ever had hoped. A fair match for your eye and hand, from what Fergus tells me. With these extra lessons of ours, you'll know as much as any other lad by fall."

"I'm only sorry my own mother told me so little of Ireland and its past," the boy said regretfully.

"Never fault her, lad," Cathbad sternly admonished. "She had her reasons. Ones you may never know."

"And do you know them?" Sentanta asked.

"I may make . . . guesses," he began. Then shook his head. "But it's not for me to pry into, nor yourself!"

"Yes, Ard-Druid," the boy said, unsatisfied but still obedient. Then, more brightly, "But could you tell me more of this champion Lugh? Is he still alive?"

"As all the Others, he is immortal. But where he is, no one can say. He wanders the world now, helping where he can. And he is a friend to mortals, unlike many of the Sidhe. But that's another tale, too long to be gone into now. The sun is descending. Go on up to the dun. Wash, dress, prepare. It will be time for the evening meal soon."

"And what of you?"

"I've duties of my own that will occupy me in the woods for a little time. Go on ahead."

So it was that Sentanta climbed the slope of Emain Macha toward the fortress alone.

He reached the outer rampart and the wall on the north side and began to circle it to the main causeway and gates on the south. But before they came in sight, a group came suddenly into view, blocking his way.

It was Cormac Conlingas and half a dozen of his comrades.

"So, finally you are alone," Cormac said with satisfaction. "Do you know how long I've watched and waited for your watchdogs to leave you?"

"And what are you wanting now, Cormac?"

"You know it well enough, whelp. You've made a fool of me too often. I mean to teach you a lesson for it here, where you have no hurley stick, no sword, no chariot, no friends."

"You've made a fool of yourself, Cormac," Sentanta replied. "None of this needed to be. We're cousins. I meant us to be friends."

"Friends?" Cormac repeated angrily. "We can't be friends!"

"And why not?"

"You know!" Cormac snarled and stepped forward, swinging out with his fist.

Sentanta sidestepped it. As it swept by he moved in, shoving Cormac aside, reluctant to strike, though he could easily have done so. Cormac staggered and fell.

But then his comrades rushed in around Sentanta, striking at him from all sides.

This served only to fire the temper that dwelt just beneath his calm, pleasant manner. He glowed with the heat of violence, his face contorting with rage. He became a madman, a wheel of energy. He managed to hold them at bay, breaking the nose of one, sending another staggering away clutching his stomach. Still, the force of numbers was against the lone boy, and blows split his lip, cut his eye, and bruised him in many places.

When Cormac regained his feet and saw the pack wildly attacking and battering his lone cousin in such an unfair way, he hesitated, his look of anger giving way to one of uncertainty, and then to a new kind of anger.

"Wait!" he cried out, moving into the battle, grabbing the shoulders of his friends to pull them back. "Stop this. It's my fight! Stop!" But they ignored him in the frenzy of the battling.

Then a new force was added to the fray, a force that descended like a whirlwind upon them, bodily yanking back the boys with amazing power. The surprised boys looked about to see who this new attacker was, then ceased their struggle at once. For it was Meave herself, queen of Ulster, who had come upon them.

"You should be ashamed!" she berated them. "Young noblemen, bent on becoming warriors? And you seeming more like brigands, coming upon this one boy? Where is your honor in that?"

They exchanged sheepish looks or stared down at the ground, unwilling to meet her glaring eye.

"It . . . it was Cormac who wanted revenge," one offered in lame defense. "We only meant to help. . . ."

"He led, and you sheep followed," she said scathingly. "I might have known." She turned to give her stepson a hard look. "And I suppose it was your father who put you up to this?"

"I . . . well . . . the boy deserved a lesson," Cormac tried to bluster, but he did not sound so sure of himself now, his usual arrogance vanished.

"Did he?" she said. "And don't you feel any shame? Think for yourself. Don't be a crawling puppy that only obeys Conchobar's will."

"As you do, Lady?" the wounded boy fired back.

At this she colored.

"It's surely clear whose son you are. But I'm not the one who's dishonored my grand name with this cowardly act. Think what a fool you look again, Cormac. And know that you and your friends will answer to Fergus MacRogh for this."

This brought an immediate and dramatic response from the rest. All feared their hard training master. Even Cormac blanched at the threat.

"No, my Queen," Sentanta said quickly.

She and the others turned toward him in surprise. "What do you mean?" she asked.

"I want nothing said of this," he told her firmly. "The others

. . . they were only drawn along. I've no quarrel with them. I've sought none with Cormac, but if there is one, it's between ourselves that it must be settled. Please, say no more of this to anyone."

She hesitated, her gaze going from him to Cormac. She ached for the chance to cause Conchobar's son some grief, to smash that haughty manner she had been forced to tolerate for so long. But the pleading in the young man's face decided her. She nodded.

"I suppose it is up to you." She waved a dismissing hand at the little band. "Then be off, you pack of curs, and quickly, but remember that if it happens ever again, no power will stop me from revealing to Fergus what a cowardly lot you are!"

They slunk away, but Cormac delayed a moment, looking at Sentanta.

"Cousin," he said slowly, clearly with great effort, "I . . . I thank you." And then he went hurriedly away, shaking his head.

"And now you," Meave said to Sentanta. "Come with me. I'll see to those wounds of yours."

"But I'm supposed to be . . . Cathbad said . . ." he tried to argue. But she would have none of it, firmly guiding him to the causeway and the gates.

"I've known for days that those boys were stalking you," she explained as they went. "I knew that you were out with Cathbad, and I saw them waiting."

They entered the yard, unaware that Conchobar was watching from the shelter of the armory's doorway. He had seen his son and battered friends come in, and now his face darkened with anger as his wife entered with his nephew. As they crossed the yard toward the royal quarters, he followed.

Her chambers, separate from Conchobar's, were modestly appointed for a queen's, but comfortable. She took the boy to her bed and sat him down. He was a little groggy still, winded from a punch to the stomach, blood streaming from the cuts on his eye and lip.

She found rags and water and cleansed the wounds with gentle hands. As she did so, her eyes met his.

For the first time they were very close. The effect of the proximity was electrifying. A force linked the two, an energy coursing through them both as if their blood, their souls, were for that instant twined.

She gasped in surprise, jerking back her head, and the contact was broken. Quickly, as if badly flustered by the phenomenon, she finished her cleansing.

"Th-thank you, my Queen," he said, also clearly bewildered. He started to rise. "Now I must go."

"No," she said, pushing him back. "You have to rest. At least for a few moments. Get back your wind. Let your blood quiet."

Sentanta had a feeling that, with her so near, that might never happen. Even without seeing her eyes, there was something most . . . well, *disturbing* was the only word he could put to it, about her presence. He could feel the warmth of her, smell her sweet scent, see every bright glint in the copper hair, the smoothness of her skin, the curve of her . . .

He mentally shook himself. What was he doing? It was like nothing he'd experienced before. A strange heat like a boiling liquid flooded into him, pleasurable and alarming at once. He felt his chest tighten, his breath shorten.

"I . . . I've wanted a chance to talk to you since you arrived," she said. Her voice was low, throaty, and she suddenly had become shy. "It's why I've been watching you. It . . . it's difficult to explain why. But I've felt a certain interest in you. A certain closeness, somehow." She turned those intense, bright, blue-gray eyes on him again, almost pleading now. "Do you understand?"

And again there was that sensation as their gazes met—the exchange, the mingling of energies, now a more subtle warming, tingling, not so intense, but still disquieting.

"I do," he said, rasping it out through a constricted throat.

"You look a young man, but you are yet a boy."

"I am thirteen, my lady," he said proudly, drawing himself up to look as manly as possible.

She smiled, then turned serious again. "But who are you, young Sentanta?" she asked with intensity. "I want to understand why I feel this way."

"You know who I am," he said. "Son of Sualtim and Dechtire, who is sister to your own husband."

"There is more," she said, shaking her head. "I know there must be more."

"And what of you?" he asked. "I know that you are the daughter of High-King Eochaid. The songs of the bards ring with his famous deeds. He must have been a great man."

"I recall him only as an aging, worn, and very sorrowful

man," she said, "forced to destroy his own sons, my older brothers, when they rebelled against him. Still, he was handsome and strong, and he had my mother's love to sustain him until the end."

"I . . . I've been interested in you, too, since I first saw you," he admitted. "I have asked Cathbad about you. He told me there was a story about your mother. Was she really of the Sidhe?"

"Many don't believe it," she said.

"I would," he told her earnestly.

"I believe you would." She smiled. "Yes, she was of the Sidhe. Etain was her name. Though I was a child, I retain an image of her as if she were before me—so beautiful. . . ."

"Please tell me," he urged, fixing his intense gaze on her.

"Shining hair she had, like burnished red gold, glowing in the summer's sun."

"Like your own."

"Maybe. But I wish I could have inherited my mother's spirit as well. It's more like you that she was. . . ."

"How do you mean?"

"Strong, sure, unafraid." She laid a cool, slim hand upon his forehead, stroking it gently. Then she went on.

"My father saw her one day when he hunted alone on the green of Bri Leith. He told the tale to me himself when I was small. He loved to describe the meeting, his eyes shining with the memory. She sat by a well, dressed in a gown of green silk embroidered with gold and a purple cloak trimmed in silver. The sun was shining on her, making her glow. Her bright hair was plaited, each plait in four locks, and with beads at each point. When he saw her, she was letting it down to wash in a silver bowl before her, her white arms out through the sleeve holes of her shift. He saw the fineness of her skin, and her soft hands. He saw her fairness, and her eyes like a clear spring sky and her lips red as rowan berries. He saw the high, proud arch of her eyebrows and the dimples of delight in her cheeks and the warm light of wooing in her eyes, and he was hers.

"He went to her and promised his love to her. She told him she was Etain, daughter of Etar, King of the Riders of the Sidhe, and had loved him since first hearing the tales of him. And so he brought her home to high Tara and a great welcome was made for them there.

"She was more beautiful than any other woman, mortal or

Sidhe, and many men wished her, but always she stayed loyal to my father, and only once did she leave him.

"One wild night, just before Samhain, a strange young man appeared in the hall of Tara, after all others had gone to bed and left the king alone. Gold hair the visitor had, and blue eyes shining like a candle flame, and a cloak of purple on him. In his hand he clasped a shield with golden knobs, and a five-pronged spear with silver rings about its haft that jingled as he strode across the vast, empty floor.

" 'Who are you, stranger?' my father asked him, 'and why have you come to me now?'

" 'I may be stranger to you, but you're none to me yourself,' the man said. 'For it's well known that you are a finer player at *fidchell* than any in Eire. My name is Midhir of Bri Leith, and I've come this wild Samhain Eve to have a game with you.'

" 'Tonight?' my father said, surprised.

" 'It's a long way I've come, and little time I have. I would play now, unless you are afraid?'

"Of course, such a challenge my father couldn't ignore. And so the young man took from a pouch tied with red-gold thread a board of silver and playing men of solid gold.

" 'Let us play now,' Midhir said.

" 'I'll not play without a stake,' said the king.

" 'Of course,' the man said lightly, as if it were of no difference. 'And what will it be?'

" 'We will decide after I have beaten you,' my father said with some arrogance, for he'd never lost a game.

"Neither did he lose this one, and it was fifty brown horses he asked in payment. But Midhir asked for his chance to be even, and my father could not resist. They played again, again my father winning, demanding more rewards, growing more arrogant as the young man grew weary and sorrowing. But then they played a third time, and the third time the stranger was brilliant in the game, winning easily.

" 'The luck of this night has turned for you,' said the king. 'What will you wish? Your riches back? Your horses?'

"Midhir smiled. 'It is your wife, Etain, I want,' he said.

"At this my father grew angry. 'I'll give no such thing to you,' he said.

" 'Then,' Midhir said graciously, 'all I ask is that you let me put my arms about her and kiss her once.'

"My father was a man of great honor, and he saw that he'd been surely trapped by his own arrogance.

" 'That I will allow,' he agreed, 'but you must wait until the spring to claim your prize.'

"When the time came, my father grew afraid of the strange man, that he might try to take Etain away by force. He gathered all his fighting men in the hall and shut all the doors against Midhir. Still, the young man appeared in the midst of them, shining and handsome.

" 'I've come to be paid what's due me,' said Midhir. 'To hold Etain in my arms and to kiss her once.'

My mother was most amazed when she heard this. " 'It's for myself to say what I will do,' she told him, 'not for my husband.'

" 'Then understand, Lady, that if you refuse, it will be known through Ireland from now to the last day that Eochaid broke his bond.'

" 'I'll ask for nothing that's against your will,' my father told her, but she saw the anguish in his eyes, and her heart softened.

" 'I will allow it,' she agreed unhappily.

"So the young man moved to her, and she looking to my father with fearing eyes, but he unable to interfere. Midhir took her in one arm and kissed her. And suddenly the two rose up as if they were straws caught upon the wind, and rushed toward the high smoke hole. When my father and his men rushed outside, they saw only two swans already high up, flying away, linked by a chain of gold.

"For seven years after that my father searched for her. Finally Codal of the Withered Breast took four rods of yew and wrote oghams upon them and used the enchantment to discover them, in a Sidhe hill in Bri Leith.

"He went there with all his army and for nine years more he set a siege to it, digging in to its banks until finally Midhir was forced to relent and send her back to him. He brought her to Tara, and there she spent the rest of her life with him, not growing a day older herself, but never deserting him. It's said that Midhir laid a curse upon my father, that somehow he would bring our family great despair and take revenge. And so it has proved."

"And your mother?" the wholly entranced Sentanta asked.

"When my father died, she was forced to return to the Sidhe, for it was only her great love of him that had kept her in the mortal world so long. I saw her last when I was very young, and she looking no older than I do now after living thirty years with my father."

"And so you are of the Sidhe blood?" he said, gazing at her in awe. "Is it really gods they are?"

"They are beings of strange powers, but they are people, such as ourselves, with our same emotions and pride and foolishness. Their blood's given me no wisdom, no powers. No help." Her voice became bitter. "It didn't keep my last brother, Eterscel, from selling me away to Conchobar like one of his bulls as a way of buying Ulster's loyalty. It didn't work, of course, but little that poor Eterscel did worked. Ireland became poorer and the more divided. And I was condemned to my life here."

"I'm sorry, my Queen," the boy said most regretfully.

"It doesn't matter now," she said, shaking off the dark mood. "It's you that matters." She again fixed her gaze on him searchingly. "Yes, I feel the Sidhe is in you somehow as well. They've touched you. You must find out."

"I do feel something within me," he told her. "Cathbad calls it a destiny. I know only that I mean to be a warrior."

"I have heard. It's a cruel life for a boy so fair."

She gently stroked his brow again. Then, seized by some mad impulse that drew her to him with a force she could not resist, she bent forward, dropping her lips to meet his own.

At first astonished, young Sentanta quickly found the warmth of her lips inflaming him. A like impulse, an ardor that he didn't understand and couldn't control, took hold of him. He responded to her kiss, rising to meet her. A hand lifted from the bed to the smooth curve of her leg, slid upward to encircle her waist and hold her closer. He felt the heat of her body against him, felt his own body filling up with fire. . . .

"Why, you treacherous wanton!" came a voice.

In surprise they pulled apart and turned to see Conchobar in the doorway.

"Is it small boys your lust's driven you to now?" he stormed, advancing upon them.

She rose from the bed and faced him, her face white with her dismay. "What are you saying?" she asked.

"I saw you bring that boy back here. Now I find you seducing him with your wiles. How many others have there been?"

"I have been helping this boy," she told her husband. "Nothing more."

Sentanta had risen too, watching the scene in shock. He was bewildered by the events, wondering if what she had said was true. Still, he knew without question that he must come to her defense.

"My King," he said, "we were only talking here. She was tending my wound. . . ."

"Keep quiet, boy!" Conchobar shouted, then moved threateningly upon Meave. "There's nothing to say here. I know. I've seen. I understand why you've been no wife to me. On how many others have you spent your passions? Who were they all? My warriors? My friends? More children like this one?"

She swung up a hand, her palm striking soundly against his cheek with power enough to twist his head sideways.

He snarled and swung up his own hand in reply, the massive palm slapping across her face with such power that it knocked her back and she collapsed upon the bed. He moved forward, lifting his hand as if to strike again.

Sentanta leaped in, seizing the king's arm to pull him back. "No, my King!" he cried.

Conchobar angrily wheeled and threw him off. He staggered away. The king crouched like a great bear ready to attack.

"Stay out of this, I'm warning you!" he growled meanacingly, then turned back to his wife, who still lay where she had fallen, a hand to the reddening welt on her fair cheek, eyes brimming with tears of anger and pain.

"You are useless to me," he told her in a low, hard voice, as if meaning to strike a blow at her with each word instead of with his hands. "You've given me no warmth, no love, no sons. You're a woman of no honor, no nobility, no strength. You've only one value to me or to any man, but the cost for it is far too great. I want this worthless marriage ended now. I will ask the Brehons for a divorce, and you will agree. I want you out of my house, my dun, my province, with no delays, or it will go hard for you, Meave. Hard!"

He turned away from her to see Sentanta glaring at him with anger. "Are you still here?" he said. "Get out of here. Now!"

"But, my King—" the boy began.

"What, pup? Are you defying me?" Conchobar challenged, stepping toward him. From the blazing look of rage in his eyes and his clenched fists, it was clear that he hoped the boy would give him an excuse to strike.

Resentful, hostile, and confused, Sentanta looked up at the taller figure of the man. He felt a need to help Meave, though he knew that to try was foolish here. He felt a desire to strike out at this man, but his oaths of loyalty, his bonds to his king, held him back. He said nothing, made no move.

"All right then, boy," the king said, moving to him and dropping a hand heavily upon his shoulder, "we will leave here together." And he turned Sentanta, propelling him toward the door.

There he paused to look back to Meave, to add with a last touch of venom, "Crawl away and hide yourself now, Lady, until you leave this place. I've no wish to see you again."

The last Sentanta saw of her before the king shoved him out the doorway was her slender form draped across the bed in an attitude of total defeat, shaking with the force of her broken sobs.

Chapter Ten

Retribution

"I am sorry for this, Meave," said Fergus MacRogh.

He stood in the doorway of the room, overseeing her as she and some servants packed up the last of her goods.

"I've some regrets in this myself," she said. She was putting on a brave front, but the effects of strain and sorrow were clear on her. "I hate him, and I am glad to be rid of him, but I also hate being driven away like some mongrel bitch in heat sniffing about his prize hounds."

"It was his argument to the Brehons, Meave."

"And they accepted it," she said disgustedly. "Of course. All men, all of Ulster, all so righteous, and all such fawning subjects of the king. Likely they already believed what he said, or wanted to."

"You made no effort to dispute it," he pointed out. "That did little in making you seem the innocent."

"I . . . couldn't," she said in frustration. "You know why. It's a violent man he is. A man of overpowering will. He'd have nothing else but his way."

"I know that you've done nothing in letting him dominate you but hurt yourself more."

"And I suppose even you now think of me as the others do?" she said, looking at him in despair.

"I never believed it, Meave," he said gently.

She looked at his broad, earnest face. "Of course not, Fergus," she said as she moved to him. "I know." She put a hand upon his arm. "One other regret I'll have at leaving here is that I will miss you. You have been a friend to me. Maybe the only one I've had here." She realized then that the servants were eyeing them surreptitiously as they worked, and she blushed and quickly took away her hand. "I must take care. Or else I'll have the jealous rage of Conchobar falling upon yourself as well."

"You don't really think he's jealous of that boy?" asked Fergus with disbelief.

"Can you think otherwise? Even in normal times he's a man of great anger and raging jealousies, but in this he's become truly a madman." She met and held his eyes, her voice low and urgent. "Fergus, I am convinced he hates that boy. He has already tried to use Cormac against him more than once. Used his own son!"

"I know there's been a rivalry between the two, but that's natural," he said dismissingly. "Cormac's lost his favored position over the other boys. And Sentanta's holding his own well enough. I can't see Conchobar doing such a thing."

She shook her head sadly, defeatedly. "No, of course not. Trusting Fergus. Well, it's the only other of my regrets in leaving that Sentanta will have one less person to watch over him. The need falls more on you now, Fergus. Look to the boy, and beware of Conchobar. Be suspicious of everything he does. He's dangerous."

"I know you and he had no life together, and that he has some temper," Fergus protested, "but he's still a fine king and a good man at heart."

"Fergus, I like and admire you as a warrior, but you are naïve and far too trusting. Don't blindly accept him."

"You sound like Cathbad now," Fergus said, smiling, trying to make light of it.

"He's right. Please listen to him and to me. It's the last thing I ask."

With that she turned away, casting her gaze around the room. "Well, the packing is done," she said. "Now I can go."

Fergus gave orders to the servants to carry the cases and sacks and bundles out and she followed after them. But as she reached the door she stopped to give him a final, private word.

"He is a special lad, Fergus. I feel it. There is something— something of the Others in that one."

Then she went out, leaving Fergus to stare after her. He was recalling other cautioning words from Cathbad about the king and his own still-vivid memories of a day in a tiny liss deep in a snowy wood.

Outside, a curious crowd had gathered to witness the final humiliation and departure of the now infamous ex-queen.

Divorces were simply and swiftly granted under the Irish law when both parties agreed, and only a few days had passed since the event. But that had been more than enough time for word to spread widely.

As she came out of her quarters into the yard, she stopped to look around her at this crowd. They returned her gaze openly, insolently, as if she were some fabulous creature at which they had a right to stare. She looked at the faces: self-righteous women condemning her licentiousness; fascinated men leering at their own lustful fantasies about her.

Fergus came out behind Meave and looked around as well, then grimaced in disgust. "Like blackbirds flocking about a dying hind," he spat out. "Why are they here?"

"They're the good and the pure people of Ulster, Fergus," she said bitterly, "making certain justice is done. I was their queen, remember. My 'crime' was against them too. Their own honor has been put at stake, and won't be avenged until I am run from this place. So, no delays."

She started across the yard, head up, striding proudly to the waiting chariot and cart where her belongings were being loaded.

From the sunroom of the hall, Conchobar watched her, smiling triumphantly. He could, like some god of judgment, gaze down aloofly upon the condemned woman's exiling, but never demean himself with any farewell to her. His eyes scanned the crowd. He saw their looks of revulsion, of condemnation, and he was satisfied.

His eyes moved across a small group almost lost among the

others and paused there. These were students from his own training school! He looked more closely, and then his eyes flared with his rage. There, with the sons of Usna, stood his nephew, the cursed Sentanta!

How had this happened? He had told Fergus to keep that boy away, hadn't he? Had his chieftain failed him, or was this an act of defiance from the boy?

Meave too had noted the boy, but was also very aware that the gaze of the king was on her. She kept her eyes averted from Sentanta, knowing that any more contact between them, no matter how innocent, could only make her ex-husband's insane jealousy the worse.

But Sentanta had no care for that. Fergus had told him he could come, ignoring Conchobar's order, but had said that he should keep himself far from Meave. He had obeyed, but now as he looked at the forlorn woman he felt a sharp, painful tug within him, as if something of himself were being torn away. He watched, and a great sorrow came in him, overwhelming him. Not even thinking, he moved forward.

"Wait!" said Naoise, trying to hold him back.

It was too late. Sentanta broke from the group and strode out boldly across the yard. Behind him, a flutter of wondering voices rose in the gathering as astonished eyes followed him. Above, Conchobar's gaze was like hot iron riveted on the boy, while his hands gripped the rail as if to crush it.

Neither Fergus nor Meave, engaged in supervising the last packing, noted Sentanta until he was close. The chieftain saw him first, wheeling in alarm toward the boy.

"Sentanta!" he said in a sharp voice. "I told you to keep out of this!"

But he was too late. The boy sidestepped him and moved to Meave's side, laying a hand upon her arm.

She had turned at Fergus's words, and now looked at the boy with an expression of dismay.

"Sentanta, what are you doing?" she said. "Fergus is right." Her eyes darted to the balcony, to the grim, taut figure visible there. "Conchobar will not like this!"

"I don't care," Sentanta said defiantly. "It's a great injustice that you must leave. I . . . I don't want to lose you. Not now!" His eyes were bright with starting tears. His voice trembled with his anguish. "Oh, Meave, I'm so sorry. I feel as if this is my fault."

She tried to smile at him, forcing comfort into her words.

"No, Sentanta. What has happened has been coming for a long time. In a way you've done me a favor, done something for me I've been afraid to do myself."

She put a hand upon his shoulder.

"Until you came, I thought that no one could defy him. I thought everyone was as I was—afraid, bullied, and controlled. You showed me that he could be challenged. Now you must go on doing as I couldn't do. Be the strength I can't be. Be your own person always, Sentanta, and let no one control you. I'll have one comfort knowing you've won that for me."

She leaned closer to him then, adding more intensely, "But be wary, Sentanta. He is a ruthless, bloody man, your highking. Be careful, and look to Fergus."

At this, her emotions finally overcame her control. Not wishing him to see the tears welling in her eyes, she quickly hugged him to her, then turned and climbed into her chariot.

"Away from here," she ordered the driver. "Take me out of this place swiftly, charioteer."

The man urged his animals forward. Sentanta stood watching her as she rode out across the yard and through the gates without looking back again.

"You should not have done that, lad," Fergus said grimly.

Sentanta did not hear, so absorbed was he in her leaving, in watching the slender, vanquished figure being carried away.

"Where will she go, Fergus?" he asked.

"To Tara. To the court of her nephew, Conaire Mor."

"There's no fairness to it, Fergus," he said despairingly. "She was a fine woman. Kind and wise and gentle . . ."

"Too much so to be wed to Conchobar," the chieftain replied. "Think no more of it, lad. She was right. You did her a good turn. She's well away from him."

He turned and glanced up toward the window of the hall. The figure was still there, still glaring down upon the back of the boy whose open defiance of him had now become intolerable.

"Whatever it may take, you strange and bastard whelp," he muttered darkly to himself, "I will be rid of you!"

Chapter Eleven

A Hunt

The boar turned back suddenly, slashing upward with its tusks in a savage thrust at the horse's underbelly as it passed beneath the chariot team.

It was a clever and dangerous move, taking all the company by surprise. The horse was ripped open from side to side and stumbled forward, its scream echoing through the forest. The second horse, in terror, pulled hard to the left. The chariot continued on, colliding with the team and twisting over to crash heavily on its side, throwing the warrior and his driver free.

In an instant the boar was at them, determined to have satisfaction upon its pursuers. It was half a man's height at the shoulder, its great tusks backed by weight, muscle, and the wily mind of one of the most dangerous of animals.

The warrior struck desperately upward at the beast with his spear as it came toward him. But its attack was so swift, so agile, that the man had no chance. It brushed past his spear point and drove its tusks into his shoulder and chest. With a twist of its powerful neck, it lifted him and tossed him aside, a ragged, crimson-stained bundle. Then it turned its attention on the hapless driver, who was trying to crawl away from the broken wreckage of the car and the wildly plunging horses.

The rest of the hunting party was in a tangled mass. The hounds had scattered before the beast's counterattack. The horses of the other chariots had panicked, bunching, turning, tangling their harness as they fought madly to pull away from the rampaging creature.

But in one chariot a figure moved, leaping over the car's side, a long spear clutched in its hands.

It was a slender figure that leaped to the charioteer's defense, clad in a simple tunic, a great mane of red hair caught back behind the neck in the warrior's manner. Only a boy, it seemed, beardless, pale-complexioned, smooth-featured, but still with a cold determination flashing in the blue-gray eyes.

In another of the entangled cars farther behind, a young man struggling to work his team free stopped to stare in alarm as he saw the figure move. It was Conaire Mor himself, high-king of Ireland, and he knew that for all the warrior's trappings, it was no boy who made this bold attack but his own aunt, Meave.

As she jumped into the charging animal's path, it halted, turning from the fallen man, allowing him to scuttle away to safety. The boar hesitated only an instant, then it charged again. The woman waited calmly, solidly planted, spear up, motionless, until the moment when the beast would be close enough.

The boar was almost upon her when she finally made her cast. She could clearly see its tiny, glittering eyes fixed on her from behind the yellow tusks. Her spear was driven forward with all her power behind it, aimed at the spiny backbone just behind the lowered head.

Yet her weight and her speed were not enough. The wily boar swerved slightly at her move. The spear slipped past the side of its leathery head and planted itself deeply in the sinewy muscle of the beast's shoulder.

It was not a deadly wound, but it was severe enough to bring the animal great pain and cause it to wheel away from its adversary. Before it could recover to strike again, others of the hunting party, finally free of the tangle, leaped toward it. The animal turned and fled, tearing free of the embedded spear as it plunged into the brush.

Meave stood watching the boar disappear into the deeper woods. She cursed herself for her bad aim and for the interference of the others that had kept her from finishing the battle herself.

A chariot pulled up beside her. From the car the young king who had watched in fear now glared down angrily at her. "Meave, is it mad you are?" he asked hotly.

She looked up to him, her face expressionless. "I saved a man," she answered shortly. "I'd hoped to save two."

"They were fools to overrun the hounds!" he argued. "For you to be risking yourself—"

"—is like no risk at all!" she finished. "No more, now, Conaire. I've no time for it. I must be after tracking down that boar."

She signaled her driver, who pulled her chariot forward at once. She climbed into it and began carefully to check over the hunting spears racked inside.

"Let the beast run," Mor told her. "He's bleeding now. Let him be weakened a bit by it. We'll find him easily enough."

"There's no 'we' in this," she said, pulling two of the better spears from the rack. "I'm going on after him alone."

"Now I'm certain you're mad. All of us are going on this hunt." He waved his hand about to include the score of other chariots with drivers and warriors, including his own foster-brothers, the scores more of servants on foot, and the large pack of lean, long-headed dogs straining to be on the trail again.

She shook her head sharply. The bushy tail of hair hanging at her back flared like leaping fire.

"My spear left him alive," she said firmly. "My wound made him more dangerous. I'll have no charioteer, no man on foot, not even any hound be risked again. There'll be no more guilt upon me, Conaire Mor. I will go alone!"

He knew from hard experience that it was useless to argue with his aunt. He sighed and nodded. "All right then, Meave. But I'll be going with you."

She started to protest, but he held up a hand. "I go, or you do not."

"You're being a fool to take this chance yourself," she said, fixing a disapproving look on him.

"If you can make yourself a fool, then I'm surely free to exercise the same privilege," he answered stubbornly.

"Let's be wasting no more time then!" she shot back, her patience gone. "Come on!"

She ordered her driver forward, and he urged the team ahead. The chariot rolled away from the rest, on into the woods in the path of the fleeing boar. Over their protests the young high-king told his foster-brothers and the others of the party to wait there and commanded his own driver to start after her.

The way was easy at first—the trees widely spaced, the floor of the forest largely free of undergrowth. The chariots moved side by side, Meave and her nephew able to follow the boar's trail of blood from within the cars. As they went, he tried to engage her in talk in hopes of easing the peculiar tension he saw in her.

"It was a fine throw you made, Meave," he said in a cheerfully admiring way.

Her gaze had been fixed intently on the way ahead, seeking

the boar's path. Now she turned it on the young man who rode apparently so at ease, so carelessly beside her, beaming at her, in his boyish, unaffected way.

"Only you could be wanting to make idle talk while stalking a quarry as dangerous as this," she said harshly, and turned her attention back to the woods before them.

He was unabashed. With a cheerful doggedness he plunged ahead. "I only mean to compliment your skill. Was it Eochaid taught you?"

This reminder of a rare time of pleasure in her youth touched Meave's thoughts. Grudgingly she answered, "Yes, it was. He was an old man when I was a young girl. But he was a fine warrior yet, and he showed me the tricks of war as he'd shown my brothers."

She considered her brothers ruefully. Those tricks of war hadn't helped to save them from her father's wrath when they had rebelled against him. Perhaps the same weakness that had plagued her life had been a part of Eochaid's other children, too.

Conaire saw that fresh pain had been raised in her by the reminder of her brothers. He shifted the subject quickly.

"Eochaid must have been a great man," he said thoughtfully. "I wish there had been a chance for me to meet my grandfather."

"He would have approved little enough of you now," she answered critically, glancing over his dress. "He felt that a ruler should always seem one in appearance."

It was true that, for a man who was now ruler of all Ireland, Conaire Mor looked more a common warrior, and one of low station at that. His hunting tunic was rumpled, tattered, stained brown with the old blood of past kills. His cloak was of the meanest, rough gray wool. Save for the silver-hilted longsword buckled about his waist, he wore no ornament, no torque of gold, no crown, no jeweled brooch to proclaim his rank or wealth. He felt such decoration was frivolous, especially on a hunt.

So Meave's comment served only to make him laugh, his youthful face lighting with amusement. Still not more than twenty years of age, his role as king had not caused him to take on any new vanities, and he retained all the exuberance and idealism of youth. To him, the old symbols of power were valueless. The only proof of his ability to rule came in what good he could do for Ireland.

He expected Meave to laugh too, for she had often jokingly nagged him about his too-casual dress. But this time she remained sober, her gaze turning back again to fix stonily on the boar's trail.

Mor's amusement died and he watched her thoughtfully. He was becoming very worried about his aunt.

Since divorcing Conchobar MacNessa and leaving Ulster the summer before, she had lived at Tara with him. The two were very close in age, Meave being the last child of Eochaid, and Mor the son of the first. They were more like brother and sister in their relationship, and he had welcomed her to Tara warmly, making her a part of his court.

But, for the year she had been living there her mood had been a strange one, marked by long, deep depressions punctuated by short bursts of violent activity. She'd thrown herself into dangerous hunts and violent games and hard, hazardous races with the chariots, as if driven to channel all her energy into reckless enterprises. And now, this risk today!

"Meave, is it your own death you're seeking here?" he asked her bluntly.

This seemed to startle her. "What question is that for you to be asking me?" she retorted, the gray eyes wide.

"Only that I've been watching you since you came to me," he answered gravely. "It seems you've bent yourself toward things that will destroy you."

She stared at him for a moment without reply. And then a rueful smile tugged at the corners of her wide mouth. "And what loss would it be if I were destroyed?" she asked.

He shook his head uncomprehendingly. "I don't understand you, Meave."

Her reply came in a tight voice. "I don't expect you to understand me, Conaire. For all the years I lived with Conchobar, he never ceased proving to me my uselessness. I tried to fight him, but even in that I failed. And when he finally branded me a wanton, all I could do was flee him."

"You accepted the divorce from him, Meave," Mor argued. "You left Ulster without argument or attempt to defend yourself. It took courage to do that, to take that step to free yourself."

"But am I free?" she said in anguished tones. "He's made his wound in me, and it won't heal. My life's been like that of the beast we're hunting now—surrounded by enemies, hounded and hurt, reduced to hiding and waiting out the end. At last the only hope left is that the end is swift!" She looked down at the spears ready beside her and her voice turned chill. "That's why I want to bring a quick end to the suffering of this creature I know so well."

Mor felt the touch of death in her chilling tones. He saw the implication in her words. His fears for her increased.

Yet, as he watched her he found it difficult to accept that here was someone totally defeated, regardless of what she said. She rode so proudly, her fine head thrown back, her bright mane of hair glowing even in the overcast day as if some inner energy charged it. And that same energy fired her gray eyes, like sunlight burning behind a heavy cloud, ready to burst through with a blinding brightness.

There was life in her. The excitement of the hunt had clearly aroused it.

The trail of the boar led them deeper into the forest. The woods began to close in, the undergrowth increasing in density. Finally the chariots found no passageway. Meave halted hers and climbed down from the car, taking up her spears.

"Are you meaning to continue the hunt on foot?" Mor asked.

"I am."

"Then you know I'll be going on with you."

"I know that," she said, "but your life is your own. Look to it yourself and stay clear of me."

With that she turned and strode away into the brush. Hurriedly Mor took up his own weapons, jumped from his car, and started after her.

The trail of blood continued to lead them on, and they could see clearly the passage the heavy body of the animal had made through the tangled growth.

Mor's instincts told him to go more cautiously, and he was aware of the silence that had fallen over the surrounding woods. But Meave moved boldly ahead, not taking any care, and he was forced to a near run to stay close to her.

They passed through an open area where the blood trail showed clearly on the earth, pointing like an arrow toward the thickets ahead. Meave started forward, but Mor restrained her suddenly with a grip on her shoulder.

"Wait, Meave," he said softly but urgently.

She gave him an impatient look. "Why are you stopping me?"

He pointed ahead. "The boar is lying in that thicket, waiting for us. He's there as surely as the waves beat Ireland's coast. I can feel him there. And the same way I can feel what's in you, Meave."

She met his eye, but her look was veiled.

"Don't waste yourself, Meave," he pleaded. "You're not defeated. Your need to act proves that. You still want something more."

She jerked away from his restraining hand and stood stiffly, looking toward the boar's hiding place as if not heeding him.

"Conchobar may not have needed you, but I do," he continued earnestly. "I need your cunning and your strength to help me shape Ireland into a strong land."

His insistence forced a harsh denial from her.

"You've no need of me. You've Father's strength and cleverness in you. It will be enough."

"But you've his blood too, and stronger than I," he argued. "It must drive you!" He stepped up to her and turned her to face him. "Tell me, Meave, that you have never wished to hold some of his power for yourself!"

He saw that he had touched her then. The truth glittered just for an instant in her eyes. He smiled in satisfaction.

"It's there, Meave. Don't be denying it. You want life. You want to stay alive."

But a covering shield came down over her eyes, blocking her emotions from his view. Her response to him was like the thrust of an iron spear-point.

"Now your insights have taken you into a realm where you've no rights. You're too bold being here. Death comes when it comes, and we've only to accept it. Now, let's be seeing if your feelings told you rightly about that animal."

At that, she wheeled away from him and headed for the thicket at a run.

Taken off guard by the swiftness of her move, Mor was left far behind her. She was nearly to the thicket before he had taken a few steps.

The boar was there. It didn't wait until Meave had reached it to make its move. While she was still more than a good spear's throw away, it burst from the thicket, charging to meet her.

Meave stopped and stood before it. Her spears were down beside her and she was motionless, totally relaxed. Mor saw with horror that she apparently intended simply to let the beast run her down.

But when it was nearly upon her, she came suddenly to life. There was no time to raise or throw a spear. All she could do to save herself was to dodge from its path. And she did so in the boldest way, leaping forward over the back of the charging beast.

With relief Mor watched her clear the animal and roll safely onto the ground behind it. Then he realized with some consternation that the problem had become his, for the attacking creature plunged straight on, picking out the next adversary in its path.

Mor flung his first spear when the boar was within its reach, but the point skittered over the curve of the hard, smooth back without penetrating. The beast was too close then for another careful throw, and a miss would leave him facing the attack with nothing in his hands. So he grounded the spear and pulled his longsword, bracing himself for the collision.

The boar was battle-wise enough to avoid the sword it saw flaring in the king's hand. It made a sudden turn in an attempt to come at Mor from the side before he could move and go in at his vulnerable legs.

With lightning reactions, Mor swiveled, sweeping the sword around him to keep the running animal away.

It seemed that they played a children's game then, wheel turning within wheel, striving to touch and not be touched, but for a deadly stake. Soon the boar grew desperate. Weakening from loss of blood, mad from its pain, it dived in with a last burst of speed and strength, passing behind the blade. Mor twisted to escape, throwing himself sideways.

He fell across the boar and found himself suddenly clutching the thick, sinewy neck. He forced the head down and they rolled forward together, thudding heavily onto the earth, the animal's weight rolling atop him.

He couldn't use his sword. He needed both hands levering up from beneath to keep the beast away as it thrashed violently in its attempt to get at him.

Then, abruptly, the animal's struggles ceased.

The great head dropped upon him, and the powerful body relaxed. With an effort, Conaire Mor rolled it off of him and climbed wearily to his feet.

He saw that behind the boar's left foreleg a spear had been driven in deeply, piercing the creature's heart.

Beside the carcass Meave stood, smiling grimly at her nephew.

"It was a fine job you did in holding the animal so tightly," she told him. "You gave me time to place my spear."

"Meave!" he wheezed, trying to work the cramps out of his arms. "You could have killed both me and yourself here!"

"Take heart, Conaire. I could have, surely, but I did choose not to . . . this time!"

Chapter Twelve

Politics

"You must give me some help!" The emphatic words were punctuated by the sharp *crack* of an iron pellet against the timbers of the high palisade.

Conaire Mor carefully fitted another walnut-sized pellet into the leather pocket of the sling and looked up at the circle of brightly cloaked druids who watched him.

"I'm sorry to be bringing you out here to talk about it, but this is a matter that needs some privacy, and I thought our meeting here now could give us a bit of that."

He turned back to the timber wall again. His first throw at the man-sized target marked against its base had been quite wide. He tried to estimate the power needed to adjust his aim.

While he was thus absorbed, the druids shifted uncomfortably, and some exchanged irritated looks. It was a bit presumptuous, they thought, for this young king to bring them to this training ground below the fortress hill of Tara in the chill of dawn. He was far too easy in ordering them about. After all, as ard-druids, the most learned men in Ireland, their own power rivaled his, and even surpassed it in some things beyond the natural. A few of them had held their positions as counsel at Tara since his grandfather's time. Too often he seemed to forget that.

Still, all of them came, and none complained aloud.

A second pellet cracked against the wood, both high and wide this time, bouncing back some distance from the resilient surface. Mor shook his head. This new sling brought him from the Alban kingdoms was difficult to master. Tossing it aside, he turned to face his waiting advisers.

"I know this is inconvenient and uncomfortable for all of you," he said soothingly, noting a few who shivered with the cold, "but it is a matter of urgency to me. It's many days I've been troubled by it, and with no answer coming to me. That's why I've turned to you. Something must be done to help my aunt."

"My King, Meave holds no favor here," the gray-haired chief of the druidic council replied boldly. "More than a few feel you've no need to be helping her yourself. She seems . . ." he hesitated, seeking the proper word, "well . . . unstable," he finished frankly. "I'm sorry, my King, but it's clear to everyone! And she may bring that disease of mind to us. She certainly did no good for Ulster's king. The rumors of her relationships . . ."

"Enough!" Mor said sharply. "I've no interest in rumors of her past. This woman is my aunt, daughter of a high-king of all Ireland. She has an intelligence and a strength within her that must be used. And I'm asking you to suggest some enterprise which will give her self-esteem and her sense of usefulness back to her."

There was no response from them, and this time he was aware of the looks of irritation that several exchanged. As often before, he regretted not being able to include younger men on the druidic council. But the rigorous process of training an ard-druid took over sixteen years. It produced a learned man, certainly, but one of middle age and conservative views.

"Look here," he ventured in a more congenial way, "I know that we've found it difficult to have a close relationship, and I can understand that approaching you on a personal matter like this could make you ill at ease."

"It could indeed, my King," another druid said. "Your assessment of at least my own feelings is correct. I feel, and I'm sure others here do as well, that our involvement should be in matters of state, not in advising you upon your private woes. More than that, to speak the entire truth, most of us agree with the opinion of our leader." He nodded at the druid who had spoken first. "We've no inclination to concern ourselves with your aunt."

"I see," Mor said with some irritation. He glanced over the rest. "And is this really the feeling of all of you?"

There were some nods. Most met his gaze with looks of grim

certainty. It was the defiance of powerful men bent on asserting their power in teaching an upstart a lesson. No one spoke.

So, after several uncomfortable moments of silence, Mor decided to release them.

"I'll not be pressing you further on this question, then," he told them in a terse way. "But keep in mind that I'll be in the debt of anyone who can find a way to help. Be off into the dun now and find yourselves some warmth, as you've such a need for it!"

Without further ceremony, he turned away from them and took up the sling again. Though many clearly disliked being so brusquely and summarily dismissed, they were relieved at escaping his presence and the piercing cold.

One of the group, however, lingered behind. He had considered the ard-rie's words carefully. As one of the newest and thus lowest ranking on the council, he had so far been distant from the king's ear. Now he was seeing presented to him a chance to make himself better known.

Since coming to Tara, he had been gathering information, cultivating sources, using his power in many ways, preparing for just such an opportunity as this. Those other old fools couldn't see it, so blinded were they by their own arrogance. None of them understood how much could be gained.

Mor had loaded the sling and now took another calculated throw. It was as far off target as the others, kicking up the earth some way in front of the wall.

"It's hard for me to believe a weapon so hard to control would ever be popular, my King," the druid remarked.

Mor looked around at him in surprise. "Still here? I thought you had all flown off to your snug nests."

"No, my King. I stayed to speak with you about this problem. I may have a way to deal with it, and more."

Interested, Mor moved closer to the man. "So, perhaps there is some hope for my druids yet," he said. "Your name is Calatin, isn't it?"

"It is, my King. We've not talked much before. I've been on your council only a little while."

The ard-rie eyed him appraisingly. He certainly was a strange, dark fellow, and quite alien in manner. As Mor recalled, he was said to have come to Ireland from Espan. No one knew why, although there were certainly tales about it and about his use of the darker druidic powers. But none of that was of real importance to the young ruler now.

"Calatin, if you've a way to help my aunt, we will surely talk a great deal more," he said earnestly. "Come on. I'm finished here. We'll go up to the dun ourselves."

"And what about the privacy you wished to keep in this?"

"I'll need to return my toy to the armory," Mor said, swinging the sling in his hand. "We can talk there without being disturbed."

He lifted the weapon and eyed it critically. "It's surely a great deal harder to manage than the one I used as a boy."

"I have heard, my King, that there are those so skilled they can bring down a flying bird with it."

Mor laughed at that. "Perhaps, Ard-Druid. But certainly not myself. At least, not anymore. This is one who'll make no more casts at birds. I've enough troubles in my life as it is."

He threw the sling over his shoulder and the two men started up the pathway toward the fortress gates.

"Tell me, why is it you've come to live in Eire?" the ard-rie asked casually as they walked along.

Calatin's reply was straightforward and simple and quite true, so far as it went. "I see in this realm of yours a land that can become united and strong. I know the same dream is yours. For that reason I wished to join your court."

Mor considered a moment before responding carefully, "I'll be open with you, Calatin. I've been told by many that I shouldn't trust you. My warriors appear to have some fear of you, and even my other druids are uneasy about the powers they feel you have. But I'll tell you now that my only concern is what you can do for Ireland, and for me."

"My King, I hope that today I'll prove my worth to you."

They reached the fortress gates and passed inside. Mor led them to the large oval structure which housed the fortress's arms and trophies of battle. As they entered it, Calatin stopped to gaze about him at the massed paraphernalia of war.

Upon the timber walls hung a wide range of weapons, impressive in their workmanship, repelling in their potential destructive power.

Bronze-fitted axes were there, and spears ringed with bands of bright gold. Racks filled with swords ran below racks of shields whose devices represented clans and tuaths throughout Ireland. And the vast floor was crowded with chariots of war, the deadly machines agleam with fittings of finely wrought silver and polished bronze-rimmed wheels.

Overlooking all the rest, filling one wide section of the wall from floor to high roof timbers, row upon row of white skulls grinned down upon the two men.

Mor had walked to the room's center. Now he paused to look back at the druid.

"Calatin, you haven't been in this room before?" he asked.

"No, my King. That privilege is usually restricted to your warriors. It is a most awesome sight."

"To me it's a reminder of the condition which always fragments Ireland," the ard-rie said darkly.

He walked to the wall of skulls and lightly touched three in the lowest rank.

"These are my own uncles'. My grandfather decreed that they must hang here with the heads of all other traitors to the king." He looked up at the scores more stretching far above. "I could wish that we'd never need to add more trophies to this company." He glanced evaluatingly at Calatin. "Or do you think I'm speaking heresy to deny the value of our ancient rites?"

Calatin crossed the floor to join him. He lifted one of the skulls from its peg and held it up.

"Our worship of the head is not a worship of this hollow thing," he said, looking into the eyeless sockets. "It is the warriors who feel that taking the head is to somehow magically take its power. But it's within this chamber that the real magic lies," he stroked the smooth, white dome, "in the mind of the living man. To control that . . ." he gave Mor a small, cunning-filled smile, "that is to truly have control."

Mor was intrigued by this druid's ideas. Calatin was being very bold in departing from the traditional beliefs and seemed much in sympathy with the ard-rie's radical notions.

"Tell me then, Calatin," he said, sitting down on a chariot pole, "what do you believe I can do to help my aunt Meave?"

Calatin hung the skull back on its peg and considered carefully before he turned to face Mor again.

"It is a complex thing, my King," he quietly replied, "but I believe it can also help you realize your greatest dream for Ireland."

Meave walked upon the ramparts of Tara, looking out across the mist-shrouded countryside that flowed away on all sides from the dun, a softly swelling sea of meadowland, rising into the haze of distant hills.

Winds blew the mist into gray-white swirls that drifted gently up into the overcast. As she walked she felt the soothing dampness of the air caress her face.

On the western side of the great wall she stopped and stood staring out across the half-hidden land below. Out there, beyond the mist, lay the Brugh na Boinne. It was there, at the tomb of Newgrange upon its banks, that her father had been put to rest, his ashes mixed with those of other kings inside the ancient royal burial mound.

She stared out toward it, seeing it in her mind, longing within her for such a quiet, lonely, untroubled place to rest, within the green hill, beside the flowing river.

The sound of feet upon the plank walkway interrupted her drifting thoughts. She turned her head to see Conaire Mor approaching her. As she watched him come she was again reminded of her father, Eochaid. Mor had the same lean, long-limbed body and loose, almost awkward movements that so well disguised a great agility and strength. She knew that despite his talk of peace, the spirit of the warrior lived in this young king.

"Meave, I knew I'd find you walking here," he said as he reached her. "I've seen you doing little else for days."

She turned her gaze back toward the countryside and answered in a strangely detached way.

"Do you know, they say it was across those fields that the Riders of the Sidhe came, before my mother went away. My father was gone, and she was lifted like a fallen leaf by a storm's wind and swept away to where the Others dwell."

"Meave, your mind's too clouded with these fantastical things," he said with vigor. "They cast strange shadowy clouds over you. Let the sun which I know burns within you shine out and drive them away!"

She looked at him, her expression lifeless. "Conaire, there's no fire left in me."

"There is, Meave, and I've come to fuel it. There is a task that only you can do for me and all of Ireland."

This announcement was delivered in a grand tone of voice, and Meave gave him a look of incredulity.

"What kind of madness is it you're speaking now, Conaire? What is it I could do for all of Ireland?"

"You could help me unite it!" he said enthusiastically. "Meave, you know my one great task since taking the royal seat has been to create a true bond among the provinces."

"Yes, I know."

"And you know I've been successful, perhaps more so than any other high-king before me—even your father!"

She nodded, not sure where this was leading.

"I'm close, Meave. I can smell the reality of it as I can smell a storm on its way. But there is one thing that's kept it from arriving."

She thought she knew what he was going to say. "You mean that Conchobar MacNessa has kept Ulster from joining you?"

He shook his head emphatically. "No, Meave. We know what kind of man he is and what his private madness did to you. We know what arrogance we have to deal with there. But his reluctance to let Ulster join us isn't shared by his chieftains. His finest champions, Fergus MacRogh and Conal Carna, are pressing him to agree to it. And he will do so, I think, once he sees he has no other choice."

He had confused her. "Then, I don't understand how I . . ."

"You will see, Meave," he interrupted, caught up in the excitement he felt about this new idea. So enthused was he that he couldn't be still. He threw an arm about her shoulders and began to walk her briskly along the parapet as he continued.

"So Ulster is not the problem. She will join, but Conchobar will hold back as long as he can, waiting to see if I can succeed in uniting all the rest of Ireland."

He stopped abruptly and met her eyes.

"I've succeeded everywhere but in one crucial place: Connacht. You know Connacht, don't you, Meave?"

A vague suspicion awakened in her mind. She eyed him narrowly. "You know well enough I do, Conaire. Part of my life was spent out there. Of all the provinces, she has perhaps the greatest potential for richness and power. It's only the long wars with the Firbolg tribes that have kept her weak."

"Yet, she'll not accept our help or even talk to us. And though Aileel was one of my grandfather's most loyal chieftains, he'll not meet with anyone I send to him."

"Enough of this, Conaire," she said with force. "Tell me now what it is you're expecting me to do!"

Mor considered a moment. Then he spoke bluntly. "He'll not meet with anyone I send, but he might meet with you."

"With me?" she cried in astonishment.

"You knew him well enough. He even asked to marry you, before your brother betrothed you to Conchobar."

"That was years ago, Conaire. I was only a child. It's likely he'd not even remember me."

"But he does, Meave. One of my druids has found out that it's so."

She laughed shortly and turned away from him, throwing back, "And how would he be knowing that?"

"He has the power to know, I'm certain," he said earnestly, following after her. "He said that Aileel had often sent agents into Ulster to inquire about how you fared with Conchobar."

She whirled to face him and he nearly collided with her.

"And now I'm to use his old interest in me to beguile him and convince him to join you? Is that it?"

He was abashed by this bluntness. "Well, I . . . I wasn't intending for it to sound that way."

"But that's what it is, isn't it!" she shot back. "And is that how you see me, Conaire? That this woman's body the gods have cursed me with is for nothing more than the twisting of men's minds?"

He laid a hand gently on her shoulder. "Meave, no! I'd never mean that!"

She knocked away the hand. "I thought you at least were my friend, that I'd found a place here where I might be accepted. Now you sound as if you believe the lies spread by Conchobar."

He grabbed her by the shoulders, this time in a hard grip. "I don't believe them, and I've not thought to use you. But I'll also not lie to you. Yes, I do hope that Aileel's past love for you will at least give you a chance to talk with him. I expect nothing more. I'm asking you to go as my ambassador and secure Connacht's support for my rule here. Doing that will require your mind, your will, and all your strength. It's only those things I see when I look at you."

Her hard gaze softened as she realized his sincerity. Then, as if suddenly drained of energy, her eyes dropped and she shook her head. "No, Conaire. I'm no good to you in this. I'm not even able to judge what I am anymore."

He shook her. "Meave, look at me now!" he fiercely demanded.

Her eyes came up again, meeting his.

"You can't stay here and just waste or even lose your life!" he told her urgently. "This is a chance I'm offering you to act for yourself again."

"I can't take it!" she cried in anguish. "Don't you see? I'm afraid to decide. Any will I ever had for doing that is gone."

"Please, Meave," he said beseechingly, "help me in this. Without Connacht, I can never unite Ireland. It's a fine country we might have here one day, and you can be a force in shaping it. You must decide."

"I can't, Conaire! I can't!" she shouted at him angrily.

She tore lose from his grip and ran from him, along the walkway, into the concealing mists.

"You can't keep running either, Meave!" he called after her. "Think of that! You can't keep running!"

Meave wandered aimlessly in the fields below the dun. She cursed her nephew for his interference. She'd hoped—hoped with all her being—never to be faced with such a thing again. How did he dare force her to have to think again, to have to take some action in her life?

The mist was thicker now. It had turned all the meadows to one sea of gray where objects floated undefined.

She realized that she was lost, and she felt a kind of relief in that. She had no choice now in where she could go. She wished that she could always remain that way, not even having to decide whether to return to Tara again.

The mist could drown her, or drift out like the tide and carry her along. There was nothing else left to her but that escape. She had no hope, no comfort, and no place to hide.

Then something solidified in the mist ahead of her.

It was a moving shape that seemed to sail toward her, drift down upon her like a swooping bird. It darkened as it came, its outlines becoming more distinct. It seemed to grow long legs that danced upon the swirling billows of the gray.

Before she could react, it swept past, nearly striking her, the slender body of the white-gold deer clear to her for an instant before it was away again into the mist.

It slowed down as it passed, and then it paused—a shadowy figure just within the veiling fringes of the mist—and she was certain it was looking back toward her expectantly, waiting to see what she would do.

Curious, Meave took a few steps forward, expecting it to dart away and disappear. But it waited until she had come very near before it pranced ahead, and only a short way, pausing again to wait.

That only fired Meave's curiosity all the more.

She became fully involved in the strange hunt then, pursuing the tantalizing beast through the whirling mist—never quite close enough to touch it, but a bit closer each time she tried, a bit more determined to catch the creature each time she missed.

At last she followed it into a stand of great oaks, the thick trunks rising like twisted giants about her. It led her into a clearing with a circle of rough, standing stones of near man-height. They marked the center of the wood and told Meave she had come upon a sacred grove.

The deer stopped there and stood unmoving, watching her. But as she warily approached, she realized that now the slender figure which faced her across the encircled space was not the same. Suddenly it was a human one, clad in a pale gold cloak. And Meave's startled blue-gray eyes met blue-gray eyes that glowed with warmth.

"Mother!" Meave gasped.

She remembered the cherished face without error. It had not changed. Though now blurred by the clinging mist, its slender fineness still seemed like that of youth.

"My daughter," said a voice that caressed like a summer mist and whispered like the rain. "I'd never thought to see you again in this mortal world of yours."

Meave started forward, but Etain held up a hand.

"No, Meave. No closer. It's only this image I can be to you now. Only the pain I felt in you over the gulf between us could gain even this much for me."

Meave stood leaning forward, hands up, pleading. "Mother, please, take me back with you! Take me out of this cruel and ugly world which you escaped. Save me."

"I had no wish to escape it," Etain gently replied. "I loved this world, Meave. And you love it too. It has the passions, the struggles, the glories that only frail mortality can give any importance to. You need them. You need life!"

Meave shook her head violently. "No! I don't belong here!"

"You do, Meave. You have the beauty and the sense my blood has given you. But there is also a strength, an iron in you that must be used and honed or it will rust to uselessness. That is your father in you, and the heritage of your father's mortal life. It's a life I was torn from without any choice. You have the choice. Meave, don't be wasting it!"

Meave stared at the shimmering figure, her mind a turmoil like the twisting billows of fog. "Do you believe I should take this chance which Conaire has offered me?" she finally asked.

"That choice must be your own, Meave. But you must believe that you can act. You were lost, wandering in this fog until the deer challenged you, and you accepted the challenge at once. That is your spirit, Meave. Follow that!"

A wind lifted suddenly, blasting through the woods, carrying the mist with it in a stream. It lifted the slender figure and seemed to whisk it away into the high treetops, spreading its image on the droplets of the mist.

Meave had no time even to call after Etain.

She walked out of the sacred grove and found that the wind had thinned the clouds above. Faint sunlight fought through, lighting the fortress walls of Tara, which loomed over her.

Conaire Mor had gathered his foster-brothers and some of the dun's other young warriors together in hurley teams and was in the midst of a spirited game on the muddy field before the hall.

He had driven down the field to score through a rather soggy but determined defense and was walking back to join his cheering team when he saw Meave standing nearby.

"Will you join us in the game, Meave?" he asked her cheerily.

"I'll go to Connacht, Conaire," was her terse reply.

Chapter Thirteen

Connacht

The burning hut sent up a thick column of smoke to branch into the overcast above, like some monstrous tree whose leaves were the clumped darkness of the clouds. Around the gray trunk wheeled the black angles of the carrion birds, their rattling cries sharp in the still air.

The little settlement had been nearly obliterated. The outer wall of rocks had been shattered in several spots and most of the houses within had been torn down. Amid the rubble were strewn the bodies of the residents. Few warriors were there save for some old men and boys. The rest were women and small children, put to the sword with ruthless practicality.

Meave watched from her chariot as her escorting party carried the bodies to the blazing hut and cast them into the flames. It was the simplest way to deal with the dead and also the swiftest. They had no time for more.

They had seen many homes and villages like it since crossing the Lough Rea into Connacht. Most had been long abandoned or destroyed. But often enough they saw the distant spire of smoke and the circling ravens to tell them that this war was still being fiercely waged.

The whole country seemed to have been swept by the ravages of war. She had never seen such widespread and thorough savagery.

The two sides seemed less concerned with conquering than with wiping each other from existence. Living people were less in evidence than beasts of prey. Most of the inhabitants she saw were homeless, worn, starved to spiritless shadows. But the wolves were many and fat and bold, even haunting the track of Meave's armed escort party.

Cruchane, Connacht's capital, was no more comforting a sight when they reached it. The lush Plains of Ai which surrounded it were empty of the vast herds which Meave remembered as grazing there before. The thick grasses had turned brown in the autumn chill, untouched.

The village below the slopes of the high dun looked almost deserted, its streets choked with heaps of refuse. And from behind the shutters of its homes, its few remaining citizens peeked out timidly at the band of alien chariots as they made their way through the town and up to the fortress gates.

Here it seemed that some semblance of order was being maintained. The timber walls of Cruchane were strong and looked well tended, and guards waited at the gates to challenge them.

"I am Meave, sent by Conaire Mor, high-king of Ireland!" she announced to them with all the authority at her command.

"Yes, my Lady," said the young captain of the small company of men. "We've been expecting you here. Aileel is awaiting you at the central hall."

"Where are the rest of your household companies?" she asked with curiosity, looking over the handful of men.

"With our host, my Lady. We're all that're left here."

"Are you leaving Cruchane so defenseless then?" she asked in astonishment.

"There're none who'd want it, Lady," one of the warriors answered with a bitter smile.

"Quiet, Kinkaeth," the young captain warned sternly. Then, to Meave, he said, "The host is nearby, my Lady. The Firbolgs have neither the strength nor the interest in attacking us here."

"With that assurance and a good team of horses, I might be far away from here now," Meave dryly replied. She signaled her party ahead and they rode past the guards into the dun's enclosure.

Once inside, she realized that the strong outer walls were deceptive in giving Cruchane's true condition. Within the walls, the fortress was a near ruin.

Everywhere Meave looked there were signs of neglect. Weeds grew thickly and undisturbed around the wall's base, across the walks and gardens. The outbuildings, made of wood and wattle and thatch, sagged with wear and with decay from the near-constant dampness. Their roofs had been ripped to tatters by the winds, their wattle fallen in chunks to leave ragged gaps in their walls.

The stables seemed in somewhat better repair. The horses, at least, would receive some shelter there. But no grooms appeared to take the horses of Meave's party when it pulled to a halt before the buildings.

Meave left the chariots to their drivers' care and walked up toward the main hall of Cruchane. She brushed through waist-high weeds that filled the playing field so carefully tended in the past. Then she stopped before the central hall to stare, the desolation of it nearly overwhelming her.

Here was the Tec Mi-Cuarta of a great dun, the gathering point for a once rich, once proud province of Ireland. This sorry-looking circle of timbers, like some child's wooden toy left to molder in a field, was the most poignant symbol yet of what had happened to Connacht.

And that thought triggered another new one for Meave. If the grand and prosperous province she remembered from her youth had come to this, what might she expect to have happened to Aileel? Had he, too, become a sad ruin, like his dun?

She tried to construct an image of him from memories six

years old. He'd been a tall, broad-shouldered man with a grace of manner and a strength of face she'd found pleasing, even intriguing, as a girl. And she knew his fine manner had been coupled with a spirit that had sustained him through over thirty years of establishing his rule and sustaining it against the constant attacks of the rebellious Firbolg tribes.

But six years was a long time. She guessed that he was nearing fifty now. What kinds of changes would she find in him? Her nightmares told her he could be withered by war or, worse, horribly disfigured as so many were in these days of tearing weapons and crude medicine.

She felt herself tighten with her fear as she looked into the blackness of the hall's main door. But she had chosen the path that she would take, and she was not going to back away again.

She drew a deep breath, forcing air into her constricted lungs. She took a firm hold on her fears, pulled herself erect, and marched boldly into the tec.

Dun Cruchane's main hall was as dismal within as it looked without. The neglected roof thatch kept little rain from seeping in. The circular room was oppressively humid, smelling strongly of mold and decay.

It was quite dark, for only a handful of stubby tapers guttered in scattered sockets throughout the room. But even the shadows could not hide the festoons of cobwebs overflowing from the rafters or the bronzework that had tarnished to black.

Meave experienced that peculiar tickling of the skin created by the impression that what she saw around her had begun to creep upon her, too.

The urgent need the room created in her to flee back outside into the air and light nearly made her forget her more basic fear. She had to force herself to move forward, around the fire pit filled with muddy ashes and refuse, through the jumbled tables where glossy rats larger than her head glared at her with arrogant black eyes that recalled to her her past husband, Conchobar.

She stopped when, from the darkness at the back of the hall, the figures of three men appeared. One was Aileel, she was certain, accompanied by a druid and a young warrior. But at first she could see little else.

She waited with stomach-twisting expectation as they mounted to a raised platform. There, several candles allowed her to see him more clearly. Then she felt relief, like a clean wind from the sea, flowing through her.

He was a grayer man, yes, in the sides of his brown hair and in the long, carefully tended mustache. But there was nothing else. He still moved with that casual grace she remembered. And his face still held a youthful leanness and strength.

She waited for him to speak, but he only stood there looking down at her, his expression devoid of emotion. She wondered if there was some rite to be followed here that she did not know.

"My King," she ventured at last, her words echoing hollowly in the desolate cavernous space, "it's good of you to meet with me."

"It is a great nuisance for me to have to meet with you," he retorted sharply, irritably. "I have a force gathered to strike the main Firbolg tribes in two days, and I am here!"

She was confounded by his callous response. "My King, I didn't know . . ." she began.

"It can't be that you didn't notice the desolation of my fields or the emptiness of my dun," he snapped impatiently. "Of course my men are gone. For over a year we've been in the field almost constantly."

"I'm sorry," she said sincerely. "There was no need for you to meet me if you were so engaged. I could have . . ."

"You could have stayed in Tara!" he finished curtly.

"My King, it was my understanding that you would be willing to see me here," she said, struggling to make some sense of this.

"A foolish idea, and a foolish reason for you to make a journey from Tara. We're at war! I've no time to spend on the amenities of entertaining you. And I've no interest in taking assistance from your nephew or giving that boy my promise of support until my own battles are ended! Take that message to him! Maybe this time he will believe it!"

"My King . . ." she began again.

"No!" he thundered. "This was a mistake. You may stay here to rest if you wish. Tomorrow I'll be returning to my warriors. If you need a further escort to assure your return to Tara, it will be given you when you're ready to leave."

Not waiting for any reply, Aileel turned on his heel and strode from the hall, leaving Meave to stare after him in stunned silence.

Was this how her momentous new chance was to end, before it had even reached a starting place? The decision to come, the hopes, the fears, the perilous journey here, were they all for nothing, then?

She could not think, so much had this unforeseen blow devastated her senses. She stood motionless, powerless to act, until the two men whom Aileel had left behind him came down from the dais and approached her.

The druid was an elderly man, stern-faced and cold of eye. But the warrior was a young man of fresh, almost boyish looks, round-cheeked, green-eyed, his pale skin flushed by obvious embarrassment.

"My Lady, I'm sorry," he said.

She had not given him any notice before he spoke. Now she shifted her gaze to him, staring blankly. "What?"

"I'm sorry you've come so far and through such dangerous country for so little."

"It's not for us to be making the apologies here," the druid said sharply. "It wasn't our request that brought this lady to us." He eyed her challengingly. "Isn't that so?"

She didn't know how to respond. Why was he so anxious to be certain that she accepted all the responsibility for this?

"You look weary, my Lady," the warrior said, moving forward to lightly take her arm. "You must need rest."

"Yes, she should rest," the druid agreed. He lifted an arm and pointed toward the main doors. "Let's be leaving here and taking her to some suitable quarters where she can spend the night."

She didn't argue. There was nothing to say. There was only the desolation in her mind, as black and ruined as this vast, lifeless hall.

She allowed the two men to direct her out, lead her away like a groom would a spent steed. They moved around the outside of the hall to a separate house reserved for visiting nobility. Here Meave's escort had already been shown quarters, and some effort had been made to put things in order. The room to which they took her was stark in decoration and almost bare of furniture, but it was dry and warmed by a small peat fire.

She walked in, stopped, and looked back at the two men, who peered in at her from the doorway almost like hounds peering warily in at a badger trapped in his hole, curious about what he would do. She was aware now of a faint uneasiness in them that added a sharp edge of falseness to their solicitous actions.

"Is that really the end of it, then?" she challenged coldly, trying to mask her despair with the rational face of diplomacy. "There's no chance I could speak to Aileel again? Or will he simply leave while I'm 'returned' to Tara?"

"My Lady, I wish there were more," the young man said. "It's my own feeling that Aileel might have spoken more with you."

"Careful, Lewy," the druid warned.

"But my king is hard pressed," he argued. "He has reasons for his actions here and she should know them."

The druid turned upon the warrior with heat, laying a restraining hand on his shoulder. "The king will be angered to hear you speak so!"

"But you know I'm speaking the truth!" the young man responded angrily.

Meave saw the pain twisting the open face and realized that here was a person of sincerity, so troubled by his king's treatment of her that he risked punishment to make some explanation of it to her. At least one person in this alien place seemed to have sympathy for her.

"Be easy, both of you," she told them in more soothing tones. "I've no wish to be causing any trouble here."

"You hear that, Lewy?" the druid said. "Now come away and let the lady rest."

He tried to pull the young warrior back from the door, but Lewy jerked free and took a step toward Meave. "My Lady, if you've need of anything, please call upon me."

Meave knew the signs of early infatuation. His interest in her coupled with his apparent honesty made him a person who might be helpful to her. Despite her present feelings of hopelessness, that fact was carefully stored away.

"Who are you then?" she asked him, smiling for the first time.

His flush grew deeper. "Lewy MacNeesh. My father is a chieftain of the Clan Falva, and I'm in fosterage to the king."

"I am glad to know you, Lewy," she said with what warmth she could kindle. "I'll not be forgetting you."

Nodding, abashed to speechlessness, Lewy withdrew after the irritated druid.

Alone now, Meave gave in to her weariness. She dropped down on the mean pile of furs which served as a bed and let her despair fall around her like a smothering black cloak.

She knew that somehow she had to reach Aileel. And it seemed as if only one way was left to her.

Chapter Fourteen

Hostages

"I'll tell you again, Fergus, I'll not put myself and all Ulster into bondage to this high-king!"

Conchobar MacNessa, king of Ulster, paced angrily along the sideline of the hurley field, the flame-haired champion striding at his side.

Out on the field, Sentanta drove the wooden ball swiftly along, flanked by several teammates who swept easily through their opposition. In the heat of their own contest of words, however, neither king nor champion was giving much attention to the match.

"But the tales of him are becoming impossible to ignore," Fergus argued. "The ollavs are composing poems of him. He's becoming like a legend through all Ireland. They're saying that in these few seasons since he came to rule, he's brought a plenty like none ever seen. Seven ships at a time are coming to Inver Colptha. Corn and nuts were up to the knees last harvest. Trees bend from the weight of fruit. The Buais and Boinne are crowded with fish."

"I am growing very weary with hearing about him, Mac-Rogh," the king said testily.

On the field, Sentanta's goal was just ahead now. Two youths of the other team came up before him, sticks lifted in defense. He plunged between them, shouldering them aside, sweeping his own stick around to hit the ball with a sharp *crack* and send it shooting ahead. It rolled unerringly to the goal, dropping into the round hole in the sod.

"Well, you'll be hearing more of him, whether it's to your liking or not," Fergus doggedly told Conchobar, raising his voice to be heard above the cheering of Sentanta's teammates.

"Miraculous they're saying he is. The powers of the Sidhe are surely in him, they claim now. More clans and tuaths vow allegiance to him every day, wishing to join in this new bounty. And there are grumblings from our own chieftains that we do not."

"The Bloody Raven take our chieftains for their treachery," Conchobar swore. "They'll not force me to this . . . this humiliation because of their greedy dreams."

"Will they not?" said Fergus. "Well, Conal Carna will be coming here to petition you again at any moment. With the Tailteen Fair coming on us in nearly—"

"I know when it's coming," the king interrupted tersely. "It means nothing to me."

"It means you must have some reason to deny Conaire Mor."

Another whoop of triumph came from Sentanta's team as the boy succeeded in stealing the ball from an opponent with a deft flick of the stick. Again he was racing toward his own goal.

Conchobar stopped to face his chieftain, legs set apart, body tense, head up in a defiant attitude.

"He hasn't yet succeeded in uniting Ireland, MacRogh," he said fiercely. "Until Connacht gives its support to him, I will not."

"But . . ." Fergus began, only to be drowned out by the explosive cheering of players and onlookers as Sentanta scored yet another goal.

"Another goal," the king said in disgust. Using the game as an excuse to end the bothersome argument, he moved away from Fergus to where his son, Cormac Conlingas, stood watching the game. "What does that make now, Cormac?" he asked.

That young man now wore the harness and weapons of a full warrior, his long hair plaited and beaded in adult style, a crimson cloak of the Red Branch clans about his shoulders.

"Thirty-three, Father," Cormac supplied.

"And not a single one for the other side." Conchobar shook his head. "Is there no one who can challenge him?"

"He makes the game as even as he can," Cormac pointed out.

This certainly seemed more than true. With the goal made, the ball now went again to the opposing team. Sentanta's teammates spread far out on the field, leaving the young man alone to guard the goal with no defending line.

"Even?" Conchobar said. "When a team of our best warriors can't best him? Ah, there's just something wrong about the boy. Look at him. Since he came, he's grown with a colt's speed. He already rivals some of my seasoned fighting men in size."

This was no overstatement. Since the spring, Sentanta had grown in height and his lean body had filled to one of smooth, sinewy muscle. Still, for all the man's body, he had retained the boy's smooth and handsome looks. Indeed, his looks had already elicited much open flirting from the women of the dun.

"And he's too clever," Conchobar muttered on. "Too clever. In one summer he's learned more from that cursed druid Cathbad than the other boys have in a lifetime." He glanced at Cormac. "You, my son, are likely quite happy to have taken the warrior's vows. You'll not be needing to compete any more with him."

"You're unfair," Fergus said defensively, moving up at Cormac's other side. "There was never a need for the two of them to compete. And your son's acknowledged as one of the finest fighters in the training school, maybe one of the best I've ever seen. He's a most promising new member of the Red Branch."

"Save your words, Fergus," Cormac said bitterly, clearly stung by his father's harshness. "My skills will never be great enough for my father." Then he faced Conchobar boldly. "But I've had enough of your belittling me," he went on, voice flaring with anger. "I know my failures were a humiliation to you. But I've accepted the skills of Sentanta. There's nothing I can do about them. He's a fair competitor and I'm glad for the chance to measure myself against him."

"Of course, you'd have to say that, wouldn't you?" his father said nastily.

"Look here, Father, for all my cruelty to him, he's been nothing but friendly to me. I've been the fool, and it may be I got what I deserved for it. I'd rather have him for a friend."

"A friend?" his father said in irritation, casting a disbelieving look at Cormac. "I never thought I'd hear such talk from a son of mine! With what he's done to you? With the way he defies me, tasks me?"

"Father, what is wrong with you?" Cormac said. "I don't see what he's done to you to make you dislike him so. He is your own nephew. He is of our own blood."

"Our own . . ." the king said darkly, turning his burning gaze back on the field, "and someone else's."

"Look there," Fergus said, pointing behind them. "Conal Carna."

Cormac and Conchobar turned to see the champion moving down from the great hall with Cathbad beside him.

"And the druid," Conchobar said darkly. "There's a most dangerous pairing."

"Have you considered your reply to Conaire Mor, my King?" Conal Carna asked as he reached the others.

"You know my feelings well enough," Conchobar brusquely replied. "Your journey here from Tara was a wasted one."

"You can no longer ignore this, Conchobar," the champion returned with great force.

Keenly aware of both Carna's insolence and of the expectant gazes of the others awaiting his response, the king's reply was accordingly hostile and arrogant. "I can do as I wish. I am Ulster's ruler. Ulster answers to no province and no man against its will!"

His voice was a rising thunder this time, rolling across the field, bringing other onlookers of the game to glance around toward him.

"But this *is* Ulster's will," Conal stubbornly insisted. "There's no man who wouldn't welcome peace if it brought happiness and wealth."

"A fighting man of Ulster finds happiness only in battle," growled the king, "and the only wealth he needs is his enemy's head."

Now it was Cathbad's turn to speak up, and he did so with great passion and eloquence.

"It's more than a warrior's needs at stake here, Conchobar. It's the good of all the people we should be thinking of now. That's what Mor's seeking, from all I've heard. Why, even the druids of Tara, who don't seem to understand this brash young king's ways, are awed by what he's done. I've heard from them that never in Ireland's bloody history has there been such peace and goodwill among its people, that each thinks the other's voice as sweet as a harp's strings. Even the wolves themselves are held hostage not to kill more than one calf in every pen. There's no thunder or storm about him. From spring to harvest there's not so much wind as will stir a horse's mane, and cattle go without keepers for the greatness of peace."

"Oh, by the blessed Dagda!" Conchobar said in a tone of immense weariness. "Not more of that! More tales spun out by your fellow druids of Tara—the druids of this boy high-king trying any scheme, any lie to keep him on his throne!"

"I've seen the signs of it myself," Cathbad shot back. "I've felt the portents in the smoke and wind. The people of Great Danu herself support this one. He can do great things, if he has help. In his reign I see three crowns in Ireland: the crown of flowers, the crown of acorns, and the crown of wheatears. Do you challenge the truth of the foreseeing of Cathbad, my King?"

His defiant gaze was fixed on Conchobar. But even that domineering man did not dare dispute the ard-druid's word.

"No matter what his power or your visions," he irritably returned, "I still will not humble Ulster by giving ourselves in hostage to him until all the rest of Ireland has done so." He fixed his glittering black gaze on Conal Carna. "I said this to Fergus, and I say it to you now: until Connacht, our most ancient rival, submits to him, I will not!"

"But he expects to hear word of Connacht's support at any time," Conal said. "It is that new hope which brought me back here to you. Conaire Mor has sent an emissary there who he believes can bring Aileel to accept his rule of peace."

"An emissary?" Conchobar repeated in disbelief. "And who would have such a skill to convince that iron-headed bull?"

"He sent . . ." Conal began, hesitating to glance toward Fergus before going on, "he sent his aunt, Meave."

"Meave?" Conchobar said, momentarily shocked. Then he gave a great, bellowing laugh. "That useless woman? To rein in a stampeding Aileel? It truly is a madman we have for a high-king. Now I surely know it!"

"But, if she does succeed?" Conal said.

"Ha! If she succeeds in bringing Connacht to heel, then I'll send any hostage to Tara that Mor wants," the king blithely declared. "Why, I'll send my own son, Cormac, in proof of my support."

Cormac looked both surprised and pleased at being given such a responsibility. "Father, thank you for that!" he said sincerely.

"There should be at least one other," Fergus put in.

"I suggest that it be Sentanta MacSualtim," said Cathbad quickly and forcefully.

"What?" cried Fergus in astonishment. "But it's a warrior that should go in hostage to Tara, not a boy. It's two years at least until he'll be of an age to earn the cloak of the Red Branch."

"He is a nephew to the king, and one day will be a tuath ruler in his own right, MacRogh," Cathbad reminded him.

"Yet he knows little of Ireland and has seen nothing of it but his own home and Emain Macha. It is his chance to learn something of the court life, gain wisdom and seasoning as vital as anything we can teach him here. I say he is a fine choice to go."

"I agree," said Conal, after considering this speech. "The high-king certainly would accept Conchobar's son and nephew as more than adequate proof of Ulster's loyalty. And I would like to see this Sentanta discover more of the world he was kept from so long. I felt for him from the first time I saw him, locked away in his mother's dun."

"But he's not fully trained," Fergus protested. "Something might happen. . . ."

"He already has the assurance and skills of most adult fighting men, Fergus," the druid reasoned. "You know that as well as I." He fixed a meaningful gaze on Fergus, adding emphatically, "My friend, I feel the rightness of it. I know this is a part of what he must do—what he is meant to do. Don't fight against it."

Fergus sighed and shook his head, but said nothing more. Cathbad nodded and looked to Conchobar.

"And so, my King, it is only for you to agree to this. Will you send Sentanta with your son as hostage to Tara?"

Conchobar hesitated. He clearly did not like the sound of the druid's words, nor the idea that this would be another victory for the boy he so loathed.

He looked out to the field. Sentanta was again driving the ball down the field, almost casually scattering his opposition on his way to yet another goal. He scowled at the sight, then wheeled back to them.

"All right," he snapped. "At least I'd be free of the troublesome whelp for a time."

"Ah! Good, my King!" Cathbad said, smiling with triumph and relief.

Conchobar quickly raised a warning hand. "Don't be so pleased about it, druid," he admonished. "Remember, neither he nor any hostage will go from Ulster to Tara until Connacht has sent its own." He gave a little knowing smirk, looking off to the southwest, toward that distant province.

"And that," he added with conviction, "is something Meave will never bring Aileel to do!"

Chapter Fifteen

Seduction

Aileel sat alone in the vast, decaying hall of Dun Cruchane.

Night had fallen, and his simple dinner of boiled pork and vegetables and bread was lighted by a pair of stubby candles and the red glow of a small fire. These meager lights had very little power to push back the host of great, brooding shadows that loomed about him. It made him feel all the more alone here, and he wished he had chosen to spend the night in the company of his men, even if it meant sleeping beneath the threatening sky.

He took a bite of the overcooked, gray meat of the pork joint, chewing the sinewy piece thoroughly for some while before managing to swallow. He looked at the pork thoughtfully for a moment, considering another bite, but gave it up as too much trouble and tossed the joint down on the platter. The clatter of it echoed hollowly in the room, emphasizing its emptiness again.

Aileel rose from the table. He moved with a certain weariness now, the vitality Meave had seen replaced by a sense that some great weight rested upon him.

There were no stewards, no servants here. Even the food had come from the cookfire of his men. He leaned forward to pinch out the flames of the two candles, leaving the fire's pale red glow alone to battle on against the host of shadows.

He walked back toward the rear of the hall where a wickerwork petition closed a chamber off from the central space. He pulled the wall aside. Beyond, the red glow revealed a stark and sparsely appointed room, the abode of an unwed warrior-king. A low pallet topped by some robes and furs, a plank table, and a stool were its sole furnishings. Its only ornaments were an ancient spear and shield and sheathed sword hung upon the outer wall. The dust of long abandonment coated them, as it did all else, and every cranny was strung with thick cobwebs.

How long had it been since he had slept in his own hall? He couldn't recall. A lifetime, surely. Several. As he moved into the room, he shook his head sadly over the sorry state of things. Beside the bed he stopped and began to undress.

First he removed his heavy cloak of wool, unfolded it, and spread it out upon the musty coverings. As in the field, the five-folded cloak, quite large when fully opened, would be his protection against the night chill. Then he unbuckled his sword belt. That he was glad to do. It seemed days since he had not worn it, had not felt the weight of the weapon against his thigh.

By long habit, he would place it close beside him, its hilt ready to his hand as he slept. He was reaching out to put the weapon down when he heard the sound.

It was only the faintest rustling, but he reacted instantly with warrior instinct, sweeping the sword from its scabbard as he whirled about to face into the hall.

"Who's there?" he demanded, peering through the wide opening he had left into the vast, shadowed space. The blade of his weapon was a thin line of red light in the fire's glow.

A patch of deeper shadow shifted in the black, moved forward, detaching itself, gliding into the light of the little fire. It was a slender and lithe form, its outlines clearly defined by the simple, clinging shift of white linen, tinged to warm rose by the flames.

"Meave!" said the king of Connacht in surprise.

"I had to talk with you again," she said in a tone of desperation, moving toward him, past the fire. "I had to see you alone. I thought it might be our only chance."

"You should not be here," he said, pulling himself upright, forcing back the fatigue, again putting on the harsh, unbending manner of their previous meeting.

"Please, listen. It's not much I ask," she said, holding out her arms in a gesture of supplication.

The effect of this was most provocative. With her arms lifted, the firelight shone through her thin gown, clearly revealing the soft, curving lines of the figure beneath, and the ruddy glow touched her wealth of unbound hair to a molten river of red-gold. She looked both vulnerable and alluring at once.

The combination was too much for Aileel. The gruff manner faltered. He lowered his sword. "I am sorry, Meave. I don't mean to be so cruel."

"Then don't be," she said, moving toward him. "Just give me a few moments. Hear me out. Then I will leave you if you wish, without more arguments."

"All right," he conceded.

She moved forward, past him, into his chamber, stopping by the bed.

"Come," she said, sitting down on it, atop his cloak. "Please sit beside me. It will make things . . . easier."

He complied, moving over and dropping down at her side on the pallet, tossing the naked sword behind them on the cloak.

"I wish to speak, not as the enemies you seem to think we are now, but as friends. The friends that we once were."

"That was long ago," he said in a slow, careful, noncommittal voice.

"But you do remember," she said with soft insistence, fixing him with her shining, blue-gray eyes. "You must remember, as I do. Remember the days when you walked with me on the broad Plains of Ai, so lush then and so green. It was peace and bright summer then. The herds grazed softly, drifting on the seas of grass that swelled in the sweet wind. Connacht was rich, her clans were powerful, and you were the most handsome man I'd seen. You were a king, but still you walked with me and told me of your grand adventures, and I felt the thrill of them in me, like nothing I'd known before."

She swayed toward him. His eyes were drawn to her by her voice. They met hers and he was caught, held, looking into the blue-gray glowing as if the images of that brighter, warmer, easier time were showing there. And like a man parched to agony by long thirst, he drank in the soothing visions of past comfort.

"I loved you; did I tell you then?" she went on softly, warmly, bathing him with her words. "I loved you from the time I first came here, at twelve, after my father died. You were like him in many ways. Smitten I was by the renowned warrior, the great king, so grand in your bright dress. I wanted you to sweep me up. To carry me away and build a house for me on the green hills above, where we could live, and you would keep me safe from all my fears."

"You were a child then," he said, trying hard to restore a sense of reality to this enrapturing reverie.

"But I am not a child now," she said, leaning toward him, her body pressing against his bare arm. He could scent her fragrance now, and feel the intense heat of her through the thin shift.

"Once, you wanted me," she said. "I know it's true. Don't turn me away now." Her hand went to his bare leg, resting upon his thigh. It seemed to burn there against his flesh, to pass its heat into him, sending it rushing through his veins, firing his whole body. He could feel her heart throbbing within her breast, feel his own heart throbbing in reply. His breath grew shorter.

"You want me still, now, don't you?" she asked. "I can feel it." She lifted her head, her lips rising to meet his. He did not resist. He returned the kiss with increasing ardor. One arm slid out to encircle her slender waist and pull her to him. Her hand slid upward, along his muscled thigh. His own free hand moved to her shoulder, slid down the long curve of her back, over the smooth curve of hip.

They fell back upon the bed, locked together now in a passionate embrace. The demand, the fire of it, was building in him, a temptation to cast all aside and give himself fully to it, to let the emotion sweep over him, carry him away, to lose himself, his weariness, his fears in this woman's arms.

His hand slid down the long, firm line of her thigh, found the hem of her dress, pulled it upward. She lifted slightly, allowing him to slide it up over the hip, up across the breast. She raised her arms and it was off, fluttering down beside them. She lay back, waiting while he sat up, pulling off his own tunic in one quick move and casting it away. He turned to lean down over her. She lay ready, eyes bright, lips parted, arms up in surrender. Her young body glowed with the warm, ruddy illumination of the fire. Her hair shimmered with bright coppery lights.

His eyes roved across her hungrily, in anticipation. He felt his heart hammering wildly in his chest. Then another shining caught his eyes. He lifted his gaze to see his naked longsword lying upon the dark cloak just beyond, its black-iron blade sharply reflecting the flames' crimson radiance.

He stared at it, seeing it in his hand and smoking with the blood of enemies in a chill dawn, seeing scenes of wild, desperate battle in rocky hills or tangled woods or swirling mists. His face tightened, his eyes narrowing. He looked back down to her, so pliant, so inviting, so great a temptation to surrender.

"What's happening here, Meave?" he demanded with a sudden return of harshness, pulling back from her. "What is it you're doing to me? Are you seeking to seduce me to you now? That child, that fresh and innocent child I loved, you now wish to draw me to you, to give yourself to me?"

"Aileel, don't draw away!" she said in alarm, surprised by his sudden change. "I need you now. You can't deny me now."

"Why? Is it for yourself, or for Conaire Mor you're doing this? Is that what it's come to, Meave? Are you selling yourself to me now for him?"

"No, no!" she said in anguish, sitting up. "Please, you must listen to me. You must believe me." She reached out to him, touching his arm, his leg. "I only meant to talk to you, to . . ."

"I know what you meant," he said brutally, pushing away her hands and rising to his feet. His large, muscled body looked towering, threatening against the firelight as he glared down at her. "You meant to seduce and draw me in. To buy my confidence. To bring me to accept you, and to accept that cursed Mor. Well, if you thought our old love or my foolishness or your body could buy me, you were wrong! You'll start back for Tara at dawn, and I will go back to my clans tonight!"

He took up his tunic, slipping it over his head.

"Tell Mor that you failed, Meave. Connacht will stay separate until her own battles are done!"

He grabbed up his cloak from the bed, savagely jerking it from beneath her, rolling her violently sideways onto her stomach. He stalked to the partition, then paused to look back. "I'm going to tell my men to make ready now," he thundered. "Be out of here before I return. I want to see no more of you before I leave!"

He swept the cloak around his shoulders and strode out into the darkness of the hall.

Stunned, she lay as she had ended among the dusty bedclothes, staring ahead into the shadows, her mind a chaos. Only one thought was clear amid the ruins of her thoughts: this was the end.

He'd asked her if it had come to this. It had. She was finally reduced to this lowest state. She had become what Conchobar had called her. She had done what she had angrily accused Mor of sending her to do. She had taken and lost her last, desperate chance, and there was nothing left.

She realized that his sword was lying before her eyes, thrown off the bed when he had yanked away the cloak, forgotten in his anger and his need to get away.

She reached out and picked up the weapon, her hand closing

around its hilt. She sat up, turning toward the fire, drawing her legs beneath her, crouching upon her knees, the weapon cradled before her in her hands.

"I'm sorry, Conaire," she murmured. "You were wrong to trust me. I'm sorry, Mother. You were wrong too. I've nothing now at all."

She sat there motionless a long moment, body rigid, the sword in her hands, head bowed in defeat, the red light of the fire still warmly burnishing the smooth, rounded flesh of her naked form.

Then, slowly, she lifted the sword, inverting it, bringing the point up to touch the hollow between her breasts. The hilt was against the bed, the weapon slanting up to her. It would take only a quick, forward jerk to drive it home. She could feel the sharp prick of the keen tip against her skin.

She looked down along the blade. It shone with the red light, a thin, blazing line of fire along the well-honed edge, running to the lethal point.

A half-burned log fell to the embers with a soft *thunk*, the exposed fresh wood crackling suddenly to flame, sending a flare of light tearing high up into the heavy cloak of black. Startled, she looked toward the sound. In the crackling of the renewed fire and in the fiercely blazing light, she saw the gloating face of Conchobar and heard his mocking laugh.

"No," she said with sudden vehemence, knocking the sword point away. She rose proudly, glaring into those imagined eyes. "You almost succeeded, Conchobar," she spat out. "You almost made me into what you said I was. You almost finished destroying me. But you'll not succeed."

She grasped the hilt again, raising the sword high in her hands, the point up now in a defiant gesture, the blade flashing a brighter, angry light.

"I'll beat you, Conchobar," she promised. "You'll never defeat me. Somehow, somehow I'll beat you!"

A blade of white-gold morning sunlight slashed sharply down between the stakes of the palisade and struck the overgrown yard of Dun Cruchane.

Its glare illuminated the small party of chariots and men who waited there, Lewy MacNeesh striding back and forth before them impatiently. Since first light he had waited for Meave to come from her quarters and start the journey back to Tara. What was the delay? Aileel himself had left well before first light, giving chill command to his young warrior to see Meave home.

Finally she appeared, coming out the doorway of her quarters and striding across to him. At first he felt relief. But this soon turned to wonder as she drew near. For she was no longer dressed in the gown and cloak of a noblewoman. Instead she wore the rough tunic and trousers of a manservant, topped by a rude but serviceable warrior's cloak of heavy wool.

These clothes were large upon her, the cloak's hem dragging on the ground, the tunic reaching to her knees, the pants long and baggy. But she had rolled up the voluminous legs, and was now strapping a wide leather belt about her slender waist to catch up the spare fabric of the top.

"My Lady, what are you about?" Lewy asked in bewilderment. "Where did you get these things?"

"I've spent half a night scavenging them from the disused quarters," she said.

"Such rags?" he said with dismay. "They're likely filthy, full of—"

"Enough, Lewy," she said sharply to cut off the rest of the unpleasant description. "They will serve me."

"Serve you how, my Lady?" he asked, more confused. "Your other garb was fine for the ride home."

"Tara is not my home, young warrior," she corrected quickly. "And I'll not be riding there. I mean to join the host of Aileel."

The young man looked massively stricken, as if she had taken a club to his head. He stared in disbelief. "Join . . . the host?"

"Yes," she said firmly. She knew the first obstacle was coming now. Like a good hunting hound, she must be ready to make the leap. She braced herself, chin thrust out aggressively.

"But . . . my Lady . . . you can't do that!" Lewy managed to get out. "Aileel . . ."

"Aileel does not own me," she replied. "He has no power over me. My father gave me lands in Connacht long ago. I lived here many years. I am as much a part of this province as yourself. And I will stay!"

"Stay to do what?"

"To fight. Connacht needs help. Aileel says he cannot make an alliance with the high-king until he has peace. So, I mean to help him gain that peace."

"How can you join the army, my Lady?" the young warrior protested. "You're no warrior."

"Give me a spear," she requested.

"What?"

"I said a spear!" she demanded this time, putting all the haughtiness and command into her voice that she could muster.

It worked. The young warrior swiftly obeyed. He went to his chariot, pulled one of the weapons from its rack within the car, and handed it to her.

"Now, look there," she said, pointing across the yard toward the outer wall. "See that white spot?" She indicated a patch of mold upon a rotting log. It was no more than the size of a palm, and a tiny spot from a score of strides away.

"It's too far," he said calculatingly.

She gave him a little smile, drew back, set herself, cocked her arm, and threw. The cast was smooth, slightly arching, true. It sang to the spot, sinking its point through the center of the white, deep into the spongy wood.

"Now that's surely a most fine throw!" Lewy said in frank appreciation, accompanied by sounds of admiration from the other men.

"My father, Eochaid himself, taught me the warrior's skills as a child," she told him with a note of pride. "I've not forgotten them."

"But skill against timber isn't skill against a man," Lewy said, turning toward her.

She leaped forward. Before he could make a move to defend himself, she had gripped his sword's hilt. In an instant she had drawn the blade and the point was against the tip of Lewy's chin.

"Do you really want to make me prove my readiness to kill?" she asked coldly.

He looked into the blue-gray eyes meeting his with a determined, icy stare. There was no wavering, no weakness there.

"I would not," he told her with great sincerity.

She lowered the weapon, handing it back to him.

"I will not force you to this," she said, continuing to hold his gaze with one both earnest and compelling now. "But please, Lewy MacNeesh, help me. You told me you would do so if you could. Take me to Aileel. It is my life I'm putting in your hands today. My life!"

The young warrior was moved by her appeal, as she had hoped he would be. He nodded. "All right, my Lady. I will lead you to his host." Then he gave her a rueful grin, adding,

"But it'll be a wonder if the king doesn't have the living heads off both of us!"

Chapter Sixteen

The Warrior

"You cannot simply go off and do as you wish," Aileel was ranting.

The subjects of his tirade, who stood before him in a small hut of crumbling wattle and thatch, were a trio of youths, similar enough in type and age to be brothers. All were lean, dark, and somewhat ferrety of look, with small, pointed chins and noses, flaring brows, and broad, low foreheads. Their mouths were wide and mobile and thin-lipped, their eyes wide-set and large, and of a smoldering red-brown.

The eyes of two were shifting about constantly, nervously, as if guiltily unwilling to meet those of Aileel. Indeed, the whole manner of all of them was nervous, fidgety, as if they were charged with some irrepressible energy.

But one of them—an especially sharp-nosed one with slim, drooping, braided mustaches—was facing boldly up to the outraged king, returning the scolding in an arrogant tone.

"We cannot be made to live as these others. We are not common warriors. We are a king's sons!"

"And . . . I . . . am . . . the king!" Aileel said forcefully. "And while I am, and your father—as much as I despise admitting to the fact—you will act as every other warrior in my army. You will not go off alone. You will not raid homes because it suits your desires. You will not loot duns nor take your pleasure with any woman you fancy, nor harm anyone I do not say is our enemy. We are here to help the people of Connacht. To save them, not to be adding to their pains."

"Save them?" the other echoed haughtily, as if this idea was of great distaste. "Well, they're hardly worth that. In fact, there's only one thing they are worth. Their women at least

—right, lads?" He smiled in a cruel and leering way, winking at the other two. They laughed coarsely in reply. "Of course," he went on, looking back at his father, "there're precious few of those left. Too many starved. So scrawny it seems hardly worth the—"

"Enough, Morgor!" Aileel shouted. "I don't know what I have to do to make you understand, to act as a king's son must. You must learn responsibility to the—"

"My King," said a warrior, popping his head in through the doorless opening to the hut, "a company has just arrived. It's Lewy MacNeesh leading them, and he . . ." the man looked puzzled, hesitating before going on, "well, I think he has a woman with him."

"A woman?" the king cried, transfering his rage from his sons to young MacNeesh. "He brought her here?"

He crashed out of the hut. Behind him, the three sons of Aileel exchanged looks of great interest. "A woman?" said Morgor. "This we must see."

They followed the king outside. There, around the hut, a large camp of several hundred men stretched away across the soggy meadows, beneath a thickly overcast sky. And from the slight rise where the little building sat, they could see a party of chariots just entering the perimeter from the north.

In one of the cars there stood a shorter, more slender figure than the rest, whose red hair, even in the dim light, even bound as it was behind her neck, still marked her like a flaming beacon in the night.

"So he did bring her!" stormed Aileel, his face as dark and threatening as the ominous sky. "That young fool! What is he thinking of?"

Meave was looking about with great shock at the camp as they rode into it. It was a most gloomy sight. She had expected to find a warrior camp as she remembered from the hostings she had seen as a child with Eochaid. Then, the host, even when on the move from day to day, made a fine camp each night—a skill and habit kept from their nomadic ancestors. They laid out streets, built market stalls and lean-to sheds and even huts. And the warriors of Ireland fastidiously washed every day, vainly grooming and dressing their fine hair, and wearing the most flamboyant and carefully kept clothes. For no real warrior could go out to battle an enemy without the grandest look upon him.

But this host seemed more a gathering of vagabonds. Their

camp was slovenly, crudely built, the streets meandering, muddy tracks. There were few stalls and no dwellings of any kind save for the derelict hut Aileel had claimed as his quarters. And the men themselves—worn, battered, ragged, many bearded and most filthy—squatted about pitiful fires whose thin, frayed threads of smoke trailed up to meet the gray-black clouds. They were listless and subdued. There was none of the warrior's banter here, no jokes or laughter or playful taunts. They sat silent, brooding, motionless, not even looking up to see her party roll past.

She felt great dismay at this, for the poor camp, for the condition of the men, but even more for the thinness of their numbers. In a province like Connacht, the warriors of the clans should number some thousands, not the twelve or fifteen hundred she saw scattered about.

The chariots of her party slowly wound their way through along the muddy, deeply rutted track. Finally they mounted the low hill and pulled up before the hut.

"What's happened?" Aileel said accusingly to Lewy. "You were to take her back to Tara!"

"My King . . ." the young man began, jumping down from his chariot.

"It's my fault!" Meave quickly put in, leaping from her car and moving toward Aileel.

Mentally she was steeling herself. She had, in fact, been preparing for this meeting since the night before. She knew she must put on the boldest front ever in her life. And now she faced Aileel squarely, making her voice even, calm, and firm.

"It was I who made him bring me here, my King. Let no blame fall on him."

"Made him!" Aileel repeated in astonishment. "And when can you force my chieftains to do what you want?" He looked at the young warrior. "Lewy, you know my order. You will obey it!"

"It's a bit too late now, don't you think?" Meave said.

The three sons of Aileel had been looking her over with openly appraising gazes. Now Morgor moved forward. "Is this your Meave?" he said leeringly. "I remember her, but only as a girl. She's become a most alluring lass."

"You keep your mouth shut, boy," Aileel shot at him.

Meave ignored this, sweeping an arm about her at the camp. "This is why you were so anxious to send me back, isn't it?"

she asked. "This is why you want no contact with Conaire Mor. You're afraid that he'll find out how weak you are!"

"I'm afraid of nothing," Aileel said with bravado, drawing himself up. "Connacht is strong now, as it's always been."

"Still, you imagine him discovering how much this war has wasted you," she persisted. "You believe he would just come into Connacht and take control. You're protecting it from him. That's why you refuse him, isn't it?"

"Until this war is ended and we control, until Connacht is whole and strong again, I'll deal with no one," Aileel told her brusquely. "That's all I'll say about it. And you—you will leave here at once!"

"I will not. I mean to stay and fight!"

"Fight?" he said in surprise. "But, you can't!"

"I can!" she countered. "I've a right. I have lands in Connacht, from my father. I lived here until my brother forced me to wed Conchobar. I am a part of this province, as much as any warrior here. And I can fight as well as most."

"I don't care," Aileel said, shaking his head. "It is too hard. You see our forces. Three years of war with the Firbolgs have done that. You've seen Connacht, all ravaged, its people starving. Thousands have died. Many clans have given up the fight and gone home to defend their own tuaths. It is a brutal war. There is no rest, no breathing time to sleep or bathe or bind our wounds or eat. There's only death, and that of many unpleasant kinds. You've seen. You know."

"I've seen." She looked past him at the three young men, all in dark wool of the finest work, jewelry glinting on arms, at throats, in the carefully tended hair. "But those three seem well enough for all that hardship."

"These are my sons," he said without enthusiasm. "Maine Morgor, Maine Mathra, Maine Aileel. You remember them. The sons of my first wife. They were children when you left Connacht."

"And how is it you stay so well when the rest seem so ragged?" she asked them.

"We are most . . . enterprising," Maine Morgor told her with an impudent grin, "and we hate discomfort."

"The fact remains, Meave," Aileel put in, drawing her attention back to him, "that I will not let you stay. I have no comforts for you."

"I want none," she replied firmly.

"You have to go," he grated. "I will not see you risked."

"But you can't really want that," she said slowly, coolly. "Not now. Now that I've seen." Upon her arrival in the camp, she had gained a new, powerful piece in this desperate game she played. She boldly used it now. Meeting Aileel's eyes searchingly, she asked, "Aren't you afraid I'll take word back to Mor?"

"She's right, Father," put in the opportunistic Morgor at once, smiling lewdly. "Keep her here. We can find some use for her. From the tales I've heard . . ."

Meave looked at him in shock. Aileel, enraged, wheeled on him and shouted, "No more from you!"

Still smiling, Morgor drew back.

Aileel looked around to Meave again, clearly troubled by the problem she presented. "I don't know what to do," he admitted. "It's my province, all my people at stake here."

"You've nothing to fear from me," she told him earnestly. "I'll stay, and gladly! I'll not tell Mor the true state of things here. He'll believe your fight is going well." She moved closer, putting a hand upon his arm, meeting his unsure gaze with her own sincere one. Her voice was firm, assuring. "Aileel, I'll keep your secret! I'll be a part of this with you. Mor will send no more emissaries here to interfere. Believe me: all he wants is your loyalty, some sign that you accept his kingship. Let me stay, and you have my oath that you'll have no more to fear from the high-king."

"Look here, don't listen to more of this," Morgor said impatiently, stepping forward again. "Just let me deal with her. I'll see to it that the bitch is tamed. It will be my own pleasure."

"You remind me of someone," Meave told him icily, seeing in him an image of the swaggering Conchobar. "He was an arrogant bully as well."

"What's that?" Morgor said angrily, moving closer. "The likes of you have no right to be speaking so to me, woman."

"Get back, Morgor," Aileel said warningly.

"No," Meave told him. "I need no one's protecting." She faced Morgor squarely. "From now on I see to myself."

"Do you?" said Aileel's son with a scornful laugh, stepping closer to her. "Then you'll have more than your match from me."

"Take care, Morgor," Lewy MacNeesh warned.

"Let the braggart strut," Meave said nastily.

"Why, you . . ." cried the stung Morgor, swinging out a hand, palm out, to slap her face.

Though his move was swift, Meave's was swifter. One of her hands came up to block his. The other drew her sword in a lightning move and he suddenly found the end of her blade sweeping up between his legs, stopping with its well-honed edge pressing in tightly against his groin. He met the icy look glinting in her eyes and he blanched, going up on his toes.

"Don't move too quickly," she advised. "Slide backward very slowly, or you'll find yourself a gelding. And I give my word that you'll be one for certain if you try any of your bullying on me again, king's son or not."

"I did try to warn you," Lewy observed, grinning.

The two other Maines guffawed loudly at their brother's expense. Even Aileel fought, with only partial success, to hide a smile. Morgor could do nothing but carefully tiptoe backward, free himself, then turn and stalk away, red-faced, humiliated, and, for the first time, silent.

"You notice that she can handle weapons well, my King," Lewy said. "I've seen her. She's as good as any warrior. I think you should let her stay."

"Do you?" Aileel said, still with a tone of doubt. He looked at her. "Well, we were planning to go on a hunt now. Some signs were found in the woods nearby. Why don't you come along, Meave? See what fighting the Firbolgs is really like. After that you can decide."

They moved cautiously forward. A massed wedge of some hundred warriors pushed slowly into the dense woods like a broad spear blade being forced through a thick hide. Another hundred were scattered out in a ragged line at either side, and a score more scouted the way ahead.

At the point of the wedge strode Aileel, Lewy MacNeesh and Meave at his sides. She looked around curiously at the wood as they pressed in. It was largely of pines, spaced evenly by nature's decree. Tall, slender, branchless trunks soared up for some distance from the level, open, needle-carpeted floor like tapering columns in an enormous hall. The umbrellas of furry branches sprouting from their tops interwove to form a thatchlike covering. With the overcast above, the lacery of limbs seemed almost a solid roof.

It was extremely, almost eerily silent here. Footsteps were hushed by the thick brown carpeting of needles. The damp air, the foliage, and the oppressive sky seemed to form a blanket that muffled the usual clattering of arms. And there were no sounds of speech—no mutterings, no curses, no jests or laughs—from the host of men.

"Our warriors have seen small war parties of Firbolgs moving in the woods," Aileel explained in a hushed voice as they picked their way through the maze of trees. "All were moving toward or away from a place just ahead. They may be gathering now for a larger raid. But if we can come upon them first, surround them, surprise them . . ."

"You can destroy their host?" finished Meave.

He shook his head. "No. They've no one host. It would be like simply killing one wolf from a scattered, roving pack. Still, it's that many fewer enemies."

They crept on stealthily for a time. The warriors, she noted, moved very slowly, almost with an air of reluctance. Their weapons were out and held in fierce grips, ready for instant use. Their eyes searched the woods about them constantly, carefully. A pall of grim intent seemed to hang over them like the overcast sky, and the tang of their nervous sweat tainted the humid air.

"It has the feel of a boar hunt, not a battle," she softly observed to Lewy.

"It is more like a hunt, with these Firbolgs," the young warrior agreed. "They're more like beasts than men. But more savage and more dangerous than any beast you're likely to ever see."

"Hold on," Aileel whispered suddenly. He lifted a hand in signal. The host behind him came to a halt.

Ahead of them, an opening showed in the trees. "A clearing," Aileel said softly. "They may be there."

He moved back through the gathering, passing orders to his chieftains. Soon the host was spreading out, forming a broad curving line of warriors.

"We move in carefully," Aileel said. He looked to Lewy. "You stay with Meave."

She opened her mouth to protest, but he had already moved away, leading the advance.

"Sorry," the young warrior told her. "I know what you're thinking, but now's not the time to be defying him."

"You're right," she agreed. She looked at the men moving forward about them. "But where are his own sons?"

Lewy shook his head. "For such a hunting, Aileel chooses only his best men. Those three are good fighters, Morgor may be the best, but they'll look first to themselves when the battle's most fierce. It's telling no secret to say he's got no trust or love for that misbegotten lot."

"I'm sorry for that," she said, looking toward the proud figure of Aileel, striding forward so purposefully at the head of his ragged host.

"Aye," said Lewy. "He's a fine man. He's deserving of more. But we'd best be quiet now. We're getting close."

They were approaching the clearing. The warriors crept carefully through the last screen of trees and peeked out into the opening.

It was a small clearing, roughly circular, halved by a small brook. Some two dozen crude bothies of woven sticks huddled in its middle. Plumes of smoke rose from a score of fires. There were no signs of movement, but a few figures were visible, seated about some of the fires.

"They are here!" Aileel said, peering intently ahead through squinted eyes. "We attack!"

"Something is wrong here," Lewy said in alarm. He moved toward Aileel. "My King, we shouldn't . . ."

But he was too late. Aileel had raised his arm, signaling the men in.

The host swarmed in from the sides of the clearing, converging on the huts. Meave and Lewy ran in behind Aileel. They came up upon a fire. The men seated about it made no move to rise or defend themselves.

"What's wrong with them?" shouted Aileel, moving in and kicking out at one with his foot.

The figure limply tumbled sideways. The wool cloak about him fell away, revealing another one beneath.

"It's our own man!" cried a warrior.

They looked about. All the figures were dead warriors of Connacht, propped up with their own spears driven into the ground.

"Our scouts!" shouted Lewy. "It's a trap!"

And from about them, wild, shrill battle cries rose wavering into the sky, forming a weird chorus. Figures began to stream from behind trees and to rain from the upper branches, joining in a flood that poured in upon the host, surrounding it.

For the first time Meave looked upon the Firbolg enemy, and found herself appalled.

Swarthier and more thickly built than her own people were the Firbolg warriors. And this coarser look was even more greatly exaggerated now by the savagery of their dress. Dark, unbound hair flew wildly about their heads in thickly tangled waves. Hides and furs clad many, giving them a barbaric, bestial look. As they attacked, snarling and shouting their battle cries, they seemed indeed more like a pack of maddened wolves than men.

Their fighting was as ferocious. They tore into the Connacht host, and the clearing quickly became the scene of a bewildering melee, warriors pairing off in single combats. Lewy tried to come between Meave and every attacker, but each attempt was a vain one. Soon both of them were hotly engaged with foes, and Lewy found the woman's skill truly a match for his own. Overcoming her initial horror at these creatures, she concentrated her whole being on facing them. A well-aimed swing sent one staggering away minus an arm. A thrust pierced a second's throat. A blow of the shield sent a third crashing down upon a fire, to roll away smoldering, screaming in pain.

The initial attack took a large toll on the Connacht host, nearly overwhelming them. But Aileel managed to turn the balance almost single-handedly, recklessly hewing his way into the thickest part of the enemy horde, swinging out with his sword to strike opponent after opponent from his way. As the Firbolgs began to waver in their assault, Aileel's warriors disentangled themselves from the melee, pulling in to form a tight ring, facing the enemy and guarding one another's backs.

Then, abruptly, the Firbolgs were gone.

Meave watched in amazement as the circle of fierce, threatening faces seemed to melt away, the warriors fading back into the shadows of the trees as swiftly as they had come, so noiseless they might have been wraiths of mist dispelled by a ray of sun.

The only evidence of the grim reality of their recent presence was in the few dead and dying men littering the clearing among the greater number of Connacht casualties.

"What happened to them?" Meave asked.

"They've not our numbers," Lewy explained. "Their tactics are to strike and run away. When things begin to go against them, they quit the fight." He looked around at the dead sorrowfully. "They've done us what damage they meant to do."

"Gather our wounded," Aileel was ordering. "Make litters for any who can't walk. Finish their wounded. Take all the heads and make a cairn of them. Put all the bodies, theirs and ours, in these huts and burn them! Move quickly now. We want to be out of these woods before nightfall."

With this wish the warriors clearly agreed, moving with great swiftness to their tasks. The king walked over to Lewy and Meave.

"I feel the fool for walking into this," he admitted, shaking his head. "I was certain they were here."

"My King," said Lewy, "didn't you see—"

"What?" Aileel said sharply, cutting him off.

"Nothing, my King," said Lewy. "It was a clever trap. I was fooled as well."

Meave gave the young warrior a searching look, but then her gaze was drawn to Aileel as he addressed her.

"Well, Meave, you've seen what we face here. They are beasts. Ravaging creatures, terrible and cruel. Had there been a greater host of them, it's all of our bodies that likely would be measuring their length upon the bloody sod."

Meave looked about at the carnage, at the warriors ruthlessly dispatching their wounded foes, at others severing the Firbolg heads to form a ghastly pile. Then she looked back to meet the king's eyes, her gaze steady and lit by her determined fire.

"This doesn't change me, Aileel. I mean to stay and fight. I ask you only if you still think I'll not be of worth to you."

He looked into the blue-gray eyes fixedly for a moment. Then he shook his head. "No, Meave," he said resignedly. "You have a fighting skill and a courage and a readiness to kill that matches even my best fighting men. I'll not turn you away if you choose to stay."

"And will you send some word to Conaire Mor?" she asked. "Some sign that you will give your support to him?"

He smiled at that. "It's a most stubborn woman you are, Meave," he said. "Yes, I will. I'll send hostages to Tara to prove my loyalty. A man clever enough to send you here must be worthy of ruling Ireland. And I have just the proper hostages in mind, I think. They'd surely not be missed here."

She felt a wave of relief, of triumph, wash through her. It was a thrill as she had never known before. She had won at last. She had beaten Conchobar. Was this the wonderful sensation that young Sentanta had felt when besting Ulster's king?

And as this sense came to her, her thoughts went to that boy. She wished he could know of her victory. And she wondered if he still battled to win his own place.

Chapter Seventeen

The Arrivals

The great heads of the four horses strained forward. The two teams drove ahead, side by side, so close that the inside animals thudded often against each other. Their sleek bodies pulsed with the intense rhythm of their stride.

The chariots behind the teams flew recklessly along the roadway, their iron-rimmed wheels clattering on the stones, skittering sideways, bouncing, rocking wildly. But the two charioteers whose skills kept the cars close together reveled in the speed, for they were young and masters of their craft. And the two warriors who stood the chariot poles between the horses paid no mind, for they were absorbed in their attempts to reach each other with their swords.

Over the backs of the animals their battle raged. The graceful, lethal lengths of polished iron swept dangerously close to the running horses as each man thrust, cut, and parried the other's blows. They did so as they danced precariously along the narrow poles, trying to use the chariot's movements as their drivers jockeyed for position.

Both combatants were very young. One was little more than a boy in looks. His face was beardless, his features very fine. A boy, but with a skill in the sword's use and a trained agility in his movements that revealed a veteran's experience.

The other lad, older by only a few years, was darker in coloring, red-cheeked, with bright brown eyes. His movements were also those of a veteran, but he was slower, less agile than his opponent. Still, they were a close match, and their battle seemed to be an even one.

Then the younger warrior made an unexpected move. He dropped suddenly from the pole, sliding under his racing horses.

Surprised, the darker youth leaned forward to see what had happened to his foe. He didn't realize that the other boy was swinging under the animals and up, seizing his own inner horse around the neck and throwing himself up onto the pole. He didn't realize it until he saw the figure flying up toward him, feet first, striking him solidly in the chest, knocking him back over his outer horse.

He tumbled from the speeding chariot, narrowly missed by the flying hooves, thudding heavily to the ground and tumbling over several times before he came to rest, crumpled and motionless.

At once both charioteers pulled in their steeds and brought their vehicles to a sliding, dusty stop. The younger warrior leaped from the pole and strode back to his opponent. He lifted his sword and touched it lightly to the unprotected neck.

Then he pulled away the sword and laughed. "That's three heads you owe me now, Cormac," he said.

The man on the ground, fighting to regain his breath, threw the youth above him a dark look and gasped out, "A very nasty bit that was, Sentanta! Help me up, then!"

Sentanta reached down a hand and the other took it, pulling himself up with an effort.

"Just look at this," Cormac said ruefully, looking down at himself. "My best cloak, torn and brown with dust. You might give me some warning if you mean to be heaving me about in the roadways!"

"And what kind of a sport would that be?" the boy answered. "You're only angry because I bested you."

"You've been doing the very same thing since we first met," Cormac returned irritably. "I don't know why it is I even play with you." Then, more reasonably, he added, "But I would like to learn that little piece of trickery sometime."

"I'll teach you, Cormac," the other promised, helping his companion to brush off the dust. "You really aren't such a bad fighter, you know."

"Why, thank you, whelp!" Cormac replied in a tone of mock gratitude. "A bit of praise from such a modest warrior of Ulster overwhelms me."

The two chariots had pulled up beside them now. The young, curly-haired driver of one asked the warriors impatiently, "Are you two ready to be getting on, then?"

"We are, Laeg," said Sentanta. He looked around him at the countryside. "Where is it we are now?"

"It's only a bit farther," Cormac told him, climbing somewhat stiffly into his car. "We should be seeing it soon."

He was right. They had gone only a short way along the road

when they topped a low hill and Cormac pointed ahead. "There it is," he announced grandly. "Tara!"

Atop the distant swell of hill Sentanta could see the line of the great dun's walls. To the young man it was a most awesome sight, this dwelling of heroes, the seat of Ireland's high-kings, the setting for the marvelous tales he'd heard the bards singing all his life. Tara an Rie. Now, finally, he was to reach it. He was to become a part of its life.

He was seized by a sudden nervousness. "Cormac, what will I do there?" he asked anxiously. "How will I behave?"

"Easy, lad," Cormac said with confidence, puffing himself up in an overbearing way. "You just stay near to me. I'll try to see that you don't make *too* many mistakes."

Now it was his turn to play the leader. Here, the student in fighting became the leader in protocol. For, as the son of a king, Cormac had had the greater experience in matters of state. However, Cormac was also a young man who had never believed in taking life too gravely.

He pointed off toward the west of Tara. "Look there," he said. "You can see the pavilions of the fair, as well."

Sentanta could see them, like a small patch of bright flowers in a green meadow, topping another hill not far away.

"You've never seen a Tailteen Fair, have you?" Cormac asked casually.

"No. No, I haven't," the boy admitted.

"It's the greatest fair in Ireland," the other said with great gusto. "Maybe even in the world." He paused, then went on in a sly and musing tone, "But, you know, once we've been introduced at the court, we'll have very little time for visiting it."

Sentanta knew that tone of voice very well. He laughed and looked at Cormac. "You want to go there first. Is that it?"

"Well, no one knows we've come yet," Cormac reasoned cheerfully. "We're still free. And it is my task to introduce my poor, ignorant charge to such new and remarkable things."

"I would like to see it," Sentanta agreed with youthful eagerness. "What do you think, Laeg? Should we go to the fair?"

"You'll get no argument from me," the driver said, beaming. "And the sooner there, the more time we'll have."

"Then, attack speed, driver!" Cormac commanded.

Both chariots were quickly racing along the roadway once again.

* * *

A log the width of a man's waist thudded into the circle of the fire pit, landing upon a heap already there.

The stocky servant straightened himself with a grunt and looked ruefully toward the gray-haired steward who watched him critically.

"There'll be enough timber here to heat half the province before we're through," he grumbled. He wiped a sleeve of his tunic across his broad face, which was streaming with sweat.

"The high-king wishes to keep everyone warmed thoroughly tonight," the steward told him haughtily.

The servant looked around at the many other servants readying the vast hall and shook his head. "Don't know why Mor's so quick to play up to these province emissaries," he complained loudly. "Used to be called hostages in the old days. Came by fear they did, or were taken by force!"

"There's none of that now," the steward reminded him sharply. "The ard-rie wants them thought of as friends."

"And what about those coming today?" the feisty servant boldly challenged. "Ulstermen! The worst of the lot, I'll be wagering. It's an arrogant clan those Red Branch warriors are."

"It's Cormac Conlingas, son of Ulster's king, who's coming here," the steward answered, greatly shocked. "A very fine warrior."

"Yes, I've heard of him," the worker said indifferently. "He's fair enough by all accounts, but a bit of a jester. And likely a blowhard, as all of them are. Why, look at those sons of Connacht's king that he sent here. It's nothing but drinking and pestering our women they've done since they came."

"I think you'd best be watching your tongue," the steward warned, gesturing upward. "Just get more wood."

"You've got too much already," the man grumbled.

"I said, get more wood!" the steward commanded.

"You! Down there!" another voice cried out.

Both men looked up. The caller was hanging out over the rail of the balcony above the hall. The steward stiffened.

"You've too much wood on that fire!" the man exclaimed. "I don't want my guests roasted. Just evenly warmed. See to it, steward!"

"Yes, my King!" the steward fervently promised. He looked down in chagrin to see the servant grinning broadly as he lifted a burning log with the fire tongs.

"I'll just take one or two of these off, then, shall I?" he asked in a taunting voice.

Above them, Conaire Mor watched carefully to be certain they made no further mistakes.

Even his few years as high-king had brought maturity to his features. High cheekbones and strong chin were now well-defined. But there was no harshness in the wide mouth or the clear, mist-gray eyes. From his high forehead, his thick blond hair was combed back in great waves on either side and plaited loosely at his neck. He wore no special ornament, his clothing still as simple as a common warrior's. Grand, outward signs of authority meant nothing more to him than they had before.

When he finally turned from the railing, he faced a warrior who watched him with a faint smile. Mor noted the expression.

"I really am mad, after all. Is that what you're thinking, Conal?"

Conal Carna was a veteran of much warfare. His lean and weathered face gave evidence of every season of combat. But good humor still gleamed in his pale blue eyes.

"I've long since given up doubting you, Conaire. No matter how mad your methods seem to me, they appear to work."

"My methods wouldn't have come to much without your loyalty," Mor told him earnestly. "Still, I sometimes think that only Calatin truly understands what I'm trying to do."

Conal's eyes flashed an icy light at that.

But the high-king didn't see it. He had turned back toward the balcony rail. "It doesn't matter," he said easily. "They'll all see the good of it soon. I know they will."

Conal moved forward to stand beside his king and look down into the room below. The army of servants were cleaning, hanging the clan shields on the timber walls of the circular hall, and strewing the earthen floor with fresh rushes.

"So, we're nearly ready, my friend," Mor said solemnly. "Another affair of state. The greatest yet. All fragile, like an egg. And we're the ones who'll have to juggle it." He smiled suddenly: a broad, boyish grin that wiped all the care from his face and seemed to fill him with new energy. He clapped a hand to his champion's shoulder, saying brightly, "But we will do it, Conal. That we will!"

As always, Conal marveled at this buoyancy of spirit, this fire of enthusiasm never completely extinguished in Mor. He was never frustrated, always optimistic, and it was that in his character which had made Conal loyal, made the worn and cynical veteran believe this lad could really succeed in uniting Ireland.

A warrior appeared in the hall below and called up to him, "My King, a lookout has reported that two chariots carrying Ulster warriors were sighted on the North Road. He believes one man is Cormac Conlingas."

"Our last emissaries have arrived, then!" Conaire said with vast relief. "Where are they now?"

"They turned away from Tara toward the fair," the warrior replied.

"Typical of Cormac," Conal said disapprovingly, knowing too well that young man's character. "He'll never learn to mind his duty first."

"Don't be too harsh," Mor told him. "I'd like to see this fair myself. Why don't we go down and meet them? There's little enough for us to do here now. It'll fill up the time until our feast."

This idea did not surprise Conal, accustomed to a king who still played hurley with the boys for sport, still hunted, raced, and wrestled with his foster-brothers like a boy himself.

As usual with Mor, once a decision had been made, he wasted no time. He and his champion set off immediately, down the stairway from the upper room, across the floor of the hall, pausing only long enough for him to give final instructions to his head steward.

"Remember: no weapons in the hall!" he admonished. "I'll take no chances. If any argument begins to brew, tell me at once."

As he and Conal moved on, he said to his champion in a confidential tone, "You know, I'm tempted to find some weaker ale for our warriors. Sometimes I think it's that alone that makes Ireland's tempers hot at these gatherings."

"No warrior worth the name would be fooled by watered drink," replied a shocked Conal. "And they'd trust you less for it than if you'd stolen their herds."

Mor laughed. "I know it, Conal. Your precious ale is safe from me!"

They went through the main doors of the hall and stopped just outside.

"Have some chariots made ready and brought around here," Mor instructed his champion. "I'm going to look for Fionualla."

"I think she's with the children, Conaire," Conal called after him as he set out to seek his young wife.

He found her near his living quarters, the Royal Seat, with some other ladies of the dun and a large collection of Tara's smaller children. They were engaged in many types of amusement, which included some early schooling as well. A young bard of the lower ranks was telling stories to a circle of enthralled four- and five-year-olds. Older children, boys and girls alike, played games of war with wooden swords and shields and chariots made of carts pulled by comrades.

The youngest ones the ladies entertained, and Conaire arrived to find Fionualla pursuing a small gaggle of them delightedly.

Each time she caught one, she would swing the laughing child high above her head, then lower it back and go after another one. The children were not trying very hard to escape.

She didn't see Mor come, and he stood for a while, watching her, fascinated as always just by the sight of her.

It was a fine young woman Fionualla had become, although characteristically she was unaware of it. As she lifted up a child, her slim body moved and stretched with a natural grace. As she arched back, arms high, her wealth of black hair, glinting colors like a raven's wing, fell back to reveal the smooth curve of her throat, the fine skin so white in contrast.

She caught two children together, swinging both up, and Mor used that moment to steal in close behind her. When she put down the children, he seized her about the waist, lifted her up, and swept her around.

She cried out in surprise. Then, seeing who it was, her face lit with pleasure. "Conaire!"

"I thought it might be your turn," he said, and swung her faster, to the immense enjoyment of the surrounding children.

Finally, with a loud "Woosh!" he dropped down into the grass with her, and the little ones swarmed over them in a joyous confusion.

Nearly breathless from laughter, Fionualla turned around to look at her grinning husband. "Conaire, what is it you're doing here?"

"Why, I've come to take my lady to the fair!" he said, playfully wrestling several children at once. "You'll go with me, won't you?"

"You know I will! But what about the celebrations tonight?"

"They're well in hand." He got up, gently detaching several children who still clung to him, and helped her to her feet. "It's time we took a little pleasure to ourselves. Come with me now. I've chariots waiting."

She made her goodbyes to the ladies and the children, who were devastated at losing their playmate. As the two walked back toward the main hall, he threw an arm about her to hug her close.

"I've not seen you so happy in many days," she said, slipping her arm about his waist.

"I feel I rule the world today," he said joyfully. "I can't hold all the excitement in. I think it's going to work, Fionualla. Meave has sent word that things are going well in Connacht, Aileel has sent his sons to me as tokens of his loyalty, and now emissaries have arrived from Ulster! It looks as if all I've been working for can really come to be." He looked down at her and added earnestly, "Now maybe there'll be more time for us."

At the front of the main hall Conal waited with the chariots. Conaire and Fionualla climbed into one, and the young ardrie took up the reins. He'd just started the team forward, across the training ground to the central gates, when another chariot pulled up alongside.

Its driver was of a sickly pale hue and bony form, a most strange and withered-seeming creature. Behind him stood a large and dark-complected man, dressed in the imposing striped cloak and elaborate golden torque of a high-druid.

Mor pulled up and greeted the newcomer cheerfully. "Calatin! What is it that you're about?"

The man's dark eyes passed over Fionualla, and she drew back behind her husband. The druid looked to Mor, smiled a slow, humorless smile, and said in a soft, low croon, "I have heard that you are going to meet some of our new emissaries at the fair. I thought that I should accompany you—for the sake of ceremony."

"You've certainly got sharp ears to have heard so quickly," Conal Carna muttered.

But Mor's response was a hearty one: "Why, you're surely welcome to come. Fall in with us!"

He urged the horses on again. Calatin's chariot pulled in behind him, next to that of Conal, who rode on in stony silence, ignoring the ard-druid.

Fionualla shuddered. "I feel a strange chill coming from that man," she told Conaire. "I'm frightened of him."

"That's foolishness," he chided. "He's been only a help in my work."

"It's in the way he looks at me," she persisted. "As if he's seeing into me. And what I've heard said about him! Conaire, they say he has strange powers, and I believe it. I can see them there, glinting in those black eyes like light glinting in an animal's eyes at night!"

He hugged her tightly to him. "Forget Calatin now," he said lightly. "The fair's just ahead. Let's think about nothing but pleasure for a while. The day is all for us."

Chapter Eighteen

At the Fair

The juggler leaped from the table into the avenue, sending up a roar of delight from the assembled watchers as he kept control of several spinning globes of brass.

Sentanta and Cormac stopped in astonishment as he dropped down before them. They paused with many others in the main thoroughfare to watch this skillful artisan send the gleaming spheres higher and higher in the air, forming a spinning ring around his smiling face.

All the avenues of the fair were filled with such diversions. Acrobats and conjurers, wandering harpers and pipers and bards plied the streets among the pavilions and the market stalls which covered the green hill of Tailteen. There, wares from all about Ireland and from far beyond were displayed, to the great delight of the thousands of visitors. For it was only once in three years that the great fair was held, bringing folk from even the farthest, most rugged corners of the island.

Tunes floated like bright birds above the humming of the crowd. At many spots around the margins of the fair, booths offered food and drink to the throngs of warriors, noblemen, and commoners who mingled there.

People from all the provinces of Ireland who had never met before talked, played, and laughed together, heedless of the differences in dialects, clothing, or customs that otherwise often made them deadly rivals. A grand oneness they became, and it was a sight like nothing the young Sentanta had ever seen, or even imagined, before.

He and Cormac moved through it all, marveling, feeling, listening, inhaling the heady atmosphere. They drank coarse, full-bodied ale, fingered rich tapestries from far-off Espan, tested the balance and edge of finely worked swords.

They were fully taken up by their enjoyment when they rounded the corner of a stall and collided with the first of a band of young warriors headed the other way.

The three men in the lead were clearly brothers, all with tightly curled dark hair, sharp features, and quick, nervous gestures, like ferrets on the prowl.

"Your pardon, friends," Sentanta said politely, barely glancing at them.

But as he started away, one of the dark youths stepped into his path.

"And do you think you can just knock a warrior of Connacht about and walk away without making amends, whelp?" The tone was arrogant. Deep-set eyes glittered with a dangerous light.

"Hold on there, Morgor . . ." began a red-haired youth.

The other ignored him. "Ulstermen!" he spat out contemptuously. "That's enough in itself to make them apologize."

"What do you mean!" Sentanta demanded, stepping forward. But Cormac raised a calming hand between the two.

"Please, warriors. I know there is an old rivalry between our provinces, but this is not the place to argue it. Tailteen is a place for us to come together as men of Ireland. As friends. Now, come along and have an ale with us."

He lifted a hand to the shoulder of the other man, but the warrior slapped it angrily away.

"And when did Ulster ever feel itself a part of Ireland?" he asked harshly. He spread his legs and stood stiffly, arms away from his body. "To you the rest of us are only barren sod to run your horses on. Get down and beg my pardon from your knees. Then I'll be satisfied. And you can be thankful you were let go by a better man than you."

"Is that the truth?" Sentanta said in a peculiar, airy tone Cormac knew well. He saw the boy's hand alight casually on his longsword hilt. He squeezed his eyes shut for an instant as he made his prayers, and then he began to brace himself. For Cormac knew by hard experience what would happen now.

"It's a great wonder to me that such fine talk should be coming from such a spare and spavined-looking object as yourself," Sentanta said in a light way. "And you with only eight others to help you face two such poor warriors as we are."

"Sentanta!" Cormac warned.

"Your Ulster arrogance will see you dead, that's sure!" the dark youth grated, nearly choking with his rage. His sword hand dropped to his weapon, and Cormac watched it, knowing that once even a hair's breadth of blade showed, there would be no stopping this.

The red-haired youth understood that too. He stepped forward and seized his companion's elbow. "Morgor, we can't have bloodshed here. Think what you're doing!"

Morgor jerked his arm away. "If you've no stomach for this, Ferogaine, get on away!" he said scornfully. "I've no need of your help."

Sentanta tensed. Cormac leaned close to him and hissed, "Remember our mission here. Please, don't kill them!"

Sentanta listened and nodded in assent. And so, as Morgor began to draw his sword, the young warrior's response was to sweep up a ripe melon from a stall and fling it into his opponent's face.

It was, in truth, quite overripe and exploded wetly as it struck. Morgor staggered, his sword dropping back into its scabbard. Sentanta moved swiftly in, swinging him around, flipping his cloak forward over his head and then using a solidly planted foot to kick him into the other young warriors as they surged forward.

"Very nice work," Cormac shouted encouragingly. Then he was forced to deal with two of the enraged warriors who came at him from the tangle.

No swords had yet been drawn, and the two Ulstermen maneuvered desperately to avoid it. Sentanta kept three at bay for a time with fruit and vegetables picked randomly from the stalls. When the warriors surrounded him and closed in to seize him, he vaulted a passing cow.

He landed amid several women who were baking bread, scattering them. One man leaped after him, but Sentanta tossed the man on over his head, and he landed face first on a table filled with wet dough. This material made an excellent throwing weapon, the boy found, and he used it to drive off two more adversaries. When Morgor came at him a second time, he went down a second time, his head imbedded in a massive lump of the clinging stuff.

The brawl was spreading now. Other warriors, not knowing the cause but unable to resist any chance for a scrap, were joining in. The market area was fast turned to a shambles, trestles and stalls overturned, produce flooding across the ground.

Cormac had snatched a long pole from a fish-drying rack—bringing it down in a tangle on several men—and was fending off anyone who tried to close with him. But Sentanta lost sight of his original adversaries and, in the confusion, found himself unchallenged.

He moved into a clearer area between two rows of stalls, then stopped when he heard a voice behind him.

"There you are!"

He turned to face Morgor, free now of the dough, which still marked his face and cloak. He was, however, anything but a comical sight as he stalked forward, face hot with rage and humiliation.

"Now, Ulster puppy, you will use that iron of yours or you will surely die," he snarled, drawing his sword.

Young Sentanta was left with no other choice. The play was ended. His blade flashed into his hand and he set himself to meet Morgor's attack.

The high-king's party, moving along the avenue in their chariots, now suddenly found themselves in the midst of the melee.

"By all the gods!" Conaire exclaimed, pulling up. "Conal," he called to his champion, "we've got to stop this now!"

He seized a round shield from the car and vaulted over its side, plunging into the fray, Conal close behind. He pulled fighters apart, commanding them to stop. Persistent ones he simply knocked down with a swing of the shield or a well-aimed blow. But then, not far ahead, he saw two warriors confronting each other with swords. Drawing his own, he rushed upon them.

Sentanta and Morgor were by this time hotly engaged. The Ulsterman found his opponent a wily fighter, tenacious as a wolf. The two tested each other and then dived in, locking their weapons in a high arch between them.

Seemingly from nowhere a third weapon swept upward,

knocking the other two apart. Both warriors stepped back, bringing their weapons toward this unexpected threat. But Sentanta found his blade pushed aside with a deft parry, and Morgor was felled for a third time by a swing of the shield.

Even without knowing the man he now faced, Sentanta recognized the authority in him. He lowered his sword in acquiescence.

Conaire Mor turned to face the others. "Stop this fighting now!" he ordered. The voice was not loud, but its power reached above the clamor. Many of those still brawling heard it, knew it, and instantly obeyed.

Mor walked into the center of the avenue, looking about the shattered marketplace and at the now silent men. He noted Morgor's two brothers there, then glimpsed another face he knew—that of the red-haired lad.

"Ferogain!" he exclaimed. "Are you in this too?"

"We all are, Conaire," the other replied.

The high-king looked more closely at the disheveled figures and realized it was true. All of his foster-brothers were there, save one.

"Where is Lomna Druth?" he asked.

"Here, Conaire!" a sheepish voice responded.

From beneath an overturned fruit cart a round, red face appeared. With some difficulty a stout body followed it as the young man good-naturedly called The Fool crawled forth, an apple in each hand.

"I'm sorry to leave there," he remarked. "It was safe, and cool, and very tasty."

"A very pretty sight all of you look," Mor told them irritably. "And can anyone tell me what brought you to a brawl here, in the center of the Tailteen Fair, where all of Ireland is to come together in peace?"

None of them answered, and as he glared around at them, each one avoided meeting his eye. Finally his gaze came back to rest on Morgor.

"You seemed to be one of the most hotly engaged," he said. "What began it?"

"It was the Ulstermen," the warrior muttered.

"Ulstermen?" said Mor. He looked to Sentanta. "You mean this lad?"

"And I, my King," said Cormac, moving out from the others.

"Cormac Conlingas," said Conal heavily. "And knowing him, I might believe he was the cause of this."

"I take offense at that!" Cormac protested. "We did everything we could to avoid a fight."

Mor dropped a cold eye to the pole Cormac still held. Flushing, the young warrior dropped it quickly and stepped back.

"This is beyond belief!" Mor said, looking from Cormac to Morgor and shaking his head. "Tonight chieftains and emissaries from all of Ireland will meet to join in peace, and the sons of two of my greatest kings start a battle in the midst of the fair marketplace!"

"But they are Ulstermen!" Morgor cried bitterly.

"No!" Mor shouted at him. "They are men of Ireland, as you and all of us are." He stepped back close to Morgor, his words growing harder. "And if you forget it once again, I'll see you and your brothers sent beyond my borders."

"I am a high-king's son," Morgor countered haughtily.

"Yes. But I'm certain Aileel would see you punished even sooner than I would. And who is your young opponent?" he asked, looking around to Sentanta, who had stood quietly through this.

"He is my companion, my King," Cormac volunteered. "His name is Sentanta MacSualtim."

"The one that Conal Carna told me about?" Mor said, looking the lad over with more interest. He glanced back at Morgor. "From what I've heard, you should be thanking me for stopping this. You might be dead now."

"Sentanta tried to avoid using his sword," Cormac said defensively.

"I can agree to the truth of that," said Lomna Druth. "The Ulsterman is especially skilled in fighting with ripe fruit and dough, as you can see by Morgor's adornment."

That warrior threw a chill look at The Fool.

"Enough!" said the high-king impatiently. "It makes no difference who began this. All of you should feel shame for it. Maybe my own foster-brothers most of all!" He passed a disapproving gaze over the lot. "The men of Ulster and Connacht I can excuse a bit because of their ancient rivalry. But for my foster-brothers, my closest friends, to become involved . . ."

In his irritation with them, Mor could think of no further words that would not be angry ones. He chose not to carry on this discussion now and instead, waved them sharply off.

"Just be away from here, the lot of you!" he said loudly to the entire collection of brawlers. "That means you Maines and all the rest of you as well." But to his foster-brothers he added sharply, "But we'll speak more of this later. That I'll promise you!"

Soberly, silently, the chastised men moved out of the market area and up the avenue. Only Ferogain lingered behind. "Conaire?" he said hesitantly.

"Ferogain!" Mor responded in a disappointed tone. "You especially I had hoped would understand what I'm trying to do."

"But, Conaire, I didn't mean . . ." he began.

"You didn't think!" Mor said sharply, cutting him off.

That wounded Ferogain deeply. His face went red as if he had been struck. He stiffened, then turned abruptly on his heel, striding off along the avenue without another word.

"You were too harsh with him," said Fionualla, coming up beside her husband.

"I know. I saw his face," Mor said with regret. "I should never let my anger speak for me."

"I'll go and talk with him," she said gently. "He'll understand."

She started to follow the lad. But Mor called after her, "Wait! What about the fair?"

"I'll meet you soon. At the hurley field." She smiled knowingly. "You'll go there anyway."

He smiled in return as he watched her move away. She knew his heart and mind better than he did himself.

He turned to Cormac and Sentanta, who stood waiting with Conal Carna to see what would come next.

"I'd like to think this brawl was not of your doing," he told the pair.

"It was Cormac who tried to keep peace," the boy said honestly. "My own temper gave me up."

"If your temper had been lost, this place would be awash with blood now," Conal Carna said. And, to Mor: "It's likely Morgor who was guilty in this. You know what a troublesome lot those Connachtmen are!"

"Now, Conal," Mor said carefully, "though you're my trusted friend, you are of Ulster. Let's make no more accusations here. Let's simply welcome our new emissaries as we should." He smiled at them, adding, "And since you are so interested in seeing our fair, shall we continue to do so as we walk?"

The young warriors agreed. Mor left the chariots in Conal's care and, with one of the Ulstermen on either side, moved off along the avenues.

Behind them, the people of the fair began to set the market right again, uttering a few dark epithets on the conduct of young noblemen, now that they were all safely out of earshot. The area was quickly returned to normal.

None of the workers paid notice to a figure that still lurked in the shelter of a covered stall. From there he had observed the confrontation with tremendous interest. And now, as he watched the last participants walk away, the ard-druid Calatin's look was thoughtful indeed.

When Mor and the rest had gone, he left the stall and returned to his own vehicle. He whispered an order to its bent, cadaverous driver, and the chariot sped away, out into the countryside.

Fionualla, meanwhile, had caught up with Ferogain in a section of the fair given over to craftsmen of many kinds. Over the din of sculptors, smiths, and jewelry makers at their work, she had pleaded with him to stop and talk with her. But he had stalked on, ignoring her. Finally, the girl had seized his arm and yanked him bodily around to face her.

"Ferogain, you have to talk to me!" she demanded.

"Be away from me!" he shouted back. "I've no wish to talk to anyone."

"When you were a child, I'd thrash you for speaking that way to me!" she said in exasperation. "I'll do it again now, if I have to!"

He glared for a moment at the young woman who faced him stubbornly, hands on hips. Then his rage faded and he slumped down in defeat onto a large wooden sculpture of a bear.

"Why don't you go ahead with it then?" he told her wearily. "You can't make me look more a fool than Conaire already has."

As he looked up at her, she saw in his face the anguish that gripped him, and her irritation died.

She had always had a special love for him. Youngest of Conaire's foster-brothers, he was also the slightest in build, with an open face whose artless, boyish look was emphasized by the dusting of freckles across his high cheekbones. Always a sensitive lad, he lacked the hard, aggressive nature of the rest. So she had become his closest friend, his comforter and protector when his own brothers taunted him. Now, as often before, she sat by him and laid a gentle hand upon his arm.

"Oh, Ferogain," she began, then paused. The noise from

a nearby woodcarver was causing her to shout. "Excuse me," she called to the man, "could you please stop a moment?"

The carver—who was hurrying to finish a large, two-faced wooden head for the impatient druid who had ordered it— was about to reply rather caustically when he recognized the high-king's wife. He snapped his jaw shut, smiled instead, and lowered his hammer and chisel. Then he nudged another worker next to him and pointed out the pair. Soon word was being passed throughout the area.

"Ferogain, Conaire never meant to hurt you," Fionualla said earnestly to the boy. "He is your friend."

"My friend?" he returned bitterly. "There was little enough happening back there to make me think he's a friend to me."

"You can't believe that. Wasn't it Conaire who was always your champion when the others were hard with you? Has he ever abandoned you since? And you talking now as if he were an enemy whom you'd given no cause at all to be angry with you."

"But I had no part in causing that fight!" he protested. "I even tried to stop it!"

"You were fighting with the rest," she reminded him.

"And what else was I to do once it had begun? Stand and watch? It's surely great sport the others would have made of me then."

"What about Conaire. Had you no thought to how he'd feel about it?"

He shrugged. "I don't believe any of us knew it would cause so much anger in him. We've all seen brawls like that all of our lives. Conaire himself has been quick enough to join in more than a few."

"But now he's trying to bring peace!" she explained. "It's a thing he cares about more than you know, maybe. That's why he was so upset at seeing his closest friends in a fight."

Ferogain eyed her thoughtfully for a time, then shook his head slowly, saying carefully, "Maybe we didn't realize how serious he had become. He's brought Ireland together so quickly and, it seemed, so easily. And he's never shown any worry to us, always seeming the same Conaire we knew as children. I didn't think until now that things might be changed."

"They aren't changed," she assured him. "We're all the same friends we were then."

"I wish I could be certain of that," he said in a troubled voice. "If he is serious, things may be hard."

"Hard?" she repeated, puzzled. "What Conaire's doing is for all of Ireland."

"I can't say if the others will see it that way. They're already restless with this peace. If it goes on, things may never be the way they were."

"Do you really think that?" she asked, meeting his eyes with a searching stare.

He sighed and laid a slim hand on the hilt of the longsword that seemed so large against his slender side. "I've waited all my life to be a warrior," he told her gravely. "I've wanted little more than to prove myself to the others. If doing so means I must anger Conaire, how will I ever feel a warrior?"

"There's more to a warrior's courage than skill with a sword," she said. "There's honor and loyalty as well. And there's nothing you must prove to anyone but yourself. Don't let the likes of Maine Morgor lead you into something that isn't by your choice. Do only what *you* believe in."

He didn't answer her at once. He sat silently a moment, then said quietly, "I'd better be getting on now, or I'll lose the others."

She nodded. "All right. I've said what I meant to say." But as they stood, she took both his hands tightly in hers and added, "Remember, Ferogain, if you have any doubts, come talk to me. You know I'll listen to you and help you, as I always have."

She realized, then, that it had become very quiet. She looked about her to discover that all the craftsmen in the area, not wishing to disturb her, had quit their work and were standing respectfully, waiting, trying not to look curious.

"But let's choose a bit more private place next time," she said, laughing, her cheeks flushing with embarrassment.

Ferogain smiled only slightly, then turned and left her. With a feeling of uneasiness, she watched his slender figure disappear into the crowds. Then she set out to find Conaire Mor.

Chapter Nineteen

Solemn Promises

In the center of the dark oak grove, two score of strange beings gathered around a sacred fire. About them in the branches of the trees, a hundred fleshless skulls grinned down on them.

Like a nightmare host the figures were, in that ghastly scene. Some looked more animal than man, and some like long-dead, weathered trees with their gray-white skin and gnarled, bony limbs. All grotesque beings, but no matter how deformed, one thing was similar in all of them: a large head covered with black, lanky hair and set with dark eyes that glowed eerily as from some secret energy.

They were the sons of Calatin, fathered, the tales went, in obscene rituals and alchemical experiments as part of the druid's attempts to harness powers alien to man. It was the rumors of such terrible things which had caused Calatin to be shunned by others of his rank, despised by warriors and nobles of Ireland. Some whispered that the bizarre rites had even caused his being cast out of his native Espan.

But it was the magic he had gained which had helped him to secure his station at Tara, at the high-king's side. And these misshapen sons were a vital part of his sorcery. Combined, they created among them a single force that he could command. It gave him abilities the other druids had no inkling of, could never harness or even understand. And it was for that reason that he kept his monstrous brood hidden away.

Now he strode before them angrily, his voice a low, ominous rumble as he spoke.

"Fools! Arrogant, mindless warriors! Their swords are their only means for acting. They'll never accept Mor's peace or his rule of law. They'll cause more troubles, stir up discontent, destroy all my work."

He stalked back and forth restlessly like a trapped beast or prey. The circle of eyes followed his every move with dark intensity.

"Well, I'll not wait for that!" he rapped out, stopping abruptly, raising a clenched fist in wrath. "I'll not let what happened in Espan happen again here. I'll see all of them destroyed first!"

Then he dropped his hand and turned toward the fire. He stared broodingly into the rising smoke and his voice took on a thoughtful tone.

"But how? That's where the difficulty lies. The high-king won't easily be brought to act against his own foster-brothers and his nobles' sons. Unless . . ." he paused, considering, his gaze resting on a skull with a wide gap between its grinning front teeth, then went on with more force, "unless he has no choice."

He swung back, his cloak swirling out at his sudden move, the fire leaping higher from the gust.

"Of course!" he announced triumphantly, his glinting eyes sweeping around the circle of watchers. "Their own violence will doom them. And more than this few. The others of their slaughterous kind who think the same will be trapped with them. At one stroke we'll be rid of all the troublesome, all the ones whose violent hearts draw them to blood, and we'll show those who remain that warriors have no more power in Ireland. And it'll not be done by my hand. No." He smiled with gloating satisfaction. "No, it shall be the hand and lips of Conaire Mor himself which shall condemn them."

He drew himself erect and lifted his hands high to either side, his gesture taking in the gathering.

"Come around me, my sons," he called, beckoning to them. "There is a new enchantment we must raise."

Like a company of wasted corpses summoned from their graves, the figures rose to their feet and closed in around him.

He stooped to open a heavy chest bound with stout bands of iron. From its depths he lifted vials, uncapping them carefully, tenderly measuring a sprinkle of this, a dollop of that into his palm. At last he replaced the vials, closed the chest, and rose. He held out his hand above the fire, so close it seemed the licking flames must scorch it.

He opened his hand slowly, letting the mixed powders trickle through. The sons raised a low, mourning chant, swaying like trees in an autumn wind, while the druid intoned the spell.

"Powers of sky and wind and sea, spirits of earth and fire and light, come at our call. Give me the magic of the shape-shifters. Give me the form I wish. Come to me now!"

As the powders were sprinkled upon the fire, it flared up higher, in fingers of multicolored flame. They enveloped Calatin's hand, his arm, twining about it with seeming life of their own, like blazing serpents, writhing upward, across his shoulder, dividing into thinner, sinuous lines that crawled across his body up and down, weaving and enmeshing it in a fiery network, thicker and thicker, until the glowing material of the garment of flame hid him completely.

The light rose to a near blinding intensity, flared altogether, then began to dissipate. It seemed such a fierce blaze must have consumed the man within, but the fading glow revealed a form still standing erect there, and the low, slow, triumphant laugh of the druid rose from it to fill the clearing.

The sons of Calatin moved in close around it, again hiding the figure in a solid ring of bodies that still swayed with the soft wailing of their eerie chant.

The wriggling pile of bodies broke apart. Curved wooden sticks flailed madly as a score of boys tried to knock the hurley ball free of the press. One lad staggered back, bleeding across the forehead from the blow of a stick. Three others were on the ground, nursing wounds.

"A tame enough match, that one is," Conaire Mor commented as he and his two young Ulster emissaries moved across the hillside above the hurley field.

Elsewhere on the plain below the dun, warriors from clans in every province and even from Alban competed in the games. Chariot races, tests of skill in the sword and lance, and several other games of hurley were in progress there. At the many pavilions surrounding the playing fields, chieftains and champions greeted the high-king warmly as he passed.

"Three years of careful work it's taken me to unite them all," he told Cormac and Sentanta, gesturing with satisfaction at the assemblage of fighting men. "Three long years of work. No winds have blown about Ireland as much as I have. No bird has pecked at so many tough-husked fruits to get at the tender meat. But tonight a hundred chieftains will gather at Tara to proclaim a peace for all of Ireland!"

Young Cormac raised a skeptical eyebrow at these optimistic

words. He turned away to watch the hurley games. But Sentanta listened intently, raptly, to the high-king. He was unabashedly in awe of Conaire Mor. For despite Mor's youthful looks, his carefree ways, his air of total ease, the force he radiated was more intense than that of any other man Sentanta had ever met.

Ironically, the boy from Ulster was unaware that the same force shone in him, like sunlight masked by the cool gray of a misty dawn. It was part of the kindred spirit that had quickly drawn the two close.

"It was a happy choice of King Conchobar's to send you and Cormac to me," Mor remarked. "But how was it he chose you to accompany his son?"

"It was Cathbad, our ard-druid, who asked that I be sent," Sentanta answered, "along with Conal Carna. They felt that I should see the court at Tara."

"However it was decided, I'm glad to have you here," said Conaire. "You are my hostages, my sign of allegiance from Ulster. But if you choose, I would have both you and Cormac as my friends as well, as Conal Carna is."

Sentanta hesitated. "I owe my sword and my life to Conchobar MacNessa," he said.

"I know that well enough," Mor assured him. "And I'd not think of asking you to make a compromise. But I work for the good of all Ireland, not any single province. Your work would be for her too, as well as for Ulster."

Sentanta met his earnest gaze, then turned with him to look out over the land. It was a bright and quiet day. Clouds teased the sun, capturing it for brief moments, then letting it free to flash broad wedges of golden light across the meadowlands rolling away on every side.

"It is truly the Land of Promise our ancestors sought," Mor said. "And no finer land could there ever be, once we're united in peace and seeking only after its good. I'd have you help me see that happen, if I could."

Sentanta's eyes were glowing with the vision of it, and he felt a fullness in his heart and mind that he had never known.

"When I was a child within my mother's dun," he told the king, "a young woman came to me and told me I must become a part of the happenings in the world beyond our sheltering walls. It was then I heard that you had taken the seat of the ard-rie. Since that time I've been seeking something: to become a warrior. But I've still not felt content. I've known there was something more. And now, here, I feel that I've truly found what I was sent to seek." He looked back to Mor, his expression sure. "So long as you live, I will give my help to you," he said. He lifted a hand to the hilt of his sword.

But Mor's hand dropped to clutch it, restraining him. "You've no need to pledge your sword to me," Mor said. "More than a hostage bound to me, more than a subject sworn to me, I'd have you as a friend, by my side through love."

He lifted a hand and Sentanta clasped it tightly. They stood this way a moment, the two young men making a single, solid figure against the sky, each feeling the strength of the other's grip, feeling the bond that was formed between them there.

Conal Carna came up the hill and joined them.

"Conaire, it's time these two went up to the fortress to settle themselves," he reminded his high-king. "They've had a long journey, and they'll be wanting to clean and rest themselves."

"All right, Conal," Mor agreed. He moved between Sentanta and Cormac, throwing an arm around each. "Come on then!"

They started down the hillside toward the chariots Conal had ordered brought up. On the way they passed a playing field where a group of young warriors were decimating a team of students from Tara's training school.

They paused to watch, and Mor casually observed, "Those lads are getting quite a beating."

"They are that!" Sentanta agreed. "It's not a fair match."

"It's surely not," said Mor.

"One or two good players would even it," said the boy.

"I was thinking that very thing myself," said Mor.

They looked at each other in agreement. Then, grinning broadly, both set about stripping off their capes and harnesses.

"My King, you can't be doing this now?" Conal protested.

"My friend and adviser," Mor responded soothingly, "it's as tightly strung as a colt before its first race that I feel now. I need a bit of a run to calm me. There's time. Be sure of it. Ready, Sentanta?"

"Ready," the boy replied.

While Conal and a grinning Cormac watched, Sentanta and Mor borrowed sticks from the disabled players and called the

teams in to reorganize. The young players weren't happy with
their new opponents. They'd played against their king before.
He was skilled and ruthless on the field and insisted on no
special rules for himself, as he needed none. And the tales of
Sentanta's prowess in the game were already known to many
of them.

Their concerns were well founded. When Fionualla came
upon them, she found that Sentanta and her husband had
soundly defeated the team of warriors, doing nearly all of the
hapless lads some damage in the process.

She shook her head over the devastation as the two beaming
victors came off the field, to the applause of a crowd that had
gathered to watch the unusual contest.

"Imagine the likes of you two playing against those boys,"
she scolded. "And you, Conaire Mor, with your old man's
tricks. Like tormenting babies it must have been for you."

"It wasn't an easy match," he protested. Indeed, from the
condition of Mor and Sentanta, that did seem true. Both were
filthy, their linen tunics grass-stained and soaked with their
sweat.

Mor introduced Fionualla to his new emissaries. Both Sentanta and Cormac were quite taken by her, and she found the
Ulstermen pleasant enough. She was especially intrigued by
young Sentanta, beneath whose boyish looks and charming
manner she sensed a melancholy spirit unusual in one of his
age.

"Now, Conaire, can we be getting up to Tara?" Conal asked
impatiently.

"Yes, Conal," Mor said in a humoring tone. "I think we're
ready now." He looked at Fionualla. "Did you manage to talk
to Ferogain?"

"I did," she replied. "And I think that you and I should
speak a bit more of it."

"A very good idea." He slipped into his harness and cloak,
saying to Conal, "Would you take our friends back to the dun
and see them settled? I'll not be going back yet after all."

Conal moaned but then reluctantly agreed, taking the Ulstermen into his charge. They made their farewells and headed
toward their chariots, leaving Conaire and his wife unaccom-
panied for the first time.

"Where can we talk?" she asked. "I'd like to find more privacy than this." She looked around at the crowded fields and

the gathered spectators, more of whom were now watching the high-king than the games.

"I think I know your feeling," he said, following her gaze. "Why don't we be truly alone? I could welcome a bit of cooling too, after that match. And there's a perfect place where we might do both."

She smiled. "I think I know it."

The little glade was dappled yellow, like a new fawn's coat, by the sunlight filtering through the surrounding trees. Through its center ran a tiny brook which tumbled and laughed over the rocky ground with the abandon of a child.

It was a sheltered place where the high-king and his wife came often to escape their cares and be alone. Now, at a spot where the brook swelled to a pool, Conaire washed himself in the cooling waters and listened thoughtfully as Fionualla, seated on the bank, recounted her talk with Ferogain.

"He's only a boy still," she concluded. "His involvement wasn't by his own choice."

"It's not him I'm concerned with," Conaire replied in a troubled voice. "It's the reason why the others were involved."

"Ferogain says they're restless."

"I expected that in the younger warriors at first," Mor said, "but not in my foster-brothers." Then he shrugged and smiled with new assurance. "Ah, but once they see the benefits of this peace, they'll be content."

Fionualla remembered Ferogain's words and wondered. But she said nothing, not wishing to worry Conaire with it. Not today.

"Come on and swim with me for a while," he invited.

"Won't we be missed?"

"It's soon enough we'll be having to put on that cursed finery, all shining with silver and gold like some tapestry," he said. "I'm in no hurry to dress myself into something other and grander than we are. For now we're alone and nothing but ourselves, as we've not been for many days. Couldn't we let it be that way for just a bit longer?"

In answer she pulled off her long gown and plunged into the pool in a clean, arching dive that brought her up beside him.

They swam together for a time, then came out onto the bank

to lie in the thick grass and let the sun and warm breeze dry
them. He leaned back on his elbows to watch her as she shook
out her long hair, letting it fall loosely over her shoulders and
back.

"Do you know how often in these past days I've wanted
nothing more than to be with you like this?" he said. "If
that birdman of the Sidhe had come to me and asked if I
would give up all I've done for such a thing, I'd gladly have
agreed."

She lay back, rolling on her side to face him, her eyes meeting his in a frank gaze. "And would you give it up if I asked
you now?"

He placed his hand on the soft, high curve of her hip, ran
it slowly down the smooth slope into the valley of her waist.
"You know I'd deny you nothing in my power," he told her
gravely. "But until the task I've undertaken is completed, I'm
bound to it. My only fear has been that you might cease to
understand."

"I've had a fear, too, that has always stayed with me," she
responded. "That Ireland would become everything to you and
leave no place for me."

He dropped his head forward, touching his forehead lightly
to hers. "Fionualla, you are my love and my friend as well,"
he said. "Ireland may hold part of my mind and heart, but I
can't talk with her, sleep against her on a winter's night, or
make her laugh at my foolish tales." He grinned. "And I surely
can't make love to her in the rushes!"

She moved close against him and he held her tightly, feeling
her life in the warmth and pulse of her.

"Will things ever be as they were?" she asked.

"They will, soon. And tonight will bring it closer. That I
promise you."

"Then, for that time, I can share you with Ireland."

He rolled back and she moved up over him. Her hair fell
around him in black, fragrant waves, shutting off his sight of
everything except her glowing face.

Chapter Twenty

The Raid

Maine Morgor slammed his cup down on the rough planks of the table, rattling them with his force. "It's not children we are that he can order about!" he cried angrily.

They were gathered in one of the many of the fair's pavilions which was being used by the visitors as a drinking hall. This one had been largely claimed by the Connachtmen and their friends. They had been there since their encounter with the king, trying to drink away their humiliation and outrage.

Across the table from Morgor one of Mor's foster-brothers, Ferger, sat in a sullen lump, shaking his head ponderously and muttering in a bewildered voice, "I never thought to hear it. I never did. My own comrade, my brother, raised up by my side! The one I slept with, fought with back-to-back, shared every meal with. To hear him ordering me not to be fighting!"

"Right along I've been telling you this would come, haven't I?" Morgor said sharply. "You wouldn't believe me. But maybe now you will." He drained his cup, then glared around the table at the others. His voice was bitter. "He's tamed every king and chieftain with his promises of wealth. Why, he's even used that sly aunt Meave of his to pull the teeth of my own father—my father! That old wolf! Your 'brother' has cunningly stolen the freedom from all of us. And you'll be made to come at his call, same as the rest!"

"Morgor, it's drunk and ravin' that you are!" said Fergel, eldest of Mor's foster-brothers.

"And what is there left for us to do but drink?" the dark Connachtman answered.

He seized the leather pitcher to refill his cup but found it empty. Climbing with great effort to his feet, he called out, "More ale here! Let's have more ale here!"

"No more of it for me," said Lomna Druth, struggling vainly to lift his head from the ale-soaked wood.

"Ah, man, Conaire's not taking anything away," Fergel told Morgor. "He was only stopping our fighting for the look of things. For this great gathering tonight. He's not really meaning to hold us to it."

"And, Mor or not, it was wrong to be fighting at the fair," Ferogain added in a chiding tone.

"You just don't see it yet, do you, boy!" Morgor said harshly, leaning over the young warrior. "Your fine high-king will see all fighting banned once his peace is formally declared. Disputes will be decided by his druids instead of by courage and skill with a good blade!" He leaned closer, his face thrust near Ferogain's, delivering his words like hard blows. "There'll be no more raiding, no individual challenges, no feuding between separate tuaths or clans." He pulled erect and shouted at them all, "By the Raven's Bloody Maw, what will be left to us then?"

"And him never letting on to us at all," Ferger said, sinking deeper into his sodden despair. "All the time playing and hunting and making such great show of us as if we were his friends. And all the time planning to turn against us."

"He's not against us," Ferogain tried to explain. "He's for the good of Ireland. He's only wanting to see her prosperous and strong."

"But where will her strength be once her warriors have been left to rot away?" Morgor countered.

"He can't mean to do that!" Fergel persisted. But there was now a note of doubt in his voice, and he added, "I mean, even if he were to try, he'd see quick enough that we'd never accept it."

"How would he see? Will you challenge him? Or you? Or you?" Morgor ran his gaze about the table, but no one met his eyes. "Or maybe you, Ferogain," he looked at the boy, "who've never been on a raid, never matched iron with another, and now are left without the chance to prove yourself a man!"

When none of them replied, he gave a short, derisive laugh and dropped down heavily on the seat.

"I thought that'd be the way of it. So, we'll just let him make geldings of us, and we'll grow tame and fat while the harness rusts upon our backs."

"And a terrible, terrible thing it is that we'll have no glorious causes left to be dying for," Lomna Druth sleepily observed. "We'll all die in our beds, full, warm, and with our heads. Oh, how, how sad."

Morgor gave the drunken Fool a look of chill disdain. Then,

in frustration, he dropped his head forward onto his arms, crying despairingly, "By all the gods, just get me some more ale!"

"Once, the young men of Ireland had more to do than play at fairs and drink and whine like beaten pups," said a gruff, deliberate voice.

It came from the far end of the long table. There, a lone figure, large and shapeless within a heavy cloak, had sat over a cup of ale, unnoticed by the rest. But now they all looked toward him.

"And who are you, stranger, to be speaking so to the likes of ourselves?" Morgor challenged. "It's chieftains' blood we have in us. Champions' blood."

Slowly the man turned his head toward them. His thatch of dark hair was stiffened with lime wash, in the old warrior's style, and bristled about his head. Great gray mustaches flared below his thick nose, and sharp eyes glared upon them from a face deeply creased by time, as water cuts channels in a rough hillside.

The man rose, levering his ponderous form upright. It bulked even larger then. And though the wide shoulders were rounded a bit by the weight of age, he was still a broad and impressive figure.

"I am a man who has seen fighting all his life," he answered, his voice the ominous rumble of distant thunder. "From the lands in the east to the rim of the world I've traveled and met fighting men. But never have I met those less worthy of the name than you."

Morgor kicked back his stool angrily as he jumped to his feet. "Watch out, old man," he warned. "We're in no temper to take insults from the likes of you."

"Don't make threats to me, boy!" the man returned. "Not after the pitiful show you made today! Sit down!"

The voice was quiet, but the dark eyes behind the shaggy, overhanging brows flared with an energy that struck through Morgor like a white-hot iron pellet. Suddenly afraid of the power in this strange, grim warrior, Morgor sat back down without protest.

The warrior's gaze flicked over the others then, and they each felt his power seize them, drawing all their attention to him as he spoke.

"There's no courage in any of you if you let this man who says he is ard-rie give you such commands," he told them, the massive outrage in his voice like a hot current surging into them, flooding them. "The right of a warrior of Ireland to battle and raid and duel is as old as the clans themselves. It was the pleasure of your fathers and grandfathers before you. It is not for Conaire Mor or any man to deny it!"

"He is our high-king!" Fergel told him.

"If he forces you to deny the spirit that makes a warrior, he severs all bonds of loyalty with you," came the hard reply.

"He is our friend as well!" Ferogain protested.

"If he means to take your freedom from you, he is no friend, but an enemy of Ireland." There was no compromise in the rumbling voice.

"Conaire would never do that—never betray us—would he?" the now uncertain Fergel argued weakly.

"Not if you act! Prove to him that he is wrong, if you dare. Then see what he will do. Show him where the warrior's spirit, the true spirit of Ireland, really lies. You must be free! Prove to him that you'll tolerate nothing else."

He picked up a large flagon of bronze whose handle was a strange, sinuous, leaping beast and moved toward them. His voice became ever more forceful, ever more compelling, as he went on.

"You can't allow the glories to be lost or you are lost yourselves. Remember what they are. Remember! Good ponies racing in your chariot traces. The high-arching flight of a balanced spear. Sleeping with the weight of a fine sword in your hand and a loyal comrade always at your back. Challenging your enemy, naked but for your blade and shield, taunting him to single combat, testing yourself against his strength and skill. And feeling the victory, his hot blood steaming on your sword, the keening of his women in your ears, the pounding heat of it flooding you like the finest ale filling you up! Remember it! Feel it!"

They did feel it, fully caught up by his words as they had never been even by those of the greatest of high-bards. He moved around the table, filling their cups with a strange, dark, pungent ale from his own flagon as his voice rolled on.

They drank and they listened raptly as he related ever more vivid tales of champions and gods of glorious ancient days. His voice shaped the air about them into images of battles and heroic deeds where massive figures moved in a golden haze that lifted to surround them. The blood surged hotly in them, and the battle glow rose in their faces as his grand visions filled their young minds.

"Remember," he exhorted again, now himself only a massive shadow in the shining mist. "Remember and rise from your weakness and show your discontent to this ard-rie. Vex him in his peace. Dare him to act. See what he will do."

And the warriors, fired by their need, responded.

"We'll not give up our freedom!" Fergel cried with great ardor.

"We'll repay his humiliation of us," Morgor promised. "We'll find a herd and raid it, just for sport, as our own fathers did."

"I know the one," Ferger told them excitedly. "A rich herd in a tuath north of here that has long defied our clan. It's very close."

"Too close," Fergel said. "It's dangerous."

"That will only add more spice to the deed," Morgor replied. "Let's strike there now!"

A roar of approval went up from the others at this.

Ferogain listened and watched with growing confusion. Was it the drink that had thrown this clinging haze about him? Had it raised in him this agonizing desire to fight?

But something else within him still held him back: his loyalty to Mor, recalled by Fionualla's words. He struggled to hold on to this as it faded away in the enveloping mist.

"We can't do it!" he managed to protest. "We're bound to Conaire!"

"Why not, boy?" asked Ferger. "Think of the sport! It's your chance to prove yourself a warrior!"

"And Conaire won't stop us," added Fergel. "You'll see. He'll not do anything against us!"

The faces were all close around him now, red, monstrous, glowing faces in the mist, urging, demanding, confusing him more.

"No! No!" he shouted, trying to force them back, force back the clutching tendrils of this awful haze.

"Boy, will you ever be a man?" Morgor said cruelly. "Or is it too frightened that you are?"

"He's not frightened," a voice said defensively. He thought it was the old warrior's voice, but it had now taken on a soothing tone. An enormous, black figure pushed back the others and moved to his side.

"He is ready to fight," the voice said, so assured, so friendly.

A voice to trust. "He wants to fight. He knows he must prove himself. He needs only the spark to kindle him to flame. Ferogain, here is your spark."

A light flared suddenly in the haze. A shining blade was before him, fire glinting along its cutting edge. He lifted a hand and gripped the hilt. At once energy flowed from it, streaming into him and through him, spreading out to tingle across his skin.

"See, feel, and know what you must do," the voice urged him. "Your chance is now!"

The mists swirling about him were alive with sounds and movements. Spear points flickered light. A chariot swept by, nearly striking him. There were running men, shouts, screams, the clang of weapons all around. Then, a man before him, so close Ferogain could hear his harsh breathing, see the sweat, like tiny points of light, beaded across his upper lip, and the nicks in the edge of the longsword already sweeping toward him in a savage cut.

He parried and attacked, a battle madness lending him the strength to drive back his opponent and swing home a hard, downward blow.

And, in that instant, the shrouding mists were gone.

Gripped by a sudden horror, Ferogain realized he faced no figure of a dream, but a real man whose blood now spurted past the blade driven deeply into his neck and chest.

The lad stood frozen, staring, as the man fell back, his weight wrenching the buried weapon from Ferogain's hand.

The lad stared wildly around him, seeing the others of his company in combats of their own. Several still figures and a shattered war car littered the ground between himself and the bunched cattle herd. He saw, and he remembered everything clearly—leaving the fair, raiding the herd, encountering the party of defending warriors. He knew that it had all happened, that it was happening now!

A chariot rolled up beside him and stopped. "Well, boy, you did it!" a voice called heartily.

He looked around into the dead gaze of a severed head. The eyes had rolled upward to show the whites. The mouth hung fully open, and blood still dripped from the neck. It was dangling over the chariot's side by its long hair, grasped by Maine Morgor, who stood in the car, a sword in his other hand, grinning triumphantly down on Ferogain.

"Do you feel it now?" he asked. He spoke quickly, his voice

pitched high, his eyes glowing brightly as if with fever. "By all the gods my clan swears by, there's no feeling like the excitement gripping me. It pounds in my ears like a *tiompan!* We've taken the lot of them, and it was glorious! Glorious!"

"No! No! It's wrong!" Ferogain shouted. "It shouldn't have happened!"

"It's no matter how it happened," Morgor shot back. "We're in it now!"

"But it's wrong!" Ferogain cried again, his young face twisted in anguish. "We have to tell Conaire!"

Morgor's face went cold. He dropped the severed head and jumped from the chariot, seizing Ferogain roughly by his cloak, jerking him close. "Listen, boy," he snarled, "it's begun now, and you're a part of it! If you mean to survive, you've no choice but to stay with the rest of us!"

He leaned down and, planting a foot on the fallen man's chest, wrenched the lad's blade free. He thrust it into Ferogain's hands. "That's blood you've got on you now!" he said. "Remember it! Go on with the others and make certain that we've left no one alive!"

He pushed the dazed lad away from him and stooped to lift his gruesome prize from the blood-soaked ground.

Chapter Twenty-one

The Peace

The boar's head thumped down onto the planks of the table. But this stuffed and steaming delicacy was waved away by Conaire Mor.

The servant sighed, lifted the huge, laden platter with an effort, and moved it down the long table. There, others of the high-king's company voraciously attacked it, battling over tender bits of snout and tongue and eyes.

Mor himself, who had little food and less drink before him, looked around the hall of Tara an Rie at his banquet of state. At the tables within the ring of outer compartments, entourages from the provinces of Ireland were gathered: all province kings—save aloof Conchobar and embattled Aileel—many clan chieftains, great champions, ard-druids, and the highest ranks of bards. And in the area between this ring and the central fire pit, hundreds of men of lesser rank crowded scores of other tables.

"It is going very well, my King," remarked Conal Carna, speaking loudly to be heard above the din of merrymaking in the vast hall. The Ulster champion, who sat at Mor's right hand, had noted the young ruler's constant, anxious surveys of the crowd. "Be at ease. You've had nothing yourself."

"I want no bloated belly or head swimming with ale to trouble me this night," Mor replied. Then he gave his friend a little smile. "And I'll not hide from you that I do feel my spirit cowering back within me just a bit at the vastness of what I've created here."

"I understand, Conaire. It is a great thing you've taken upon yourself to do. But it has worked. Look at them." A tone of amazement came into the once cynical champion's voice as he gazed about. "I've seen no quarrels, no signs of rivalry. Why, it's like they're one great clan tonight. I've never seen the like."

It was the truth Conal spoke to his king. There was an air of camaraderie pervading the hall, so strong it could almost be felt, like a fine mead in the blood, or a warm fire on an autumn's night.

The feasting was now at its height. The sounds of revelry, spiced by the festive occasion and by the stimulating day's activities at the fair, filled the hall. There was much exuberant talk, much boasting of great feats and bragging of great wagers won. They exchanged new jokes and tales among clansmen from widely distant parts of Ireland—the bright colors of their cloaks not collected into solid patches this night, but blended in one shifting, speckled sea.

Conaire looked down on this from his raised table and felt the irritating sensation of bird's wings fluttering within his chest give way to a calmer sense of satisfaction mingled with relief. This blending of the colors of the clans was to him the greatest sign of his success. These men who had for so many years killed one another, often for so little as the difference in the color of their cloaks, did indeed seem to be mingling peacefully, even thriving. Was all his careful work, all his preparation, really coming to fruition here?

He looked around at his own table. There the province hostages—more diplomatically called "emissaries" now—feasted and talked with one another and with the highest-ranking bards and druids.

"Our guests seem content as well," he remarked. He noted Sentanta laughing with a young chieftain of Munster, and Cormac regaling others with a bawdy tale.

"All but our lads from Connacht," Conal replied, shaking his head.

The three Maines were sitting sullenly, Morgor glaring around him at the company with obvious distaste at being forced to rub his elbows against theirs at table.

"It's a great trouble they've been since they came here," the champion went on. "I wonder at Aileel's siring a spoiled lot like that."

"Aileel's had many troubles these last years," the high-king reminded him. "Just be blessing my fine aunt Meave that they are here, and that we have Connacht's support. And bless good Danu as well."

"True enough," Conal agreed, still with some reservation in his tone. "But I'll keep close watch on those three all the same. Trouble ripples out from them like from a pebble dropped in a still pond. Why, look what they've already brought your brothers to."

As he gazed on the sons of Donn Dessa, ranged to the left of Conal Carna, Mor felt a pang of concern. Like the three Maines, they stared ahead glumly, nearly immobile, partaking of food and drink in only a listless way. Even rotund Lomna Druth seemed unable to eat and sagged at his place as if ready to pitch forward into his bowl of broth.

"They seem unnaturally sullen tonight," Mor said, and felt now the prick of a new irritation. "Still angry over my scolding are they? This is a fine time for that!"

"No," Conal said. "Too much ale, I'd say." He looked toward young Ferogain, who sat slumped beside him, bleary eyes staring into the dark red-brown pool of ale within his cup. "What's wrong, boy?" he asked. "Feeling the drink?"

"Let me alone," the boy all but snarled in return.

Conal sat back, surprised by the hostility. But Mor's temper flared. He leaned across the champion, and spoke in a low but intense voice.

"You'll not speak to him that way, insolent pup. Had too much drink, is it? Well, that's no excuse. Not today. You know how important this is to me, yet you violate my trust at the fair, and now you come here like this, to be shaming me before the whole company! You're no child. You should know how to act. Look at that young lad of Ulster!"

Ferogain turned his gaze toward Sentanta, so lively and laughing, so free of gnawing cares and bloody visions in his ale cup. Once he had been like that boy, Ferogain thought resentfully. Now his one act had cut him off from that life and from Conaire Mor. His stomach turned and he was nearly sick. He fought it back, masking the despair with cold scorn.

"Make *him* your brother then, and let us free of your nagging," he spat out.

"Enough!" a now outraged Mor said sharply, causing eyes to turn to them, especially those of Calatin, who sat far down the table. He watched with immense interest as the high-king went on, "I want nothing else disturbing this night. You'll give up your drinking, as will the others."

In reply Ferogain raised his cup and, fighting back revulsion, took a deep draft, shooting Mor a glare of defiance over the rim.

"Why, you . . ." Mor began, lifting a clenching fist from the table.

"Enough," Conal said, putting a hand upon Mor's arm and speaking urgently. "Not here, my King. Not now."

The cooling waters of reason washed across the heat of rage. The king subsided, nodding in agreement, sitting back to look out at the company, forcing a pleasant smile.

Calatin hid his own smile of satisfaction, but Morgor grinned openly and with malicious glee at the boy's successful show of rebellion.

Sentanta and Cormac had noted the little altercation too. The boy shook his head with righteous disapproval. "It's too bad that the high-king's own brother should be acting so," he commented to his fellow Ulsterman.

"It's those Maines' doing, I'll wager," said Cormac. "Look at the weasely smirk on old Morgor there. A bad lot they are, I've heard. Wild enough to lead country-bred lads like the king's brothers astray."

"They shouldn't be allowed to cause the high-king hardship," Sentanta said indignantly. "Why, a man like Conaire Mor . . ."

"Is still just a man, my friend," Cormac said in the gently lecturing tone of the worldly-wise elder. "Don't be forgetting that. And don't let your awe of him or of this place blind you. You're here to learn about such things, remember? Look at them fully, and know their truth. Stop gawking about at it all as if you were in some palace of the Sidhe. It's quite embarrassing."

Sentanta realized that Cormac's cautioning was a fair and a sensible one. Since coming to grand Tara he *had* felt a child again, marveling at the sights, recalling the golden legends, as if it were some dream.

"Just keep it in your head that Tara is only a place," Cormac went on, as if reading his thoughts, "and Conaire Mor only another king."

"I understand you, Cormac," Sentanta told him. "But I still believe he's more than that."

"Do you?" the other said in a sardonic tone. "Well, I thought the same thing about my father once."

"Cormac, look around you," the boy told him. "Doesn't this prove anything?"

"Nothing," his skeptical friend replied. "Tailteen's always been a time of fellowship. It's when they leave here that the test will come. A warrior can put aside his sword for a time, but not the iron in his blood. The rivalries and the fighting spirits of Ireland are as old as her green hills."

"And you think we can't forget them?" Sentanta asked earnestly.

Cormac met his eye with one equally serious. "Do we want to? Maybe that's the question you should ask."

Sentanta wasn't certain how to reply to that, but there was no further time for arguing. The feasting was at an end, the immense platters of remains being carried away. At the main table, Mor was rising to his feet. Clearly, he meant to address the company. The talk faded as all eyes turned toward him.

"My friends," he said in a calm but powerful voice that echoed across the hall, "we are met here on the occasion of Tailteen's final night. But tonight we are also met on a greater occasion yet. For from this time, the spirit of cooperation, of peace, and of plenty will extend throughout all the days, and into every corner of our Ireland!"

A great roar of acclamation greeted this, filling up the vast space, booming like thunder.

"You all have a right to cheer," he told them, "for it is you—you together—who have brought this peace. For once in many years all of the provinces, the tuaths, and the clans of Ireland are joined. Each king and chieftain has given his allegiance and his signs of support to Tara.

"So from now on, it is not the sword but the arbiter of law who will prevail. From this night forward, all clan rivalries, disputes, feuds, conflicts over land or herds or power will be decided here, in Tara's hall, before myself and a court of our learned men. A code of laws more broad and more specific than ever before will be enforced. It will ensure us all a lasting peace. No longer will the flower of our fighting men be wasting one another's lives. No longer will our sod be drenched in our own people's blood.

"My friends, we now face a world grown new, filled with both promise and threat that we can face together. Our children will grow up without violence or fear, and—Danu grant—may one day live their lives never knowing the weight of a sword, or the sight of enemies' heads upon the stakes."

For young Ferogain, this raised a dreadful image of the bloody raid. All the words of Mor were torture, wrenching painfully at his insides. He saw the wall dividing him from Mor—his closest friend, protector, brother—soaring higher. He longed for some escape from this nightmare.

The other sons of Donn Dessa, while not in such great agony as he, clearly also found the speech a distressing one, sinking further into their sullenness. And the three Maines only glowered all the more.

The rest of the audience, however, was totally rapt. Mor's words rang with his authority, his optimism, his pride. They held the audience, both in mind and heart. That Sidhe-given power surged in him again, giving his speech the quality of a lightning storm, charging the vast room's atmosphere.

Then, in an instant, that atmosphere changed.

A sound arose outside, thundering around the peaked roof with great force, rattling the shakes. The fire and torch flames fluttered violently. Their light faded. A great darkness swept into the hall from the doorway, circling around the central pit, sweeping above the heads of the diners, drawing about them the cloying, pungent scent of damp earth and chill skies and decaying flesh. A low, keening wail filled the room.

Mor looked up as the black shadow swept low over his head. He could smell the foul-sweet carrion breath of it, see the blood-tinged curve of beak, the glinting black eyes, and the wide-swept wings of an enormous bird.

"The Morrigan!" someone cried in shock, and gasps of terror went up around the room.

It swept around again in a great, slow, graceful turn, covering them once more with its cloak of shadow and its stench of death. Then it was gone as swiftly as it had come, drawing its darkness, winds, wailing, and scent out the doors and into the night. The flames regained their full and steady glow, refilling the space with light.

The room's silence exploded in a sudden bedlam of excited talk. Tara's druids fell into immediate and heated discussion of the phenomenon.

"What does it mean?" asked Sentanta, who yet knew little of the meaning of such things.

"Nothing good, I can surely tell you that!" Cormac answered. "For the Bloody Raven to appear means battle and death for certain. Not the finest omen for our high-king's new world of peace."

"And now what's happening?" Sentanta asked, turning toward a fresh source of tumult at the main doors.

Men were moving in. Around them, the feasters were rising at their tables, exclaiming at what they saw. Sentanta and the others on the king's dais rose too.

Mor, reanimated by this new development, strained futilely to see above the bobbing heads. "What is it? What's happening?" he shouted across the uproar in frustration. "Give way there. Let me see!"

The command was heard. The crowd slowly pulled away. Figures moved out into the open area about the central hearth where all could see.

There was a collective expression of dismay from the gathering. Surrounded and supported by a trio of keening women stood a warrior, his body streaked with the blood of a dozen wounds. One arm hung useless, and one eye was closed by clotted gore. He clutched the shattered haft of a spear in one hand, using it as a crutch. The women released him and he stood, if unsteadily. They sidled back into the crowd.

"What is this?" Mor asked him. "What clan are you?"

"My clan?" The warrior laughed bitterly, then grimaced with pain. "My King, I have no clansmen left. They are all dead. Our herd . . . it was raided. We took arms and rode to save it. But we were destroyed. All our fighting men . . . slaughtered . . . slaughtered. Only I survived. Left . . . for dead. These women found me . . . brought me . . . here."

He tottered. A score of men rushed in to help, easing him down. But his head lolled back limply, his one eye staring up.

A warrior looked up toward Conaire Mor. "He is dead, my King."

Ferogain looked away, his face tight with his pain. How could his crime have come to haunt him here?

"Now we know what the Morrigan's visit to us was foretelling," Cormac said grimly.

"What clan is he?" someone called. "Who knows him? Or his colors?"

"Ask the women," another suggested.

There was a stirring in the crowd as all looked around for them.

"They've gone!" came an astonished shout. "They've just vanished from the house!"

"It's a terrible thing," Sentanta said, shaking his head.

"But maybe no more than we should have expected," Cormac said knowingly. "Tonight—tomorrow—sometime." He nodded toward the king. "And so should he have."

Down the table, Conal Carna had also looked to Mor. "Conaire," he said, and then, more urgently, "my High-King!"

But Mor wasn't listening. He was unmoving, staring at the dead man's bloody face, his own a mask of dismay and bewilderment.

Chapter Twenty-two

Meave and Aileel

The ominous form that had wheeled about the great hall of Tara flew out from the high dun and headed west.

It soared through the night, the sharp black sweep of its broad wings slicing through the softer black garment of the sky. But soon dawn was rising just behind it, the light first seeping up from the world's curved ridge to dilute the purity of the dark, then rays shooting outward like gold spears meant to bring down the soaring omen of doom.

The Morrigan flapped ahead of it, the immense wings pumping with a greater urgency, the lean, sleek body straining, seeming to race to stay ahead of the pursuing day. But it was a race even this powerful being could not win. Soon the ground below grew lighter, black giving way to gray, then to gray-green faintly glowing with the light frost of a chill fall dawn. Objects appeared. Hills, lakes, and forests could be defined. The varied countryside of Ireland became gradually visible, sliding by beneath the rushing bird.

At last the rays of the lifting sun dropped low enough to strike the body of the creature. It fired the glossy feathers to a blue-black glow, startling against the brilliant pale blue of the brightening sky. Then the rim of the ruddy sun popped above the far horizon, and more light flooded across the landscape.

The bird of death banked steeply and began to spiral down. The dawn had caught it, but its goal was here. Below, garishly illumined by the sun, was the thing whose sounds and scent —a clarion call that no mortal might hear—had drawn the Bloody Raven across the whole of Ireland: another scene of death, a field of desperate battle.

It was above the camp of Aileel and the Connacht host that the black cloak of the Morrigan's wings now glided. A large raiding party of the Firbolgs had struck it before dawn, smashing through its perimeter at one side and swiftly penetrating deeply into the camp itself.

Now the still-groggy Connachtmen, wrenched from sleep to reach blindly for weapons, were trying to mount resistance in the avenues.

"My King!" cried an urgent voice.

Aileel awoke and sat up. The interior of his hut was still dark, the form above him a vague shadow leaning down. He shook his head irritably and stared with squinted eyes. The face of a young, disheveled warrior slowly grew more clear, as if surfacing from great depths. And sounds came clearer too: shouts and screams and the clattering of arms.

"My King," the lad blurted, "the Firbolgs have attacked in great numbers. They have broken into camp on the west."

"By the gods!" Aileel cried. "Meave!"

He cast aside his blanket and leaped to his feet. He was clad only in a light tunic, but took no time for dressing. Grabbing his shield and spear, he plunged from the hut into the cold fall morning.

From the high ground he could see the area under attack. There was a confused milling of warriors. Smoke was rising in several places. The area in which Meave had been camped was indeed the scene of a wild battle.

"Gather men and join me, quickly!" he ordered the warrior and then sprinted away.

Lewy MacNeesh, just awakened himself and rising from his fire near Aileel's quarters, looked up to see his king speeding recklessly off.

"Oh, no!" moaned the young champion, grabbing his own weapons.

In the meantime, Aileel was plunging into the fray. The area was a chaos of men battling savagely in the camp's streets and stalls. Scores of Connachtmen, caught by surprise, lay already dead or wounded. The rest were now putting up a courageous resistance against much greater numbers. The rampaging Firbolgs were taking full advantage of their position. What they couldn't smash they were setting afire. A haze of smoke was filling the still morning air.

Ahead was Meave's campsite. A crowd of Firbolgs surrounded something like a pack of hounds about a trapped boar. He hurled himself upon them, his sword and shield swinging out to clear a path.

The Firbolgs, surprised by his fierce attack, gave way. Within their circle he found an embattled Meave, like him unshod and clad only in a light tunic, her unbound hair like a flame in the morning light, her lithe body straining as she swung out with sword and lance to keep her foes at bay.

He moved to her side. Even in her desperate state, she flashed him a smile of welcome. Then the savage Firbolg warriors were closing in again.

The two fought back to back in the cool and hazy dawn, adding to the clouds with the steaming breath of their labors, and swords smoking with hot blood, and the white vapor rising from the wounds of those who piled up around them.

The attackers began to lose heart against such a lethal pair. Their numbers thinned. Then Aileel's gaze fell upon what seemed a gap in the circling wall of enemies—a chance to break free.

"Here, Meave! This way!" he shouted to her and plunged into the gap.

Meave stared after him in disbelief. For what he had taken to be a break in the circle of men only led into an even greater maelstrom of flashing weapons, the confusion of battling men, the red blaze of flaming stalls.

"Aileel! No!" she cried, plunging after him.

He had already managed to move forward some paces without real resistance, his sword swinging before him. But then a huge, shaggy-haired warrior loomed up on his left, lifting an immense ax and swinging out.

Meave, moving up behind, was horrified to see Aileel take no offensive action. He seemed not even to be aware of the man plunging in at him, but gazed intently ahead, eyes narrowed as if concentrated wholly on some danger there.

She leaped forward. The short jabbing lance in her hand swept up and was fired out in a desperate throw.

The throw came too quickly and the Firbolg moved too fast. The spear went wide, missing his chest, but tearing through the flesh of one of his his upper arms. It was not enough to stop the blow, but the man's flinch of pain diverted the falling ax's course slightly. Instead of cleaving through Aileel's shoulder, its keen, leading edge merely slipped along his breast, slicing a shallow groove from shoulder bone to belly.

Aileel grunted with pain and surprise, staggered sideways, and crashed down, lying momentarily stunned and helpless. The Firbolg instantly moved upon him. But before he could lift his ax again, Meave was closing. He wheeled toward her, startled for a moment to see a young, comely, and nearly naked woman, her great mane of hair billowing out behind her as she flew toward him through the haze.

She used his surprise to strike, giving him no chance. She dived forward, holding her sword out before her in both hands. It slammed into his belly just below the ribs, her whole weight driving it deep. He exhaled in a great explosion, and his upper body jerked forward into a bow.

Her sword's hilt touched his stomach. The matted fleece of his sheepskin jerkin pressed against her hands. She could smell the bitterness of his sweat, see his stringy, thinning hair so close before her eyes.

She started to pull back. But one of his hands lifted suddenly and gripped her wrist. It was a massive hand. The grip was viselike, the death grip of superhuman strength. She could not break it. Slowly, his massive head lifted. She could see his face, twisted as he fought the pain. His eyes met hers. Deep, red-brown eyes looked not hatefully but curiously into hers, as if wondering about the one who had slain him. Then a ghastly smile of both savagery and satisfaction stretched his wide mouth. His other hand lifted his ax to strike a final blow in just revenge.

She fought to pull away, but had no luck. No mortal effort could break the strength of one already dead. She watched the ax rise, its curved blade glinting in a ray of morning sun.

A sword flashed down through the shaft of light, the keen edge of its blade striking across the Firbolg's forearm, severing it in one powerful blow. Still tightly clutching the ax, it thudded to the ground.

The added pain made no impression on the face of the dying man. He seemed only disappointed that he could not complete that final swing. Then his eyes rolled upward and he collapsed limply to the sod at Meave's feet.

It was Lewy MacNeesh who had struck the saving blow. He and a hastily assembled band of warriors had come at last into the fray, fighting to her side.

Around them the Firbolgs were retreating, their surprise raid, now met in force, prudently abandoned.

She ran to Aileel, who was sitting up, a hand to his breast, grimacing. He looked to be more angry than in pain.

"Are you all right?" she asked.

"Only enraged at myself," he growled. "Stupid to let him come on me like that. Yes! I'm all right!"

He pushed aside her helping hand and clambered up. But he was bleeding heavily from the long slash across his breast.

"No!" she said fiercely, moving in and gripping his elbow. "You need attention for that."

"I will not," he told her. "The men . . ."

"Your men needn't know of your wound," she said firmly. "I'll see to it myself. Or would you rather they see you bleed to death before them?"

At that he wavered.

"I'll see they don't know," she said more insistently. "Go back to your hut now."

"The Firbolgs . . ." he began.

"They are gone, my King," Lewy said as he came up beside them.

Meave noted his quick, evaluating eye taking in the wound and the situation at once, though his face remained expressionless.

"They did the damage they wished," he went on. "I can see to the righting of things here. There's little to do."

Around them, men were already busy dousing the fires and tending to the wounded.

"Very well," Aileel agreed. He was looking suddenly pale, and it was clear that, after the first shock, he was feeling the effects of the wound. He turned back toward the hut.

"You'll see to him?" Lewy asked anxiously.

Meave smiled assuringly. "Be certain I will."

She stayed close beside Aileel on the way to his hut, ready to support him. But his pride kept him erect and striding stolidly until he came through the door. Then he sagged, and she helped ease him to the low pallet.

Meave fetched hot water and cloths. She stripped his tunic from him and bathed the edges of the cut, then pressed a pad upon it to stanch the red flow.

"You saved me," he told her as she worked. "I was a fool."

"He came at you from behind," she glibly lied. "You could not have seen."

"A good warrior—"

"No one but a good warrior could have fought to my side," she interrupted. "It was you who saved us. You who held them back."

"With help from you," he said, pausing, then smiling. "But . . . we did fight well together, didn't we?" He lifted a hand to her arm.

"We did that," she said, smiling too and putting her hand on his. "Together, I say we cannot be beaten."

"Maybe," he agreed, but more gravely. "Maybe you are right." He considered, then went on somewhat hesitantly. "Meave . . . Meave, I am sorry about what I said to you at Cruchane. I didn't mean to hurt you then."

"I know," she said soothingly. "Think no more of it."

"But I want you to know . . ." he told her with greater urgency, "I still feel a love for you, as you guessed I did. It's only that . . . now . . ."

"Now. I know. The war."

"Aye. This cursed war," he said bitterly. He met her eyes, so close above his, holding her gaze, his voice intense. "But I could wish for more. I could wish that after this is ended— great Dagda granting our victory—once Connacht has been made strong again . . . that you . . . you could . . ."

"Could be your wife, my King?" she finished and smiled most tenderly. "I'd want nothing more than that. To be at your side. To help you build Connacht again."

This seemed to comfort him. His face relaxed, and his eyes closed as he fell into a sleep.

With great gentleness she bound the pad tightly against his wound to close it. As she did, gazing down at his face, she remarked how much more frail, how much more aged he looked here, with the facade of rule and the strength of pride gone in sleep.

She leaned over him and kissed him softly upon his lips. Then she rose and quietly made her way from the hut.

She found Lewy MacNeesh waiting just outside, his expression one of great concern.

"I brought your sword," he said, clearly by way of excuse.

"I thank you," she said, taking the weapon. She looked from its bloodstained blade to her own arms, splattered elbow-high with drying red-brown gore. "You'll not mind if I wash myself now?" she asked.

She moved to a nearby fire where a caldron of water was on the boil. Setting down her weapon, she took up a ladle to transfer some of the steaming liquid to a large copper washing basin. She knelt before it, splashing the water up her arms to wash away the blood, turning the clear contents of the basin to bright pink.

Lewy moved up beside her, crouching to watch her work so matter-of-factly at this grisly task. He wondered at the great coolness, the great control this young woman had.

He watched her, considering. She was aware of his gaze, sensed his indecision, guessed his need to speak. She waited, knowing it would come.

"He would have died for you, you know," he finally stated flatly.

"I know." She paused and turned her head to fix him with a searching eye. This was only leading to something else.

Lewy grew shy, hesitant under the bold gaze. But he forced himself on. "He . . . must love you a great deal—more than life—to take such a risk. I . . . I wonder if you understand that?"

"I do," she said calmly, continuing her wash.

"Do you?" He moved closer, speaking more urgently. "I don't know. But I must make you understand. I've no choice now. You must know all of it. You must help and protect him with the rest of us. Keep him from things like today."

"From leaving your care, you mean?" she asked. She stopped

washing again to look at him, adding bluntly, "And how long has his eyesight been failing him?"

At first startled by the question, he recovered quickly, smiling in acceptance. "So," he said, "you are surely a most clever woman. Just how did you know?"

"I first suspected in that ambush," she replied. "He should certainly have seen it. And there've been other times since then. But it was today that proved it finally." She eyed him with new interest. "And you, Lewy—you are most loyal to protect him. Other warriors might have challenged him instead."

"He is a great man and has done great things, and still does, for all his weakness," Lewy said stoutly. Then he added with a grin, "And there are few who could yet beat him in a single combat, face to face." Then he turned serious again, moving yet closer to speak in most confidential tones. "But, Meave, will you keep our secret as well? Your ties to Mor . . ."

"You know what I promised Aileel about Mor," she said with great earnestness. "And I will keep to it. You say Aileel loves me. Well, I love him as well. And I esteem him for the same things as you do." She put her hand, hot and wet but now clean of blood, upon his own, clenching it hard as she held his gaze. "Lewy MacNeesh, I vow to you now that as long as I have strength to help, I will do all I can to see that he stays king!"

He saw the truth of her words in her straightforward gaze, and he nodded.

"But what now, Meave?" he asked. "How badly wounded is he?"

"He'll heal. But he'll be weak for some days," she answered, rising from the basin, tipping out its blood-tinged water onto the earth.

Lewy shook his head in despair. "Ah, that's very bad. With him hurt, I don't know what may happen now. The last of our chieftains, their warriors, they're all wearied of it, ready to go home. His strength may be the only thing left binding them now, especially after this attack today."

She paced about the fire, frowning thoughtfully. Then she stopped and looked back to him where he still crouched, staring glumly into the fire.

"Then we can't let them know," she said decisively.

"What?" he said, rising and staring at her in surprise. "But how?"

"We must give commands for him," she said. "We must prove he still rules, and with even more strength than before. We must make a bold move."

"What kind of move?"

She stepped back toward him, her bright gaze capturing his, her voice low, intense, compelling. "You said it. They all are weary. But it's weary of sitting here they are! Of not being able to strike out at an enemy, of sinking in this mud while the Firbolgs move at will."

"Aye," Lewy agreed. "Aileel has been reluctant to strike out."

"Likely his failing eyesight has made him fearful in their woods," she guessed. "But now that will change. Now we will take this war to them. Divide the clans. Set them free to fight as they always have, man to man. Let them hunt the Firbolgs in their lands, seek out their dens, keep them in fragments and always on the run. Prove to our enemies that we can fight as they do, and as savagely."

"Yes!" he said with force, caught up in her enthusiasm. "The clans would welcome it. A chance to move. To fight! Yes, Meave. It might work!"

"If not, then pity poor Connacht," she said, looking up to where the black carrion crows now circled lower in the morning sky.

Chapter Twenty-three

Searching

The black forms flew down, their great shadows swelling, filling up the sky, swallowing the light. . . .

Cathbad, ard-druid of all Ulster, jerked violently in his sleep and sat up, suddenly awake, every sense alert, body soaked in sweat.

What had he dreamed?

It was most disturbing: dark figures moving in a bloodred

mist, the flash of weapons, the mingled images of leaping flames, of terrible wounds, of severed heads, of worn and weary fighting men in sad procession, and the shrouding shadows of great, black birds sweeping over all.

The portents in these images were many, complex, obscure in their details, easily dismissable as nightmares. But the collective impression came through clearly, and its import could not be ignored. He knew that something of great and deadly purpose was under way, and that it involved both his own young Sentanta and the high-king of Ireland!

In haste the druid scrambled from his covers and began to dress. He had no need to light a candle. The room was bathed in a silver glow cast in a wide shaft through his half-opened shutters by a full, cold-white fall moon.

The moon drew a wide, shimmering path across the calm ocean's surface, like a silver roadway that might be traveled from the base of the high cliff out to some magic country beneath the waves.

But Conaire Mor, standing atop the cliff, had no mind for such fancies. He stalked irritably up and down along the precipice.

"More raids! More raids!" he barked, the breath that puffed out into the chill air struck to glowing white by the bright moon.

Nearby on the cliff stood Conal Carna, while on a spur of rock jutting precariously out beyond the edge, Calatin perched, the wings of his dark cloak furled around him, his face impassive, his glinting black eyes fixed on the young high-king. A bit further from the cliff edge stood the one-man chariots which had brought them here, their tethered horses shuffling and snorting uneasily in the cold.

"It makes the third raid I've heard of since Tailteen," Conal said gloomily.

"And why is it they can't be stopped?" Mor demanded, stopping to face his champion.

"There's little that can be done," the frustrated warrior explained. "They come randomly, at places widely separated. We've no way to anticipate them."

Mor tapped his foot impatiently. "And have you discovered anything about the raiders?" he snapped.

"No, my King. They've left few alive to speak of them. Those who have seen them can speak only of dim, shadowed figures, without clan colors to mark them, coming upon them like a host of the Sidhe—or of the dead."

"I could wish they were so," the king said bitterly. "Better that than to think they're mortal fighting men of our clans." He clenched a fist, shaking it before him violently. "Each raid is like a dagger driven into my own back. Another blow against the newborn peace I've labored so hard to spawn."

"Few in the rest of Ireland but ourselves see what this means," Conal said by way of comfort. "The places raided so far were isolated strongholds. Those who may hear of them will likely think it just clan rivalries. Only we have put these scattered reports together. I've been careful to see that others don't know."

"I understand that," Mor testily replied. "That's why I agreed to slip from my wife and bed and ride here in the heart of a freezing night, like a thief myself, so none in Tara would know of our talk."

"It will not be long before they do know, for all our care," the druid said in a slow, ominous voice, speaking for the first time, "and everyone else in Ireland as well. From what I understand, it seems that the numbers of these raiders, these outlaws," he emphasized the word, "are growing. From a handful at Tailteen, they have grown to some twoscore through the fall. How long until all Ireland *must* know of them? And know that they can violate the peace with impunity?" He slid down from his rock and faced Mor, his voice growing urgent now. "My King, they must be stopped. They must be caught, condemned, and destroyed, with the greatest ruthlessness!"

"Hold on!" Conal protested sharply. "Is there a need for that? Raids like this have always been the way in Ireland."

"Not in my Ireland," Mor said brusquely.

"Someday perhaps," Conal said in reasoning tones. "But, Conaire, I've told you that such things wouldn't be stopped by the declaration of one night. It'll take time, and careful judgment, and great patience to change the fighting spirit of a hundred lifetimes."

Calatin turned, fixing his hard gaze upon the champion. "If Mor will remain king and keep his peace, he has no choice," he tolled in a deliberate, emphatic way, as if this warrior must be handled as a slow-witted child. "He has made a law. My own place as druid is to uphold that law. As his champion, so is yours. The law makes clear that those who would violate this new peace must die."

"Is there a need for such bloody, vengeful talk from you?" an angered Conal shot back. "These are fighting men, only acting as others have for ages past—"

"Exactly that!" the druid cut in. "And they must be shown that those ages are ended—and shown most harshly. Any weakness on the part of Conaire Mor will bring disaster." He moved back closer to Mor, fixing him with a challenging eye. "My King, are you up to this task?"

"Why must they be condemned?" Conal argued hotly, moving up close on the other side of Mor. "These raiders have fought their battles man to man, by all accounts. Open challenges. Single combats. No dishonorable means were used. Why, in all the reports I heard, the numbers were even against them!"

Calatin gave a snort of derisive laughter. "Fair combats! What of that? By law, *all* differences must be arbitrated by the king. No fighting, no matter how minor, can be tolerated. And these are no isolated cases of clan rivalry. You said it yourself. It's clear to see! The same band of men, but attacking too widely, too randomly. No, this is open defiance—rebellion! These men are brigands, criminals, traitors to Ireland. And their numbers are growing!"

He leaned in toward Mor, his low voice ever more compelling. "My King, you must act. Believe me! You must capture and punish without mercy. Anything else would seem weakness, proof to your people that your peace will never work. It is these men—or it is Ireland!"

"No, Conaire," Conal urgently countered, also leaning closer to the king. "Don't listen to him. It can't be so bad, so deadly as he says."

Mor looked at the druid and then at the champion, clearly torn between them. There was great anguish showing in his eyes.

"Conal, I can't ignore this," he said at last in a desperate attempt to make him see. "Can you understand? Calatin is right. This is open rebellion, endangering my whole rule of law."

"No," Conal returned firmly. "No. Not yet. It is still isolated. I told you: Ireland knows little of it, and few see it as one threat. If we could stop it now—find out what's involved before you make judgment—then it might be there's a way to deal with it. At least let me try!"

Mor met the beseeching eye of his champion, the stout and loyal warrior who had sworn to help him and had never failed his trust. Then he nodded. "All right," he said, his voice reflecting his relief at being given this way to delay the fatal judgment. "I will give you your chance."

"But, my King . . ." Calatin began in protest.

Mor raised a hand to cut him off. "I'll make no judgments until we know everything," he said, now with decisiveness. "Maybe Conal is right. Maybe it can be solved without bloodshed or great strife or loud outcry." He fixed an eye on the druid. "You'd not want all Ireland to know of it unless we had no choice, would you?"

Calatin swallowed his disgruntlement and shook his head. "No, my King," he agreed, putting on an air of humble acceptance. "Certainly not." He stepped back, turning away to hide the scowl of rage he bent upon the blameless sea.

"I'll give you time, Conal," Mor told his champion, "but I can't give you much. Many more raids will surely rouse a public outcry which even we can't hide. For the same reason, you must carry on your search with care. No one must know why or for whom you act." He shook his head regretfully. "I loathe acting in this deceitful way, or asking you to do so, but it is for Ireland's own good." He looked appealingly at Carna. "Does that set well enough with you?"

"Yes, my King," he said stolidly. "I understand."

"It is near to Samhain time," Mor said, glancing up at the icy globe of moon. "Winter is fast coming upon us. Good Danu grant that with it these raids will end. If not, I can give you only until the spring to discover those involved. Until spring, Conal," he repeated emphatically. "By the festival of Beltaine, if the raids continue, if nothing has been done, I'll have no more choice but to act as Calatin asks. Do you understand that as well?"

"I do," my King," said Conal reluctantly. "But this task will be no easy one for me alone. I'll need help."

"Help?" Mor said in puzzlement. "But whom can you trust? Any warrior could be involved. And each one who knows might spread the word. . . ."

"Not these," Conal said with certainty. "Not the two Ulstermen, Cormac Conlingas and the one called Sentanta."

"Your own Red Branch comrades?" sneered Calatin. "How convenient for you."

"Do you imply anything by that?" Conal asked ominously, stepping toward the druid.

"Take care, Calatin," Mor warned pointedly. "Conal has my trust above *all* others."

"You can have trust for the Ulstermen as well, my King," Conal said. "Both were with you when the first raid took place. That should prove their innocence, even to your own druid." He shot a glare of defiance at Calatin.

"It does that," Mor agreed. "And I know them to be good warriors, and my loyal friends, especially Sentanta. Very well, Conal, you may have their help."

"If the arrogant Ulster pups will give it," Calatin said with a skeptical air.

"They will," Conal assured him.

"I've come to ask your help," Conal said gravely.

He stood in the doorway of the quarters of Sentanta and Cormac. The dawn sun, a deceptive warm gold that masked the biting fall air, poured in behind him.

The Ulstermen, recently awakened, had just risen from their low pallets beside the fire. Clad only in their linen tunics, Cormac was lovingly brushing out his fine, long hair while his comrade stoked the low-burned fire. Both looked up in surprise at the champion's abrupt entrance.

"What's wrong, Conal?" Sentanta asked, seeing the grim expression on the stolid warrior's face.

"I must have you help me to stop these raids," was the blunt reply.

"Raids?" Cormac echoed in puzzlement. "Have there been others?"

"Four now, that we know of," Conal said, coming into the room. "I've been receiving reports. I've managed to keep them quiet."

"I did hear rumor of one," said Sentanta, "from a traveler. I thought little of it."

"Well, the king thinks *much* of it," Conal said irritably, pacing the room. "He says the raids must stop, and he's given me until Beltaine to stop them. That's why I must have your help. If only I had more. . . ."

"May I help you?" said a voice behind him.

Startled, he whirled about to see a figure emerging from a curtained corner where another pallet lay.

"Cathbad!" the champion said with mixed surprise and delight. "What magic brought you here?"

"He came last night," Sentanta explained. "He told us some dream of trouble here made him come."

"Well, his dreams were right enough," Conal said, adding warmly to the druid, "and you're most welcome to join us, my old friend. Maybe with your helping us as well, we will have time to stop this terrible thing."

"Terrible thing?" repeated Cathbad with concern, moving forward into the room. "What do you mean, Conal?"

"That if we cannot discover who has carried out these raids and stop them, then Conaire Mor will condemn the lot to death!"

The chariots moved forward slowly, the warriors within them swinging out with spears to swat the rumps of cows and drive the close-bunched herd ahead of them.

The reluctant animals were slowly funneled into a cave mouth, a ragged slit in the face of a rocky cliff. Beyond the mouth the cave opened suddenly into an enormous space. Like a natural hall, its acres of level floor were roughly circular, with outer walls sloping up and in to form a domed roof, narrowing to a small hole where a glimmer of outside light showed. Most of the light, however, was provided by a large wood fire built in the center of the stone floor, and by flaring torches set randomly about the outer edge. Most of their smoke found a way through the hole above, but enough was trapped to create a hazy, gray atmosphere within the chamber.

At the back of the room, a few cattle were already penned. Beside them a second pen held some twoscore chariot horses of especially fine quality. Their war cars were lined up not far away, being cleaned down and tended by industrious drivers.

Most of the warriors from these cars were gathered about a few crude plank tables set close beside the fire. Here some were engaged in stripping off the sameness of unadorned trappings and dark cloaks, transforming to glinting individuality. They donned fine tunics richly decorated and handsome wool cloaks of bright colors and bold patterns that declared a dozen different clans. They belted harness and richly fitted scabbards about them and fastened hair and cloaks with most elaborate jewelry. All were young men, their numbers including Ferogain, Lomna Druth—The Fool—and the other foster-brothers of Conaire Mor.

Those already changed were engaged in eating and drinking heartily while exchanging laughing tales. A few of them were wagering at a game of *brandub*, "black raven," rolling the carved bone cubes for ownership of finely wrought swords and a strange, peaked helmet trimmed in silver.

Along the nearby wall, other trophies of battle were ranged as for proud display: a gleaming array of swords, shields, and spears, and a grisly pyramid of severed heads.

The last of the cattle moved through into the cave, followed by the chariots. While the other cars continued herding the cows around the central fire to the pen, one of them pulled up at the tables. The black-robed and hooded warrior within jumped down, throwing back his hood. The move revealed the grinning face of Maine Morgor.

"Well, lads, it was a fine one that time!" he announced triumphantly. "We've got their herd, and we had a most grand fight for it. And I've got the finest prize."

He went to the front of his car, untying the head that dangled there and holding it up by the hair to show them. The slack-jawed, staring visage was broad, weathered, and scarred by years of hard battle.

"Their chief!" Morgor declared proudly. "A harder fighter than any of you are likely to come across. Killed more men than old Conchobar himself, so they say."

He swaggered to the pile of heads and with great flourish perched his prize atop its peak, then turned to his comrades.

"What about it, then? Can anyone say I've not led you to the best of our raids yet?"

"Don't you think these raids are becoming a bit too much of a risk?" asked one of the young men.

"Aye," Lomna Druth agreed between voracious bites at a rack of beef ribs. He nodded to a brother who nursed a bandaged arm. "Ferger nearly lost his hand today."

"It's no matter," Ferger quickly replied with spirit. "I did for him in the end. A good fighter he was, too."

"You see that?" said a grinning Morgor, moving up to slap The Fool heartily on the back. "You're too cautious and too fat, my worried friend."

The slap nearly caused Lomna Druth to choke. He forced down his mouthful of beef, looking up indignantly at Morgor.

"And if someone should die?"

"Nobody has. Nobody will!" Morgor arrogantly pronounced. "There's no one in Ireland who is our match, and that we'll one day show to everyone. Even young Ferogain here has proven himself, right, lad?"

Ferogain looked uncomfortable, but he nodded.

"We are the sons of chiefs! Of kings!" Morgor crowed, beaming about him at his company. "What have we to fear?"

"Fear being caught by the high-king too soon!" came the ominous rumble of another voice.

They turned to see the familiar, dark-clad figure of the old warrior in the entrance to the cave. He stalked toward them, his face set in stern lines.

"You acted without me, and you might have destroyed our carefully made plan!" he growled.

"Nonsense!" Morgor blustered, putting up a domineering front before the larger man. "We succeeded, and under my leadership. We've no need of your constant shepherding, old man."

"Do you not, young whelp?" he said. A hand shot out, pointing toward the head. "That man was a renowned chieftain of Ireland. His death cannot go overlooked by many. You could bring all of Ireland upon you with such acts."

Morgor's arrogance was untouched by this. "What matter is that?" he sneered.

"What matter?" The dark man thrust his face closer. "And do you want them all hunting you down now? Mor has already set Conal Carna to seek you. And he's to be helped by Cormac Conlingas and Sentanta MacSualtim."

At the name of Sentanta, Ferogain winced inwardly. Of course! Conaire Mor's new favorite would now be hunting him.

"We'll make fools of those Ulstermen," declared Morgor. "They'll never find us here."

"Why not?" countered the old man. "You've made it easy enough." He skewered Morgor with a lancing glare. "Tell me, can you guarantee you left no evidence?"

Morgor faltered under the gaze. "I . . . I didn't look," he said weakly.

"And you didn't think," the warrior added harshly. "You risked your fellows' lives along with your own."

"Maybe we should give this up," suggested Ferogain.

There were some murmurs of support for that.

"No," said the old warrior quickly, turning to them. "No. You can yet succeed. You have done much. Already your numbers have increased more than a score. There will be more yet. But you must be careful. You must strike where I say, where you won't be known or run fool risks. I have learned many things in my years of traveling. I have many tricks to hide and cover you. You must do as *I* say, always. Then you will be safe. No mistakes and no discoveries. That I promise you."

His gaze swept over them, drawing them, holding them, its power seizing their spirits while his words convinced. When he had finished, there were no more looks of doubt, no more mutterings of uncertainty. Once more they were his.

His eyes went back to Morgor, challenging him again. "And you, Morgor," he boomed, "do you understand as well? Do you agree?"

Even the towering arrogance of the youth could not withstand such power. He tried to return the stare defiantly, but felt a tremor through him, turning him weak. He gasped and stepped back, dropping his eyes in defeat. "Yes," he said meekly, fighting for breath. "Yes, curse you. I agree."

"Good!" the man said briskly, turning to address them all. "Then be careful from this time on, the lot of you. Remember there are those now hunting you. When you return to your own duns, say nothing and do nothing to reveal yourselves or this cave. No drunken talk, no fool bragging, even to lovers or closest friends. Divide these cattle and get them away from here. Bury those weapons, and destroy those heads as well."

"Our spoils?" Morgor said in dismay, looking toward the chieftain's head.

"And would you rather keep them about you, like badges signaling to all the world what you've done?" the old warrior asked sarcastically. "Destroy them. Now!"

"And what about Conal Carna and the others?" asked Ferogain.

"Those three," said the dark man ominously, "you can leave to my own care."

Chapter Twenty-four

Winter Fight

The creatures scrambled with desperate haste through the snow-covered rocks. They were clearly being pursued, pausing often to cast savage but also fearful looks behind them.

The scene was a most harsh one: the rugged countryside covered with past fallen snow, melted and refrozen to a smooth, crackling glaze by fierce winds that shrieked and blasted and scoured across the surface. Here and there the jagged ends of gray rocks showed, like shattered bones thrusting painfully from the icy white body of the earth.

The threescore of running creatures were fit denizens of this bleak domain, their hides shaggy and matted, their bodies lean and sharply angular—like great wolves long starved by the winter's cruelty, now hunted by relentless packs of deadly hounds.

But these were men, not wolves, and it was not hounds who hunted them, but other men.

They passed on, disappearing up a vale between two stark spines of hills. Soon other sounds were heard—much louder, more aggressive sounds of passage—and another party some two hundred strong came into view.

Though nearly as starved and as ragged of look, these were more easily identifiable as human beings. Instead of tattered hides and matted furs, they were clad in the much-worn trappings of Connacht fighting men. But the more important difference was in the expressions of their faces. These were not hunted but hunters, their look not fearful but filled with the once rare glow of victory.

At their head moved Meave herself, Lewy MacNeesh and several of the Connacht chiefs close beside her. She strode ahead boldly, strong and erect and sure, sword swinging in her hand.

"They're making no stand at all," said Lewy, gazing searchingly ahead. "We surely have them fully on the run."

"But where is it they're going now?" she asked.

"They've no choice but to retreat deeper into these hills and hope to lose our host," a chieftain said.

"Aye," said Lewy in a more cautious way, "but they should have scattered. Something is keeping them together."

"Maybe they're heading to a fortress," another suggested.

"We've found no signs before of their having one," Lewy replied. "But I'd say it's certain they have some goal in mind."

"That's what concerns me," Meave said gravely, looking about her at the rocky hills. "Keep all our warriors alert, but keep them moving. We must press the Firbolgs as hard as we're able. They can have no time to rest."

They climbed upward for some while, moving along the rocky vale toward a crest where a jumble of rocks made a sawtooth line against a dull iron sky. As they grew near to it, Lewy pulled up suddenly, raising a hand. "Wait!" he said sharply. "They've stopped."

They gazed upward. Several figures were visible upon the points of rock. They were waiting now, looking down upon their foes.

"And I know why they have," said a burly, red-faced chieftain, moving up beside him. "I know these hills. They've nowhere else to go save through us. They're trapped."

"At last!" another chieftain cried in elation. "We've cornered a band of the cursed beasts at last!"

"You can be thanking Meave for that, Murchadh," the ruddy chieftain put in. "It was her taking the clans out against them that has forced them to flight."

"It was the choice of Aileel to do so, Donnchadh," Meave reminded him modestly, though this was a lie. Then her scrutinizing gaze fixed on the quarry above. "The question is: why have they become trapped? They know this land better than any of us. They've made no such foolish move before."

"Perhaps they thought themselves well hidden here," said Lewy. "This vale is nearly impossible to find. Only our pursuit of them has brought us to it."

"And that pile of rocks is a natural fortress," added the one called Donnchadh.

"Right enough!" a warrior said grimly. "We'll be many broken spears and many dead men scratching them out!"

"But this is our chance at them!" snarled the chieftain named Murchadh, glowing with a battle light. "This is our chance to finish the lot of them, show the rest of the stinking savages what we mean to do to them all!"

This bloodthirsty declaration drew exclamations of ferocity from those about him, from warriors too long frustrated, too long beaten, ready for revenge.

"We should do nothing without knowing the full situation first," Meave said cautiously.

"She's right," Lewy agreed. "We must move up closer. And be ready for any attack."

The men of the clans spread themselves out and moved cautiously upward toward the natural palisade of rocks, weapons ready. When they were nearly within a spear's throw of it, a single figure leaped up upon a flat ledge above them and shouted down, "Warriors of Connacht, wait! I wish to talk."

The voice was clear and strong, the words well spoken. Meave found herself actually marveling at the speech. In the hard days of fighting, she had come, like the others, to think of the Firbolgs only as ferocious beasts. She examined the figure above more carefully.

He was a young man, of sharply hewn but handsome looks, discernible even through the long beard, mustaches, and wild, unbraided hair most Firbolgs sported. His clothing was leather, but a cloak of wool with a bold green pattern hung about him. He stood up proudly, his lean and sinewy body poised with a warrior's easy grace upon the point of rock.

"We'll waste no time in words with you, Firbolg!" shouted warlike Murchadh. "Our iron will do all our speaking for us."

"I wish to talk," the other persisted. "It is my right as a warrior."

"The likes of you can't call yourself a warrior," Murchadh snorted in contempt.

The man above, clearly wounded by this, drew himself up stiffly. His words came ringing with pride. "I am Fardia, son of Daire, chieftain of the men of Domnand. Since before the first Milesians came to Ireland, before even the first Tuatha de Danann came, my people have walked this sod and matched their swords against all others man to man. Our right to be warriors is better than your own!"

"Fardia!" Lewy said, staring up with greater intensity at the man, then nodding. "Of course!" He looked at Meave. "I know him, from my childhood. We played together. His father was a good friend to my own."

"What kind of man was he?" she asked.

"A good fighter, a strong man, and a fair one."

"And this Fardia?"

Lewy gave her a little smile. "I've still a bruise or two from his hurley stick, I think. A sturdy lad he was."

"Honest?"

"His father would have nothing else. He's surely no savage beast, my Lady."

"Then speak to him now," she told him.

Some of the chieftains protested, but she ignored them, and Lewy stepped forward and called upward, "Fardia! It's Lewy MacNeesh."

"Lewy?" the other echoed with surprise, peering down. "So, it is you." He shook his head, his voice touched with regret. "It's sorry I am to see your face in the host of my enemies."

"I've your own feeling myself," Lewy truthfully replied. "But what is it you're wanting to speak about?"

"It is a hard thing, Lewy. No Firbolg warrior would ever shame himself by showing weakness to his foe this way, were things other than they are. But here, now, I've no other choice. I'm asking you to talk."

"Because you're trapped, you miserable creatures," Murchadh shouted. "You're run to earth, and you're whining not to die!"

"We do not fear death!" Fardia fired back indignantly. He put a hand upon his sword hilt. "Come face me, Milesian, and see for yourself."

"I believe you, Fardia," Lewy called, throwing a warning glare at the warlike chief behind him. "But why is it you wish to talk?"

"I cannot tell you," came the response. "I can't trust you. Not yourself alone, Lewy, but any of that lot with you. There has been too much betrayal. Too much savagery."

"From your side. Not our own!" cried the outraged Murchadh.

"So you'd believe," Fardia said. "But I'll not speak before you. Let someone come to me."

"And be slaughtered?" Murchadh asked with a harsh laugh. "None here is mad enough!"

"I promise safe passage to any who will come," the young Firbolg replied.

"It is a hard thing to ask us," Lewy told him. "Are you certain you can't come here? Or speak to us from where you are?"

"That I am. And that man behind you makes me the more sure of it. But if someone will come up, unarmed, and we can talk, then you may save yourselves some few lives."

Meave liked the look and the manner of this bold young warrior. She believed what Lewy had told her of him, and she believed the promise that Fardia had made. "I will go talk with him," she said with decisiveness.

Murchadh looked at her in astonishment. "You're mad for certain to be saying that! You can't go up. It'd surely be your end."

"Then you can watch me get my end," she told him brusquely, pulling the round shield from her arm.

"Are you certain of this, my Lady?" Lewy asked with some concern. He glanced up to where Fardia waited above. "I think *he* can be trusted, but there are many more Firbolgs up there."

"I know," she answered, setting down her shield and spear and unbelting her sword. "And I'll be needing all the edge I can get." She dropped her scabbard and fixed her gaze on his. "That's why you'll be going too."

"I was expecting you to tell me that," he said unhappily. He glanced upward again, shook his head, then sighed and pulled off his own shield. "Well then, let's be about it."

It was not long after that he and Meave were climbing up the last rugged bit of face onto the level stone of the high ledge.

They found themselves facing young Fardia, backed by three others, burly warriors, all heavily armed. And from the shelter of rocks above and around them, many more faces peered down. The gazes they fixed on the two arrivals were hard and suspicious.

"A woman!" Fardia said, eyeing her narrowly. "Is this some kind of trick?"

"It is not," Lewy assured him. "She is Meave, aunt to Conaire Mor, who is now high-king over all Ireland."

"*Your* Ireland," Fardia corrected, "not our own."

"Still, she has earned high rank within our host. She speaks for King Aileel, as I do myself."

"Please, believe what he tells you," Meave added with great earnestness. "We've come to you, unarmed, as our sign of faith. I do truly wish to speak to you."

His gaze met hers, searching for any hint of deception in

the blue-gray eyes. Then he nodded. "Very well," he said, some of his wariness vanishing. He stepped back, waving an arm along the ledge past him. "Come this way."

He led them ever higher and ever farther back into the rocky hillside until at last they came out onto a relatively flat plateau covered with weather-smoothed gray stones half-covered by drifted snow. It took Meave several moments to realize that some two dozen round huts were scattered across the area, for they were made of the same stones on which they sat, and very nearly invisible. Only the thin streams of gray rising from their smoke holes and the figures moving about them showed her what they were.

As they drew nearer to the dwellings, Meave had another surprise. For the figures she saw were not those of more warriors, but of women and children.

"By Danu," exclaimed Lewy. "Your families!"

"Aye," Fardia agreed. "More than a hundred here. This is the final hiding place for the families of three clans. We hoped that you would never find it."

"Is your father here?" Lewy asked.

"My father's dead," Fardia replied. "I'm chieftain of the clan now."

"I'm sorry," Lewy told him.

"He was a warrior," the other told him brusquely. "He died in battle, as he'd have wished. If you've sorrow, then it ought to be for these."

They were just entering the camp, and Meave had her first close look at its populace. She did indeed feel both sorrow and a great shock at what she saw.

The Firbolgs here were dying.

Not dying quickly or from battle wounds, but dying slowly and most painfully from hardships, cold, weariness, and starvation. Even in their wrappings of worn furs and cloaks the women looked gaunt, hollow-eyed, and wan, moving slowly, drifting by like wraiths. The children seemed too weary and too cold even to move, much less to play, sitting huddled within the huts or at the outside fires, clinging to one another or their mothers for warmth. Some looked more skeleton than living being, the only sign of life a fading glow in the dark pools of the enormous eyes that lifted, with an effort, to stare at the two strangers in their camp.

Meave felt the eyes and could not return their gaze. There was a revulsion in her at the state of these poor creatures, but it was strangely blended with a wrenching sensation of pity and a desperate need to comfort, to give aid.

They made their way through the camp to a meager fire before a central hut. Here some caldrons were suspended from tripods on heavy chains, their liquid contents barely brought to steaming by the low-burning flames of the peat. The soft, autumn fragrance of this sodlike fuel gave the air a pleasant tinge that was in sharp contrast to the grim winter surroundings.

Fardia crouched down at the fire, signaling the two to do likewise. The three warriors who had followed them there stayed upright, ranged behind the visitors, their wary gazes fixed on the backs of the pair. The young Firbolg chieftain took up a ladle, scooping the hot liquid from a pot into some crude pottery bowls. These he handed to Lewy and Meave.

"I hope it's warm enough for you," he said. "Fuel is a difficult thing to come by up here." He scooped a bowl for himself, looking down into it. "It's only thin broth," he said with the tone of an apologetic host. "Little more than water really. We've little meat now, either, save maybe a poor rabbit now and then." He smiled ruefully, gesturing around him at the snow. "Water, though, that we have in plenty."

"We don't need to be eating your food at all," Meave said. "Not when you've such need."

"It is our custom to feed guests, both friend and foe," Fardia told her, stiffening with pride. "Not death itself would change that. You'll eat, and we will talk."

"Is this why you couldn't speak before?" Lewy asked, looking around at the camp. "Because of your families?"

"It was," Fardia admitted. "If that lot of yours knew of them, they'd likely be up here all the quicker to slaughter them. One more nest of Firbolg vermin done with for good."

"They wouldn't do that," Meave said, shocked at the thought.

"Would they not?" Fardia replied. "And have they done anything else since the start? I know they haven't. I've seen their work myself. And Lewy knows the truth of it as well."

"I've seen what your people have done to our lisses and duns," Lewy countered.

"In retribution only," was the response. "Your side began it. You Milesians have never thought us people. When our fighting men couldn't be found, their families were slaughtered. So we hid our folk. They've suffered for it, but at least some have survived."

"There has been much horror on both sides," Meave said in a cooler, moderating way. "I've seen enough of it since I came to Connacht. All have suffered. But what is it that you want of us now? Are you meaning to surrender?"

"Surrender?" He gave a harsh laugh at that. "Why, even if they didn't slaughter us, we might as well be dead. No. No surrender. We only mean to save our children and their mothers if we can."

"Save them?" Meave said. "How?"

He fixed her with a grim and earnest gaze. "Let them go free, unharmed, from this place, and the rest of us will come down from these rocks to fight you openly, iron to iron."

"But we've more than three times your strength," she told him. "You would die."

"Maybe. But with greater honor. We've no wish to fight a coward's defense from these heights. We'll likely die, but earning a gallant death and the lives of our families."

Meave felt an amazement and a sense of awe at the nobility in this young man. These were no savages, no mindless ravagers they faced here, but a desperate people driven to war, holding on to honor in the face of the near destruction of their race. She looked at him, and a new idea, an exhilarating and most reckless impulse, seized her.

"Fardia," she said, leaning toward him and speaking with great intensity, "we can do something much greater, you and I. I've seen both sides now. I am not of Connacht or of you, but from outside. Let me help you. Work with me, and together we can bring peace."

Lewy looked toward Meave in disbelief.

Fardia stared. "Peace?" he echoed, clearly nonplussed by her sudden notion.

"Yes," she earnestly went on. "If your Firbolgs and the others of Connacht could talk . . ."

He shook his head emphatically. "No. No. The crimes are too great. Our lands stolen, our people enslaved . . ."

"But if we could talk," she persisted, "maybe we could find ways to agree."

"Never!" he shot back.

"And what do you gain by not trying to talk?" she asked. "Would you rather see all Connacht destroyed, watch all its children die, as yours are dying now? Isn't saving them worth any chance?"

He looked around him at the wretched camp. He seemed

to waver. Then he shook his head again. "I've no reason to trust you."

She smiled. "And would you if I let you go? If I let all of you go now?"

A shocked Lewy opened his mouth to speak, but she shot him a warning look and he subsided.

"Let us all go?" Fardia said, once more astonished by her words. "You mean you would do that?"

"I would. But only for your vow to me that you would speak to your own clans, try to convince them to come and talk, the whole Firbolg nation with our own."

One of the warriors behind her growled, "Why should we believe anything she says? She may not be of Connacht, but she's Milesian."

"I believed you," Meave countered. "I came here without arms. Doesn't that prove anything?"

Fardia turned to his childhood friend. "For our old comradeship and the honor I still feel alive in you, you have my trust," he said. "Tell me whether this woman speaks the truth."

Lewy hesitated. He looked at Meave, who met his eye levelly, determinedly. Then he nodded, turning back to Fardia. "She will do as she says," he said with sincerity. "That I know."

Fardia now eyed Meave speculatively, clearly fascinated by the possibility, but kept wary by the years of bloodshed and betrayal.

"What could I tell our tribes?" he asked. "What sign would they believe?"

"Aileel will withdraw the host of Connacht to Cruchane," she promptly answered. "We will cease chasing you. We will stop fighting and wait for you to come and meet us."

At this incredible offer, Lewy, past astonishment now, didn't even blink an eye.

"Aileel would do that?" Fardia asked skeptically.

"He would," she said firmly. "And you would have his word that we would meet under truce."

"You understand there are few certainties in this," he warned. "I can give no promise that I can convince, or even reach, all of our scattered clans."

"There's little any of us can lose by your trying," she replied.

"Except our lives," he corrected. "But that's what it's come to anyway." He considered, then he nodded. "All right. I will agree."

Soon after, the two were climbing back down the rugged

cliffside from the high ledge of rocks. Meave, glancing around, realized that her companion was looking at her in disbelief.

"What is it, Lewy?" she asked.

"You promised to let them go," he said.

She shrugged. "Sixty warriors, for the chance of peace?"

"You promised a truce and a chance for discussion," he added.

"Aileel will agree," she said with certainty.

"And the other chiefs? You'll not convince them."

"I must. And you must help." She stopped to look at him. "You will help, Lewy?"

He gazed into those bright, determined eyes, and then he laughed. "You know I will," he told her. "And the blessed Danu help the both of us."

Chapter Twenty-five

On the Trail

The red-black stain was startling against the background of white. The heat of it fresh from the veins had melted it deep into the smooth surface of snow.

Sentanta stood from his crouching position where he had examined the blood and looked about him at the scene. Surrounding him over the wide area of open ground were the confused marks of a wild and desperate struggle, the once-pristine field of snow torn up, the prints of man and horse and iron-shod wheel creating a muddled interlace spotted here and there by other ominous patches of dark red.

Cormac Conlingas, Conal Carna, and the Ulster druid Cathbad were, with Sentanta, spread out about the area, carefully perusing the ground just as he was. At one side of the battlefield, a lean, bent, gray-haired warrior stood watching with a sagging face of woe. Near him the four chariots and drivers who had brought the Ulstermen were pulled up.

While Cathbad and Conal continued their minute examination of the scene, Cormac sidled up beside Sentanta. "Look at them searching," he said softly, shaking his head. "What do they hope to find?"

The boy shrugged. "Something to point us to the raiders. I don't know what, myself."

Cormac moved closer, his voice dropping to a confidential murmur. "But, tell me now, what do you think of this? I mean, this searching."

The other youth regarded him curiously. "I'm not certain I understand you."

"You do," Cormac accused. "You must have thought of it. Hunting out other warriors like ferrets crawling through some rabbit's hole? Doesn't it make you feel . . . strange?"

Sentanta opened his mouth to make a denial, but he paused, knowing it would be a lie. He did have a faint feeling of discomfort in this. But that it was for the reason Cormac had said, he wasn't sure. "It doesn't matter what we feel," he hedged. "It's what we've been set to do."

"And there's another thing," Cormac went on in a disgruntled way. "Why set us to it? I surely didn't ask to be sent out hunting my fellows. Why did we agree?"

"You know there was no one else Conal could trust," Sentanta answered. "And it's part of our sworn duty to the king."

"Our sworn duty!" Cormac snorted derisively.

"It is that!" the boy told him stolidly. "And a great one to be helping so fine and honorable a man."

"Is it so honorable for him to be having us sneak about like this?" the other countered. "Why all of this secrecy anyway?" He shook his head. "I tell you, there's none of it sets very well with me. It's just not right."

Perhaps that was it, Sentanta considered honestly. Perhaps it was the feeling of some wrongness in all this that bothered him as well. His dreams of serving the great king, of being the warrior, the glowing champion of future bardic tales, wielding his sword in defense of the great peace—they grew faint here, in this winter cold, ingloriously hunting out traitors as if they were rampaging boars.

He hung on to the one truth he could not deny: "We uphold the laws, Cormac. It's the duty of all to do that. There's nothing wrong in it."

"Is there not?" Cormac answered, sounding unconvinced. "And are you so certain that his law is right?"

"It's not our place to question," the boy replied.

"A fine notion," Cormac said sarcastically. "Like the steer doesn't question being led to the butcher's block?"

"What are you two about?" Conal called to them, interrupting their talk. "Have you found something then?"

Cormac turned guiltily away. Sentanta quickly responded, "No. Nothing."

"Well, keep looking," the champion ordered, but then shook his head in frustration. "Though they surely did leave little enough to find."

"It's a great pity we couldn't have seen the whole battlefield," commented the ard-druid, looking over the confused tangle of hoofprints and wheel marks.

"We weren't to leave our poor dead warriors lying about for days here so you might see them!" the old warrior nearby cawed indignantly.

"And we wouldn't expect you to," Cathbad swiftly and soothingly replied. "It's just that I might have told much more about these raiders seeing the whole of it as it was."

"We should be lucky there's even this much left," said Sentanta. "It's the closest we've come to the raiders since we began our searching. For once we've had a snow to show the marks, and no more since to cover them."

"I suppose we should be grateful for the cold as well," Cormac put in, drawing his cloak closer around him. "At least it's kept us free of the rotting smell of that carcass."

"Carcass?" said Cathbad with interest. "Where?"

"Just beyond that knoll," the young warrior told him, pointing to a small white swell of ground not far away. "But there's no reason for excitement. It's a horse, not a man."

"Let's see it anyway," the druid said, bustling off toward the knoll.

On its rear slope the carcass lay, half sunk in the snow by its last body heat, legs thrust stiffly out and neck arched up as if frozen in its final death agony. A wide spill of blood from a severe cut in the neck gave easy evidence of what had done for it.

It was a magnificent chestnut horse with the heavy furring of winter, its massive hooves thick-shagged. Cathbad crouched to examine it.

"A chariot horse surely," Conal commented. "See the wear marks on the hide of its shoulders where the harness rubbed."

"One of your own?" Cathbad asked, looking up to the old man.

"No, it is not," he replied. "And if it is one of theirs, it's the only bit of them got by us in return for their slaughter of our lads!"

"One of theirs!" said Cathbad excitedly. He looked around at his companions. "Have any of you seen the like of it before?"

All examined it carefully. All shook their heads in regret.

"None I know has a horse like it," said Conal.

"It bears no clan markings," said Sentanta. "It's as if the owners meant to keep it secret, in case such a thing as this happened to it."

"Ah, they're clever, all right," said Cathbad thoughtfully. "Haven't made the tiniest slip that might reveal themselves to us."

"Pity this poor brute can't speak," said Cormac.

"And who is to say it can't!" said the druid, casting him a sly smile. He rose, his manner suddenly brisk and commanding. "You lads, just take off the creature's head and follow me."

He strode smartly away. The three warriors exchanged puzzled looks. Then Sentanta shrugged and drew his sword.

"Oh, well," he said, bending down over the horse's outstretched neck. "Madness or not, we'd best do as he says."

In a few moments, he and a grimacing Cormac were lugging the massive head back around the knoll. There they found Cathbad smoothing a round patch in the snow.

"Sorry about the neck," the boy said, indicating the hacked-through stump of it. "It was hard frozen. Like chopping the bog oak."

"Never mind," said Cathbad. "One of you now, drive your stoutest spear in here. And drive it deep. I must use it as a post."

The three warriors working in turn managed finally to break a hole through the frozen sod and sink a heavy spear nearly a third of its length into the softer earth below.

"Now, set the horse's head upon that post. Balance it, if you please, as best you can."

Cormac threw another glance askance at Sentanta, who only shrugged. Then the two lifted the head and set it firmly on the pole.

"A strange trophy it looks perched there like that," Conal declared, somewhat amused.

Cathbad ignored him. He went to his chariot, fetching a small, iron-bound chest from the car. Opening it, he took out some vials, mixed pinches from each of them in his cupped hand, then carefully replaced the vials and returned to the others.

"This works best with someone who's just freshly dead," he explained. "But maybe with this cold there's still a chance."

He moved around the head. Carefully, gently, he blew some of the powder into the ears, into the wide nostrils, and into the half-gaping mouth. As he did, he spoke a soft incantation to it.

"Awake, you brain within this icy skull. Bring back to life the memories of this beast. Show us the way to your last resting place. Show us the final home where you were fed and warmed. Go back again to your stable and your friends. Back to find your final comfort and rest. Back to your masters."

As the three warriors and the old man watched in astonishment, the head appeared to thaw. The frozen flesh seemed to grow pliant, the icy color faded, the glazed eyes grew moist. Then, more astoundingly, the head began to move. Tiny movements they were, but most definite signs of life. The lids shivered above the eyes, then slowly blinked. The ears twiched. The nostrils flared as if to breathe again. The jaw tightened, closing the gaping mouth. The muscles of the neck grew taut, finally shifting the massive head. Slowly, it lifted and began to swivel upon the pole of the spear. It turned steadily, and then it stopped, its long muzzle pointing northwest.

"There!" Cathbad cried. "That's the way!" He turned to the others. "Quickly! We must follow as it leads. There's not much time. That spell will be fading in a day."

At the druid's direction, they prepared to go. The three warriors pulled out the spear, taking care to keep the head perched on its end.

"Someone must carry it before us," Cathbad told them. "The spell will lift the head's weight from the pole somewhat, but it will still be a hard, unpleasant task."

"I'll carry it," Sentanta volunteered.

"Good fellow," Cormac told him, smiling in relief.

"We'll carry it in turns," Conal put in, shooting a meaningful look at Cormac. "All three of us."

Cormac's smile promptly disappeared.

So they set off, Sentanta walking ahead, manfully holding the weighty head out before him on the spear. The boy's fellows walked close at either hand, to relieve him should he tire or stumble. Close behind rolled the chariots, carrying the drivers and the Ulster druid.

The old man stayed behind, at the scene of his clan's defeat. For all his sorrow, he still stared after the bizarre procession, shaking his head as if they were lunatics, as, indeed, they did look.

But he was not the only observer of the departing company. From the shelter of a tree-shrouded hill nearby, the tall, dark-cloaked figure of Calatin watched.

He had peered down with faint curiosity as the Ulstermen searched, then with greater interest as the horse was found. When the head was severed and it became clear what Cathbad's purpose was, the watcher shook his head in surprise.

"Well, and who would have believed a druid of Ireland to have so much skill in him," he murmured.

As the spell was finished and the group started away, the watcher too began to move. He turned from his hiding place and pushed back through the brush to where a chariot waited.

"Bring my chest and follow me!" he ordered its spindly, gray-faced driver. "Quickly!"

The son of Calatin instantly took up a small, brass-bound trunk of polished wood, much like Cathbad's, and jumped out of the car. His father led him up the hillside, onto a rounded and naked crest that stuck up above the thickly foliaged slopes below.

Here, at the druid's order, the son deposited the chest gently on the ground. Calatin crouched beside it and opened it.

"So he uses the old spells," he murmured, perusing its contents. Then a malicious smile stretched his wide mouth as he selected several of the vials. "Well then, he'll surely appreciate this one!"

He took a small bowl of thinly beaten gold from the chest. Into it he painstakingly measured out doses of powders from the chosen vials, stirring them gently with a silver rod. When he had finished, he rose and walked to the crest's highest point.

Far out now on the smooth, white meadows he could see the tiny figures of the Ulster party moving away. Above them stretched a bright but chill blue winter sky, dotted with some long, billowing, flat-bottomed clouds that glided in a stately way.

Calatin's gaze rose from the tiny company to the drifting clouds. He raised the golden bowl high in both hands and called out to the skies, "Winds, winds, hear me! Please come to me and take my offering now!"

A light breeze rose to swirl about the hill, fluttering his cloak.

As it lifted around him, he tipped the bowl. The mingled powders streamed out into the wind, whisked away, drawn up into the skies.

"You have taken my offering," he cried with a triumphant grin. "Now you must obey my will!"

The breeze was suddenly convulsed, twisting and rising in force into a whirlwind that coiled around him.

"Carry my enchantment to the clouds!" he commanded. "Waken in them that fierce being of snow who dwells in winter skies. Call it to me!"

Across the meadows, now almost beyond the view of the hilltop, the Ulstermen continued on northwest.

"The weather's turning suddenly," Cormac remarked, gazing as the sun abruptly disappeared.

"It is that," Conal agreed. The sky was now quite thick with drifting clouds.

"Curious," said Cormac, looking behind them. "It looks as if they're being drawn from all sides toward the place we just left."

"It's not only curious," Cathbad said, staring back with concern, "it's impossible!"

But, indeed, the clouds *were* drawing together at one point, pulled from all the sky to collide and join, forming a dense, gray-white mass that swelled, covering the blue, smothering the sun.

And then, from out of the blackest point of it, a mass began to swell downward, dropping to the earth, spreading to form a massive, towering cloud wall.

Then it moved toward them, sweeping with rapidly increasing speed across the plain, like a massive tidal wave rolling up onto a beach.

"It's coming!" said Cathbad.

"What, a storm?" asked Sentanta.

"Something more dangerous," the druid said grimly, then raised his voice to shout, "Drivers! Form the chariots in a square! You three, come to me. Quickly, for your lives!"

"What is it?" the warriors asked, running to him.

But before Cathbad could explain, the cloud wall was upon them. In an instant they were surrounded by the mass, plunged into a snowstorm of blizzard intensity, the thickly falling flakes whipped by corkscrew winds into a great cyclone of white that whirled about them, hemming them in.

But it was more than snow and wind that swept about them.

Something else was taking form there in the swirling clouds. It coalesced from the individual flakes, its shape growing clearer as it grew more dense. Its body was the long, twisting coils of the circling storm, a lithe, sinuous tail that could enwrap all of Tara's hill, writhing constantly, whipping violently about. And atop this snakelike body, higher than a great hall's roof peak, lifted an immense head, broad and flat and serpentine, its eyes glittering with a malevolent, sapphire light, its fangs like curving swords of ice honed by the wind.

"A snow serpent," Cathbad said.

The four drivers, nearly blinded by the swirling snow, struggled with their panicked teams, managing to pull them up in a tight ring.

"Release the teams!" the druid ordered. "They'll never survive here!"

As the drivers hastened to unfasten the harness from the steeds, Cathbad turned to the three warriors.

"We must protect the head," he shouted over a rising scream of wind that might also have been the wail of the creature itself.

Sentanta grounded the spear, leaving the precious horse's head balanced atop it. And though they could already feel the swift building of an enormous cold around them, Cathbad whipped off his own wool cloak and covered the head with it.

"Now form around me!" he said to the warriors. "Do what you can to keep that thing away from me. I must have time to build a fire!"

"A fire?" Conal echoed in disbelief. He looked around at the treeless, snow-covered plain shrouded in the roiling white. "With what?"

"Cut it from your cars!" the druid commanded. "Quickly!"

"Not from our cars!" protested Cormac, casting an alarmed gaze toward his ornately fitted chariot.

"By Danu, young fool, is it your car or your life?" the exasperated druid replied. "Start with my own if yours is so precious."

"Do it, Cormac!" Sentanta told his friend. "We'll hold this thing away."

Cormac obeyed. He jumped to the druid's chariot, drew out his sword, and began to hack free the woven bulwarks of wicker that enclosed it.

"You needn't do it with quite such zeal!" Cathbad criticized as he lifted his iron-bound chest from the car.

One side of the bulwark was quickly cut loose and the shattered pieces tossed down to the druid. But Cormac's work on the other side was hampered by the tearing force of the creature of snow, which now closed upon them.

The great head with the glinting eyes and tearing fangs swept in at them. The long serpent's tail flicked out at them, slashing keen lashes of freezing air across them, blasting fine, stinging particles of ice against their skin and into their eyes, wrapping them round with coils of snow.

The warriors battled against it desperately. But they soon found their efforts nearly useless. The cuts made by their swords slashed harmlessly through the clouds of the serpent body. The defensive moves with their shields to knock aside attacks from head or tail merely turned the blows by sweeping through them, blasting them to tatters. But it took only an instant for that portion of the creature to reform. And as the coils tightened further, further, the freezing air enveloped them, soaked into them, weighed them down as if they were immersed in a winter's sea. They began to feel the effects of the strangling cold in rasping breath and weakening limbs.

Between them Cathbad crouched, piling scraps of the shattered wicker and wood painstakingly to form a pyramid.

"Wood! More wood!" he cried. Cormac wrenched the other bulwark free and tossed it down to him. "More!" the druid cried again. "Something larger. The wheels! Get the spokes!"

So Cormac attacked one of the chariot's great wheels with his sword, hacking into the hard oak of the wide spokes.

But his work was becoming harder now, as was the defensive fight of his comrades. The snow serpent was closing farther on them despite their best efforts. Its winding coils had now moved within the compass of the cars to totally enclose them. Laeg and the other drivers, defenseless, huddled with their cloaks pulled close about them, turning quickly to white lumps under the deepening carpet of driving snow. Sentanta and Conal fought on as well as they could, but the snow was plastered to them, and their own cloaks were useless as the blasting, twisting winds tore them away from their bodies, sending them flapping out to further hamper the warriors' moves. The sharp spears of the icy wind pierced deeply into them now, bringing a numbness to their limbs and a heaviness to their minds.

Sentanta wrenched out his cloak pin and let the garment flutter away in a desperate attempt to gain more freedom. But even more he felt the cold defeating him. From the tingling burn of fingers and toes, the deadly chill was creeping up his arms and legs. Ice filled his nostrils, scoured raw his face, blinded his eyes.

Behind him, Cathbad worked urgently, but Sentanta wondered what his puny fire could do against such a monstrous thing, should he even manage to get it alight in time.

And that time was quickly running out.

Chapter Twenty-six

Snow Serpent

The serpent pulled tighter, tighter, its winding coils drawing in.

Cormac wrenched three spokes free and staggered to the druid. "Here!" he panted, dropping them. "I can't do more!"

The druid had painstakingly piled tiny splinters of wicker topped by larger ones. He laid what wood he had atop the whole.

"By the gods, hurry, man!" gasped Conal, wearily flinging up his shield in an unsuccessful move to ward off a blast of the tail. It staggered him back and he dropped to one knee. He seemed unable to rise.

Sentanta too felt the last fatigue coming on him. The sword and shield were intolerable weights. He saw only a white blur swirling before him. His body seemed no longer part of him.

He looked toward Cathbad. The druid crouched over the pile, his chest opened, hands moving over the vials within. Cathbad was working carefully, his chilled hands fumbling with the chemicals. A pinch of this, a little more of that. Amounts were crucial. He couldn't make a mistake.

A sudden, treacherous gust of wind swept the powder from his hands. He moaned and reached for more. . . .

The serpent's head swept down at the boy. Its eyes were blue-white glows of power. Its mouth spread in a baleful gleam of ice as it opened, seeming ready to devour him.

He could not raise his shield in defense.

Cathbad got out more powder, his hands almost useless now. No time for careful measures. It must work! He poured it on. He fumbled a small pellet of red metal from a pouch and tossed it down.

A spark. It flickered, faded, then caught on a splinter, brightened, caught the powder.

A red light flared. Instantly fire crackled through the pile of wood and wicker, flames licking up.

The creature convulsed, its white coils of snow jerking back from the sudden heat. The head reared high, the vast mouth opening as it gave out a scream of rage and shock, shrill as the sound of the blasting wind.

The fire blossomed, soared higher, sending out an aura of warmth that penetrated the bodies of the nearly frozen warriors, bringing their chilled blood back to life.

The serpent withdrew its coils farther, like ice melting back about a heated brand. But in its vitality, the fire was consuming its fuel too fast. In moments it would fade, allowing the creature of wind and snow to strike at them once more.

The head swayed above them, its malevolently glinting eyes watching for an opening so it could dart in again.

Cathbad rose beside the fire, glaring up defiantly at the towering being. He grasped a cut wheel spoke in one hand, pouring liquid from a vial on it with the other.

"Now, creature of the cold," he said with a savage satisfaction through his chattering teeth, "taste this and die!"

He thrust the spoke's drenched end into the fire. It flared up with an intense, white-gold glow. He swung this torch back in a swift move and flung it upward with all his power.

It flew into the gaping maw of the serpent that hung over them, vanishing into the swirling mass of white. There it exploded into a giant bloom of silver sparks. The head jerked upward, turning the open mouth to the sky as it voiced a great, long, piercing cry of agony, like midnight winds in a bare mountain crag.

The white coils of its body shivered, as if slashed through by enormous blades forged from the icy winds. The shrill cry died away, and with it the creature. Its coils suddenly dissipated, and the winds abruptly faded, leaving the last of the snow to drift down in gentle spirals.

In only moments, to the amazement of the warriors, the sky was clearing, the heavy overcast breaking up, gliding away.

A lump of white moved near Sentanta. It rose, the snow

covering falling away as the head of Laeg was thrust out from
the sheltering cover of his cloak.

"What happened?" he said, looking around in disbelief.

"Cathbad destroyed it," the boy said proudly.

"Aye," Conal added. "And saved us all."

"A snow serpent." Cathbad said, looking thoughtfully up to
the skies. "It takes a great power and a wide knowledge of the
old Sidhe lore to bring such a being to life." He looked ahead
of them, across the countryside, his face drawn in a troubled
frown. "It's not mere raiders that we're facing now. Somewhere
in this there is a great and a most evil sorcery at work!"

Calatin peered down from the hill's crest. His eyes, fixed on
the suddenly cleared skies, were narrowed in puzzlement.

Then a movement on the ground below caught his eyes. His
gaze dropped to the snow-covered hills of the countryside. He
started in surprise.

Figures were moving there, around the chariots. Tiny at that
distance, they were large enough for him to see that their
number was complete, their company clearly having survived
intact. A faint thread of smoke still lifted from Cathbad's fire
to the remaining, now-tamed clouds.

"By all the Raven's Powers!" Calatin rumbled, both anger
and admiration blending in his words. "That little druid is
strong indeed! Maybe he is even an adversary near my worth.
I'll take no more chances with him."

He strode down to his son. "Take up that chest," he ordered.
"Quickly now. Make our best speed to Tara. I must hurry if
I'm to reach the others before they do."

"Leave here?" Maine Morgor said in disbelief. "What do you
mean? We've just gathered to plan another raid!"

The warriors of the raiding band were gathered about the
tables in their hiding place. A blazing wood fire drove back
the winter's chill that seeped in through the stone walls. It
cast a ruddy light across the young faces of the three Maines,
the sons of Donn Dessa, and the rest of their company, some
sixty strong now.

Between them and the fire, the form of the old warrior
loomed, massive and dark against the flaring light.

"You've little choice," the dark man rumbled. "Conal Carna
and the others are drawing very near. Leave now and you may
just be safely away before they come."

"And what happened to your vow that you would keep us from discovery?" Morgor asked sarcastically.

The warrior fixed him with a glinting eye. His voice was a growl as he said, "And what do you think I am doing now, boy?"

"Asking us to give up our hiding place," the unintimidated son of Aileel shot back. "How did you let it happen, Great Protector?"

"It was unforeseen. This druid Cathbad who helps them has more powers than I thought."

Maine Morgor looked about him at the others. "Well, I say we're fools to run. What's an old druid and three warriors to us? Let them come here. They'll never leave again."

"What, all of us against them?" Lomna Druth said in horror. "It would be murdering them."

"Would it?" the dark warrior sneered. "The last time, I recall the Ulster pup Sentanta all but doing for your whole lot by himself."

"It was no fair fight!" Morgor retorted indignantly.

"And neither would this be," the old man said with force. His hard gaze swept the group. "Listen and believe. With three warriors like these, and aided by a druid of no small skills, the risk is just too great. Leave here at once, and let me find you a new hiding place."

"And wait for them to discover that one too?" Fergel asked gloomily.

"The gods are warning us!" an anguished Ferogain blurted. "We've taken this too far. It's a great wrong we've done. Now we have our reason to give it up!"

"No!" the old man returned with force. His bright, compelling gaze swept them again. "There is no need for you to panic. You are too close. Look at what you've already done. And I have scores more of young nobles like yourselves who are ready to join you. By spring you will be so strong, the king cannot defy you."

"And now?" asked Morgor.

"Let the raids end for these deep winter days. Let Mor dream of peace until the weather turns. Then you will strike again, in greater force. You will suprise him. You will show all of Ireland your force. But for now—now you must go, and with great haste!"

Once more the man's strange power held the young warriors, filled them with belief in what he said. All, even the defiant

Morgor, agreed. Hastily they gathered what they could, hitched their chariots, and rode out from their cavern, dividing at its mouth to speed away to their homes.

Only the old warrior remained until the end, seeing the last ones safely away. They were just in time. As their chariots vanished from sight across a northern ridge, other figures loomed into view from the southeast.

He watched them coming closer, waiting to identify them. Soon he could see them clearly: three chariots with riders following three walking men, one of whom carried a strange object on a pole.

"No man before who made me run has gone unharmed for it," he grated. "You've made me run this time, Cathbad. But I promise you, you'll yet pay!"

Waiting no longer, the dark man wrapped his cloak around him and slipped stealthily from the cave's entrance, climbing swiftly through the rocks of the hillside to where his own chariot was hidden above.

But his departure did not go unnoticed.

"What was that?" said Conal, who was taking his turn at carrying the head before their party. "I thought I saw the flash of some black form sweeping from that cleft in the rocks ahead."

"Likely ravens using the place to nest," Cormac said dismissingly.

"Don't be too casual, my lad," Cathbad warned. "See, the head's pointing us to that very spot."

And so it was, the poor dead creature's nose leading them up to the entrance of the cave.

They paused some distance from the ominous, black opening, leaving chariots and drivers there, moving forward, the three warriors first, swords out.

"Careful now," said Cathbad. "There are some twoscore of them, remember. Too many even for you three."

"Not likely we'll meet then," said Conal, pointing to the ground before them. "By these tracks, I'd say they've left, and not long ago."

"In a dozen directions, too," Sentanta added.

"Which tells us that they were no single band," Cathbad interpreted.

"Maybe," Conal said more cautiously. "But we'll learn nothing more of them from outside. If you're ready, my lads, we'll be going in. Cathbad, please wait here."

Cautiously the three approached the opening. Nothing appeared to challenge them. Swords and shields up, the warriors moved boldly through, pausing just inside to gaze about them.

The torches and the fire had been extinguished, plunging the vast space into a shrouding gloom. But the faint light from the cave mouth and the hole high in the dome was enough to reveal the interior once the men's eyes had adjusted. There was no sign of life, no movement save the frail remnant of smoke that fluttered up from the central pit.

"Come in," Conal called back out to the druid. "It's deserted, as we thought."

Cathbad moved into the cave to join them. "Well, it certainly offers little promise," he said, peering around in disappointment. "Still, we'd best search. There's no saying what we might find here."

"Better than another dead horse, I hope," Cormac said, wrinkling his nose in distaste at the heavy, musty odor of the place. "Though it surely smells like one in here."

They separated, Conal moving to the left and Cormac to the right to follow around the curved outer wall of the space. Sentanta and Cathbad went straight ahead, out across the floor to the fire pit.

While the boy kept careful watch about him at the dreary place, the druid circled the pit slowly, examining the ground, the doused embers, and the plank tables with great care.

"There've been many meals cooked here," he concluded, "and many men who've eaten about these tables. From the signs, I'd say several dozens. A greater number than our earlier signs showed were in the raiding band."

"Could it be a different group?" Sentanta asked. "A company of brigands or pirates, maybe, who used this place?"

"Cattle have been penned here," came the voice of Cormac, echoing from the far side of the vaulted room. "Looks like a hundred or more. And horses too! It's clear what's caused the smell." He moved on a bit farther and stopped again, peering at the ground. "Here's where they kept the chariots. Big war cars, by the tracks. Fifty or more."

"No pirates or wandering thieves would be using chariots of war," Cathbad pointed out. "It must be warriors."

"Over here!" called Conal, who stood by a small natural alcove in the rough wall.

The three joined him quickly. There a heap of dark material

lay upon the ground. Conal bent down and seized a portion, lifting it up. It was a heavy cloak of dull gray wool, devoid of any pattern or fringe.

"They all look the same as this," he said. "More than two-score of them, I'd judge."

"And like the ones worn by our raiders," added Cathbad. "Either abandoned or forgotten in their haste to depart this place." He turned to the others with a look of grave certainty. "Well, my friends, there would seem to be no question that this cavern was the hiding place of the ones we're seeking. They came here to hide their cattle, to eat, to rest, to change. . . ."

"To change," Conal repeated darkly. "That means they had something to hide. It means they would be known."

"I fear it does, Conal," Cathbad admitted. "Our raiders were no single clan, no simple band of outlaws. From these signs, they were fine fighting men, warriors of some wealth, who rode in chariots pulled by fine war steeds, quite likely men of some renown, and, I would say, men from many parts of Ireland."

"What does it mean, Cathbad?" Sentanta asked.

"It means that my own worst fear has been realized! Their banding here is not just a wild act by some independent few. It can mean only one thing: a clear and deliberate defiance of the king's new peace! A growing one, too. Their numbers seem to have tripled since the raids began."

Conal sighed in defeat. "I've no liking for agreeing with you, Cathbad," he said slowly, "but I must." He shook his head. "It will be hard for Conaire Mor to give pardon to this!"

"Giving punishment is not the greatest problem now," the druid replied. "We've got to find the raiders first."

Sentanta leaned down and took hold of another of the discarded garments. As he lifted it to examine, something tumbled from its folds, clacking sharply onto the stone below.

They all looked down. The object shone even in the faint light. With an expression of shock, Conal swooped a hand down to retrieve it, holding it out. It was a large brooch of gold formed in a crescent shape, filigreed ornately around the outer curve, its face a complex interlace design inlaid with bright green and red enameling.

"By the Bloody Raven," Conal swore. "It's worse than I could ever have guessed."

"It belongs to someone of great rank, surely," said Sentanta, examining the brooch curiously. "But you'd already guessed that some such could be involved."

"We did," Conal agreed. "But this is not from just any ranking house in Ireland. This design is that of the court of Tara itself!"

Chapter Twenty-seven

Truce

"They will not come!"

The chieftain Murchadh snorted scornfully, his breath a clear jet of white in the chill dawning.

The Plains of Ai were a scene of frosty brilliance under the sharp morning sun. On this early spring day the snows had vanished, and beneath the frost's silver glazing the yellow grass of the wide meadows showed the first faint tints of greening.

Just below the high dun on which sat the fortress Cruchane, the forces of Connacht were drawn up in battle array. The warriors of each clan were gathered behind their chieftains, their massed colors making the host seem a bright patchwork scarf against the glowing smoothness of the plains.

Massive war cars lined the front of the host. Their hundreds of horses, held ready by the drivers, shuffled and stamped uneasily, waiting for the battle which experience told them to expect. The sounds of their apprehensive snorts and whinnies blended with the constant martial rattling of arms and rumbling undertone of talk from the equally impatient men.

Before the host sat the cars of Aileel, Meave, and the most powerful chieftains of the clans. The men were garbed in the grandest dress and trappings that the years of grueling war had let survive. And Meave too was in full warrior's kit, her bright cloak pinned at her throat with a brightly enameled brooch of Tara's distinctive crescent shape. In the chariot beside her Aileel stood resplendent in the green, silver-fringed cloak of Connacht's kings, apparently recovered from his wound, erect and proud and looking as commanding as ever in his youth, Meave thought.

Only she knew what effort the man expended now to keep up this strong front before his host. Only she knew how truly weak the wound had left him. In fact, he should not be here, and her heart went out to him at his pain—though she herself had prepared him to come here. For he alone could bind the clans of Connachtmen and hold them to their pledge. He had to be here, she told herself again, no matter what the risk.

Behind her, the argument among the chieftains was continuing.

"You hope the Firbolgs will fail us, don't you, Murchadh," Lewy MacNeesh was replying to the warlike chief. "But I say they will come. Fardia MacDaman has sent his word on it. And if you've no trust for him, our own scouts have seen signs that their clans are gathering."

"Gathering are they?" the red-haired chieftain named Donnchadh said glumly. "If so, it's likely only to come upon us in a host. To sweep upon us and finish us. And all of us drawn up together like fine fools. Like calves waiting for the wolf pack to close."

"You don't believe their strength could be so great as that?" Aileel asked, turning to the man. "They wouldn't dare to strike at us in our full force."

"Our force?" the other echoed with an ironic smile. He looked around him at a host that numbered less than two thousand fighting men. Then he shrugged, adding in a stoic way, "At least we'll be dying in our finest dress."

"You're fearing only fancies, Donnchadh," Lewy chided. "You see them now as giants, monsters, not as just men."

"Well, I say that if they're fool enough to come here, then *we* strike *them!*" the always aggressive Murchadh put in. "Just get all those bloody animals where we can see them clear for once, where we can put iron to 'em, and we'll finish the lot!"

Aghast at his harsh words, Meave wheeled upon him. "There can be no talk of that!" she said sharply. "If they come to talk under the king's truce, no warrior of honor would use the chance to attack them."

"Not if they were other warriors," he returned, undaunted. "But there's no making truces with the likes of these. Only destroying them will finish this war and earn us a proper vengeance for what they've done."

"We've made a pact," she said slowly and with force. "You

all agreed to honor it if they came." She looked to Aileel for support. "My King, if anyone violates this truce, there will never be an end to this awful war. This is your chance for peace."

"It's the truth she's speaking," said Aileel, then raised his voice to be heard by all the chiefs, his voice commanding, his look chill and meaningful. "My own word is in this. Any man who has sworn loyalty to me will keep it as well. No one will act without my order." He fixed a challenging eye upon Murchadh. "No one."

There was some mumbling and exchanges of looks, but no one said a word aloud. Even the blustering Murchadh subsided without protest.

Aileel, however, leaned across his chariot bulwark and murmured to Meave, "Were he or any chieftain to defy me, I'd have no strength to stop him. My power is only a show now. Only a bluff holds us together. That, and you, Meave. My trust is all in you. I've put my honor, my lands, and all our lives into your hands. This much I trust you. But if you are wrong . . ."

The rest went unspoken, but she understood. If anything were to happen, it would be much more than her own desires and her own hopes that would be destroyed.

She looked off to the south, down the broad vale of the Plains of Ai toward where the Firbolgs must appear. The sun shone glaringly, starkly, clearly revealing an empty plain.

Her great gamble had come to its final throw here. A fear of a new, greater failure flooded in suddenly, threatening to overwhelm her. She felt a weakness, a burning in her limbs, a heaving in her belly. But then she pulled herself in stolidly, clutching at the single, hard reality at the center of her being. There was little she had to lose in this, she told herself with brutal truthfulness, and neither did ravaged Connacht.

And if the Firbolgs did come to attack in force, did come to overwhelm and slaughter them? Well, better even that end, fighting bravely here, than wasting away abandoned and useless.

"Someone's coming!" cried Lewy, pointing excitedly to the south. "Look there!"

Meave looked, heart pumping wildly. Yes, something was there, an object moving rapidly toward them. She stared intently as it resolved itself. Only a single chariot. One of their own.

But then, behind it, something else appeared. A black line this time, filling the lower vale from east to west, surging ahead like a wave rolling to the shore.

And then the sounds reached them, the rumble of vast movement, the rattling of thousands of spears and swords and shields.

"So, they have come!" said Aileel.

Meave realized she had been holding her breath and released it slowly, in a silent sigh of relief.

"By Danu, it must be their entire nation!" Donnchadh said in awe.

For it was not only the hundreds of Firbolg fighting men who now moved toward the Connacht host, it was some thousands of people—women, children, and ancients of each clan—trudging forward behind the warriors.

Three spear throws distant from the opposing host they stopped. The warriors of Connacht stared across at them—at these elusive and almost mystical beings they had savagely battled so long—with curiosity. There was much surprise among them. The fierce, giant Firbolg warriors revealed in the hard morning light were only worn and tattered men, with that same war-weariness, that same hollowness in the cheeks and hopelessness in the eyes as the Connachtmen saw in themselves.

"These are what we have been fighting?" the battle-hungry Murchadh said in shock. "These are the Firbolgs?"

And Donnchadh, who had feared them, said in a compassionate tone, "Look at their women and their young. They seem nearly starved."

Within the forefront of the Firbolg clans, men were now moving. A score gathered and strode unarmed but fearlessly out from their host toward the van of Connachtmen. At their head walked Fardia MacDaman.

"We must meet them afoot," Meave said to their chieftains. "And without weapons."

She, Aileel, Lewy, and a dozen other of the highest chieftains of their force climbed from their chariots, gave over swords and shields and spears, and walked out toward their foes.

They met midway, stopping to appraise one another warily for a long moment. Then Fardia spoke.

"We have come, as I promised," he said to Meave in a calm, proud, certain voice. "We have all agreed to this truce and this discussion, if you mean to uphold it. We have brought our families as proof of our faith and of our wish for final peace.

This has gone on for too long. Our infants die in hunger. Our old ones freeze in the cold. There is keening in every hut for our dead warriors. We are so weary, many would welcome their deaths as a freedom."

He paused for emphasis, his eyes traveling over them, fixing each with a piercing look. Then he went boldly on.

"I will tell the truth to you: only some few believed you. Most did not. We've been given no reason to trust you in this war, or in your betrayals or your taking of our lands. But all are resolved in one thing: if you mean to make a peace or strike at us, we mean to end it here. Either way, the Firbolg people will have honor today."

As the eye of the noble young warrior met that of the hostile chieftain Murchadh, that man, ashamed, was forced to look away.

Fardia turned his gaze on Aileel. "Well, King of Connacht, man whom my father once honored, will it be peace or war?"

"We must have terms that both your people and our own can accept," Aileel said earnestly.

He strode about the fire pit of Cruchane's main hall, where a well-stoked fire blazed, driving back the chill. Around him, at two great curves made of plank tables, hundreds of warriors of both sides faced one another in a guarded way.

Cruchane had undergone a hasty cleaning. Though still a battered, sagging derelict, the festoons of cobwebs and the rats were gone, the torches lit, the tables scrubbed.

Beef, pork, and lamb, gleaned with great labor from the ravaged countryside, broiled on spits all about the fire. Great vats of steaming broth boiled upon it.

But none had eaten. Before the feast, there must be talk. There was no drink—a decree from Aileel, insisted upon by Meave—to ensure that nothing might inflame the minds or fire the fighting blood. For that same reason, no weapons were allowed, a precaution Meave had learned from Conaire Mor.

"We will not be made slaves to the rulers of Connacht again," a broad and craggy-faced Firbolg chieftain told the king gruffly.

"And we would not expect it," Aileel assured him. "We want a peace that will be fair to all."

"Then give us back our lands!" another Firbolg demanded.

"You want us to give all Connacht to you!" one of the Connacht chieftains answered.

"All of it lands which you stole from us!"

"Be at ease now," Fardia MacDaman said soothingly, rising and moving out into the open space. "We can't be making mad demands here," he told his people in reasoning tones, "or this will come to nothing," Then he turned to face Aileel across the fire.

"We've talked this out before among us, and we've agreed," he told the king. "We've no wish to take back all Connacht. Much of that land was won honestly from us by you. But, at the same time, we'll not give all Connacht into your hands. What we're asking for here is only our own rights to the lands we have settled, that they be ours alone. Our clans, our laws, our herds. No man of yours may hunt them, settle them, even enter them without our leave."

"What? You mean to keep those lands separate from us?" an indignant Connacht chieftain cried out. "You're seeking your own kingdom within our own?"

There were some grumbled noises of support from his fellows at this.

"The finest lands of Connacht are already yours," Fardia countered in an earnest voice. "Long ago we moved our clans into its most distant parts. It's on wild seacoasts battered by the waves and craggy hilltops scoured by chill winds that we live now. But we have learned to survive in these harsh domains. We've learned even to love these places where you Milesians would never choose to live. They are part of us now. Let us have them in peace. What is that to ask for final peace, and your own lands never spoiled again?"

The young Firbolg chieftain's truth and eloquence moved his listeners. Now, amazingly, there were many murmurs of agreement from the Connachtmen. Aileel looked around him, then met the eye of Meave. Almost imperceptibly, she nodded.

"Very well," he said to Fardia, moving around the fire closer to him. "I can pledge that to you. But that's not all of it. You must realize that you can't live within Connacht and be entirely free of it. You must serve."

"Serve!" a Firbolg chieftain spat out. "Of course, Connacht-man! You'll give us our poor bits of land, but we must be your slaves to earn it, just as we were before, doing your filthy tasks for you, bowing to you—"

"No!" Aileel said with force, cutting him off. "There'll be no more of that, I promise you. But you owe some service to Connacht, just as we all do. If she is threatened, then your own fighting men must join its host."

Fardia looked to his people. There were murmured conversations, shrugs and nods, but no voices of dissent.

"It would be fair to do so," he said. "No Firbolg would expect a Milesian to defend his lands for him. Our clans would surely host with yours."

"But what about their skills with the animals, Aileel?" Donnchadh called out. "Are we to be denied them? Everyone knows that Firbolgs are near magic with the beasts. We'll need that skill more than ever now, with our herds so thinned by the war."

"He's right in that," Aileel agreed, moving closer to Fardia. "Your skills are legend with us. And they will be needed to make Connacht rich again. Will you help us?"

"As servants, or as equal men?" Fardia asked, stepping toward him.

"As free men, rightly compensated for their work," Aileel replied.

"Our own cattle herds are nearly gone, our last horses lost to the war's hardships long ago," the Firbolg admitted. "We need to replenish them ourselves. A quarter of your animals at breeding time will be fair payment for our services to you."

The two men were now close. "Done then," said Aileel, extending his hand. "We are agreed. From this day, you and your tribe will be Connachtmen, as ourselves."

"No, my King," Fardia corrected gravely. "We will never be as you. We will be always Firbolgs—separate, but a part of your Connacht."

Aileel smiled. "I understand."

With that, Fardia smiled in return, extending his own hand. The men clasped each other's wrists in a bonding gesture, standing so, locked together for a moment as the men of both sides raised a cheer whose thunder threatened to shake down the fragile hall.

The Firbolgs were departing Cruchane. As evening shadows began to fill the fortress's yard, the last band of their warriors gathered at the main gates.

Aileel, Meave, and other of the Connacht dignitaries were there as well, making proper farewells to their guests. The formalities complete, the Firbolgs started out down the slope, back to their own host. But young Fardia tarried behind, clearly wishing to make his own goodbyes.

"Well, old friend," he said to Lewy, "now I can hope to see you again soon."

"And as comrades again, as we were so long ago," Lewy said heartily, clapping a hand to the other's shoulder.

"At least we'll not be trying to kill each other when we meet—if all goes well," he answered guardedly.

"You sound doubtful," Meave said. "But I know this treaty will last. Fardia, it's a new Ireland we'll live in now. Conaire Mor has created a great peace, and we're all part of it. Connacht and Ireland will prosper together, as your people will with ours."

"You may be right, my Lady," he said, but still with a cautious tone. "I pray good Danu that you are. But these years of war have made me see only hard truths in the world. No treaty will suddenly make Firbolg and Milesian friends. We've been separate for too long."

"Both seemed content enough together at our feast," she said.

"My Lady, you're a woman of wisdom and fair judgments. You know better than you say. The warmth you saw was that of men with bellies full and the threat of death gone from them for the first time in many years. But I watched your people as we ate. I saw the looks of scorn, of disdain, of loathing behind the veils of camaraderie."

She opened her mouth to protest, but he held up a staying hand. "No, don't deny it. I know the truth of it, and so do you." He gave her a self-mocking little smile. "Of course, I'll not be saying some of their dismay can't be understood. Our people have always been a rough, unmannered lot, and it's sure our years of scavenging like beasts in the wilderness have done little to make us gentler. But there's more much deeper in this. Something in the blood. And you must believe, Meave, that it's not today, tomorrow, or a hundred years from now that the Milesians will see Firbolgs as their equals. Look to Lewy, look to your king to discover if it's the truth I'm speaking now."

Meave turned to Aileel, who had listened gravely through the young chieftain's speech. He nodded. "Only a fool would say otherwise," he told her.

For all her optimism, her new hopes, she understood what they were saying to her. She'd seen the scornful looks herself, and she knew them well enough. Hadn't she herself been the victim of such looks from Conchobar? Still, she tried to hold on to her buoyant mood.

"It may be so," she told them, "but I feel it will change. Years it may take, but we've made a fine start here. We've won peace and freedom, and someday we'll win the rest."

"We'd have none of it without you, Meave," Aileel told her. "All our people owe a debt to you for that."

"They do," Fardia agreed. He met Meave's eye levelly, his voice earnest. "No man has won more respect from me than you have, with your courage and honesty. If I pledge myself to doing all I can to see this treaty kept, I want you to know that it will be as much for you as for the good of Ireland."

She smiled warmly in return. "With such as you to lead them," she said, "I've a feeling your people will gain anything they want one day."

Lewy MacNeesh, noting the intensity of this exchange, seemed irritated by its intimacy. He frowned and then moved forward in an almost proprietary way, clapping an arm about Fardia in a comradely gesture that also moved him between the two, breaking the contact.

"Well, Fardia," he said heartily, "it's growing dark. Why don't I walk back with you to your host? We've many past years to talk about."

"All right," the other agreed with a broad grin that banished his somberness and made him seem again the young man he was. He looked to Meave and Aileel. "Good night, my Lady," he said graciously. "And good night . . . my King."

With that, he and his old friend started away, out the gates of the fortress.

Night was nearly upon them now. The others of the Connacht company departed for their own quarters.

"Shall we retire too?" Meave asked Aileel, looking up to him with some concern. "You've shown no sign of it, but I know this day has wearied you."

"Not yet," he said. "I want some chance to be alone with you. Come, walk with me."

They moved out to the gateway and stood there looking down. The shadow of the dun in the sun's last rays cast a long cone of darkness far out across the plain. Within it, the hundreds of campfires of the Firbolg host twinkled like red-gold stars. Below, Lewy and Fardia were still visible, striding away, gesturing animatedly, laughing heartily.

"You've another conquest there, Meave," the king said with amusement. "Or should I say two?"

"I value their loyalty," she said honestly, "but they're only boys."

"Boys? They're little younger than yourself."

"There's only one whose affection I've wished for," she told him, slipping an arm about his waist. Beneath the deceptive bulk of his tunic and cloak, she felt the boniness of his much-thinned frame.

"Do you still wish it, Meave?" he asked her bluntly. "Now that it's ended? Now that we've won? Or are you wishing now that you could escape from this old man, return to the glories of grand Tara's halls?"

She looked up at him, frankly meeting a searching gaze that was filled with hoping and with fear at once.

"My Aileel, I said I wanted nothing more than to stay in Connacht, at your own side. I will do that, not because you have my vow, but because you have my love."

He saw the truth of it glowing in her blue-gray eyes. He nodded, smiling with great joy. "Then now begins the time for us, my Meave," he said, pulling her close.

"It does, my King. There's time for us . . ." she paused, looking behind her at the sagging ruins of the once-grand fortress, "and for Connacht."

Chapter Twenty-eight

Revelations

"I don't know what to do," said Ferogain. He seemed on the verge of tears.

He sat in the quarters of the queen of Ireland, body sagging, head down in his hands. She sat by him, an arm about his shoulders to comfort him.

"What's wrong?" she asked, puzzled by his sudden appearance here and by his state of distress.

"I've just no way to live with this anymore, Fionualla," he told her miserably. "I had to speak to someone, and there's no one else I could think of but you. No one else who might help . . ." He broke off, shaking his head in his hands as if racked by some great pain.

"Help with what, Ferogain?" she gently prodded, rocking him as she would a stricken child. "Please, tell me what it is."

"It . . . it's just that they won't stop," he forced out brokenly. "They've gotten worse . . . worse. I've prayed they'd quit, but they haven't. And come spring there'll be even more. I can't quit them. I'm caught up in it—in the heat and the blood of it." He moaned in agony, squeezing his head now violently between his hands as if to crush it. "Ah! The blood is on me now, and I can't be rid of it! I can't be free! But I'll go mad, Fionualla! I'll go mad!"

She turned him forceably toward her, shaking him now, the gentleness gone in her sudden alarm at his state. "Ferogain, stop that! Tell me what you're talking about! Tell me now!"

His head came up slowly. His tear-filled, anguished eyes lifted to meet hers. His mouth forced out the awful words. "It's about the raids, Fionualla! About the ones Conaire's seeking. I . . . I'm one of them."

Stricken by the terrible import of his confession, she stared, frozen, for an instant, then shook him again, and with more violence. "No!" she said with force, as if such firm denial could change the truth of it. "You're not! You can't be!"

"I am. I am!" he nearly shouted back at her, the tears spilling from his eyes, running across the smooth, rounded cheeks, making him seem even more the child.

The words were like a slap across her face, making her head snap back, driving home the truth. She released him suddenly, standing up and moving away, her back to him.

He, so abruptly abandoned, reached out toward her, face crumpled in lines of despair, voice racked with sobs. "Please, Fionualla. Please!" he begged. "You're the only hope I have."

She didn't answer, standing stiffly, back to him, her eyes staring unseeing as her mind struggled to deal with the effects of this thunderbolt.

Ferogain dropped his hands and sank back, head drooping in a gesture of great weariness. "I don't blame you," he said resignedly. "What I've done is a terrible thing. All those we've killed . . ."

"What about Conaire?" she said harshly. With the initial shock now overcome, her first response was outrage. "What have you done to him?"

"I know!" he said dismally. "Don't you think I know?" He lifted his gaze again to her imploringly. "But I didn't mean it to happen. You must believe me. I only meant to prove myself. To be a warrior. And the others . . ."

The total despair in his voice reached through the anger to her heart. She turned back to him, her voice softening. "What about the others?"

"They pulled me into it. I tried to fight them, but I was too weak. I've always been too weak. It's only been you . . . you who protected me." He lifted a hand out toward her, then dropped it back limply. "And now I've lost even you."

At this her pity for him, her motherly need to protect him as before, overcame her. She returned to him, sitting back down beside him. Her arm went out about his shoulder again in comfort.

"I'd never turn against you, Ferogain. You must know that. But this . . ." she shook her head at the awful, overwhelming enormity of it, "this is too horrible. You've betrayed Conaire, Ireland, even yourself."

"It's what's been tearing at me every day," he said. "I'm tortured by it. I feel the hot blood spraying up my arm. I see the grinning heads in my nightmares. I hear the screams in every wail of breeze. I can't forget." He gripped her hand in his, squeezing it tightly, his voice near panic now. "And soon . . . soon it will be worse! Soon there'll be many more in it. More each day. And with the spring they'll start the raids again. Not small raids against scattered clans this time. Three nights from now—three nights!—and it will begin again. You must help me!"

"I can't, Ferogain," she said regretfully. "Do you see that? Not this time. This isn't a childhood prank or teasing from your brothers. You've let yourself be drawn in far too deeply now."

She put a hand on each of his shoulders, meeting and holding his eye. Firmly she said, "You listen to me now, Ferogain. There is no other way for you. You must go to Conaire."

His expression filled with dismay and fear. "No! No, I can't!"

"You have to," she said emphatically. "Only his own understanding can save you now."

"He would never understand," the boy said. "He's turned against us."

"Us?" she repeated. "So, all your brothers . . . they are in this too?"

"Yes," he admitted. "Even poor Lomna Druth, too much a fool to do anything else. And if Conaire knew, he would have us all condemned."

"He would not," she insisted. "You are all still brothers to him. He still loves you."

"I don't believe you," he said more forcefully. He pulled back from her. "You know that he has changed." His eyes narrowed in a gaze that probed her own. "Why is it you're trying to convince me otherwise? You know he'd hate me, Fionualla. You know I'd surely die."

She opened her mouth as if to argue more, but the shuttered mind she saw behind his eyes told her it was futile. She sighed defeatedly.

"If that's what you believe, then I truly can't help you," she told him with regret. "I'm sorry, Ferogain. I don't know what to do." Then a new thought occurred to her. With more energy, she asked, "But what about your brothers? Maybe *they* could be convinced to quit this madness."

He shook his head.

"No. None think as I do. Ferger and Ferobain love the danger. Fergel's become greedy for the loot. And the poor Fool is content so long as he has food enough. None will admit to any fear, and any word of it from me only gives them more reason to call me weak."

"What about the rest? Who is leader for this band? What others are involved?"

At that he eyed her with open suspicion. "And why are you wanting to know that? Do you mean to betray us all?"

"No!" she protested, taken aback by his accusation. "How can you say that?"

"I don't believe you," he said harshly. He rose and stepped away, wheeled back to her, face hard with a new certainty. "I see it clearly now. You've changed as well. It's only him you care about in this, and let the Morrigan take us."

"You're wrong!" she told him. "I love you. I want to give you help."

"Your 'help' would see our heads upon the spikes of Tara's walls," he said with scorn. "Well, if that's all you can do, I want no more from you. From here on, I'll be following only them. If I can't escape them, then my only hope is that they are right: that our raids can force Conaire to give up his foolish peace."

He turned and strode proudly, stoically to the door.

"Wait! You can't!" she called after him. "You could destroy him. You could divide all Ireland, bring it back to war."

He paused in the doorway. But his back stayed to her, and his voice was cold. "I've no other choice. And if you don't mean to help me, then I charge you, as one who said you once loved me, to keep my secret from Conaire Mor."

"It's a cruel thing for you to use my own love to trap me so," she told him in agony. "Still, if you mean to force me to a vow, I'll not betray you, as you've done to him. But think of what you're doing. Help yourself in this while you still can. Please, tell Conaire!"

He gave no reply to this plea, only stalking silently out through her doorway.

The hand ran smoothly up over the firm swell of the shoulder.

"You see here?" Laeg said, his hand pausing at the top of the muscled curve, his thumb and forefinger bracketing a spot where the short hair had been worn away. "It's right down to the soft skin now, and chafing it raw as well."

Sentanta peered over his driver's shoulder at the spot with interest. "Yes, I see it," he said. "Well?"

Laeg turned from the chariot horse to his master, face flushed with indignation. "Well?" he echoed. "Is that all you can say?"

Sentanta shrugged. "I'm sorry. What do you want from me?"

"I want your permission to quit using this new harness," the driver demanded. He moved out of the stall in the stable shed to lift the harness from a wall peg. Its straps rattled and glittered brightly as he held it up. "Look at it. The leather is stiff and all but bristling with that golden filigree. It's a wonder the steeds aren't covered with sores from it."

"It's one of the finest harnesses in Ireland!" Sentanta said in protest. "The king himself had it made for me. . . ."

"Finest harness in Ireland," Laeg repeated, snorting in scorn. "Well, the old harness was quite good enough for you before you came here, my young hero," the driver brusquely told him. "Now, with you puttin' on your grand airs . . ."

"I am an emissary to the high-king," he replied, defensive before his always outspoken friend.

"I wonder if you know *what* you are," Laeg bluntly replied.

"Once you wanted only to be a warrior of worth. Well, that kingly finery will be little use to you if your horse balks in a fight from a sore leg and you find yourself suddenly swinging into the path of some enemy's sword!"

"If Conaire Mor has his way, there may be no need for fighting chariots or swords one day," Sentanta said.

"Of course," Laeg answered in a sardonic tone. "The same day the bloody black Morrigan becomes a great white swan. But in the meantime . . ."

"Sentanta," said a voice.

They both turned to see the wife of Conaire Mor standing in the doorway of the shed.

"My Queen!" Sentanta said, surprised to see her there. "What is it?"

"I wish to speak with you, somewhere alone."

"Alone? But what about here?" he asked in puzzlement, looking around. The long stable shed with its row of stalls was deserted save for them.

"No," she said firmly, "we must truly be alone, and away from here. I've told Conaire I mean to go out and gather some spring flowers. He's busy with state matters and can't go, as I well knew. So I asked for you to take me. Of course he agreed." She stepped closer to him, her voice nearly pleading now. "Will you go? Please. It means much to me."

Sentanta gazed into the depths of those bright green, imploring eyes. Then he looked around at Laeg, who stood just behind him, observing the scene with immense interest. Laeg, out of her sight, pursed his lips in a soundless whistle and raised one eyebrow. Sentanta frowned in return.

"Laeg, will you harness the queen's chariot?" he asked.

"Of course, Master," Laeg answered in his best subservient manner. "And will I drive?"

"No. I'll be taking it out myself."

"But, can you handle it?" Laeg asked, a glance at the queen giving a double meaning to the words.

"Just harness the car," Sentanta ordered curtly.

The chariot rolled to a stop.

Sentanta looked around him at the place with appreciation. It was a small glade beside a clear, blue pool. The day was warm, and a bright sun filtered through the trees to dapple water and grass with jewels of light that shifted lazily in a soft breeze fragrant with the reborn scents of spring.

"A most beautiful place," the young man said, hopping from the car and lifting a hand to help her down.

"Yes," she agreed. She took his hand and stepped down, pausing there, meeting his eye so close, adding meaningfully, "And quite hidden as well."

She stepped away, leaving him to look after her as she moved with an unconscious grace down to the pool. She was most comely, he mused, watching her. The setting quite fit her. The brightness, the vitality of spring, the sensuous fragrance of the air, the lush swellings of the . . .

He reined in his galloping fancies sharply, blushing at his thoughts. She was the wife of Conaire Mor, his high-king, his sworn leader, and his friend.

She stopped at the pool's edge, looking around her. "Conaire and I came here many times to be alone," she said in a faraway tone. Then she shook her head, hard reality coming back. "But we've not been here since last fall. Ah, that seems so very long ago. The whole world has changed since then." A great sorrow, like a weight, seemed to come upon her, and she knelt down upon the bank, her body sagging with it.

Sentanta, concerned by her sudden melancholy, moved up beside her. "I . . . I know we've not come here for flowers, my Queen," he began awkwardly. "There's great trouble in you. Do you want my help?"

"I do," she said, looking up to him. "Please, sit."

Obediently he sat beside her. She gazed intently, searchingly into his eyes.

"You seem a handsome, strong, able young man," she told him. "But are you truly as Conaire says? Are you also a man of honor and fierce loyalty?"

He felt uncomfortable under the probing gaze. "I . . . I hope I am, my Queen," he said modestly.

She placed a hand upon his. Her voice grew more intense. "And are you compassionate as well?"

He felt the heat of her hand. It seemed to be burning upon his. He smelled her fragrance, more heady than that of the spring blossoms. He found it suddenly difficult to breathe.

"My . . . Queen . . ." he managed to croak out.

"I hope you are," she went on earnestly, "because I most desperately need your help." At his look of confusion, she explained, "Conaire's peace may be in great danger. I must do something, and I had nowhere else to turn."

"Oh!" The realization of her true intent chilled his fever like a winter rain. But his doused feeling quickly gave way to one of relief. "My Queen," he said, "of course I'll give you help, if I can."

"You must first understand," she told him, "I've been put in a most terrible position. I cannot betray my trust to a friend, but I cannot see my husband's work and all Ireland betrayed. I've come to you as my only hope. I will tell you what I know, but you must promise to tell no one what you will hear from me." She took up both his hands, clasping them between hers in a fierce grip, her gaze boring into his. "Promise!"

"I will, my Queen," he said, astonished by the desperation he felt vibrating within her.

"Very well," she said, seeming satisfied. She released his hands and turned away from him, as if ashamed to give her betraying revelation to him face to face.

"Then listen: one of Conaire's own foster-brothers, young Ferogain, is in this band of raiders. He confessed this to me two days ago. He says they will raid again, tomorrow. I've agonized over this for two long nights. I know I must stop it, but I don't wish him hurt!"

"Ferogain," Sentanta repeated with amazement. "We had suspected it might be someone here, at Tara's court. But a foster-brother to the king . . ."

"Can you see why I couldn't tell Conaire myself?" she asked. "Yet, I can't let the raids go on. I promised only to keep the secret from my husband. So I've told you."

"And what do you wish me to do with this secret, my Queen?"

"You must stop the raids, of course. My only hope has been that you might somehow save my husband from destroying these reckless men, might at least save Ferogain. He is trapped in this."

"I can't promise anything, my Queen," he told her honestly. "It would help me if I knew more about who is involved. Did he tell you more of . . ."

"No!" She shook her head emphatically. "I've said all I can. Please, don't press me for more. My heart is twisted by anything I do in this. The rest must be up to you."

"I understand, my Queen," he said, moved by her anguish. He put a hand lightly upon her shoulder. "I will keep your secret, and I will try in what way I can to save your friend."

She looked up at him. Some hope glimmered in her tear-filled eyes. "I believe you, warrior of Ulster," she said. She leaned forward and kissed him lightly on the lips. "And, whatever happens now, you have my own affection and my thanks."

This lit a new fire in the young man, but of devoted zeal this time. He drew himself up in a courageous pose, his voice taking on a most earnest tone. "My Queen, I've pledged my sword and life to Conaire Mor. I pledge the same to you. My loyalty until my death!"

Laeg looked up from his combing of a horse's mane as Sentanta strode back into the stables. His smooth, boyish face was drawn in troubled lines.

"Ready our war chariot, Laeg," he ordered sharply. "We'll be riding out tonight."

"I will," the other said with alacrity, his young master's grave expression telling him to ask no questions now but just to obey.

He moved toward the rich harness hung upon the wall.

"No. Leave that," Sentanta told him, pointing to a plain one hung beside it. "For this," he said grimly, "you can put on the old harness again."

Chapter Twenty-nine

Discovery

The chariot carrying Ferogain rolled through the opening in the wall of rock.

It and the circular fortress into which it had just vanished were only tiny objects to Sentanta, peering out from behind a ridge of stones a good distance away.

It was the flat and barren nature of the rocky landscape that had forced him to this distance. He had been able to stay much closer to the boy on most of the nighttime ride from Tara, crossing rolling and heavily wooded countryside. But then, with the dawn, they had entered this stark scene, and Laeg had reined back on his steeds, giving the other chariot a much greater lead.

Laeg and their chariot now waited in a rare sheltered spot not far behind Sentanta while he continued to stare out at the goal of Ferogain's trip.

It was a large fortress, its curved walls of carefully piled rock reaching up over twice a man's height. The space encompassed by it was not so large as the yard of a great dun, but it was greater than that of Tara's own main hall. Once it must have offered security to a fair-sized clan, he estimated. But the now-ragged wall, completely fallen at some points and overgrown by vines, was evidence of past defeat and abandonment.

There was no movement visible about the place. His guess was that the boy had come to meet with his fellow raiders, but he saw no sign of other chariots or men. Were they inside? He had only a single way of finding out.

He moved back from his vantage point to his hidden chariot. Laeg looked around from the soothing talk he had been having with his horses.

"There you are at last," he said. "What did you see?"

"He went into that ruined fortress, as we thought. And I have to go in too."

"Of course you do," Laeg said with a sardonic air. "And shall I wait, or shall I go right back to prepare your funeral?"

"Wait," Sentanta answered, not amused. "I'll be only a few moments."

"I will wait then. But is it all right if I pray as well? Just so I'll have something to do."

"Do as you wish," the lad snapped irritably. "Just wait!"

He left the chariot and crept across the rocky plain to the fortress's wall. There was still no sign of movement, and no lookouts were posted atop the wall. If the raiders were inside, Sentanta thought, they must have great confidence in the isolation of their new hiding place.

Still, it was with caution that he moved about the wall, peering upward for a place where he might enter unobserved.

Nearly opposite the gateway, he found a place where the wall had crumbled almost half its height, creating a redundant ramp of stones against the outside. He clambered up this slowly, taking care not to cause a landslide, poking his head carefully above the top. Then he pulled back quickly.

But the single glance was enough to tell him that this was indeed the place. For ranged along the curved inner wall below were nearly a hundred chariots of war.

He peered in again. The yard was a busy place, with the

scores of horses tethered near the ruins of a long stable shed and the many charioteers swarming about tending the cars. There was no warrior among them, and none seemed concerned with keeping an eye out for intruders, so he felt safe in examining the interior at greater length.

Besides the old stables, there were half a dozen other structures in the yard. Round huts mostly, half-fallen and roofless. Only one, a larger, oval structure, seemed intact, and from its roof hole a stream of smoke rose. There, he supposed, was where the warriors must be.

The drivers and chariots were all gathered at the front of the yard. Behind the hut, between it and the wall, there seemed to be no one. Keeping as hidden as he could, Sentanta made his way around the circumference, clinging to the top stones, inching his way along until he was at the rear of the fortress.

He looked down again into the yard. He was behind the oval hut. No one was about. Swiftly he lowered his body over the edge and dropped lightly down inside, then ran to the hut.

As he drew nearer to it, he heard voices from within.

"And why did you delay?" someone demanded sharply. "Your brothers have been here since last night."

"I had some matters . . ." came a defensive reply.

"Matters?" the first voice echoed. "And what would they be?"

There were several windows along the hut's rear. Weather-battered shutters sagged on wooden hinges, gaping apart. Sentanta moved to an opening and peeked within.

The hut's single room was crowded by some fivescore of men, a few seated upon the antique remnants of furniture, most standing. All surrounded a blazing central fire where Maine Morgor now confronted a timorous Ferogain.

"They're my own matters," the boy was mumbling, not meeting the sharp-faced warrior's scathing eye. "Nothing to do with you."

"If you're one of us, then it *is* to do with us!" Morgor shot back. He stepped forward, his manner threatening. "Now I ask you again: where were you?"

The boy lifted his head, meeting the other's gaze squarely. "If you must know it, I was ill," he answered in a defiant burst. "I was ill all day."

"Ill?" Morgor repeated, then laughed derisively. "Sick with fear, more like."

The harsh laughter of a few others joined his, and there were condescending smiles from more. Ferogain colored and looked about him angrily.

"Let the boy alone," said Fergel, at last coming to his brother's defense. "He's here now, and he's ready. Aren't you, lad?"

As this exchange went on, Sentanta had been scanning the company with increasing astonishment. The fire struck a ruddy light from the smooth, young faces, revealing all Donn Dessa's sons, the three Maines, plus many others whose clan colors he knew. He realized that the sons of chieftains, champions, even kings were assembled here. The flower of Ireland's young warriors. It was worse than Conal and Cathbad had ever feared. The simple band of raiders had become something a great deal more dangerous.

Then, from a shadowed corner, another figure he had not noted before moved forward into the light. The red glow revealed a stooped but massive warrior, his dark face grizzled and much scarred by war. He stepped up by the fire and swept around the room a gaze like sparks struck from a forge. His voice—deep, soft, and rolling as distant thunder—still sounded most distinctly across the room.

"We are all here now. And we are stronger than we have ever been before. All of you know me—because it was my efforts these seasons past that lit the flame in you and brought you here. You number among you now every true warrior son of the great clans of Ireland. Your presence here cries out against the foolish peace your fathers have made with Mor."

The gaze swept them again. The flaring eyes seemed to draw images before them of battle and victory. The voice grew more powerful, more commanding, seizing their minds. Even Sentanta, watching from outside, felt the compelling force of it, felt a strange energy flow through him, recalled images of his own triumphs.

"You are the fighting spirit of Ireland," the dark warrior went on. "You are its champions. Only through you can it be kept alive. You must fight on, as your ancestors did. You must show all others that you cannot be deprived."

He drew his sword, sweeping up the blade to gleam with bloodred light from the rising flames. "Are you ready to strike?" he called.

A hundred swords leaped out in reply, filling the air with their glinting light as the warriors shouted their shrill, affirming war cries to the rooftop.

Outside, Sentanta also opened his mouth to shout, but caught himself in time. He shook his head in wonder at the spell that had seized him, and looked down to find his hand clasping his sword hilt, the blade drawn halfway out.

He released it, looking toward the old warrior again. Who was this man whose voice and gaze could weave such a bloody enchantment about them all?

"Then today we prepare and plan," he was now telling them. "Tonight we rest ourselves and feast and dream of victories. Tomorrow we strike! And this time we will show everyone our power. A fair challenge and a fat herd await us in the heart of Ireland. Tomorrow we will take them both!"

Tomorrow! Sentanta thought. And a major raid in the heart of Ireland—such an attack wouldn't go ignored by anyone this time. There'd be an outcry through the land. It was madness. Yet, they all seemed transfixed, led like hounds on chains by this one man.

He must return to Tara. He must warn the king. Perhaps if Conaire Mor could confront them, break this man's spell, stop them before this raid, things could yet be righted without more bloodshed. Ferogain might be saved. But he must hurry.

He was turning from the window, casting about him for the best way to leave, when a driver rounded the back of the building.

The man, seeking only a more isolated place to relieve himself, stopped short on seeing Sentanta, clearly puzzled by his presence there. With dismay, the youth recognized him as one of the charioteers for the three Maines.

The recognition was mutual. The man's mouth dropped open as he froze in shock. But it was only for an instant. Before Sentanta could react, the man wheeled and charged away, yelling out at the top of his voice, "It's Sentanta! Sentanta! That boy from Ulster is here!"

Within the hall there was instant pandemonium and a tangle of alarmed shouts:

"Sentanta?"

"Where?"

"How could he be here?"

"He knows!"

"He'll warn the king!"

"Find him!" screamed Morgor, his voice rising above the rest. "Stop him!"

There began a confused milling in the crowded room. Drawn swords were brandished dangerously.

"Outside, you fools!" Morgor cried, angrily herding them toward the door.

Sentanta, meanwhile, had not dallied. The wall behind him was too steep to scale on the inside. He ran around the building to the front. The drivers, still reacting to the warnings with complete turmoil, now scattered like frightened birds before him as he charged boldly through the parked chariots.

Warriors uncorked themselves from a press at the narrow door and began to pour out of the hut. They would come between him and the gateway. Just ahead of him was a section of wall somewhat crumbled but still too high to clamber up swiftly enough to escape.

Several chariots were parked beneath it. He vaulted into the car of one, leaped from it to the high bulwark of another, and launched himself up. The first warriors rushed in beneath him as he caught the wall's upper edge with his fingertips. They reached up for him, flailing out to grasp his feet as he hung, swinging, above them. Then, with an effort, he drew himself above their hands, crawled onto the top of the wall, and dropped over the other side.

"He's out!" someone shouted.

"Well, don't stand gaping after him!" shouted Morgor, having finally battled his way through the crowd and out the door. "Be after him! We can't let him escape!"

"He's fast!" said Fergel. "We'll not catch him."

"He's not faster than our cars," Morgor shot back. "We'll ride him down!"

At his orders, the drivers quickly scrambled to harness their horses.

Outside, Sentanta was making his best speed across the open ground. There was no hiding place. He loathed running from a fight, but he couldn't face such odds and win. He had to survive and warn the king. His one hope of escaping was to reach his car.

But he was only halfway to its hiding place when the first chariots burst from the fortress. Morgor's car led them, that warrior already climbing out onto his pole, a spear ready, his mouth drawn in an evil smile of anticipation.

Sentanta looked back and then ahead. The sheltering ridge of stones was still too far. He would be skewered like a running boar long before he reached it.

Then his own car burst suddenly from the cover into the

open, Laeg crouched low at the reins, urging the steeds forward. The chariot flew over the ground toward him.

As it drew near, it didn't slow. Instead it passed him, Laeg deftly pulling it around in a sharp turn and back toward him.

The boy needed no instructions. As the chariot swept close to him, he leaped for its rear. He gripped one of the curved brass handholds and threw himself forward, his upper body landing in the car. His feet dragged a moment, the rock scraping at the flesh of his ankles and shins. Then he had drawn them in and was up beside Laeg.

"I didn't pray quite enough, it seems," the driver said, sarcastic even in their danger as he coolly guided the chariot across the uneven ground.

Behind, a score of chariots were bouncing ahead, just beyond spear range and slowly dropping back. But a score of others were fanning out far to the left.

"What are they doing?" Sentanta asked.

"I'd say they're trying to cut us off," was Laeg's reasoning reply.

"They can't!" the other protested. "They're not fast enough!"

"They don't need to be," Laeg told him, pointing ahead.

Before them there suddenly seemed to be a sharp line of ground beyond which showed only a blue-white haze of sky. And they were approaching it with great rapidity.

Laeg reined in hard, jerking the team into a sharp turn.

The car slewed around to the right, tipping up as if to overturn, skittering sideways on one wheel across the stone, then slamming down as the horses came to a stop.

Their hooves danced nervously at the edge of a high cliff. One wheel sat a hand's breadth from the very brink. Below, at the base of the sheer wall, great waves crashed against sharp spines of rock thrusting from the sea.

"Wrong way?" Sentanta inquired politely, looking down.

"I hadn't much choice," came the barked reply.

One group of the raiders was now closing in behind. The other was moving up along the cliff edge. Having little choice, Laeg urged the horses on the way they were pointed, paralleling the cliff, far too close to the precipice for Sentanta's peace of mind.

He looked down at the waves crashing so far below, then back at the pursuers. "Can we outrun them now?" he asked.

"Easily," Laeg answered. "At least, we can till we run out of land."

Sentanta looked ahead. The cliff curved back sharply there, forming a narrow point along which they sped. The two groups behind them, now rejoined, were already plugging the open end.

"We're trapped," he said.

"Not quite," said Laeg. "There is one other way." He jerked his head sideways to indicate the sea.

"What?" Sentanta said in disbelief. "We can't!"

"You prefer fighting sixty men?" Laeg returned. "Even you can't win."

Again Sentanta peered down, past the sharp cliff edge speeding by, down to the boiling surf. "We'll be smashed on the rocks!" he cried.

"We'll be dead anyway," Laeg reasoned. "Be ready to jump clear!"

And before the boy could protest, the driver had urged the horses to an even greater speed.

As the pursuers watched in amazement, the chariot raced out to the point without slowing, and sailed forward into space, arcing out and then down out of sight. The horses' shrill neighs of terror dwindled in the distance and were lost.

The raiders' chariots pulled up at the cliff point. The warriors gazed down at the sea below. There was no sign of chariot, of horses, or of men. Only the sea hammering angrily at the sharp rocks.

"They must have gone mad with fear," said Fergel, shaking his head.

"He cheated me of killing him myself," snarled Morgor. "A coward after all."

The other warriors now began to look at one another questioningly.

"Morgor, what should we do now?" one asked, voicing all their thoughts.

"Why should things change?" came the voice of the dark warrior. He was just rolling up behind them in his own car, guided by a robed and hooded charioteer. Behind him came the balance of the raiders, slower in readying their chariots to join the chase.

"You can't think to quit because this one found you out?" he went on, pulling up in their midst and looking about at them. "He was alone, and he is gone."

"But something brought him here," said Fergel. "It could be others know."

The dark warrior's eyes noted young Ferogain as he looked down at this, a faint flush, as of shame, coloring his cheeks. But no one else saw.

"I think that it was he alone who knew," the old man said. "But what if there are more?" His bright gaze swept them challengingly. "Is fear of that enough to keep you from your sport? I thought you meant to prove yourselves, prove to all warriors that their spirit cannot be destroyed. You're strong now. There's no one you can't defy, no one who will dare to act against you—even Conaire Mor. Do you still believe that," he fixed his eyes on Maine Morgor, "or is it a true lack of courage that's showing in you, now that the risk's become a bit too great?"

"We'll show you, old man," Morgor hotly replied. "Nothing will stop us. Right, my comrades? We'll go on as before, and the Morrigan take any who come against us, including the high-king."

The others joined in with renewed fervor. Even Ferogain shouted out with apparent zeal, though the dark warrior, eyeing him, could see that it was largely feigned.

When the band turned and started back toward their hiding place, the old man stayed behind, watching after them. A smile of satisfaction, almost of gloating, stretched his wide mouth.

"Young fools," he said to his charioteer. "They'll do as I say, even to their deaths." He glanced down at the waves. "With this meddling Ulsterman gone, there'll be no chance of stopping them now. After today, all Ireland will be joining to hunt them down. Mor will condemn them, and they will die. None of them will stir troubles again. No others will dare defy Mor's law. There will be no one left to challenge Ireland's new peace." He looked back to his driver.

"Then," he said slowly, savoring the words, "then we will have our power!"

The driver shrugged back his hood, revealing a skull-like head with parchment skin and dully glowing eyes. His lipless mouth split in a death's-head grin.

Chapter Thirty

Confrontation

The thick candle guttered low in its bronze sconce. Its flame whipped angrily, threatening to die each time Conal Carna shot by in his nervous pacing of the floor.

The fluttering light dimly illuminated the quarters of the two young Ulstermen. It revealed the room's other tenant, Cormac Conlingas, at the sole table, head resting upon his hands, eyes fixed grimly upon the shrinking stub of the beleaguered candle. Behind him, upon a pallet, the ard-druid Cathbad sat, head down, eyes closed, seemingly asleep.

"How can you sleep now?" Conal demanded irritably, stopping before the druid.

"I am not asleep," came the soothing reply. "I've been within my mind, searching for some feeling of him."

"A feeling. A great lot of help that is," Conal said derisively. "Can't you get leaves or powders or another horse's head, for Dagda's sake, and conjure something up?"

The druid sighed and opened his eyes, looking up at the warrior looming over him. "I know what you're feeling," he said with sympathy. "But I've no knowledge and no magic that can help us here."

The door flew open suddenly. All three turned to it to see two figures push through from the darkness into the faint light.

"Sentanta!" Cormac cried delightedly, jumping up. "Laeg!"

"By all the gods, what's happened to you?" Cathbad exclaimed, rising and moving toward the pair.

They were a most disheveled sight, clothes filthy and torn, limbs covered with raw scrapes, hair matted about their heads. They sank down wearily upon a bench at the table.

"And where have you been?" Conal demanded irritably. "We've been up most of the night."

"We have," Cormac confirmed. "All we knew was that you'd disappeared in the early dawn."

"Some ale first," Sentanta requested. "And a bit more heat."

Cormac moved at once to rouse the burned-down fire, stirring the embers and adding fresh peat. Cathbad poured both the youths a hearty drink.

The two drank deeply, greedily, gasping out their pleasure at the relieving effect.

"Ah, blessed ale," said Laeg. "Only liquid I've had but a bellyful of salt water since yesterday."

"We stopped for nothing in our hurry to come here," Sentanta said.

"We nearly weren't here at all," put in Laeg, shooting his master a critical look. "Our young hero didn't see fit to tell me that he couldn't swim. Nearly drowned the both of us, he did, before I got him in."

"Never mind that," Sentanta said quickly, frowning. "There's too little time." He looked around at his other comrades, announcing dramatically, "I found the outlaws."

"The outlaws?" Conal echoed. "Where?"

"They've a new hiding place—a stone fort near the coast a half-day's ride. They're meaning to go on another raid. . . . What time is it?"

"The night's three-quarters done," Cormac supplied.

"Today then," Sentanta said. "Curse it! It's taken us so long."

"Aye," Laeg said, rubbing his behind. "And by a jolting pony cart on the last bit. No roads at all."

"But there may still be time to stop them," Sentanta said with great urgency. "If we'd confront them, speak with them before they raided again, I think we could persuade them to give it up. It's not too late. This could be ended peacefully, and Conaire never know."

"And why would we not be wanting him to know?" a puzzled Conal asked. "It's against his peace these raids have been carried out. It's for him we've been seeking these brigands."

"Because," Sentanta answered slowly, "these 'brigands' number among them his own foster-brothers."

The others exchanged a glance at this: Cormac's astonished, Conal's grim, the druid's sorrowful.

"I feared something of the kind," Cathbad said. "And are Aileel's sons in this too?"

"They are," Sentanta answered, surprised. "How did you know?"

"When you vanished, and I began to ask about, I found that

they were all suspiciously gone too. Some vague mention of hunting was the excuse they gave. But I felt a disquiet."

"They're not all the ones in it," Sentanta said. "The sons of many of Ireland's greatest clans have joined them. There must be a hundred or more now."

"A most dangerous lot," said Cathbad, shaking his head. "Their revealing would send a wave of shock through Ireland that would shake the roof poles of Conaire's carefully built peace."

"Nothing can stop their being known if they carry out this raid," Sentanta told him. "It's to be at a rich tuath in Ireland's heart."

"I've no care who's in this or what it means," Conal said stolidly. "It's not for us to deal with it alone."

"But I gave a vow to . . ." Sentanta began, then hesitated as he realized his near mistake, "to try to save Mor's brothers from disgrace."

"Your first vow is to the high-king," Conal told him in a stern, lecturing tone. "All others—to whomever they may be—mean nothing here. You can't save them, lad, and jeopardize all Ireland. You must tell Conaire, and he must come. Perhaps you're right. Maybe he *could* confront them and stop the raids and make a quiet end to this. But only he could have any chance at doing that. Or do you really think these men would listen to us alone?" His eyes scanned meaningfully over the lad's battered form.

"He's right, Sentanta," Cathbad added earnestly. "And our word by itself will not be enough to prove to Conaire who these raiders are. He must see them himself."

"I understand," the youth said in resigned tones. "I thought to spare him, but I see the truth you're speaking. We'll go to Conaire. I'll show him where they are. But we must go now or we will be too late."

The stone fortress was empty.

The chariots rolled in through its gateway and pulled up in the yard, the men within them gazing around. At their head was Conaire Mor, behind him the four men of Ulster and some two dozen of the high-king's other champions and chieftains, brought along both as escorts and as witnesses.

"We are too late," Sentanta said in frustration.

The raiders had gone, were no doubt already on their raid.

Too late to stop them, to stop the irreparable damage they would do now.

Mor climbed down from his car, the others following, spreading out to search the area. He moved across the yard, gazing about him at its barenness, its air of long abandonment. He looked back at Sentanta, his gaze a probing one.

"It's certain you are that they were ever here?" he asked. His voice was neutral, but the implication was clear.

"My King, do you doubt me?" Sentanta answered with surprise. "You must know I'd not lie to you in this."

Mor sighed and nodded. "Yes, my friend. I know. It was only a last hope speaking in me. And I know that they were here."

"There're signs of many horses," a warrior called from the stable area.

"There's food inside here," Conal Carna said, coming out of the oval hut, "and clothing as well. Look at this!" He held up a cloak and sword harness.

Mor crossed the yard to him, taking up an edge of the fine, gold-fringed cloak to examine it more closely, then dropping it to turn away. "It's Fergel's," he said flatly. "I gave it to him myself."

"My King," Conal began, "I . . ."

Mor held up a staying hand. "No. There's no need for saying anything." He turned back to his champion and friend. "You know, to speak the truth, I think I'd suspected it already, feared it, tried not to look at it. Maybe I was hoping that this would never come."

"You can't be blamed for that, Conaire," Conal said in sympathy. "They are your brothers."

"They are outlaws, and nothing can be done to change that," Mor answered harshly.

The others had given over searching to join them, forming a circle about their high-king. He looked about him at the stolid faces. "Well, my loyal friends, there's little we can do now," he said. "If they have gone raiding, then they will return here. All we can do is wait."

"Ah, this stone is rough!" Cormac loudly complained, shifting himself. "I've spurs of it sticking me everywhere."

"Quiet, Cormac," Sentanta said sharply. "You'll be giving a warning to anyone from here to Lough Rea."

The two were lying upon the upper stones of the fortress's

rampart, keeping watch over the countryside for the returning men. It was late afternoon now, the lowering sun before them making the rocky plain glow like a billowing sea.

The chastized Cormac sighed and settled himself as best he could, staring out silently for a time. At last he spoke again, in softer, thoughtful tones. "Sentanta, do you recall my speaking to you before about the unnatural feeling to all this?"

"This?" the cousin repeated, uncertain of its meaning.

"This hunting of other warriors. I told you that I didn't like it then. We'll, I've even less liking for it now."

"There's surely little joy in having to face traitors," Sentanta agreed. "Still, it must be done, for our own honor in this."

"Our honor?" Cormac said with a short, derisive laugh. "There's no honor in this. We're just two poor fools set by their own fool's vow against their fellows. It's not brigands or traitors we're waiting here for. It's warriors! Young men like ourselves, of royal lines and mighty clans!"

"They've betrayed the king and broken his new laws," Sentanta answered stubbornly. He wished his comrade would give up this talk. It troubled him.

"I've no certainty in me that either he or they are right," Cormac returned. "This 'betrayal' has been only a few cattle raids. We'd have been on such ourselves, without the grand new peace. And, who knows? Without the loyal lad of Ulster at my side, I might have been brought to join this lot myself." He turned to fix a searching eye on his friend. "And would you have been so willingly hunting me now, as well?" he bluntly asked.

Sentanta returned his gaze levelly, his voice emotionless. "I would."

"Then your own spirit's been taken from you by this high-king's spell," Cormac said with disappointment. "And I pity you."

Sentanta wanted to protest. He wanted to argue on, to convince his friend that he was wrong. But he could not. Enough truth rang in Cormac's words to make him hesitate, trying to sort out his true feelings.

But then a movement far out on the rocky plain caught his eye. He turned, peering intently into the afternoon's glare.

Objects moved there, casting long shadows ahead of them across the open ground. Many chariots there were, moving toward the fortress.

"They're coming," he said urgently. "Cormac, go and tell the king!"

Out on the plain, the band of raiders rolled triumphantly toward their hiding place. The signs of their victory were plentiful and clear. Heads festooned the bulwarks of the war chariots, staining the wicker with their last draining blood. Fine weapons and rich harness filled the cars. Warriors glowed with the ruddy light of battle won. And, finally, a herd of cattle, swelled by many calves and plumpened by lush spring grass, plodded before them.

When they reached the fortress, the cattle were driven aside into a rough pen of piled rocks. The warriors then rode on through the gateway into the yard.

They climbed from their cars, leaving their drivers to the task of unhitching the weary horses, and started toward the large hut. Most of the men were still energized by the recent fight, talking animatedly, laughing, comparing battle tales.

Morgor, as usual, led the group, bragging loudly of his great exploits. But as he and the others neared the hut, they stopped abruptly, staring ahead.

A figure, followed by several others, had appeared suddenly in the doorway, then moved out into the bright, slanting glare of the afternoon light.

"Conaire Mor!" exclaimed the startled Morgor.

At his words the other raiders, still moving up behind, pulled to a halt, bunching together in the center of the yard. They stared ahead in consternation as Mor, flanked by the four Ulstermen, stepped forward to confront them. At the same time, the rest of the high-king's contingent moved out from their own places of concealment to surround the band. None had their weapons out.

After his initial surprise, Morgor recovered himself quickly and put on his usual, arrogant front. "Well, High-King," he said, giving the title a scornful sound, "you found us at last." He gaze went disdainfully over Sentanta. "I see your faithful hound survived his dunking. A pity."

"A pity for you, Morgor, and for the rest," Mor shot back. He waved a hand toward the chariots with their grotesque ornaments. "I see you've made your raid."

"We have. A most rewarding one, too. Fine combats and fat prizes."

"I'm glad you enjoyed it," Mor said dryly. "It will be your last one."

"Do you think so?" Morgor asked, unconcerned.

"You have broken the peace and violated the laws you've sworn to uphold," Mor told him. "You have been well and truly caught in your crimes. I ask you to surrender to me now."

"I've never sworn to you," Morgor spat out contemptuously. "And none of us here are bound by vows our weak fathers may have made for a bit of gain."

"No, Conaire!" cried Ferogain. "We don't all think as he does. We didn't mean—"

"Quiet!" Mor shouted, cutting him off. "There's nothing you can say. Your deeds speak for you now."

"Wait, my King," Sentanta put in, his eyes scanning the faces before him. "Where is the old warrior? The one I told you of?"

"Who do you mean?" asked Morgor.

"The old warrior. I saw him." He looked to Mor. "My King, I think he was the one who led them. He seemed to control them, as if there was some power. . . ."

"No power rules our acts," Morgor shouted. "There is no old man in our company. Your Ulster whelp has had some vision, Mor. Maybe his dive into the sea has soaked his brain. There are only ourselves here, and we've needed no other excuse to act besides your foolish laws."

He drew himself up proudly, sneering at the high-king. "We've chosen to defy you, and I know we'll win. Because facing us now and knowing who we are, you haven't the courage to act against us. You don't dare."

"You're wrong, Morgor," Mor responded levelly. "For I'm asking you all to surrender."

"Are you?" Morgor laughed derisively. "But you've missed one tiny thing, haven't you, Mor?" He gazed about at the king's small host. "There are more than three of us to every one of you."

"You mean to challenge us?" Mor said with calm, showing no sign of alarm at the threat. "It's a bold and a most foolish one you are, as I should have guessed." He turned his attention to the rest of the band. "But hear this first, all of you, and think: breaking the peace with your raids may be a crime against Ireland, but to turn upon your king is a violation of your honor that no true warrior would dare. No Ban-Sidhe would come keening at your wake, no clansman would ever speak your name again, and your unburned body would lie naked for a raven's feast."

"It's not *our* bodies would lie waiting for the crows," Morgor returned, his hand moving to grip his sword.

Mor's hand did likewise, as did those of his champions. "We may not win, Morgor," he said in a deadly voice, "but you're truly a madman if you think you'll go from this place unbloodied."

"Come on then," Morgor said. He drew his sword, his brothers following his lead. "We're ready for you."

But from behind him there was no accompanying sound of swords whisking from their sheaths. He turned his head to see his company still standing as they had been, looking around them at the grim and ready veteran warriors whose great names and deeds they had heard all their lives. They looked at the red afternoon sunlight glinting on the slim but lethal blades and flaring angrily in the determined eyes.

"What's wrong with you?" he screamed at them. "Draw! At them! Here's our chance!"

The others exchanged reluctant glances. Many shook their heads. Then Fergel spoke.

"I don't know what the others say, but I'll not fight my own brother and my king." He unbuckled his sword belt and let the weapon fall.

"He's right," another said. "It's like a dream faded away from my mind, and I see more clearly now. The battle fever's gone from me. I'll do no more."

He dropped his sword and shield. The rest followed, one by one, their weapons clattering to the hard ground of the yard.

Morgor, florid with rage and frustration, looked about him as they surrendered, finally leaving only himself and his two brothers.

"Well, Morgor, will you still fight?" Mor asked coldly. "I will give you *fir-fer*—just you and myself—if you wish it."

Morgor met the hard gaze of the other. Then he grunted angrily and hurled his sword down before the high-king's feet. "I'll give you no chance to kill me with a dozen swords behind you," he said, no less arrogant in his defeat. "I still know that you'll not dare to act against us anyway. Take us to Tara if you wish. *Try* to punish us. Yes, I challenge you to try! Because you'll soon learn that every warrior in Ireland will be against you."

"Do you really believe that?" Mor asked in surprise.

"I do, poor, dreaming fool," Maine Morgor jeered. "You've caught us, but it's yourself and your great peace you've put in jeopardy."

Chapter Thirty-one

A Summons

"You there! Get that pole centered properly now!" Meave shouted upward.

High above, a worker struggling to ease a massive roof pole into the frame that formed the roof peak paused in his labors. Irritably he cast his gaze down at her, opening his mouth as if to give reply. But even from the distance he could see the icy look of command flashing in her eyes and thought better of it. He closed his mouth with a snap and did as he was told.

Around him other workers moved atop the vast web of poles that would form the roof of Cruchane's new central hall. In the yard below, hundreds of others swarmed, like insects upon a carcass, but with the object of restoring the rotted remains, not tearing them apart. Some replaced the decayed posts of the outer palisade, some rebuilt stone walls and graded the inner yard, and others renovated or replaced the battered outbuildings. And amid this all, directing the massive repair of the fort, was Meave.

She stood with legs set wide and hands on hips, looking critically about her at the work. Though she kept a stern face and a brusque air of command for the army of workers, she felt within an exhilaration and sense of satisfaction that she had never known before.

It was all going so well: the buildings nearly finished, the fortress becoming stronger than before, and beyond, on the Plains of Ai, herds drifting on the green billows of lush spring grass. It was going well, and she could tell herself—for once unabashedly, without modesty, and with pride—that much of the credit for it went to her.

The hall itself was the great setpiece of her accomplishment, she thought, walking toward it. A glorious symbol of the powerful, rich, new Connacht that she was forging—with Aileel.

She paused in its doorway, gazing about the interior of the nearly finished structure. In size and shape it was the same as the old main hall, but here the similarities ended. In the hall she had designed, wattle walls had given way to planks of oak, and the wattle roof to oaken shingles. In each wall of the enormous octagon were set two windows, each with rare and dearly bought panes of glass, closed by shutters of glowing bronze.

The room itself was divided into seven wedges, each separate part with its own benches built from the outer wall to the inner space about the central hearth. The dividing walls were fronted with bronze sheets and with red yew deeply carved in most elaborate designs, and each of the inner circle of thick pillars that upheld the roof were sheathed with strips of bronze.

Across the room from the main entrance where she stood was the compartment designated for the royalty. There, craftsmen were finishing the insetting of silver and bronze strips around the edges of the raised platform where the king would hold court. Four bronze pillars surrounded it as well, combining to create the exact impression she had calculated: to set it off as the domain of a man of great power.

Behind her, across the yard, a sudden stir about the main gate caught her attention. A chariot had just rolled through it, and the warrior within was talking animatedly with the sentries.

She watched curiously as they both turned to point her out. The warrior looked toward her in puzzlement, then ordered his driver forward. She waited where she was, letting the visitor come to her.

"It's a great lot of work you're doing here," he said genially as his car pulled up before her. "The fortress walls look stronger than any I've seen." He nodded back toward the entrance. "And those gates! Most impressive!"

"The walls and gate are being done by Brocc, son of Blar," she told him.

"Are they?" the man said, clearly awed at the name. "Why, he's the finest dun builder in all of Ireland, they say. His father did Tara itself!"

"This will be as fine, if not finer yet," she boasted. Then she turned brusque again. "But what is it you want here? Your trappings tell me you're of Tara's household."

"I am, my Lady," he said. "And I've a message for Aileel from the high-king himself." He shook his head in perplexity. "But those warriors at the gate told me I must talk to you."

"They were right."

His confusion deepened. "But . . . my message is for the king, my Lady."

"The king is resting," she said with rising impatience. "Any message you have for him you may give to me."

"You?" He gave a short laugh of disbelief. "No, my Lady. That's impossible. It's for him alone to hear it, and from me."

"Or from his queen?" she said testily.

"His queen?" Now the man was truly taken aback.

"Yes, messenger." She drew herself up and spoke with an air of full authority. "I am wed to Aileel and queen of Connacht. I am also Meave, aunt to Conaire Mor and his own emissary to Connacht. Any message that you bring from Mor you will give to me. Now!"

"Y-yes, my Lady . . . I mean, my Queen!" the man said, fully cowed and flustered.

He took a breath to regain his composure then, and in a flat, emotionless voice intoned the terrible news: "Aileel's three sons have been captured in unlawful cattle raids, along with other young noblemen of Ireland. In five days' time they will be tried by the high-king at Tara on the charge of treason!"

"It could mean their deaths, my husband," Meave said.

Aileel sat unmoving upon the pallet in his room. The windows were shuttered against the sound of work and the afternoon sun. His hair was tousled, and in the half-light he seemed still groggy from sleep after being awakened by Meave.

"They were captured in the act, you say?" he asked.

"With some fivescore of other young men of Ireland's most royal families, including the foster-brothers of Mor himself! It's a most dreadful circumstance for my nephew and for his whole plan. They're the sons of the very men whose support he needs, yet what they've done may be punished by death under his new laws. It is for that reason he has asked the province rulers and the chieftains of all Ireland to come for the judging. He must prove himself fair, and he must have all there to watch him and concur."

"For my own sons to be a party to this," he said bitterly. "To dishonor me, to violate me, to betray me!" He got up and strode angrily across the room. "Ah, but I should have known it. That misbegotten lot. I was a fool to send the likes of them to Tara in my name."

"You couldn't have known that they would dare do such a thing," she said reasonably.

"Couldn't I?" he angrily replied. He wheeled toward her as he spoke, but one foot caught against the edge of his pallet. He staggered, nearly falling before he caught himself. "The Dagda curse it!" he raged. "It's so bloody dark in here!"

He felt his way across to the window, throwing open the shutters to admit the golden sun. Then he stood there, staring out, suddenly quiet, his manner thoughtful.

"It was another foolishness of mine," he said, resigned. "Another great mistake. But I can't seem to make anything else now, can I?"

"Don't speak that way," she said, crossing to him, placing a hand on his arm.

"It's true," he insisted. "Without you here to help, we'd have had no putting the Firbolgs on the run, no treaty, no peace. Not even this!" He gestured out at the yard. "Cruchane would still be nothing but a moldering ruin."

"I couldn't have done any of it without you," she told him earnestly. "It was you held it together. You who gave me the chance."

"*No*. It was you alone. And that's why now it must be you who goes to Tara to deal with this."

"Me?" she said in astonishment. "It can't be me. You are the king."

"Am I?" He turned to her. "Look at me, Meave."

The sight was shocking. He was not simply still groggy from his nap. His face, lit pitilessly by the hard afternoon sun, sagged as if the underlying flesh had melted away. The high, sharp cliffs of his bold features were deeply eroded by creases across cheeks and forehead and about the mouth. His eyes, now deep sunken behind the crags of brow, stared out blearily. His body, quite bony now, had become stooped.

From the robust man she had met on her return, he had swiftly dwindled. To her it seemed that it had been only his need to save Connacht that had sustained him and kept him strong. Now, with that need gone, the age he had so long held at bay had come upon him.

"You see it," he said with a knowing smile. "The truth shows so clearly in those bright eyes that even my half-blinded ones can see it. Make no protest. It's a good thing that you know."

He took her hands in his, the lean fingers clutching tightly as he spoke with urgency.

"Meave, listen. You said once you would join me and help me in my rule. I told you then the day would come when all the duties fell on you alone. That day has come already. Mor must not see how weak I am or realize how weakened Connacht was by its long war. You must be strong for me, for all of us."

She wanted to protest, to say that he was still the real power, the bold warrior who might face any man. But she knew that Aileel was right. He couldn't face the high-king as he was. And there was something else—a welling feeling that she couldn't deny: she wanted to assume this authority, to go back to Tara as Connacht's queen.

"Very well, my husband. I will go."

He threw his arms about her, hugging her to him. "Thank you, my wife," he said fervently. "I know it will be hard for you, but you are my only strength now. My regret is laying the burden of myself upon you."

"Think no more of it." She kissed him tenderly upon the lips. "You are a part of me, and will be always. I've said before that as long as we both live, you will be king. That I still swear to you."

He peered down into those brilliant eyes, blue and intense as a clear winter's sky. "I don't doubt you," he said. "There's no word you say that your will can't make the truth." He released her and moved away, his voice taking on a brisker, more official tone. "But now you must be preparing yourself to go. You've little time."

"And your sons?" she asked. "What should be done about them?"

"If they did this deed, they will pay the price," he said grimly. "Ask no mercy for them, Meave. If Mor says they are to die, I'll not argue with him."

Meave and her retinue rode in through the gateway of Tara.

As they pulled up before the stables and she dismounted, she looked about her. The great dun was as she remembered, but there was something different, some new atmosphere that she couldn't identify.

Lewy MacNeesh climbed down from his chariot and moved up beside her, gazing around with awe. "I've never been here," he said. "It is a grand place."

"It is," she agreed. "And it seems an age since I left."

"But you were only the aunt of Conaire Mor then," he told her with a smile. "You've gained a new life since."

With his words she realized suddenly that the difference she felt was in herself. She had left this seat of power a woman cowed and useless, sustained only by pale dreams. Now she had returned a victor, flushed with the sense of a worth she had truly earned, feeling an equal to any here, including her nephew.

The fortress was very busy, filled with milling people, the crowd bright with the colors of many clans, glinting with the finery of chiefs and champions and learned men. It imparted a false sense of festivity to a gathering called for such a grim purpose.

Leaving the chariots in their drivers' care, she, Lewy, and their escort started across the yard toward the main hall. From beyond the stable sheds, another group appeared suddenly, cutting across their path. Meave stopped, nearly colliding with the tall, burly warrior in the lead.

She opened her mouth to voice a complaint but was stopped as the man threw back his arms and exclaimed in delight, "Meave!"

"Fergus MacRogh!" she responded with equal pleasure, looking up into the broad, red-bearded face of her old friend. But then she sobered as another man moved out from behind him into view.

Conchobar MacNessa, king of Ulster, stood glaring down at her.

"Well, Meave," he said in his sneering way, "you look well enough, for all your exploits. I understand you've been putting your talents to their best use again."

"And what does that mean?" she demanded, fixing him with a chilling gaze.

"It means beguiling a new king to take you into his bed. The poor fool."

Beside her, Lewy bridled. Meave saw his fist clench about his sword hilt and his face grow flushed. She put a detaining hand upon his arm and spoke warningly to the king.

"Watch your words, Conchobar. You're not in your own court now."

"So, our new queen, is it?" he snarled. "Putting on your grand new airs. Come to Tara for Aileel." His voice took on a speculative tone. "And just why has your 'husband' slighted our young high-king by not coming here himself? Can it be that he's no interest even in the fate of his own sons?" He fixed a probing eye on her. "Or is it that age has finally made him too infirm?"

"We have just finished a long and brutal war, as you well know," she said coolly. "My husband must stay with his forces. He's rebuilding Connacht, making it stronger than it ever was. Strong enough even to challenge the likes of your haughty Red Branch, MacNessa."

"I see," he returned caustically. "And so he sent to Tara the one person he could most easily spare."

"You think this trial is so unimportant, Conchobar?" she shot back. "Then I'm surprised to see such a great man as yourself here. Especially as you bragged that you would never come to this king or serve his court!"

"I come because he has overstepped his bounds!" said Conchobar, inflamed by her insinuation. "He's seeking to punish warriors of Ireland for being warriors! He has gone too far with his madness this time, and I'll not allow it!"

"You'd wish traitors going unpunished instead?" she challenged, meeting his angry glare boldly. "That sounds treason itself!"

"Woman!" he said hotly, stepping toward her threateningly. "Take care now or you'll be—"

"Be easy there!" said Fergus, stepping between them. "Both of you! Save your differences for the court."

Conchobar looked past him to Meave, his face dark with his anger, body tensed as if he meant to push by his champion and drive at her. Meave watched him defiantly, body set, ready, daring him to come on.

"Ah, the Bloody Raven take her," Ulster's king said in disgust, pulling back. "She's not worth our brawling here. Let's be away."

He turned on his heel and stalked off, his other warriors following. But Fergus tarried behind, standing beside Meave, looking after him.

"So, that was Conchobar," said Lewy, shaking his head. "It wasn't tales I heard about him then."

"He's certainly not changed at all," said Meave. She forced a smile and a light air to cover the inner trembling that now seized her in the aftermath of the confrontation. "He's still the gentle, peaceful man I remember so fondly."

"But you handled him well, Meave," Fergus told her, turning to look at her with open admiration. "Few men—druid or champion or chief—have ever faced him so fearlessly as you."

She had, she realized. It had come without her willing it, without having consciously to overcome her old fear of him. For the first time she had not fled from him, and she felt an amazement in this at herself.

Fergus was looking at her approvingly. "Your time out in Connacht has done something for your spirit, that's certain," he told her, grinning. "And it's not done any harm at all to your fine looks. You're more the beauty than you ever were. The life's fairly glowing in you."

She flushed at his praise. "You're a fine liar, Fergus, as you've always been. And still a friend, I hope?"

He put a hand out to rest upon her shoulder and said earnestly, "As before, Meave. You know that."

Lewy, giving this gesture of familiarity an irritated look, moved up closer to Meave. "My Queen, shouldn't we be getting on to the hall now?" he pointedly suggested.

"I'll walk with you," Fergus said heartily, falling in beside her, much to the young Connachtman's obvious displeasure.

"Will Conchobar really fight Mor?" Meave asked the red-haired champion as they crossed the yard.

"He will," was the grim reply. "And he may succeed if the province rulers don't support our young high-king. We've been here a day or two already, Meave. I know the feelings run strong amongst those gathered here, both for the old ways and for these fool sons whose families don't wish to see them die. It'll be a true test of Mor's strength, and whether his new Ireland has a chance of surviving."

"What do you think?" she asked. "Please, tell me. I hold a great respect for your feelings."

He considered, then put a hand to his sword hilt. "I think that for a thousand years we've lived only by this," he said.

Chapter Thirty-two

The Trial

"Everyone is gathered, High-King," the gray-haired chief of Tara's druids announced from the doorway.

"All right," Conaire Mor said testily. He fumbled with the brooch at his shoulder, trying to fasten it, but it popped free, letting his heavy, gold-fringed cloak of state drop to the floor.

"Here, let me help," offered Fionualla, crossing the floor of their royal quarters to him.

"It taxes my mind to concentrate on such little matters," he told her in an irritated tone. "They all seem more distractions, and my mind . . ." he shook his head, closing his eyes as if to shut things out, "my mind feels stuffed, swelled tight with them already."

"I know, my love," she said with sympathy, lifting the ornate cloak to drape about him again. "It's been too many nights since you slept through till the dawn. And why shouldn't I know? Haven't I lain awake and restless beside you?"

As she fastened the cloak at his throat with the great brooch, he looked into her face, pale and drawn with weariness. His self-concern gave way to understanding. He took her hands.

"My poor wife. It's a fool I am not to think of you. Of course this has been hard on you as well. They were as much family to you as to myself."

"Is there no way but to be so hard with them, Conaire?" she asked in an imploring way.

His tenderness vanished and his face grew hard. He dropped her hands and turned away from her. "How can you ask me that?" he said angrily. "You know I can show no unfairness in this. I'm their king now, not their brother. It was they who forced me across that line. And they weren't alone in it. What of all the rest?"

"What of them? They're all young men, just boys, many of

them. And they're all sons of Ireland's finest clans. Doesn't that mean anything?"

"If anything it speaks out the more for their condemning than their saving," he answered harshly.

"Why?" she demanded, moving around him to look into his face again. "Why is that so?"

He met her eyes. His gaze was cold. His words came slow and hard. "Because as nobles' sons, they more than any others should have obeyed the peace. To let them do such crimes and treat them as no more than prankish boys would make a mockery of everything I've done. Who else then would stay loyal to me? Who else would trust me after seeing me compromising the very laws I had them all swear to? No one! It would mean the end. So there must be punishment. And it must be hard."

She listened to him with a growing horror. That face drawn taut with such outrage, that voice filled with so much brutality, they were not her husband's. It was a stranger to her that she faced now. She put her hands out to his shoulders, her voice pleading for him to understand.

"Conaire, listen to what you're saying. You've gone too far in this. You've lost yourself. Ireland will survive. She has for ages past, and with people just like those whose acts have now condemned them in your eyes. Why, you're even one of them. Have you forgotten that? Will you destroy Ireland's heart, her life, in the trying to save her? Has this dream taken possession of you? Filled your eyes and mind with nothing else?"

Her words did seem to touch him. His anger gave way to a look of puzzlement.

"But, Fionualla, I've wanted this for ourselves, for you as well. Peace. Think of peace! Our own children growing up without the sounds of war, of rattling iron, and cries of pain, and the keening lifting from the huts of all the slain."

"And will there ever be time for our children, for the having or the raising of them, with you forever cursed to struggle for your peace? For this may not be an end to it."

"It will be an end!" he said fiercely. "When the people of Ireland see me condemn my own foster-brothers as I would any brigand, they will believe in the truth and power of my new laws. They will obey."

"Oh so?" she said in surprise. "Obey is it? Now it's the words of Calatin I hear coming from your mouth."

"Calatin understands what I want here," Mor argued. "He may be the only one."

"What of Conal?" she returned. "It's him you should be listening to."

"He is a warrior. He thinks as a warrior does. In the end, it may be their codes and not my law that he supports."

"How can you say that? There're none so loyal to you as that man."

"There were others I thought loyal," he said darkly. "They betrayed me."

She moved in closer to him, meeting his gaze searchingly. "Is that it?" she demanded. "Would you have more mercy if your own brothers were not in this? Conaire, is it bitterness toward them for their betrayal that moves you to such cruelty? Revenge?"

"Woman, it's madness you're speaking now," he snarled. "I act by the law alone. My own anger will not change that." Then his gaze grew suddenly probing, challenging. "Are you trying to betray me now as well, my wife? I thought that in you at least I had loyal support. Now . . . I wonder."

He turned from her abruptly and stalked out, leaving her to stare after him blankly, stricken by his words.

Once more the great hall of Tara an Rie was crowded with men. But they were not assembled for festivities this time. No foods or ales sat upon the long tables. No stews and roasts cooked upon the fire. No sounds of music, laughter, or bright tales filled the air. The men who packed the rows of benches and the outer tables sat grimly, silent or speaking in low tones whose collected, constant rumbling was like the far thunder of a rising storm.

Mor passed in through the doors with his chief ard-druid and made his way across the floor. As he moved along the narrow avenue through the crowded tables he scanned the assembly.

Here were the highest ranks of Ireland gathered in an array unprecedented. The significance of the event and Mor's own hold on Ireland were both evidenced. The highest ranks of druids, the most senior ollavs, Brehons, and physicians all were there. From every province, save Connacht, the kings had come as well, accompanied by hosts of their chieftains and their champions. A more impressive collection of power even this hall had never seen before.

As Mor looked about, he met the hard, glittering black gaze of one he knew at once as Conchobar MacNessa, though they had never met before. The Ulster king had avoided an audience since his arrival, remaining aloof in his own visitor's dun.

Mor experienced a more pleasurable feeling on meeting the gaze of his aunt Meave. He read sympathy and the warmth of a supportive smile in her blue eyes, though her expression remained suitably grave.

On her part, Meave was remarking on the change that had taken place in him since their last meeting. The boyish brashness, the buoyant spirits, and the vitality that had been his then were all vanished now. In the passage of the one year he seemed to have aged many, his look now more weary and much more grim.

As he rounded the fire pit, Mor's eyes took in the dais where sat his own council of champions and high-druids. Calatin, still among the lower ranks of the learned men, sat at one end, quiet, expressionless, content to watch the events unfold.

Below the dais, at a line of tables, sat the accused men, the fivescore of young warriors from Ireland's best houses.

He passed by them, pointedly avoiding looking at them. Their gazes followed him intently, their expressions mixed. Some were sullen, some hopeful, some afraid. Ferogain's face was like that of a whipped child, swollen and flushed. Maine Morgor glared after Mor with open hate.

As Mor mounted the dais and moved along it toward his seat, Sentanta leaned back from the table and asked, "My King, a word?"

"Now?" said Mor, glancing about the roomful of waiting men. "There's no time."

"It's vital, my King," the young man said urgently. "You must withhold a judgment until this dark warrior is found. I don't believe their actions were their own. He was their leader. He . . ."

"My lad, there's still no proof this man ever existed, save your own eyes," the king said patiently. "None of the captives will admit that they even saw him. All deny that he was in control. They have taken full responsibility for their crime onto themselves, and so it shall stay." He put a hand on the shoulder of the disappointed youth. "I'm sorry, Sentanta. I know what's in your heart. But it won't save them."

As he passed on, Sentanta looked after him in frustration.

"He thinks I made up that man to help them," he said. "But he was there!"

Cormac, beside him, leaned forward to murmur in reply, "Easy, my friend. Say no more about it now. There's no one to believe you."

That was, in fact, not true. A single believer farther down the table had watched this exchange most intently, and with narrowed eyes. Calatin had found yet another reason to dislike this meddlesome youth.

Mor reached the center of the table and sat down. At his right sat Conal, his most valued champion. At his left, in deference to his renown and his great help, sat Cathbad, Mor's own high-druid seated beyond him.

As Mor took his seat, the murmuring about the room died away. Mor waited for full silence, then began.

"We are gathered to pass a judgment on these men for their crimes against the whole of Ireland. Because what they've done affects all of us, and because the accused come from the greatest clans in all your provinces, you have been called to witness and confirm their punishment. Chief Druid, will you now list out their crimes?"

The gray-haired druid rose at once and intoned, "These men have committed willful acts of war upon the peoples of Ireland. They have raided the herds of others, taking the cattle, and doing great slaughter upon their protectors."

"Wait now!" called out Conchobar, rising. "Am I to understand that you're meaning to condemn these men for nothing more than that? And did they sneak upon these people, attacking them like robbers on the road?"

"They did not, my King," the druid replied stiffly, indignant at being interrupted.

"And did they take unfair advantage in the fight, or did they challenge men in open combat, as befits a warrior?"

"Well, from the evidence, it does seem that they attacked only clans stronger than themselves, and more than a fair match," the druid admitted. "And it seems they held to *fir-fer* in the combats."

"And prevailed through their fighting skills alone!" Conchobar added, giving a laugh of triumph. "Ha! You make my point, druid!" He looked challengingly around him. "I ask you all: when has such a thing been judged a crime in Ireland?"

There were mutterings and some nodded heads at this. The

druid, uncomfortable under Conchobar's attack, looked to Mor for help.

"We have made a new Ireland," the high-king replied. "It follows new beliefs and has new laws. We all agreed and swore to them."

"They're foolish laws, and we were fools to swear to them," came Conchobar's bold retort. "Such things are part of us. There's not a seasoned warrior here who hasn't tested his iron against another clan or raided a rival's cattle herds for sport. To deny a warrior's right to do such things is to deny a bird its flight or a salmon the waters in which to swim."

"That 'right' you speak of has torn Ireland apart," Mor answered. "We can live well enough without it."

"Can we? And become a lot of peaceful farmers, or meander in the glens like our own cows?"

"What these men have done goes far beyond some unleashing of warrior spirits," Mor explained, trying to keep his patience under this hectoring. "They have willfully violated laws they had sworn to obey. They confess to openly defying me to bring down my new peace."

"No!" protested Ferogain in agony, jumping to his feet. "We never meant that. We meant only for you to be more free with . . ."

"Quiet, you craven pup!" cried Morgor, leaping up to force the other down. He glared up defiantly at Mor. "Yes, we meant to destroy it utterly then, and we'd still be trying now if we were free. So, if you mean to punish us for that, High-King, you'd best be getting to it, for it's the only way you'll stop our rebellion against your cursed, emasculating peace!"

"You will both be silent!" Conal shouted down at them. "And the rest of your treasonous lot as well. You have done enough already."

"They have done nothing!" Conchobar shouted back. "And you, Conal Carna, should know that better than most."

All eyes went to the Ulster king at that. He was a towering presence, his physical size dominating the gathering, his resounding voice filling the room.

"Maine Morgor is right," Conchobar went on. "What these warriors have done has been to prove that this peace is the unnatural thing, the real enemy to us. Denounce it now, all of you. Call Mor the fool, or even the madman, for his faith in it. Don't let him do this to your sons, to your beliefs, to your whole land! Defy him yourselves, as these brave lads have done. Give them your support before it is too late."

There was a great deal of excited murmuring in response to this. Mor could see that many in the gathering had been swayed by Conchobar's emotional appeal. Now was the crucial point. Now his peace had reached its test. What happened in the next few seconds would decide its life or death. He must act. He must counter MacNessa's reasons with his own.

But he could not speak.

The power of the Ulster king's speech had touched him too. He was confused, uncertain of a reply. The eloquence that had brought him this far had now, suddenly and utterly, deserted him.

The people were waiting, becoming aware of his hesitance. The vital moment was slipping away.

"Don't listen to Conchobar!" said another voice suddenly.

Meave was up now, her voice strong, firm, ringing out across the hall.

"Conchobar cares nothing of your welfare or of Ireland," she said, looking scornfully toward him. "He cares only for his own will. He wants an Ireland where he can raid and bully at his pleasure. He wants an Ireland divided, where he and his Red Branch can play the masters of you others as they always have." Her eyes swept the gathering. "You all know that. You all remember the years of his cruelty and arrogance. He doesn't care for peace, but Conaire Mor does!"

She threw out her arm to point dramatically toward the high-king.

"He wants only the finest life for you! And hasn't he brought it? Hasn't he made truths of his promises to you? Hasn't Ireland been brought to a peace and a prosperity it has never known? Connacht has ended its long war, the provinces work together for one good, even the lone and savage bear of Ulster has been brought to heel."

These words too had a visible impact. There were many nods and noises of agreement in the crowd. Seeing this response, Conchobar tried to counter it, a certain desperation now entering his tones.

"You'd listen to a woman cast off?" he said harshly. "She's not speaking with any authority here."

"I speak the words Aileel would say himself!" she fired back, facing him with body drawn proudly erect and eyes flashing a

challenging light. "And all here know what a man of honor and
of worth he is. He told me that to hold to his bond and show
his belief in this peace, he would agree to whatever judgment
the high-king reaches for his own sons! Would any here dare
admit to a lesser loyalty than that?"

Morgor, clearly shocked, met her gaze. In those ice-blue,
pitiless eyes he read the deadly truth. "My own father?" he
said aloud, his haughty defiance gone in his dismay.

Around the room, her words were having an electrifying
response. The truth and the power of them had moved the
listening men, reclaiming their support. The murmuring voices
of assent swelled to an affirming clamor. Around the Ulster
king, even his own chieftains were voicing words of agreement
with Meave.

Conchobar, red-faced with rage, glared at them, but it had
no effect.

"Give it up now," Fergus MacRogh advised, clearly delighted by Meave's success. "She is right in what she says, and
you'll only look more the fool now to go on fighting against
her."

The king of Ulster fixed a venom-filled gaze upon his ex-
wife, now smirking at him from across the room. His hands
clenched and a growl of rage and frustration sounded in his
throat. But then, forced to recognize his defeat, he dropped
down in his place to stare stonily ahead.

Young Sentanta, watching Meave, felt an elation at her victory. She had truly gained an amazing new strength since
leaving Ulster, and he regretted that in the confusion and the
crowds at Tara and the focus on the trial, he had had little
chance even to make himself known to her, much less to speak
of all that had happened to both since they last met.

"I thank Queen Meave for her words," Mor was now telling
her most graciously, but inwardly he was troubled that this
defense had come from her and not himself.

He forced himself back to the issue at hand, looking out over
the audience. "Now, the judgment must be made. The crime
is clear." His gaze dropped to the raiders. "There is no confusion and no doubt. They have freely admitted it, admitted
deliberately flaunting the new laws of Ireland. For this they
must be punished. And the sentence against them, as witnessed and guaranteed by those assembled here, it is now my
duty to pass."

He ran his gaze along the row of young faces—some hopeful,

some defiant, most afraid—that looked up at him. But as he did he suddenly realized that the choice before him was not so obvious a one as he had thought. True enough, the law was clear, simple, and quite ruthless. Treason meant death. Still, his thoughts continued to be confused.

A bedlam of conflicting ideas, words, and images filled his mind. There were too many loves and hates in this; too many beliefs and too many loyalties. His feelings for his foster-brothers were challenged by his rage at their betrayal. His dream of peace fought with his upbringing as a warrior. The stormy winds of Ireland's violent nature crashed against the serene hills of her poet's temperament. The voices of Fionualla, of Conal, of Meave and Sentanta and Conchobar whirled about one another in wild melee.

Just how truly willful had the acts been? Just how strong was this spirit in Ireland's fighting men? And the hot blood of youth—was that a factor too? What had the man of the Sidhe said? Let no robbery be done? Yet, he had also charged Mor to build his rule on justice. Was condemning these boys justice, or was he destroying something else, something vital, in destroying them?

"What you have done is most terrible," he began slowly, feeling his way through this maelstrom of contradicting notions. "It can't be forgiven or treated lightly. It has torn at the fabric of our peace. It has violated us all.

"Yet there are circumstances—ancient habits and long training—that cannot be ignored. And there is youth to consider. Perhaps the hold of the warrior's spirit *is* so strong in Ireland that restraining it is hard for those without maturity.

"But even so, that battle must be won, for all our sakes. We're men, not savage animals. It's our minds, not our claws and teeth, that should shape our destinies. Worse yet is the fact that some of you have expressed no regret for what you've done. You've boasted of your crimes and of your desire to carry them on. Ireland must be protected from any chance of your continued violence. I've no other choice but to see you removed from her life forever."

There was a sigh of worst anticipations realized that swept across the room. Fathers' looks grew sorrowful or stoical or stern as the cold words condemned their sons. Only Calatin was forced to suppress a smile, gloating inwardly.

So, there it was, he thought. The careful plotting, the great labors brought finally to the end he'd sought. From this moment, the power of the warrior would be forever gone. No one would ever dare defy the law again. Now, truly, his own time of power would begin.

Down the table, Mor was raising his hand for silence and attention once again.

"Please, the judgment is not finished," he told the whole company, then turned his gaze once more on the outlaws. "You must be removed from Ireland's life," he repeated, "but you have not acted in a way to forfeit your own lives. You fought by the warrior's codes, and to deny those codes in putting you to death would be no justice. Though the law decrees execution, you will instead be banished from Ireland for the rest of your lives."

There was a sensation in the hall. Calatin rocked backward as if struck a real blow, his face going blank in his astonishment. Sentanta and Cormac exchanged wondering glances. Conal lifted an eyebrow, his face staying otherwise impassive.

"A most clever judgment," Cathbad told Mor with a little smile.

"But, my King, your own law!" protested the gray-haired chief druid.

"My decision is made," Mor told him firmly. "The circumstances are too complex and the law too vague. They have been judged adequately. To Ireland, they will be as dead."

"Too great a punishment," growled Conchobar, looking across to Meave.

"Not hard enough, Conaire," Meave said harshly, looking toward Morgor. "They should have lost their heads."

Around them, the responses were mixed: joy, outrage, sorrow, relief, but in many cases a look of uncertainty. Mor scanned the faces, feeling a twisting in his stomach and a weakness in his limbs. More, there was a strange sense of emptiness in his chest, as if something had been given up.

He gazed upward, as if there were some answer in the rising smoke of the central fire.

"Man of the Sidhe," he softly murmured, "please, have I done right?"

Chapter Thirty-three

Conspiracy

"He has betrayed us!"

Calatin stormed about the sacred clearing in the oak grove. Around him the scores of grinning skulls stared down.

The druid's twenty-six sons also watched, silent as usual, a flock of scrawny crow-wraiths circling him, glinting eyes blinking in the shadows of the overhanging trees.

"Mor should have put them all to death," he raged. "He betrayed me! He betrayed the laws!"

He snatched a skull from the branch above and glared into its black sockets.

"Curse the man. He is no ally to me. He has revealed his true nature now. He will not give me the power. He is a warrior!" He spat the word out like an oath, clenching the skull in his fist as if he would crush it.

"He let them live! And he will always let his fellow warriors live. He sent no warning to the rest. He'll never strip their power. The next time he may bow to them completely. He is too weak. He now stands in my way. And he must be destroyed!"

He slammed the skull to the packed earth of the clearing with the full force of his outrage. It shattered into white splinters. Then he swung around, his cloak swirling about him as he swept the circle with his blazing eyes.

"I'll not let what happened in Espan happen again here," he told the listeners in fierce tones. "We are too close this time. The laws are still in place, the peace still a success." His voice became softer and more musing now, as if he were voicing his deepest thoughts. "It only wants the right leader, one with the strength to keep the laws, yet pliable enough to heed my counsel. One without the same mindless loyalty to the warrior class. A leader of my own choice."

His gaze swept over them again. This time a smile of

cunning and cruelty stretched his wide mouth, glowed in his dark eyes.

"And I have a way, my sons. I have seen in that hall today the forces that will yet win Ireland for me. I have seen hatred and ruthlessness. I have seen courage and belief. These I can use.

"But we must act quickly," he added, his manner now abruptly brisk. "The forces I need are already preparing to scatter. Gather around me, my sons. Kindle the fire. We must raise the spell about me once again."

The fire was rebuilt in the heart of the sacred grove, fed carefully with the woods and elements needed to create the ominous yellow plume of smoke that curled serpentlike up through the canopy of leaves. The withered sons of Calatin moved in about him, raising their dark, eerie, moaning chant. Like ravens preparing to take flight, the wings of their black cloaks lifted, forming a wall that hid the druid from sight.

The cloak billowed out as Conchobar swept it up. Then he unceremoniously wadded up the crimson, gold-embroidered garment of state and, with an angry gesture, stuffed it into his leather traveling bag.

"Why the rushing?" Fergus asked. "It's too late in the day. We should stay through until tomorrow. Why, the darkness will be on us before we've even gone a few . . ."

"I'd not be staying in this accursed home of cravens even if it meant braving a Samhain night itself!" Conchobar barked in answer. "We go back to Ulster now! Get the chariots!"

Fergus shook his head, but left in obedience, knowing there was no arguing with his king in such a mood. He went out into the yard of the visitors' dun, a small version of the main fortress of Tara situated on its own hill just beyond the great dun's walls. It was one of several such satellite dwellings where visiting royalty could maintain the privacy due their high rank.

Crossing to the stable sheds, he ordered the charioteers to draw out the vehicles and begin to harness them. The men, expecting to stay, were already preparing supper. They grumbled at the orders, but it took Fergus only a brief mention of Conchobar's state to persuade them to hurry things along.

Meanwhile, inside, Conchobar continued his packing.

"You seem in a great hurry to leave Tara," a rumbling voice said behind him.

Startled, he wheeled about to see a strange warrior, a dark

and ponderous form with grizzled, mustached face and long black hair.

"And who are you?" he demanded.

"Only a simple fighting man, great King," the other humbly replied. "But a fighting man who thinks just as yourself."

"What do you mean?" Conchobar asked, eyeing him narrowly.

"I heard you at the trial. I agree with your words there. Mor will destroy Ireland with his madness. He'll see every warrior cowed, killed, or exiled as these boys. There'll be no true fighting man left."

"So, you agree with me," Conchobar said cautiously. "And what of that?"

"So, I am not prepared to watch tamely while Mor has his way," was the reply. "He must be stopped."

"How?"

"It can be done," the dark man said cryptically, giving a sly smile.

"If you mean to try killing him, I'll have no part in it," the king tersely replied. "For me to act would bring my own downfall. You saw the others. Nearly all but myself support his rule. The fools are still blinded to the dangers by this new prosperity. And, the Bloody Raven curse it, I have sworn oaths to him that I can't break without bringing the gods' wrath falling upon me."

"Ah, but you needn't act directly in his end," the other said. "He has himself created the very forces which will destroy him. Those he has exiled will have their chance for vengeance. That I can see to. You won't have to be involved."

The man smiled cunningly, conspiratorially, his dark eyes glittering. There was something in those eyes, thought Conchobar. Some kind of force, potent and deadly. It seemed to draw him in.

"Who are you?" he demanded again.

"I have told you."

"A fighting man, you said. But there's more in you than an old warrior's soul. I feel . . . I feel a strange affinity to you. As if I know you."

"And how well do you know yourself, my King?" the man asked. "For it's your own heart and mind you're gazing into when you look in my eyes. We're one in knowing what must be done, and in using the means necessary to gain our ends."

"Maybe," Conchobar said, still cautiously. "But if you mean to do this thing yourself, why come to me?"

"You wouldn't be involved in Mor's end, but I still need your help before that comes. The time and place for our exiles' revenge I can arrange, but it can't be done quickly. Until I'm ready, our band must be kept alive, secure, and within our easy reach. My own resources are limited in such an area, but I thought that such a powerful king as yourself . . ." He trailed off, leaving the clear implication hanging in the air.

Conchobar considered, then nodded. "I see. Yes, well, I may have just what it is you're seeking. I think I can find a place to keep them for you, and maybe gain them some allies as well. Good fighting men they are, if without the honor of our warriors. I . . . use them now and again when I've a need. They'd likely shepherd your little flock, and keep up their fighting skills and fire for vengeance at the same time. I can help you reach them . . ." he raised a finger in a cautioning way, "but I can do nothing else to help you. Do you understand?"

"I do," the other assured him. "Just tell me how to find these men. Then you'll be through with it."

Conchobar stared searchingly into the dark eyes. He hesitated, seeming to ponder again the enormity of the intended act. But any qualms he felt were apparently drowned by his ruthlessness.

"All right then. When our exiles leave Tara, tell them to make for the port of Ath Cliath, for the bruidhean there. I'll send word on ahead. When they arrive, they'll find what they're seeking."

"I knew I made no mistake coming to you," the dark man said with a grin. "I will tell them."

He turned as if to go, then paused, looking back at the king. "There is one thing more."

"What?" Conchobar said with rising anger. "You said there'd be nothing else."

"Be calm, my King," the man said soothingly. "This hasn't to do with killing Mor. Well, not directly anyway. It's your druid, Cathbad. He's a danger to this business. He has powers that might reveal the plot to him. It was he who helped to track down our raiders before. He must be kept out of the way. Can you do that?"

"I can," Conchobar conceded grudgingly. "It's time he returned to Ulster anyway. But it'll not be easy," he added. "That druid is one of most independent mind."

"I'm sure you can see it done, with the great power you have," the other told him with great confidence. "Then there'll be no one who can interfere with our success."

"*Your* success," the king corrected. "I want no more part with you or with this business from here on."

"No danger of that, my King."

"There'd best not be, old man," Conchobar growled. "Or you'll find your own head being taken with all the rest."

"You speak as I would myself," the dark warrior said with a smile, clearly unintimidated by the threat. "Don't fail me, and I'll not fail you. And soon, my King, you will be the most powerful man in Ireland once again."

With this parting promise, he passed out through the door, leaving Conchobar staring thoughtfully after him.

Almost immediately Fergus entered to see his king staring ahead as if entranced. "Conchobar, what is it?"

Conchobar shook his head as if brought suddenly awake. "Oh . . . it was only some old warrior I was speaking with," he said quickly.

"Old warrior?" Fergus said in puzzlement. "Where?"

"Didn't you see him just now?" the king asked with surprise. "Why, you must have walked into him!"

Fergus looked toward the door, then back to Conchobar. "Sorry," he said, sounding at a loss. "There was no one."

"What do you mean?" Conchobar said irritably. He went to the door and threw it open.

Save for the drivers harnessing chariots, the yard of the little dun was quite empty.

"To be run out of our own land like mad dogs whipped from their kennel," complained Maine Morgor. "They cannot do it."

"To stay and be hunted like a hare by every man in Ireland," said Fergel. "That would be worse."

"Aye," said another gloomily. "We've no choice. We have to leave."

Some two dozen of the newly exiled youths sat moping in the small and crowded section of the warriors' quarters they had been allotted since their capture. A few others half-heartedly went about the motions of packing up their kit.

Lomna Druth, The Fool, paused in jamming a smoked pork loin into his traveling bag to cast back sarcastically at Morgor, "And you told us so grandly and so cocksure that they'd never dare to do anything to us."

Morgor leaped up, kicking back his stool, face suffused with angry blood, hand moving to his sword. "You fat, stupid cow! I should carve out your bloated stomach for those words!"

Lomna Druth turned, going white with fear. But his brothers Fergel and Ferobain quickly rose and moved up before Morgor in defense.

"Back away, Connachtman," Fergel warned. "He's right, and you've already caused more than enough trouble for us all."

Morgor hesitated, then looked about him at the rest of the young men. Many return gazes were accusing, resentful, even hostile.

He dropped his hand from his sword hilt, his voice taking on a defensive whine. "It's not my fault! Who of us would have thought they would support Mor so blindly? They are more cowardly or more greedy than any could have guessed. Even my own father—that great Wolf of Connacht—was enchanted to his side by that woman Meave." He looked about him for understanding. "All your own fathers betrayed you as well. Can you call that my fault?"

"Ah, no," Fergel said in sudden resignation, dropping back down at his table. "We're only looking for someone else to blame but our own selves. It's not your doing, Morgor, or that of any one of us. We all freely made our own decisions to join in. The adventure beguiled us as a comely maid, the danger made us drunk as the finest ale, and we were sure no harm could come to us. We were all fools."

"But what will we do now?" another young man asked despairingly. "We've lost our homes, our families! Where will we go?"

"I can help you in that," came a low, familiar voice, and the youths looked about to see the dark warrior among them once again.

"What, you, old man?" Morgor said, bridling in outrage. "You got us into this. You said we couldn't lose!" He looked at his companions. "See here, lads! If there is someone to blame in this, it's him!"

"I got you into nothing that went against your own desires," the dark one said. "You all know you acted willingly, and that all I did was try to give you help. Is there one of you who can call that a lie?"

The man's gaze passed slowly around the room, challenging that of each warrior. The hostility and suspicions in them faded before its strange, enthralling power, replaced once again by acceptance and belief.

"So if you can cease your bickering and listen," he said, shooting a warning look at Morgor, "I can tell you how you may yet regain your lives."

"What do you mean?" asked Fergel.

"I can give you a place to go, a place to live, but more importantly . . ." he paused dramatically, his eyes sweeping them again, "a chance for your revenge!"

"Revenge?" Morgor echoed, a sharp glitter of interest coming to life in his beady eyes.

"It was Mor who did this to you," the old man said with a cunning smile. "You can destroy Mor."

"What, the few of us?" another warrior asked skeptically. "How?"

"I can arrange it," the dark one replied. "You've only to act. You might have destroyed him once, when he first captured you, but you trusted in his lenience. You were fools to do that. Now you know he is your enemy, the one who has cheated you of everything. This time there'll be no weakness in you, only hard iron."

He pulled his sword from its sheath, laying it hilt-forward on the nearest table. It was an elaborately fitted weapon, the silver handle in a sinuous shape of two great serpents intertwined, so real they seemed almost alive. The men gazed upon them, fascinated.

"For those whose honor will not allow them to live in this disgrace, pledge now, upon my sword, to join in this revenge."

As before, his words had a spellbinding effect. In the young minds, the image of Mor grew to monstrous proportions. The fires of anger against him burned bright. With a now eager Morgor in the lead, they moved in around the table, one by one putting out their hands to lay their fingertips to the weapon's strange hilt. There came to each a peculiar vibration, as if the serpents writhed beneath their touch, and an energizing current seemed to flow into them, through them, charging bodies and minds with a new, tingling power.

Only the three sons of Donn Dessa who were with the group held back, in their gazes a coolness, an uncertainty.

"But Mor followed only the rules we broke in punishing us," Lomna Druth said. "And he might have put us to death instead of exiling us. Have we a right to seek revenge?"

"You more than any others," the old man answered, turning upon them the whole force of his compelling voice and his bright gaze. "He's shown you, his own brothers, that he cares nothing for you."

"I suppose he has," The Fool admitted, but still with some hesitation.

"And what of your own lives?" the man relentlessly pounded on. "Don't think only of revenge. Think of freedom! You can regain it in destroying him. He made these foolish laws. His power sustains them. Without him, his great peace would soon collapse. Once more the warriors would rule Ireland. Then all of you could return, free men again. Why, there are many here who would even call you heroes for your act."

He moved closer to the sons, his eyes moving from one to another, his force holding them all now. "Think," he commanded. "Is it his life—this man who has denied his love to you—or is it your own?"

The three exchanged looks, their hesitancy now replaced by new conviction, their young faces grown hard. Then they moved forward together to the table.

As one they each put out a hand, their fingertips coming to rest upon the sepentine hilt of the dark warrior's sword.

Chapter Thirty-four

Exile

Ferogain gently lifted the small, carved figure of a stag down from its shelf. It was a most delicately executed work, its running form a smooth, curving, elongated sweep of power, its great antlers a curling interlace of impossibly fragile lines painstakingly cut from the single piece.

He stood gazing upon it musingly. His eyes filled with tears and his mouth grew taut with sorrow, quivering. So taken by his thoughts and feelings was he that he took no notice when Fionualla slipped past the wickerwork partition from the central portion of the royal quarters and into the section that had been his room.

"Ferogain?" she said softly.

He started guiltily and jerked about. She glimpsed the tears shining in his eyes before he realized it was she, and, embarrassed, he used a sleeve to quickly rub them away.

"It's you," he said then, pulling himself up in a proud, defiant stance. "Well, you needn't be worried. I've only come to get my things. It's all right. I've our noble high-king's most gracious leave." This last was said with intense bitterness.

"Oh, Ferogain," she said pityingly, moving forward, "I've not come to chase you out. This is as much your room as it ever was. It was given you freely by Conaire, from his love."

"His love," the boy said scornfully. "He gave us rooms as he'd have given a shed to his horses, and in exchange it's only our freedom he takes away."

"You're unfair to think him cruel for that," she said in a more scolding tone. "It was still your own doing brought him to it."

"He needn't have exiled us," came the angry reply.

She stepped up to him, her voice fierce now. "He needn't have left you alive, either. Did you think of that?"

"Better kill us than leave us exiled, disgraced, homeless," he answered, stubbornly refusing to concede anything. He eyed her in an aloof, indignant way. "And you! Who are you to be coming to me now? I've no reason to listen to you anymore. You betrayed us. You betrayed my trust. You revealed my secret."

"No!" she protested. "I kept the bond you unfairly forced me to. I said nothing to Conaire."

The boy fixed her with a gaze that pierced her to her heart. "Then you can truly say you had nothing to do with his finding out?"

"All right," she admitted, forcing out the painful truth. "I did speak to someone. But it was not to Conaire."

Outside the room, the faintly heard sound of his name brought Conaire Mor, just entering the quarters, to a halt. He recognized his wife's voice. He knew he should go on, that he should hear no more. But he was transfixed, unable to break away from the voices that now came to him, soft but thunderingly loud to his attuned ear, holding him like some terrible spell.

"I told Sentanta about you," Fionualla went on. "He was the only one."

"Sentanta," Ferogain said, shaking his head wearily. "Of course. That perfect, loyal, humble puppy of Ulster. My replacement in Conaire's love. I should have guessed he would be the one."

"You gave me no choice," she said with force. "Can't you see that? I couldn't go to Conaire, but I couldn't let you go on. You told me you were trapped. You begged me for help. It was the only way I had left to give it. I hoped that he could stop you, save you somehow. Ferogain, I meant it for your good."

"My good," he echoed in disbelief.

"I did all I could for you," she said, growing irritated at his relentless ingratitude. "I even begged Conaire to have mercy."

"Oh, and mercy he surely had," Ferogain replied. "Instead of a swift end, I'm doomed to a living death, wandering strange lands like some wraith cast out from Tir-na-nog. I thank you much for that."

Beaten by his wall of hostility, she sighed heavily, shoulders sagging, eyes dropping toward the ground. "I'm sorry," she said defeatedly. "I can't help what happened."

He looked down at the finely crafted deer that he still held. "You see this?" he said harshly, through clenched teeth. "You gave it to me when I was ten years old, after my first stag hunt. I've cherished it since then. I had thought of taking it with me, to remember the old times . . . before."

In a savage move he hurled it to the floor. It smashed there, the fragile antlers and slender legs splintering away. She jumped at the explosion of it and at his violence, her eyes lifting to him in shock.

"But I've nothing I want to remember," he went on brutally, "of then, of Conaire, but even more . . . of you."

He turned his back, taking up some bits of clothing from his pallet and beginning furiously to stuff them into his traveling bag.

Heartstruck, tears welling in her eyes, she stood helpless, wordless, looking at him for a moment. Then she turned and pushed past the partition, back out into the central room.

She came up short as she saw Conaire across the floor and pulled back, looking with consternation into his face, which was hardened with his rage.

"So, you knew," he said in an icy voice she had never heard before. "You knew and you didn't tell me."

"You heard," she answered. "But then you know that I did tell Sentanta."

"You only told him to save Ferogain," he snapped. "I can see that's where your true love lies, and not with me. His betrayal only wounded me. Yours stabs me to my heart."

He wheeled and strode angrily away, back out the door of the royal house. She, now so swiftly and brutally stricken from both sides, slumped down upon the bench of a nearby table. Her head fell forward upon the table's top, and her slender body shook with despairing sobs.

Out in the yard, the rest of the exiled young men were making their final preparations to depart.

They were gathered under the stern gazes of Tara's whole populace. There was no help for them. There were no leave-takings, no sorrowful partings of loved ones and relatives. The clanspeople of the disgraced men were largely absent, those few still at Tara gazing ahead with stony faces or looking pointedly away. Meave, Conchobar, and the other province kings with their companies of chieftains and champions had departed the day before, wanting no part in witnessing the finish of these sorrowful events.

Near the main hall, the high-king's own entourage awaited him. Conal stood with his fellow Ulstermen: Sentanta, Cormac, and the druid Cathbad. Calatin kept himself discreetly behind the rest of Tara's druids.

Mor went first to Conal's group. His face still hardened with outrage, his gaze bored into Sentanta. "I've just found out that you first learned of Ferogain's part in the raiding from my wife. You kept that from me."

Sentanta knew that there was no denial he could make, no hedging he could do now. There was only the truth. "I swore to help her if I could and to preserve her own oath of secrecy," he answered flatly.

"And in doing so, violated your own greater oath of loyalty to me!" Mor grated in uncompromising tones.

"Now, now! That's not called for!" Cathbad spoke up defensively. "The boy only tried to help. He nearly died."

"And will he say he didn't go out with the intent of stopping them?" demanded Mor. "Can he tell me he had no thought of keeping me from discovering who was involved?"

Sentanta was taken aback by this. Both things had crossed his mind. He had not thought of them as crimes. "I . . . I did those things, my King, but—"

"Then you've betrayed my trust as well," Mor interrupted sharply.

"He did no such thing," Conal told him irritably. "He came to me at once when he knew they couldn't be stopped."

"Are you telling me that you also knew of this secret?" Mor asked, turning his accusing gaze on his champion.

"No!" Sentanta said quickly, realizing that Conal was only going to incriminate himself in the high-king's eyes. "No one else knew but myself. It was my choice alone to act as I did, and I take any blame. But what I did wasn't meant as a betrayal. I meant to help you, to save you from your need to punish them, to stop the raids—"

"To hide treason from me?" Mor cut in angrily. "To leave this cancer spreading in our gut? Eating away at the poor flesh of Ireland? Surprising help that is. I thought that you, above all others—" He paused abruptly, glancing back toward the royal quarters, then shook his head. "No one," he muttered bitterly. "There's no one."

With that he wheeled from them, striding away toward the company of exiles.

Sentanta looked after him, too stricken by this cruel attack to speak more, his mind stunned from the suddenness of the unexpected blow.

"Never mind, lad," said Cathbad, putting a hand to the warrior's shoulder in a comforting gesture. "He's had some great shocks given him at once. His own world's a chaos now. Just give him some time to sort out realities."

Mor reached the exiles. They were completing the packing of their cars. His cold, evaluating gaze ran over them. "Are you ready, then?" he asked.

"There's just one more," answered Fergel, nodding toward the royal quarters.

Mor turned to see Ferogain coming out its doorway, his kit bag slung across one shoulder. Above, on the balcony of the *granian*, Mor saw his wife, red-eyed but now in control, staring down at them.

Ferogain strode past Mor stiffly, giving him no glance. He joined his brothers, throwing his bag into his car.

"A final warning I must give to you," Mor announced. "To-day, when you ride out from Tara's walls, you will be no longer men of Ireland. It will be on your own heads to leave her by whatever means you can, and never come upon her shores again. As once-sworn fighting men, your own honor—if any such still exists in you"—his moving gaze fixed momentarily on Morgor and on Ferogain—"binds you to obey this sentence. Otherwise, know that if you are found within her boundaries in ten days' time, sentence of death will be upon your heads, and every loyal man of Ireland charged with seeking you out. Ride out now from our gates, and give thanks to Danu that you still have your lives."

Wordlessly the exiles climbed into their chariots and began to ride out through Tara's main gates. All save Maine Morgor. That one stepped forward to face the high-king, his expression as haughty and defiant as ever before.

"Before I go, I mean to say that I've no fear of you, Conaire Mor. I've no remorse for what I did. It's you who are wrong. I deny your laws and I deny your rule. One day—mark me in this—your own madness will destroy you. And I promise you, as the Bloody Raven is my god, that I will see it. May you die abandoned and in torment, Conaire Mor."

With this last, savage speech, the son of Aileel climbed into his chariot and followed the others out, the last through the great gates. As the exiles rode down the slope of the high dun, none giving even a rearward glance to their lost home, Mor turned and strode back, proudly, stoically, alone, into the main hall.

"Well, that's done then," Conal said resignedly. "For good or ill, it's done. Now, maybe, things will return to what they were."

"I hope so, Conal," the druid said with a touch of cautiousness. "But we must be careful, and we must keep watching the signs."

"Signs," Conal said with a skeptical laugh. "Well, I'll leave that to you."

The crowd was dispersing now, Tara's inhabitants returning to their tasks. The flock of druids moved off toward the Star of the Bards, their private meeting house. None took notice that one of their number was missing now. None of the elite and very clannish group associated with the outsider Calatin anyway.

It was only Fionualla who, watching from her high vantage point as the exiles circled Tara toward Slighe Cualan, noted another chariot with a dark-cloaked passenger appear from beyond the oaks of the sacred grove to join with them. And it was only she, her attention drawn skyward by a movement there, who saw the great, dark birds that swooped above the departing men, like carrion crows over a field of the dead.

Chapter Thirty-five

New Lives

With the dark warrior at their head, the exiles rode down toward the coastal village of Ath Cliath.

The huts of it clustered close about the sheltered inner curve of the great, sweeping bay and about the wharves of timber and stone constructed there. Just inland from them, on a higher ridge of ground, a large, six-sided building of shingled wood stood on the joining of the roads from north and west and south.

This was the bruidhean, a public house like scores of others dotting Ireland, provided by law and endowed by province kings to serve the wants of any traveler. And it was to this house of hospitality that the old warrior led his charges. Before it they climbed from their vehicles, giving them into the care of a contingent of eager grooms before following the old man inside.

It was a crowded place, the many tables circling the fire pit in the vast, single room filled with travelers from abroad as well as from Ireland. Rough men they mostly were, sailors from the trading ships of many lands. And since few in the band of young exiles had seen any but other Irishmen in their lives, they looked about with open interest, and sometimes revulsion as well, at the boisterous, hard-drinking company.

Indeed, some of these men were very different from the young exiles. There were those of swarthy complexion and dark hair, sporting great beards and curling mustaches. There were beardless men whose skin seemed nearly black in contrast to the pale white Irish lads. Even many of the fair-haired, light-complected men differed from the newcomers in having broader bodies and features.

The garb, too, was most exotic here. It blended ornately decorated brocades and silks in bright colors with simple garments of leather and rough wool. A high-king's treasure-house of ornaments ladening arms, legs, necks, ears, and twined in elaboately styled hair added a garish glitter to the barbaric nature of the scene.

By now the entrance of this large group of nobly dressed young warriors had attracted much notice from about the inn. A hefty, ruddy-faced little man broke off a conversation to hustle through the crowded tables to meet them.

"I'm pleased to welcome you to my hostel, my fine men," he said heartily. "I am Da Derga. And what pleasures can my house offer to you?"

"We've come from Tara," the dark warrior told him in a confidential way. "A certain man of Ulster said we were to seek you out for help."

"Ah!" the man said, his genial manner giving way to one of gravity. His gaze passed over the young warriors again, this time with greater interest. "So it's those who need to be leaving Ireland, is it? Well, I have heard from our Ulster friend. The ones you want are over there." He nodded toward a table close beside the fire. "You'll need to be asking for Ingcel the One-Eyed. He's leader."

"We will. And thank you, bruighaid," said the old warrior, moving on toward the indicated men.

The men at the table glanced around as the exiles approached.

"We're seeking one called Ingcel," the dark warrior addressed them.

"Are these boys the band of ruthless outlaws Mor was forced to exile?" one of the men said in surprise.

He was a wide-shouldered man of boldly chiseled features, their handsomeness marred by a great scar across one eye. It was as if a flaming torch had been ground into the socket, the wound healing in a twisted mass of tissue that had sealed the eye closed. But the other eye, of a bright silver-blue, blazed out with enough vitality for the two.

The single eye was the man's only mark of distinction. In dress he was quite plain, in contrast with the eccentricly colorful men about him. He wore tunic and trousers of simple dark wool topped by a leather vest. His single bit of decoration was a scarf of green and red plaid tied about his forehead, keeping a wealth of dark blond hair back from his face.

"You are Ingcel," the dark man stated.

"I am surely," the man said with a smile. "This face declares it to all the world. Come and sit down," he added heartily, waving a hand about him in a welcoming gesture. "Join us, have some drink. Then we can talk."

The young warriors found spaces about the tables, squeezing in among the men there. Room was made across from Ingcel, and the old man sat down. Morgor forced his way in beside him, only to find himself across from a squat, leathery-skinned man whose flat head and bulging eyes gave him a toadish look. Morgor eyed this being with open abhorrence.

"Ah, here's ale," Ingcel said as Da Derga and other serving men appeared laden with pitchers, mugs, and platters of steaming food.

A burly man beside Morgor leaned across him to grab a pitcher. Morgor jerked back as if slapped, exclaiming in disgust, "By all the gods! Do these men ever bathe?"

"We've enough of the water without getting ourselves into it," Ingcel said, apparently amused by the insult. "It's that sharp nose of yours, boy. If you're meaning to stay with us, we'll have to whittle it down a bit—right, lads?"

As his comrades guffawed loudly at this rude jest, Ingcel turned his attention from the now-affronted Morgor to the dark warrior.

"So tell me, old man: just what do you want? I was given word that you needed my help, but little more than that."

"You know these warriors are now exiled," was the reply. "You've likely guessed that they need a way to leave Ireland, and a place to go."

"I have, and I can understand their need. I'm an exile too, of sorts. My grandfather, King Cormac of Britain himself, drove me out for a bit of feuding within the family." He smiled and winked slyly. "Well, to say the whole truth of it, I tried to do away with my whole family and seize the throne. So now I wander the sea, making my own life whatever way I can."

"But there is something else," the dark man said in a more confidential tone. "Something much greater. When the time is right, I want you to return to Ireland and help them carry out a special task."

"Task?" Ingcel said suspiciously, leaning toward the man. "And just what sort of task?"

"We mean to kill a king," Morgor haughtily declared.

The water erupted and spattered away in bright droplets of light as the boy shot from the water.

His surprised fellows scattered, laughing, then turned to plunge back upon him in a wild fray that churned the waters of the clear stream to a white froth.

Upon a rock nearby, the lone figure of Conaire Mor sat, body slumped forward in a posture speaking of desolation, staring out at them. In his mind flashed other images, but similar to these, overlaying other faces upon those of these carefree boys. They were the faces of himself and his foster-brothers, playing here in the River Life themselves not so very long ago.

Though they were painful images, he seemed to relish dwelling upon them, recalling their details, as if the pain were some kind of deserved punishment for what he'd done.

Fionualla and the Ulster druid Cathbad stood just above him on a low bluff. Both watched the forlorn high-king, but Fionualla with a look of great concern.

"Day after day he's come here to sit like this," she said. "How long can it go on?"

"It's a terrible thing he's had to do," Cathbad explained. "His feelings about his brothers, about his life, about what he did are confusing ones to him. He just needs time to sort them out."

"But how much time?" she asked. "He came here days ago to ask my father and uncle to forgive him. They've done that. They understand what he had to do. Still, he seems inconsolable."

"He came for more than to talk with them, I think," Cathbad replied. "He came here because it was here his simpler life was left, given away when he made that walk to Tara. Maybe he wants the feel of those lost days again. Here he can think. He can be alone to work out his torments."

"Alone," she repeated, a touch of bitterness in her tone. "Well, he's that, all right. Rolled up like a hedgehog he's become, head tucked in and spines flared out to drive everyone away. Sentanta, you, even myself. He's said almost nothing to me since . . ." She stopped, her body drooping, head falling forward in a gesture of despair. "Oh, Cathbad," she said, voice heavy with emotion, "what have we done to him?"

Cathbad put a comforting arm about her shoulder. She leaned into him, like a hurt child seeking a parent's security.

"I could guess at your involvement in what happened, Fionualla," the druid said, "though I would never violate your privacy, nor that of any others, by doing so. Still I can say I'm certain that it was nothing you did that was the cause of Mor's despair. It wasn't you or even the betrayal by his brothers. It's the curse of rule. He meant to rule justly. Well, maybe the truly just can have no friends."

"Good Cathbad," she said. "I understand you're trying to help me. But, to see him this way . . ." She looked beseechingly at him. "Isn't there anything you can do? No magic that could cure him of his pain?"

"No magic I have can reach into the places his pain lives, my Queen. I can banish *sheoguey* beasts that walk the earth, but not the more terrible creatures we create in our own minds. I might intoxicate him or make him sleep, but I'd only be masking the feelings for a little while. No, it's only the medicine of time that can cure him. Come. Let's leave him now."

With her arm linked through his, they walked back across the meadows toward the circling wall of stones that protected the homes of Mor's foster-fathers.

The usually quiet dwelling place of simple herdsmen had become a hub of great activity with the king's visit. Scores of chariots and carts were parked against the outside of the wall. Around them the stalls and pavilions and cookfires of the king's vast entourage spread outward to surround the little compound with what had now become a fair-sized town. Its avenues bustled with the people of the court, the warriors, their servants, and the servants who served them, all busily about their varied tasks, largely oblivious to the troubles of their king.

"Like fleas swarming upon a tethered hound," Cathbad said, looking over the vast camp with distaste. "I don't blame Conaire for escaping to the river. Are they all really here to help him, do you think, or only to play the Battle Raven and drink his rich blood?"

"It could be love of him for what he's done," she said with sincerity.

Cathbad gave a short, humorless laugh of skepticism at that, but made no other reply.

As the two worked their way through the crowded thoroughfare toward the gate, Conal Carna and Sentanta came into sight there, moving out to meet them.

"How is the king faring?" the Ulster champion asked.

"As before," she told him sadly. "The brooding hangs on him like a cloak of iron."

"It is a melancholy sight," Sentanta agreed in a sympathetic tone.

But Conal snorted impatiently. "He sits doing nothing, and there are important affairs of state to be seen to."

"Still, Ireland seems to be running itself well enough for the moment," said Cathbad. "The prosperity continues, and no one dares challenge his peace now."

"But they may one day," the practical-minded Conal stubbornly returned, "and what then? Will this one, hard judgment bring him to let it all go? He made the right decision. Now he must carry on his rule."

"That he was right doesn't erase his pain," said Cathbad. "Be reasonable, my friend."

"Well, it's all Ireland at stake here. Sooner or later . . ."

"Try to make it a bit later, Conal," the druid advised, "if you're truly wishing to have him whole again. He will recover, but he needs time. It will be for you, his champion and his friend, to see he gets that time. You must protect him, and you must be patient."

He turned to Fionualla, taking up both her hands in his. "And you, my dear—you must love him, and watch over him, and wait. The sorrow truly is like an illness on him. It will pass. As for me," he added, releasing her to look around, "I can stay here no longer. There's nothing more I can do, and Conchobar's demands that I go home to Ulster have become quite strident." He smiled. "Even I must appease the old wolf once in a while."

"You're not the only one wanting to leave," Conal said, nodding at Sentanta. "Our lad here has also been asking to go back to Ulster."

"Not to Emain Macha," the boy put in. "I want to go back to *my* home, to Dun Dalgan."

"But it doesn't seem right to me to be having one of our hostages leaving," said Conal doubtfully.

"Maybe it was Conaire's own coming home that put it in my mind," said Sentanta, clearly not certain himself. "But since the trial, since . . ." he glanced at Fionualla, "well, since all this, I've had a . . . a certain confusion in my mind. I ran away from my home and mother, and I haven't seen her since. I don't really know quite why, but I've suddenly a great need to go back and make it right with her. It seems as if it's there I need to go to make sense of a great many things."

"My friend, you needn't explain," the queen said soothingly, putting a hand on his arm. "I understand."

She turned to the older warrior. "Conal, he has a right to this," she told him earnestly. "Listen to me: I know what he's feeling. You must let him go."

"I don't know." He looked at the druid. "Cathbad? What do you think?"

"I think there are many good reasons he should go," the druid said gravely, looking at the lad.

"All right then," Conal reluctantly agreed. "But don't be longer in your absence than you have to be."

"I won't," Sentanta promised. "And what of Conaire? Should I speak to him of this?" He shook his head. "I've no great liking of doing that, I'll say truly. I speak very little with him anymore."

"No. Don't worry, lad," Conal assured him. "You just go on. No sense in disturbing his brood for it. Likely he won't notice anyway, shut up the way he is. And if he does, I'll explain to him."

"It may be he'll be happier with me gone," Sentanta said ruefully. "One less reminder of his betrayal."

"Don't think that way," Fionualla said, taking his hand. "You are a good friend, and I cherish you, as I know he still does. Will you return soon?"

"I will think, my Queen. That's all I can promise now."

"Please, just remember that he needs all his friends," she said most earnestly.

He nodded, but it was hard for him to meet that pleading gaze.

Seeing the young man's awkwardness, Cathbad moved briskly in. "Well then, my boy, let's make ready to go. No use in delaying. The day's young yet, and we can make a good start for home. Come along." And, taking Sentanta's arm like a teacher taking charge of a pupil, he led him away.

It was not long afterward that their chariots were rolling down across the meadows from the camp to the river.

Mor did not even look up as they splashed through the ford and up the other side, heading north to Ulster. His melancholy gaze was still fixed on the playing boys.

Several of the smaller ones had just captured their one larger tormentor. Managing to grasp and lift the wet, struggling body with an effort, six of them heaved him above their heads, swung him, and threw him far. He rose and arched and then dropped down toward the sparkling waves.

Chapter Thirty-six

Homecoming

Waves beat rhythmically against the base of Dun Dalgan's sheer cliffs.

Some distance along the clifftop, on a narrow roadway that edged the very brink, a single chariot of war sped toward the high fortress. Over its reins crouched the charioteer called Laeg, while behind him young Sentanta clung to the curved bronze horns which formed handholds on either side.

As they rounded a curve in the undulating wall of cliffs, Dun Dalgan, perched upon its highest prominence, came dramatically into view. When the boy saw it, a sudden tautness creased his smooth brow and drew deep lines about his mouth.

He put a hand on Laeg's shoulder. "Pull up here," he said.

The young driver, who was having a fine time recklessly guiding the team along the perilous road at their fullest speed, looked back at him in surprise. "What! Stop here? Why?"

"Just do it, Laeg. Please."

With a sigh the charioteer obeyed, reining the galloping steeds in to a halt.

Sentanta stared up at his home. It looked no different from before: a stark line of wooden palisade, weathered to dull gray, the wall that had formed his prison for so long. He felt no more warmth for it now than he ever had. His absence from it sparked no fond images now, but only memories of his loneliness there, his feelings of emptiness.

The gray line, lifting over the swell of the clifftop, was still like a frown, as if the grim fortress disapproved of the boisterous sea. To Sentanta it also called up an image of the sternly set mouth of his mother. Was that what he would see on his return?

Laeg, curious about his companion's odd action, looked about to see his friend's face set in grave lines. "What's wrong?" he asked.

The words seemed to pull Sentanta from his gloomy reverie. "Nothing. It's just . . ." He stopped and shook his head. "Ah well, go on."

Laeg shrugged and urged the horses forward. Under his skillful hand the chariot continued along the treacherous road, up toward the high walls of the melancholy fortress.

A bent and ancient steward opened the doors of the great hall, ushering Sentanta past him into the room.

He stepped forward with a certain reluctance in his movements, peering around him warily. The hall seemed empty. Then he stopped, staring straight ahead. Across the floor, upon the raised platform of state, stood a lone figure wrapped in a scarlet robe.

He started toward it. The trip seemed endless to his apprehensive mind, the suspense making the floor grow vast as he walked across it. With what seemed painful slowness, he drew nearer to the dais. The tall, slender figure upon it still stood with back to him, conveying to him disapproval and cold rejection in the upright, rigid stance.

He stopped below the dais, standing in a strange, hunch-shouldered way, like a small child waiting to receive a blow. The figure looming above him made no move, no sound. It might have been a column hewn from red yew wood.

"Mother?" he called in a voice that, though soft and tentative, seemed to ring hollowly in the empty room.

The figure stirred. Slowly it turned, revealing the face of his mother, Dechtire. She stared down imperiously at him, making no reply.

"Mother," he repeated, still uncertainly, peering up at her, "I've come home."

"So I see," she said in a voice devoid of all emotion. The handsome face was as of stone.

Though it was disconcerting to have his mother greet him in this distant way, it was much what he had expected. But he was not going to be cowed by it. He drew himself up, striking what he hoped was a most manly pose.

"I am in warrior training now, Mother," he declared.

He hoped the words would sound ringing and grand. Instead they came out sounding flat, hollow, and foolishly boastful.

"I can see that as well," she said, still with no sign of thawing.

His pose of manhood faltered before the overwhelming power of disapproving motherhood. His will failed him, his shoulders hunched again, and he was once more the flustered child.

He gave a great sigh, shaking his head. "You're not making this very easy for me," he said dismally.

"And did you make it easy for me by sneaking away from me in the night as if I were your jailer?" she replied, now with the heat of resentment entering her voice. "Did you think of me when you ran off to what might have been your death with no word to me? To me! After I gave up my own life, isolated myself here, cut myself off from the whole world just to see that you survived!"

"But, Cathbad brought you word of where I was," he said by way of lame excuse.

"Oh yes, he brought word," she said sarcastically. "After you had been nearly the whole spring at Emain Macha, and me thinking every day through all that time that you'd been hurt or killed. Then, finally, he brought word."

"He feared that if you knew where I was before I was well established at the school, you would bring me back. That you would stop me from becoming a warrior."

"And he was right, the clever, clever druid," she said bitterly. "I should have known he'd have his way in this at the end. I should have known they all would. The cursed men!"

"Mother, please, I didn't mean to leave you in that cruel way. But now it's done."

"It's not done," she shot back. "It's only beginning for you. I know it. I've always known. It's that same, terrible fate I meant to save you from."

"I know you fear for me. I understand. But *you've* got to understand that it was something stronger, something in me I couldn't fight that took me to it. Can't you understand and forgive me now?"

"And why *did* you come back now?" she asked tersely, ignoring his plea.

"Why?" he repeated, nonplussed by the question. "I . . . I'm not certain. I felt a need. I felt I had to make things right somehow. I wanted to come home."

"But why *now?*"

"Things are . . . confused with me," he said vaguely.

"Things have happened. I don't know what to do . . . to think. . . ."

His brain seemed to be swelling, pressing against his skull, as if the wildly milling flock of troubling thoughts had jammed it. He suddenly felt a great weariness sweep through him, nearly overwhelming him. He sagged down upon the steps of the dais, his head dropping into his hands in a gesture of despair.

"Oh, Mother," he said miserably, "I just needed someone to help."

He looked so forlorn, so helpless there, that Dechtire was moved. The hard face softened a bit with sympathy. One arm lifted from the folds of her robe, hand stretching out as if to caress his bowed head comfortingly.

But then some other impulse, some stronger feeling, pulled her sharply back. The hand fell and the face grew cold once more. "You are no longer son to me," she intoned. "You made that choice. I fought to make you mine, to keep you safe. But other forces were more powerful than my own." Her voice dropped, and she seemed now to be speaking to herself. "If I'd known what he meant for me—"

She stopped abruptly, but the rancor in her voice brought Sentanta's gaze sharply up to her.

"Who, Mother?" he asked curiously.

"No matter," she said brusquely, giving her head a sharp, angry shake as if to cast away the tormenting thought. "It is over. I've no part in it anymore."

"No, Mother, please," he appealed, raising a hand. "That's not true. You have a part. I need you! I've had doubts about what I thought was meant for me. All of those years I yearned to be a warrior. Now I don't know. I meant to be a champion and help the king. But now . . . now things have happened to make me feel unsure."

"You've made your choice," she said again, unbending. "You've entered the outer world. This place which you saw as a prison is no longer home. The one who was your mother is no longer one to you. Your life is somewhere else now, your destiny beyond my reach. I must accept that." She looked upward, seeming to direct the next statement to the roof poles. "But you were wrong!" she said with a sudden ferocity, her teeth clenched. "I'll never be content!"

"Who was wrong, Mother?" he asked, rising. "Whom are you speaking to?"

She looked down at him. There was a strange light in her eyes, as if some reckless impulse rose in her. "Maybe you should know," she said in a musing way, then added defiantly, "And why shouldn't you have a right to know all of it now?"

"What do you mean, Mother?" the boy demanded. "What should I know?"

She seemed about to speak, the words ready at her lips. But then a strange, soft sound arose, like the fluttering of great wings. Though it seemed to come from outside, and all around, its wordless whispering filled all the hall. Then it faded away.

The impact of this eerie noise on Dechtire was profound. As if a sudden gust of cold rain had come to douse a blaze, the sound extinguished her fiery impulse.

"Not now," she said. "Foolish things are often said in the grip of rage or spite. Not now. I have to think."

"Then, may I stay, Mother?" he asked hopefully. "I've no wish to return to Tara yet."

"Dun Dalgan is your inheritance," she told him flatly. "Of course you have a place here, if you wish it."

"I would like to see Father, too."

"I'd not advise that. His seeing you might be a shock to him."

"Still, he is my father, and I—"

"Wait, Sentanta. Please listen to me. It may sound cruel to say, but he has been more a sane man since you left. He's even come out of his apartments at times to walk the parapet. To see you now might do him more harm."

"I see," he said unhappily. "All right, Mother. If that's so, I'll keep away from him."

"The steward will see to your things," she said brusquely. "Please, leave me now."

He turned and strode across the great floor toward the doors. As he rounded the fire pit he paused, looking back at her. "Mother, tell me—will it ever change?"

She made no answer, only staring at him from the dais, her face once again as of stone.

Defeated, he went on out the hall's main doors, leaving the slender, rigid figure standing alone in the great room.

Meave, queen of Connacht, moved briskly across the floor of her own bustling hall, directing the many servants.

"Aoibheann, take those plates out to be washed again," she

directed a young serving girl laying out the tables for the evening's feast. "They've not been cleaned at all well."

While the embarrassed girl hastened to obey, Meave turned to a round, red-cheeked man in steward's livery. "Garbhan, see that fire pit's cleared today, will you? The ashes will be spilling over the hearth with one more fire. I've spent too long seeing this hall restored to have men tracking the filth all across the floors."

Meave had indeed done a most amazing job in bringing life back to Dun Cruchane's main hall. It was finished, a new place now, clean and glowing, its walls hung with the finest tapestries, clean mats of woven rushes covering all its floors, the many surfaces of wood and glass and bronze polished to a brilliant sparkling. The servants worked vigorously, with a lively and a cheerful air about them, seeming most proud to labor for such a grand place.

A leather-aproned steward moved into the hall from the main doors, approaching her. "My Queen?" he said. She turned to face him. "There is someone to see you." He pointed toward the doors.

She looked and saw there a large figure silhouetted against the light in the wide doorway.

"I am Calatin, ard-druid to Conaire Mor," he said, his low but powerful voice rolling across the vast space of the hall to her.

He came forward, out of the glare, revealing his swarthy face and his stocky body wrapped in its striped druidic robe.

"I remember you," Meave said. "I saw you at Tara."

"I am not an easy one to forget amongst those of Ireland," he said with a smile, adding graciously, "but you, my Queen, have your own qualities—both of beauty and spirit—that make you even more memorable."

"You are a most flattering man," she said with an easy laugh, but still flushing at his compliment. "Now, tell me why you've come so far from Tara."

"To see you, my Queen," he said. He had now crossed the room and stopped close before her. "I feel that we must talk. It is most vital, and . . ." he leaned toward her, his voice dropping, "most confidential."

She peered into those glittering dark eyes, seeing a look of grave urgency. "Very well," she agreed. She looked about her at the servants, raising her voice to order, "Listen, all of you.

You can finish your tasks later. Go now, please, and leave me with my visitor."

Though the command was unusual, there was no balking, no murmur of complaint. They obediently, silently gathered their work materials and filed from the room. In moments, the two were left alone.

Meave walked away from Calatin to the royal dais. She climbed onto the silver-banded platform. There she pointedly took a seat at the center of the great oaken table surrounded by its four gleaming posts of bronze and placed her hand lightly upon a long, slender rod of silver that lay before her.

Calatin followed her to the dais, standing below it, looking up at her. "Where is Aileel?" he asked.

"He's resting now. He has worked hard lately, finishing the restoring of Cruchane."

"Of course," he said knowingly. "And so these rumors of his health—"

"Rumors?" she broke in, speaking flatly, meeting his eye without blinking. "There are none I know of, and none you should believe."

"Of course," he swiftly acceded. "In any case, it was you I came to see. I first want you to know that I've followed your triumphs in Connacht with interest." He smiled. "I feel, quite modestly of course, that I've had some stake in you. It was myself who first recommended your coming here to Mor."

"Was it?" She eyed the dark man with greater interest now. "If so, then I thank you," she told him sincerely. "I'll tell you honestly that you and Conaire gave me a new life."

"You have certainly done great things here," he said, looking about the room. "More than even I would have imagined." He fixed his gaze on her again, a greater earnestness entering his voice. "I believe that there is no other ruler in all Ireland who has acted with such courage and such cleverness, who's shown more loyalty, more honor, more belief in peace. Conaire Mor and Ireland herself could have no better supporter of this new unity. That's why I've come to you. You see . . ." he put a foot onto the step of the dais, leaning forward to speak more intimately, "that unity may be in great danger soon."

"Come up," she said, signaling him toward her. He mounted the dais, moving up before the table. "Now, tell me what you mean," she demanded. "Is there more raiding? Other rebels?"

"No, nothing of the kind," he assured her. "Ireland is at

peace. Prosperity continues. It's the future I speak of. I fear that Mor has been weakened by the exiling of his fellows. The signs have turned against him. I've foreseen his fall in the portents from the gods."

"His fall?" she said with concern. "How?"

He shrugged. "That knowledge, I am afraid, my Queen, the great Others keep secret even from me. But they have told me other things more vital to yourself: that his fall needn't bring down the miraculous peace he has wrought, if someone even stronger of will than he—more dedicated to keeping the new rule of law—takes his place. That someone, my Queen, is you."

"Me?" she said in surprise.

"Yes, my Queen." He stepped closer, his voice growing more intense. "I've seen the signs. A woman it is to be, out of Connacht. A woman of power who controls men. A tamer of wolves. That is you."

"How could that be?" she asked, incredulous. "No woman has ruled over Ireland."

"Why couldn't it be?" he countered. "The daughter of one of Ireland's greatest kings? The ruler of Connacht? The one who has brought the savage Firbolgs to accept peace? Many already see you as greater than Mor for what you've done. I saw them look to you at the trial. It was your boldness and your sense of justice which prevailed."

"No," she protested. "I could never rule."

"Yes, yes," he said, leaning down, fixing his gaze on her, his dark eyes smoldering now with power, his voice low, compelling, filled with energy. "You could do it. Can you say you've not thought of it yourself?"

Maybe she had. She remembered Conaire himself telling her that the strength of her father was in her, that she must have wished for his power for herself. She hadn't denied it then, and she couldn't now.

She looked into the druid's glowing eyes and saw visions of that power, felt the wave of exhilaration surge through her. She had proved herself here. She had tasted power and found it a heady drink. But to rule all Ireland . . .

Then a darker vision intruded before the shining ones. She shook her head, breaking off eye contact with the druid.

"No," she said angrily. "I can't be thinking of such things. What about Conaire? If there is some bad omen, shouldn't he be warned?"

"Of course I have given warning to him," Calatin said. "But he's too deeply sunk in his melancholy to heed anyone now. The course he must take for Ireland's good seems too hard for him. I fear that soon, rumblings of his weakness will begin."

"Maybe if I . . ."

"For you to thwart the gods' will would only bring ill fortune upon you," he hastily assured her. "No mortal can reweave the threads of fate's tapestry, and for you to try when you've been so chosen is greater madness. It must be as it is. You can only be ready to accept it."

"Accept it," she said thoughtfully, not yet convinced.

"Think, Meave," he went on softly, enticingly, leaning closer. "You must carry on, for Ireland. You are the only one who could do so. It may be that the portents I have seen are wrong. But if, good Danu forbid, they are right, that anything should happen . . ."

"Yes," she said gravely, both repelled and fascinated by the possibility.

"A powerful leader, Meave. That's what will be needed. Someone to rule over all the headstrong men of Ireland. To command even its province kings, even the proud, ravening bear of Ulster, Conchobar MacNessa."

To be Queen of all Ireland, she thought. *To rule over Conchobar*.

Calatin saw the enraptured light filling her blue-gray eyes. He straightened, his voice taking on a more businesslike tone. "Of course, should such a thing come to be, my Queen, I wanted you to know that I would certainly help you. The other druids of Tara are a closed-minded lot, resentful of Mor, stuck in their old ways. But I know how great you can become, and I would be at your side."

She roused from her reverie at this, her manner becoming brisk and official once again. "I thank you for that, Calatin, and I thank you for coming to me. As to my actions should such a terrible thing occur, I can give you no answer now."

"I have put the notion into your mind, my Queen," he said, smiling. "I see that it works upon you, and with that I am content. I must leave you and return to Tara now. But I will see you again. Of that I'm sure."

He turned and went down from the dais, striding away across the hall and out the door, leaving her alone.

She lifted the silver rod and tapped it against one of the bronze pillars. A clear note rang out, echoing in the room.

From the opening to one of the outer chambers a steward poked his head. "Yes, my Queen?"

"Tell the others they may resume their work now."

"Yes, my Queen," he said, and in a short time the company of stewards and serving girls was moving back to their labors.

But Meave stayed seated upon the royal dais, staring ahead musingly into space. "Queen of all Ireland," she said, and smiled in pleasant reverie. "Ah, Conchobar, what wonderful, tormenting rage would come upon you then!"

Chapter Thirty-seven

Indecisions

It was his mother Sentanta watched, but also someone else.

She sat at a great celebration in Emain Macha's hall. A wedding feast, he somehow knew, though he couldn't say how. It was as if he were himself, gazing on, and at the same time within his mother, seeing out of her eyes.

She was a girl of glowing beauty and immense vivaciousness, unlike the somber woman he had always known, aged not so much by years as by weighty cares. Here she laughed and talked and danced, swirling about to the piper's lively tune, singing joyously with the minstrels. Then, made thirsty by the activity, she sat and drank deeply of the heady mead.

But as she drank, a small, errant mayfly fluttered down, as if drawn by the strong sweet scent of the honey drink. And, quite suddenly, Sentanta was the mayfly too, seeing through its eyes as the vast cup and its mead—like a wide, bottomless well—seemed to soar up toward him, draw him in, envelop him as he sank into its pool of liquid gold.

Then he watched his mother lift the cup again. He saw her drink. The impulse came in him to warn her, but another impulse came to urge her on. She drank, the mayfly, unobserved, drawn down with the stream of mead into her mouth.

And with that, he was somehow the three at once, his mother, the mayfly, and himself, all within her, drifting in a warm, soft, throbbing darkness.

But he also continued to gaze on from without as she, suddenly drowsy, left the feast and went to her rooms. She stretched herself upon her bed and slept until a voice awakened her.

Over her bed now stood a young man, his handsome face alight, his eyes like glowing silver. He leaned down close to her and spoke, his voice soothing and sensual at once.

"It was myself came to you as the mayfly in the cup," he said. "and it is with me you must now come Away."

His beauty and his voice enraptured her. She made no protest, surrendering pliantly as he easily lifted her. Then a bright light rose about them, and within that light their two bodies transformed, taking the shapes of great, swanlike birds linked by a chain of gold. They rose, soaring from the high windows of the dun, out across the smooth swells of green countryside, across the coiling blue ribbon of the Brugh na Boinne, sinking down to disappear beneath a great heather-covered mound.

Within it was a single room, a cavern formed within the earth, but done as finely as a high-king's chamber. There they again shifted to human form. He lay her in the comfort of a cushioned bed. He lay beside her, caressed her softly, and she in return reaching out to him; and Sentanta, feeling the heat of them together as the two drew closer, seeming to blend, becoming one, becoming somehow himself, all enveloped by a vast, comforting warmth like the sea that he had once wished to carry him away, drifting . . . drifting into the depths . . .

And he awoke.

He sat up rigidly in bed, looking around in bewilderment. Some sound had awakened him, he was certain. He listened intently. It was faint, but he knew it. His mother's voice.

He rose at once, propelled by urgent curiosity that drew him across the yard from his sleeping quarters, following the voice, and into the great hall.

As once before, he stole silently in, peering out from the shadows about the outer edge toward where the low-burned fire cast out a ring of soft, ruddy light.

He stared, amazed.

Between the fire pit and the dais his mother strode angrily back and forth. And upon the platform's edge there sat a man.

Sentanta could make little of him, for his back was to the youth, and he seemed surrounded by a strange silver light that blurred his outline.

He and Dechtire seemed to have been arguing, and as Sentanta entered, his mother was just taking it up again.

"I don't know how you can dare to ask me anything now. After what you've done to me?" She stopped before him, her voice hard and bitter. "How could anyone dare? Do you so arrogantly believe that your coming to me was the greatest moment of my life? That all you had to do was appear in your bright glory and use your wiles to arouse a foolish girl and so awe her that she'd cheerfully sacrifice her whole life for you? Only one year *you* sacrificed out of your thousands, giving me a few days of passion. Then you leave me with him, cursing me with knowing that even he will never be mine. And for that do you believe I am supposed to thank you?"

"I loved you," came his voice, soft and caressing. It made Sentanta start. He had heard it before.

"You used me," she answered sharply. "And you've kept on using me. You knew that all my protecting would come to nothing."

"I warned you, Dechtire," he said reasoningly. "This was for something greater than you or myself. He is too valuable to all of Ireland. Why can't you be proud of that?"

"Because he is my son and I weep for his fate," she told him. But then she shook her head, her voice taking on a weary note. "No, not weep. I mean that I've wept for him, long night after night. But there're no tears left. It's ended, and I know I've lost. You can use him as you wish now."

"But you'll not tell him?" the man asked urgently. "You were meaning to."

"And why shouldn't he know?" she asked with a new spark kindled by defiance. "If he's to be yours now, he has a fair right to it."

"It would be more fair to him that he not know," said the other. "He lives in the mortals' world. That's where he can act while we cannot. He can do great good there, but it would not help him to know. He must be one of them . . . think himself one of them."

"Why? Isn't it a cruel thing to keep the truth from him?"

"Crueler than making him see himself as a freak, alien to both worlds?" the man countered.

He rose and moved closer to her. A hand lifted to rest

shimmering upon the smooth whiteness of her bare arm, thrust out through the sleeve of her gown. The voice implored.

"Dechtire, I know the pain I've caused you. I regret it. But I still must ask you to do this."

She looked at him, tensing as if she wished to physically cast a denial into his face. Then she nodded angrily. "I will do it," she grated. "But I curse you."

"Do you?" he said. The hand slid caressingly up her arm. It rose to touch her neck, the fingers sliding on to tenderly brush her soft cheek. "You are still a most beautiful woman. . . ."

Her look of outrage faded at the touch. A strange, faraway look came into her eyes. Her head tilted, her cheek moving to rest in his cupping hand. A flush of warmth rose up her smooth white throat. Her breathing quickened.

His other hand rose, sliding up her side. Sentanta watched, shocked but unable to move, as the hand moved up, following the curve of hip and waist to the soft swell of her breast.

To this she reacted. As if the last caress had been a slap that jarred her from a trance, she stepped back and angrily knocked away both hands.

"No more!" she told him sharply. "I will not say that I've no longing for our time together, but I also feel a loathing for what you did. Young and handsome you may be still, but you'll not be casting that spell on me again."

"It was no spell," he said. "It's what I felt, what we both felt that drew us together."

"And no more words!" she said, lifting a staying hand. "You have what you want. Cease tormenting me now and leave me to whatever life I still have."

His hands dropped to his sides. A great sorrow came into his voice. "I will, Dechtire. That I promise you. But know that you will always have my love."

He was about to go, Sentanta realized. But the boy couldn't let him. The intense need to act released him from his immobility. He stepped forward and called out, "Mother?"

Surprised, the man wheeled about and Sentanta saw his face. It was a face that he both knew and didn't know—the same as he had seen in his dream.

"Who are you?" the boy demanded, starting toward him.

But instantly the aura of shining light around the man grew intense. As Sentanta watched in amazement, the man's shape altered, turning from human to a great white bird. And as it stretched its wings upward, ready to take flight, the globe of light about it blossomed outward, filling all the room, catching him in a wave of blazing silver that engulfed him, lifted him, and carried him away.

Sentanta sank into the sea of light that blinded him, smothered him, filled his mind.

He awoke.

He sat up rigidly, looking around in bewilderment. He was in bed, in his own quarters. It was still night, with enough faint moonlight trickling in through the shuttered windows above his head to illuminate the room and show he was alone.

It had been a dream, he told himself. All of it one dream. Still, it disturbed him with its vividness, and with the strangely real quality of its last part.

But, what had it been about? He wasn't certain now, the details fading even as he tried to grasp at them, to hold them long enough to examine as a child tries to do with snowflakes.

He turned and pushed open the shutters. The moon shone on the quiet sea, lighting a few clouds to glowing silver. He stared at them, frowning as he tried to think.

There had been a man with glowing silver eyes. A man and his mother. But, what about them? What was it they had said?

Frustrated, he lay back, staring up into the wedges of deeper shadow between the roof poles. He had no idea what the dream meant, or if it was more than that maddening beast of turmoil in his mind crawling out to plague him in his sleep. But he did know one thing: dangerous or not, he meant to speak to his father.

The sun lifted, casting its light through a red-tinting veil of horizon clouds to cut a crimson trail across the waves and strike fire against the wall of Dun Dalgan's cliffs.

The man perched with what looked like great precariousness atop the palisade at the cliff's edge, staring out. He was a wild figure, his ragged cloak and long hair fluttering about him in the stiff morning breeze off the sea.

Sentanta approached him along the parapet walk slowly, cautiously, as if to come upon him too abruptly might startle him and cause him to topple.

"Father?" the boy called softly.

The man turned toward him. He was lean almost to the point of cadaverousness, cheeks hollow, eyes sunken deep behind shaggy brows.

The eyes—golden brown and filled with melancholy—fixed

on him, first with disinterest, then with a rising curiosity. Suddenly they narrowed, the face tensing as if a sharp, intense pain had shot through the wasted frame. Then, abruptly, the eyes went dead again, their gaze wandering back to the sea.

Undaunted, Sentanta moved up beside him, sitting down on the wall not far away.

"Father, please listen to me. I know what you're feeling. I've not come to cause new agony for you. I only wanted someone to speak to. I thought that . . . maybe . . ."

He paused, looking for some sign of response. Still there was none.

"I'm training to become a warrior now," he went on, lifting his cloak to reveal his sword. "I wanted to be one, and that's what I'm to become." He dropped the cloak, his expression growing more troubled. "I thought I wanted to help the high-king, too, to win great renown as his loyal fighting man. But now . . . now I don't know."

His father continued to stare out to sea, seeming not to hear.

Sentanta took a deep breath and forged on. "I found out that there was no real glory in being a warrior. Not anymore. Instead of using my sword in battles for my king, I hunted fellow warriors, captured them, and took them before him for punishment. There wasn't any joy in doing that. Cormac was right. And now things have changed with Conaire Mor as well. I thought I was his friend, that I was a part of his great dream for Ireland, but now I've come to doubt that, doubting everything I've wanted. Should I become a warrior? Am I traitor to what I've meant to be? Or am I traitor to Mor, and somehow to myself at the same time?"

That strange feeling of intense lethargy flooded over him again, swamping him, drowning his mind. He dropped his head forward into his hands.

"I just don't understand, Father. What is it I'm to be, to do? I've felt that my life was set out for me, but the way isn't clear anymore. There's something in my mind that says I've no free will, that I'm a tool to be used toward some great end. But, if that's so, why is my path so twisted, so confused?"

He looked to his father, who was still staring fixedly out to sea. An anger filled him, born of his frustration, driving away his lethargy. He grabbed the man and forced him around, looking into his eyes.

"Father, speak to me! There's no one else to help me. But you can. I see it in you. You know, and you can speak to me.

Don't hide like this. Help me! By good Danu, you are my father. I need answers. Please, please, why don't you speak to me!"

Finally there was a response. The eyes focused on his. They seemed to see him, and the light of recognition dawned in them. The mouth moved, and from the lips came a voice, rusty with disuse, hollow as if coming from the dead.

"I'm no father to you."

Conaire Mor stood below the slope of the southern visitors' duns, well out of sight of the walls of high Tara.

Alone and quite isolated there, he was engaged in loading his sling and casting at the upper branches of a large fir in the nearby woods.

His aim was quite good, the iron pellets trimming branch after branch as he worked his way down the tree trunk, though he seemed to take no interest or pleasure in it. He only loaded, cast, and reloaded in a rhythmic, automatic way, as if the process occupied his mind, keeping other, more painful thoughts away.

From behind the rounded dun on which the visitors' enclosures sat appeared Conal Carna, striding rapidly, purposefully ahead, his expression stern.

"So here you are," he said disapprovingly as he approached. "And do you think you can just steal off unknown and come here by yourself this way?"

"Look here, I came back to bloody Tara, didn't I?" Mor replied tonelessly, casting the sling again. "What else do you want from me?"

"I want you to rule," Conal said sharply. "You *are* the king."

"Then why do anything?" Mor said, shrugging in apathy. "Things are going well, aren't they? So long as I'm king, everything will prosper, just as the Sidhe vowed. And no one will dare cause trouble now that I've proved my ruthlessness."

"And what about running things?" Conal persisted. "There are other decisions to be made: judgments, arbitrations, payments, distributions of goods, management of herds. . . ."

"All that can be done by Brehons, druids, and chieftains of the court, as always before. My father surely never put a hand to any of it."

"Your father was a weak man. I thought you meant to be different. To help Ireland."

"Oh, but I have," Mor answered with a rueful smile. Don't

you know? Just listen to the bards' tales. I'm a legend already, Conal. I'm the high-king who united the provinces. I brought Ireland the great benefit of peace. I've brought her riches like she has never known." He looked at Conal, still smiling, but with tears of anguish in his eyes. "I've torn apart my life for Ireland. I've lost my brothers, my closest friends, my wife. Isn't that enough?"

"I've grown weary of your endless agony over this," Conal said brutally, his patience gone. "You've had time enough to overcome your grief. Do you think you're the first to learn that ruling can be harsh? Didn't your grandfather, Eochaid, kill his own sons when they rebelled? Yet he went on and ruled as a great king." He gripped Mor's arm, his voice growing more urgent now. "Conaire, you can't let this drain your spirit. You must be strong and take command again."

"Not at that cost," Mor said angrily, jerking away his arm. "I've fulfilled the cursed prophecy. So why don't you and the rest just leave me alone!"

"You've seen to that well enough yourself," Conal bluntly replied. "Even driven your own poor wife to hide herself away in that *granian*. You sound more and more like Meave when she first came to Tara from Ulster, broken and caring about nothing, not even her own life. But look at what she's done since."

His words recalled for the young king that boar hunt of long before: his argument with Meave, her wish for death, their savage battle with the maddened beast.

"Meave is strong," Mor shot back. "She has the fire of Eochaid in her. It's not in me."

"You're wrong, Conaire. Look at me. I was a warrior with belief in nothing but a good sword in my hand. Your plan for peace seemed like a madman's dream. It was your own fire, your faith in it, that changed me. It was your words that convinced Ireland's kings and chieftains to give their bond to you, and you who gave that new, strong life to Meave. *You* did those things, not the gods or prophecy or fate."

"I thought I could do them," Mor said, shaking his head, "but I was wrong. I know that now."

"Oh, do you?" said Conal, at last exploding in frustration. "Well, *I* know that if you've given up believing in yourself, if you mean to hide away and play the pouting fool, then you should pass on the rule to someone else and go out grazing with the cattle in the field!"

With that he turned on his heel and stalked away.

Mor looked after him thoughtfully for a time. Then his gaze went back to the sling dangling in his hand. Slowly, carefully, he loaded it again, then looked to the tormented, half-denuded tree.

A movement above it caught his eye and he looked up to see a large, white, gold-speckled bird wheeling overhead. He hefted the sling tentatively, feeling an urge to make a throw at it. But the words of the Sidhe-man Nemglan, uttered those years before, came back to him:

"It is not for you to be making casts at birds, if you'd be king over Ireland."

"Ah, but if I were there again," Conaire muttered, "and knowing what I know now, it's no *gessa* of yours that would have held back my hand, Sidhe-man."

He heaved the sling with all his power, the pellet shooting out to crack against the bole of the poor tree.

Chapter Thirty-eight

Preparations

The body slammed down through the water, sinking deep. A hail of fine rocks loosened from the cliff face hissed into the sea all about it.

The stone fortress that perched on the very edge of the high cliff was stricken. The spires of smoke rising from within its curved walls and the doleful moans of wounded men were clear signs that it was in its last death throes.

Bodies of scores of warriors were draped across the stone ramparts where scaling ladders and ropes showed how the defensive barriers had been overcome, and the small number of bodies outside the wall were proof of the experience of the attacking force.

Now those attackers—the horde of exotic and savage men who made up Ingcel's sea-raiding band—moved freely about the fortress's inner yard, busy at a most grim work. They were searching through the bodies of the fallen, ruthlessly finishing those badly wounded, methodically stripping all the bodies of anything of worth.

The young exiles of Ireland were among this company. Some were joining the raiders in their plundering, a few with great gusto. But others, in whom finer sensibilities or noble breeding still held sway, remained aloof, eyeing the activities with disdain, distaste, and even horror.

The boy Ferogain watched with particular revulsion as a squat and toad-faced pirate finished a wounded defender with the quick slash of a knife across the throat, then began to strip him of his brocaded cloak and a gold-embroidered tunic. The man's single hand and clumsy hook of iron were woefully inadequate for the task. He looked up, fixing liquid, bulbous eyes on the young Irishman.

"Help me here, lad," he appealed. "Come on. He's a rich one. We'll share!"

Ferogain looked from the awful face to the poor dead man, whose pale, blood-streaked stomach and chest had already been bared by the pirate's efforts. The young warrior's throat constricted suddenly and he felt his stomach knot. He turned away, eyes squeezing shut, chest heaving as he fought to control his nausea.

"Agh! Useless lad!" the other growled, and went on alone with his grotesque struggle.

Observing this from across the yard, Ingcel strode over to the panting, white-faced boy. "What's wrong, lad?" he asked, slapping a hand to Ferogain's shoulder. "You act as if you'd not seen dead men before."

"Of course I have," the other forced out. With an effort of will, he managed to overcome his queasiness, turning to face the leader of the sea raiders squarely. "It's nothing. I'm all right."

"Are you?" Ingcel said, eyeing the boy closely, then shaking his head. "I think you're not. I'm certain it's not the killing. You do well enough in that. It's afterward. You've held back like this more than once."

Ferogain looked into that keenly probing gaze and knew he could not lie. "You're right," he admitted. "And it isn't because of the killing. It's the cruelty, and the plundering of the dead."

"Come on now, lad, what are you saying? You were raiders yourself."

"For us the raiding was only a part of it," Ferogain returned with a certain righteous indignation. "The cattle were a prize, not stolen but won, and in honorable fight."

"Honorable was it?" Ingcel seemed amused. "And where was the dishonor in this? We fought here man to man. The best survived. Now we're only taking our prizes too."

This seemed to confuse the young warrior. He struggled to make the difference clear: "It . . . it's not the same. You're outlaws. We were warriors, doing what others have done for ages past—"

"Sea raiding has a long past of its own," Ingcel interrupted. "Ask my lads, the Lochlanners especially. Why, they were raiding these coasts long before the first of your people or mine ever came to them. No, lad, you can't use those arguments on me. It's only your belief in that warrior 'honor' of yours that makes you any different from ourselves. None of that foolishness exists here. You'll learn that soon enough. Look there." He pointed. "Your brothers know it's true."

Across the yard, Fergel and Ferobain were searching through the scattered bodies with the zeal of all the rest. And as Ferogain watched in shock, Fergel swooped down to yank a jeweled bracelet from a corpse's hand and hold it aloft with a whoop of triumph.

"Believe me, boy, I understand," Ingcel went on more sympathetically. "I've noble blood in me. I had visions of honor once, the same as you. They were a sham. All men fight to gain—if not wealth, then a sense of power. But the power is all illusion. It's the wealth that helps you survive. That's all I want now: to survive!"

"But I don't want survival this way," the boy told him despairingly, "and I want no wealth. I'll fight for you, and do my share, but I want nothing from you. I only want to go home."

"I know that feeling too," Ingcel said, a faint longing in his voice. "For me it can never happen." He looked at the boy and smiled. "I hope it can for you."

A sudden scream brought both of them quickly around.

From a high window of the square-sided keep which sat at the cliff's brink a man was hurled, flailing out, shrieking in terror as he fell, the shrill voice fading away as he dropped below the edge.

"By the tempests of Llyr, what's going on?" cried Ingcel. He started off at a run for the keep.

Behind him, Ferogain still stood, staring up at the window, his face a mask of horror.

Inside the keep, Maine Morgor was laughing with immense delight. He sat at a table in the keep's great hall, leaning back in an ornately carved chair that was clearly meant as the seat of state. His legs, now trousered and heavily booted like those of the seafarers, were up on the tabletop before him, creating a posture of arrogant ease.

Around his long, lean neck was a great torque of twisted gold strands, properly to be worn only by a chieftain of great rank. About his wrists and upper arms were several golden bands set with jewels, and the ornately crafted hilt of a dagger thrust into his belt lay against his belly, the carbuncles studding it winking crimson light as he breathed.

"Good!" he cried out, waving an arm in a gesture of royal command. "Let's have another one!"

The keep was a large room, its stone walls rising two stories to a vaulted ceiling of heavy timbers. Around the circular hearth of its central fire, Morgor's table and several others were arranged in a large square.

Crowded tightly into one corner of that square were a dozen women, all clad in rich gowns but devoid of cloaks or jewelry. Three grinning seamen watched them, one sitting cross-legged on a table nearby and running leering gazes over the youngest and most comely of the women. There was little question where the jewelry of the captive women had gone. Brooches, necklaces, bracelets, rings, and other booty lay in a glittering pile before Morgor.

Outside the square, by a large open window in the hall's seaward wall, a score of men were grouped. Captive warriors of the fortress they clearly were, some elderly, some quite young, but all bloodied in the recent, desperate fight. Like the women, they had been stripped of cloaks and jewelry and all weapons. Around them four heavily armed sea raiders stood on wary guard.

At Morgor's command, two of these guards looked over the group of men. They hesitated, not certain of the choice.

"Come on, come on!" Morgor prodded. "Get on with it. You want to get to the women, don't you?"

With this incentive the two seamen wasted no more time, laying hold of one of the older men. But as they did, a boy rushed up, grabbing at their arms.

"Father!" he cried. "No, not Father!"

Though of no more than thirteen years and slender of build, he fought with spirit, trying to yank them away. But his struggle ended when one burly pirate savagely cuffed him back.

"No, wait," Morgor called, smiling with a malicious pleasure. "I think you ought to give the boy his wish!"

"I see your meanin'," the burly one answered, grinning in return. "We will, then."

He and his fellow released the man and grabbed hold of the boy. One of the older women in the group cried out in terror. The elderly man moved forward, but the prodding spear of a guard forced him back.

As the two men lifted their struggling captive, Morgor saw a flash of gold from the boy's hand. "Hold on," he told the men. "Not so quick now. Just take off his ring first."

They wrenched it from the boy's hand and tossed it to him.

He looked at the plain band, shrugged, and tossed it carelessly atop the rest of the booty. "Go on then," he said.

They lifted the boy and hauled him to the window. Below it was the long drop to the sea. The older woman broke down completely now, crying uncontrollably as the other women tried to comfort her. The men sat the boy on the windowsill. His arms shot out, hands clutching desperately at the rough stone edges as the men began to force him through.

His fingers were slipping. He cried out despairingly, futilely, for help. Maine Morgor only laughed.

"Stop that!" came the voice of Ingcel.

The two pirates eased their pressure on the boy and turned to see their leader striding into the great hall. It was clear from his look that even this hard and ruthless man was appalled at the barbarity he now witnessed.

"What are you doing?" he demanded of Morgor. "We don't kill our prisoners unless they're badly hurt. These people have surrendered to us."

"What sport is there in that?" Morgor answered. "Anyway, I've thought it a mistake to leave them alive to speak of us. And the women," he cast a licentious gaze toward them and smiled, "well, they've surely other uses that you're letting go to waste."

"The lad's got ideas, Ingcel," said the raider seated by the women, putting out a hand to tease at the lush brown curls of a cringing girl. "You can't say he doesn't."

"He does, Captain," the burly one put in. "And he's a hard one, so he is. I thought I'd never see one so hard as yourself."

Ingcel looked down at the still-lounging Morgor, who now smiled, gloating at him. "My men know you well, it seems," he said with heavy sarcasm, "and I agree. You truly are as vicious a little vermin as I've seen."

Morgor only smiled more broadly, as if this were a marvelous compliment. "I've only followed your lead, great Captain."

Ingcel's arm shot out, sweeping Morgor's feet from the table. As the chair thudded suddenly down, jerking Morgor forward, the pirate chief leaned over him, face close, voice chill.

"Not my lead, you bloody-minded boy. I raid for booty or for pay, not for sport. But you . . . you like it! You like it far too much!"

At first surprised by Ingcel's swift move, Morgor now resumed his insolent air. "Too bad you've no choice but to put up with it."

"But not for much longer, I hope," Ingcel said tersely, straightening. "I pray to the gods my fathers prayed to that that old warrior of yours calls you back to Ireland very soon."

"You've no greater hope of that than I do myself," Morgor returned.

"Just gather what loot you can and come along," Ingcel brusquely ordered. "And let the rest of these people alone!"

"What?" Morgor said in disappointment. "The women too? But . . ."

"I said come!" Ingcel commanded with more force. "And I still lead. Come now!"

He turned and stalked from the hall.

"He still leads," Morgor muttered, watching him go. Then he rose, moving around the tables toward the captive men. "All right," he called to his guards and waved both hands above his head, "let them all go. You heard Ingcel. He still leads."

The two men holding the boy released him and moved away. The captives exclaimed their great relief as Morgor stepped up as if to help the boy down from the sill.

Then, in a sudden move, Morgor drew the ornate dagger from his belt. He rammed it forward, its sleek point jabbing through the boy's narrow chest to pierce his heart.

The boy jerked, staring at Morgor in surprise for an instant before falling back, pulling off the blade as he toppled out the window.

As the crowd, shocked to silence by the swiftness and savagery of the act, stared silently, Morgor turned to shoot a look defiantly after Ingcel, his mouth curling in a cunning smile as he spoke.

"He still leads . . . for now."

Wind swept around the black tower upon the cliff, keening against the ragged pile of stones.

Within the tower, Calatin moved before the gathering of his sons. His figure seemed looming, massive, and dark against the flaring light of the fire licking up behind him. From the great vat bubbling upon it, an oily column of black smoke snaked up to the roof hole, scenting the air with the hot, acrid smell of pitch.

"It is all prepared," he told them with satisfaction. "Everything has gone just as I wished. I've even tricked bloodthirsty Conchobar into thinking he has helped me destroy the peace." He laughed heartily at that. "The fool! His treachery will turn upon him. He'll soon find his help has only replaced Mor with a leader he'll think more dangerous to him: a ruler with the courage to make his kind of mongrel live forever on a chain."

"And who will this leader be?" a son asked him in a dry, chilly breeze of voice.

"It will be Meave, queen of Connacht." He laughed again. "What delicious irony! The one person Conchobar has most reason to despise. But I've seen no other in Ireland stronger, more willing, and—though she does not admit it yet—more thirsty for power. I have used that, awakened the lust for it in her. With my help, she will take the rule and end the age of warriors forever."

"When will it come, Father?" another son asked.

"Soon now," he said. "All has been most carefully primed. Meave is prepared. The young warriors who will do the deed for us have been recalled. It only remains for us to set the trap that will draw Conaire Mor in, stake him, and leave his throat bared for the knife, like a bull ready for sacrifice."

He stopped, facing them, his burning gaze running over their white, intent faces.

"So now, my children, it is time for you to play your parts in this. When the darkness has been raised and dispatched on its mission, some of you will depart on your own also. You, Feardorcha, will go out with five others into the countryside of Munster and prepare. Fearganainm, you and two others will go to the river Muilchean to see that Mor is drawn there as I wish. Dubhan and Dugald, you will go to the last place near to Ath Cliath and set Mor on his final course for his doom. The rest will stay with me, to join with the exiles and see that doom is met.

"But before that, we have our work to do here. Come, gather in the ring, my children. Raise the spell."

They formed a circle about the fire and its bubbling caldron. Their sepulchral voices joined in a low, rolling chant—the words guttural mutterings of some ancient speech, lost with the dying of its people, forgotten to all save the sinister Calatin and his hideous brood.

As their eerie song drifted upward with the oily smoke, the ard-druid moved between the table and the pot, slipping in platters of shiny flesh and entrails, scattering crushed leaves and the minced pieces of strange herbs across the churning surface, tipping bowls of viscous green and yellow fluids into the mixture until it thickened to a yellow-brown ooze, like mud boiling about a hot sulfur pool, each erupting bubble belching out a puff of stench.

Then, from a small gold-bound chest of black oak wood, darkened by ages, polished by the wearing touch of countless hands, he lifted the object.

It was oval, the size of a large apple. Its surface, however, was as that of no fruit but rather like a reptile's skin—a thick, leathery gray-green covered with overlapping layers of shiny, disk-shaped scales. It was suspended on a chain of glinting silver, and he lifted it by that most tenderly.

"Now comes the time," he intoned in his low, soft croon. "Now do I use my most precious amulet, the Serpent's Egg."

He lifted it higher, the flickering red lights of the fire reflecting from the many disks, making it scintillate.

"No power in this land or in the whole of the world is so strong as this, hard won from the serpents' frenzied twining in the sea. But now, to gain the end of a high-king, I sacrifice it in completing my greatest spell."

A heavy chain hung from a tripod of iron rods set over the caldron. A hook at its one end was suspended close above the bubbling surface. The other was caught on a bracket set in the floor beside the fire pit. Calatin gently hung the amulet upon the hook. Then, freeing the chain, he slowly lowered it until the egg had vanished beneath the heaving concoction.

At once the liquid around the amulet began to boil with a new frenzy, churning the grotesque ingredients that floated in its depths, foaming up in billows of yellow froth that spilled

over the sides of the pot, running down the curved iron sides
in thick rivulets, fat drops pulling loose to drop into the fire
with a sharp hiss that sent up more foul smoke.

"Be born of this egg, spirit of the night," he said. "Rise and
appear to us, child of the serpents' twining, spawn of fear and
treachery and death. Come now!"

The column of smoke grew thicker. Its coils began to un-
dulate with a distinct rhythm, matching the deep-toned chanting of the sons. Within its depths a shape began to form. A
massive head came into view, sleek, long, and reptilian, its
bony jaws glinting with its curved fangs, its eyes like immense
black pearls glowing at each side of the flat skull. The body
that curled down through the smoke behind it seemed formed
of disk-shaped scales, like the egg, but shiny black, flashing
uncountable facets of red light.

Once it had formed, it expanded, its coils sweeping outward
to surround the fire, Calatin, then the circle of his sons. The
darkness of it seemed to fill the room, swallowing its light. A
new scent pervaded the already odor-filled air, its strength
overwhelming all the rest: the scent of fear. The head dropped
toward the encircled men. The vast jaws opened to reveal a
cavernous black maw.

Calatin took up a long rod from the table, thrusting its silver-
shod tip up toward the creature's face. It reared back as if
struck.

"Your evil will not be used against us, black spirit of the
egg," he said. "It was my hand brought you here, and my
orders you shall obey."

It held itself motionless above him, black eyes fixed upon
him intently.

"You will go forth from here," he continued, "into the tuath
of Mumain. Spread yourself upon its countryside. Let your
clouds of terror and deceit fall upon every rath and dun and
liss. Bring your darkness and your direful sights before the
eyes of all its men. Fill up their thoughts with terrors drawn
from the inmost minds—the hidden monsters of their own
most secret fears—and parade them in the light. Bring the
sounds of strife, fill the air with disquiet and the noise of battle:
clashing arms, moaning wounded, thunder of chariot wheels.
Give portents to the air as if gods keened and Ban-Sidhe wailed
upon the dead. Make the land burn as if every fortress were
under siege and the whole land laid waste by war. Do all of
this for me, dark spawn: direful sights and sound, the world

upset, the countryside made waste, all nature in upheaval, as if Ireland herself were in rebellion against the sins of this weak and wretched king."

He plucked from his cloak a massive ornament, the brightly enameled, jeweled crescent pin of Tara's royal brooch. He lifted it high. "See here the symbol of the man you will help me to destroy. Then go!"

The creature lifted, slithering up the smoke column as if it were swimming up through the sea, its length sliding out through the roof hole and into the sky.

Calatin watched until it was out of sight, then dropped his gaze back to the gleaming brooch of Tara in his hand. "Farewell to you then, Conaire Mor," he said, and cast the ornament into the caldron.

It sank slowly, vanishing into the depths of the thick, bubbling ooze.

Chapter Thirty-nine

Premonition

The thick brown liquid bubbled in the iron caldron, churning indefinable chunks of yellow, gray, and green that drifted in its depths, sending up white streamers of coiling steam to fill the air with its heavy odor.

Cathbad stirred the concoction carefully, delicately sprinkling a handful of dried, crushed leaves across the surface. Around him in the druid quarters, a fascinated company of his fellows watched him work.

"A most wondrous thing it is, Cathbad," one said, coming up beside him to peer down into the pot.

"Well, I do say there's no finer maker of real lamb's stew in all Ireland," the druid answered with a touch of pride.

"The smell of it alone is making me faint with hunger," said another young druid, so lean and famished of look it seemed the whole pot might be needed to satisfy him.

"Yes, me too," a third said eagerly. "When will it be ready?"

"Nearly done," Cathbad promised cheerfully. "Just a bit more rosemary to it, I think."

The atmosphere in the quarters of Emain Macha's druids was, thanks to the chief druid, a most congenial one. The place itself was bright, with many windows opened to the sun and light, and gaily patterned rugs and tapestries. Cathbad thought it a most healthy thing that his fellows gather here to talk and laugh and free themselves of the ponderous weight of their profession for a time. And when no state affairs demanded their presence at the feasting in the main hall, it pleased him to cook a meal for them.

Now he sprinkled another touch of seasoning into the stew and stirred it slowly, lovingly. Then he bent down toward the bubbling surface to fill his ladle for a taste.

A monstrous black form erupted from the stew, shooting upward toward his face, jaws wide, fangs aiming for his throat.

He jerked back, exclaiming in shock, dropping his ladle to the stones of the hearth with a clatter.

"By the gods!" he cried. "What was that?"

"Cathbad! What?" said a man nearby, moving up to grasp his shoulder.

"Didn't you see?" he said. "It came up . . . from the stew. . . . Something alive."

"Using lamb a bit too raw, maybe?" a druid said with a smile.

Cathbad looked around and saw others smiling too. They thought it was some joke, he realized. He looked to the man beside him. "Devin, didn't you see?"

"No, Cathbad," the man said, then realized the seriousness in the older druid. "You really did see something?"

"I thought I did."

Cautiously Cathbad bent down over the stew again, examining the surface. Only the chunks of meat and vegetables were to be seen swimming in the thick broth. He took up the long ladle and experimentally poked it down into the liquid.

"A monstrous thing it was," he said musingly. "No creature of the earth, but something from a nightmare, or some ancient, terrible . . ."

And then suddenly he stood upright, stiffly, face drawn in tense lines.

"I feel an evil," he said. "I feel it rising. I've been given a glimpse of its coming. It was meant as a sign to me." He turned to the others. "Quickly, you must help me raise the Seer's spell. Cumhea, fetch out my pallet. The rest of you, gather round."

"What, now?" the lean young man said, casting a longing, famished gaze at the stew.

"Forget your stomach for a time," admonished his chief. "This is most urgent. Get on with you."

In moments the pallet had been brought from its compartment into the center of the room. He lay back upon it while his fellows gathered about him and began raising a low, melodic chant that wafted upward with the savory steam from the cookpot, out the roof hole into the evening sky.

The ard-druid relaxed, creating a void within his mind. The sound of the lilting music filled it up. Faint images danced and soared there, becoming clearer, as wraiths drawing into the light. And suddenly, jarringly, he was besieged.

Bright, glaring images shot into his mind and he went rigid, nearly swept away by their violence, fighting to control them. In quick succession he saw the creature of his vision, but grown massive, blotting out the sky and earth. He saw fires and heard the screams of women and children, heard the clash of arms, saw other, vague but dreadful shapes moving in a mist, witnessed a great building going up in flames while men battled savagely, flooding the earth with streams of crimson blood glowing luridly in the firelight. And through it, in the very midst of the worst of it, he saw Conaire Mor battling desperately to survive.

The fire rose then, its flames seeming to collapse upon him, smothering him in a sea of blazing red, and he sat up.

"The high-king," he said. "He's in great jeopardy."

"What?" said the druid Cumhea. "Again?"

"Not again, Cathbad," Conchobar said impatiently. "It seems you just returned from helping that boy king out of his *last* jeopardy. You can't be running to Tara every time you have some twinge of pain or a bad dream. You're *my* ard-druid, if you'll recall. You need to be seeing to our own affairs."

He was in the Speckled Room with Fergus and other of his champions, looking over some new weapons that had come from their smith. The druid's so casually bursting into the sacred province of the warrior without invitation had outraged the king, but Cathbad's announcement that he meant to go to Tara had roused even greater ire. That, however, made no impression on his druid.

"I tell you Conaire Mor is in mortal danger now," Cathbad insisted. "Powerful forces are gathering against him. He must have help."

"It's not for us to be forever solving that boy's predicaments," Conchobar complained, swinging a sword sharply against a hanging shield as if to emphasize his point.

"It's for every man in Ireland," Cathbad indignantly replied. "I know your feelings, but he is our sworn high-king."

"Maybe Conchobar is right," said the hulking warrior Dubthatch. He was experimentally balancing a casting spear of great size, its bole as thick as his wrist, its iron head broader than even his massive fist. "If he is in trouble, it seems he's bringing it on himself. If he's strong enough to rule, he can see to his own problems without your helping him."

"But it's more than himself in danger," argued Cathbad, "it's his whole peace. Our peace! And it's not only what he's done that's bringing the trouble on. I can feel some magic working here, drawing him in, playing black tricks upon him. That's why he needs my help. His own druids haven't the skills to fight a thing like this."

"And if you don't help him?" asked Conchobar.

"Then I foresee destruction for him, and for many of his champions," Cathbad replied bluntly.

"Your own son Cormac is among them, Conchobar," Fergus reminded him.

"He is," said the king thoughtfully. He wondered if this danger was the plot that old warrior had spoken of. It had not occurred to him before that it might involve his son.

Dubthatch had been closely examining the massive spear's broad point. It was a long, slender pyramid, four-sided rather than flat. The four edges were separate pieces, hinged into the central part, flaring out slightly at the bottom. But at Fergus's dire words, the champion looked up from the weapon, laughing skeptically.

"Come on now, MacRogh," he said. "Do we need to be getting ourselves into a great lather just for some nightmare Cathbad has had?"

"It was no nightmare," the druid said with force.

"No one comes before me in questioning the real powers of most druids," Fergus replied, "but I trust in Cathbad's skills. If he's had a vision of this, it can't be ignored."

"I don't like anyone, even a high-druid, doing such a thing without leave from me," Conchobar put in testily.

"I don't need your permission," Cathbad shot back. "As a druid, my highest loyalty is to the high-king, as your own should be. I will go. I plan to leave at dawn. But I'll have to ride to Dun Dalgan first to fetch Sentanta."

"Sentanta?" said Fergus. "Now wait there, druid. Why involve him?"

"Do you think he'd forgive us if he was left out of this? He should be there, as he's a sworn hostage to Mor, and I feel his presence there has some great import. His fate's tied to Mor's somehow. We can't deny it."

Fergus sighed. "Yes, I suppose you're right. Conchobar, you have to let them both go."

"I don't *have* to do anything!" the king said, glaring defiantly at him. "And I don't like being told I do."

"You've no other choice," the druid told him flatly. "Or do you mean to look a traitor if something does happen?"

At this threat Conchobar knew he was beaten. "All right, go off to Tara with the boy, and curse you," he growled. "If you're destroyed with him, it's no more than what you've sought, and I'll be well done with the both of you."

"If we're destroyed, your own son may be too," said Cathbad reprovingly. "Remember that in your cursing." He turned and stalked out of the room.

The king glared after him, then shook his head angrily. "Well, I'm tired of all of this," he said. "If there's to be some more trouble, I want no part in it."

"How can you avoid it?" asked Fergus.

"I simply won't be here to know of it," he answered. "I mean to do some deer hunting in the north."

"You want a hunting party?"

"No. I mean to go alone and lose myself from the whole of it for a few days. Fergus, I'll leave Emain Macha in your hands. Do as you wish about this. I want to hear no more of Conaire Mor."

"And you really mean to go now?" asked Fergus, still nonplussed by the king's abrupt decision.

"I can still make *some* choices for myself," Conchobar said defiantly. "And I mean to go tonight!"

"Say, look at this!" said Dubthatch, who had ignored this last exchange in his absorption with the new spear. "It's quite a weapon. Maybe our smith's greatest cleverness."

He drew back the spear and hurled it at a heavy, oval shield propped against a chariot. The point slammed home, tearing through the thick layers of leather as if they were a linen sheet. He jerked back on the spear's leather thong to pull the weapon free. But the flared ends of the point caught, the separate flanges pivoting out into long, wickedly curved barbs that hooked the shield, preventing him from yanking it toward him.

"Tear out a man's whole chest, that would!" the king said with a most cheerful grin.

The silver playing piece settled upon a new spot on the *fidchell* board.

Conal Carna looked up from his move toward Mor, who stared with brooding disinterest upon the game. Above them, the king's wife sat alone in the *granian* of the royal quarters, sewing.

Mor was finally lifting his hand toward a piece in preparation for a move when the outer door opened. The ard-druid Calatin glided into the room.

"My King, I don't mean to be disturbing you," he said in his most ingratiating tone, "but a messenger has come, and his news is very grave."

"What is it, Calatin?" Conaire asked, rising with Conal as the man approached.

"He's brought word from Munster that the two Carbres are at war in Tuath Mumain."

Above, Fionualla, hearing the mention of war, dropped her sewing and went to the *granian* balcony to look down into the room below.

"Great slaughter's being done on both sides," Calatin went on. "The countryside is all ravaged, and they say no man will end their quarreling until Conaire Mor himself goes there to make a fair truce between them."

"Well, my King," said Conal, looking to Mor, "there is your everlasting peace. I knew it would come to this. Now you *must* make a choice. Do you mean to act, or do you give it up?"

"I . . . I don't know," said Mor, still taken aback at the calamitous news.

"If you hesitate now, it will spread," Conal went on insistently. "Soon all Ireland will be warring again. Remember your own words that fired me? You were weary of the violence and wanted it to end. Well, you were not the only one. What about all those who trusted your word, believed in your peace? Where will they be? You gave an oath to them. You are no king, no man at all, if you deny it."

"For once Conal Carna and I are agreed," put in the druid. "Only you can uphold the law."

"You're right," Conaire said with a heavy tone of resignation. "I have to act."

"No!" said his wife. They looked up to see her descending the stairs, her look one of great concern. "You can't risk yourself again."

"I've no other choice," he told her. "Conal warned me. Now I see he was right. It's likely my own selfish withdrawal, playing the hurt child, that's brought this on. I'm responsible. I have to try to stop it."

"Let it go," she said, moving toward him. "What matter? Ireland will survive. Think of yourself this time!"

"You still don't understand, do you?" he said. "I'm pledged to this. I didn't want it, but I took it by my own choice. I can't turn away. It's what I have to do."

She came up to him, put a hand upon his arm, and looked up into his face. Her expression and her words were pleading. "You've given enough to it, my husband. You can't do more. Give it up. Have your own life again."

"You don't care about Ireland? About her people?"

"Let them see to themselves. I care about you. I only want you." She put her head against his chest, clutching him tightly. "I want us as we were."

"Us? What 'us' can there be now?" he said, standing stiffly, unresponsive to her. "The hope for that's gone with most of my other foolish dreams of warmth and peace. I've only this cursed bond left, and my duty to the souls who foolishly looked to me for safety, for security. And if I let it go, I'll be nothing at all, worse than my wretched father, whom I so despised."

Defeated by his cold words, she released him and turned away, sinking down at a nearby table in an attitude of dejection. Her voice turned bitter now as she said, "So, in the preservation of your peace, you mean to go out and make war?"

"No," Calatin hastily put in. "The high-king cannot go out as if to fight. Only by his authority as king, and by his invoking of the law, can he stop this. He dare not take an army."

"You can't stop a blood feud that way," protested Conal. "They must be shown iron."

"That's strange talk from one who once argued to save the traitors from the sword," Calatin said sarcastically.

"They were a few score, raiding for defiance and to prove

their fighting skills," Conal shot back. "This is two warring clans. Hundreds of men burning with their battle fever. You can't have the king walk between them unarmed."

"And you can't have him come on them with his own host. It would only bring them against him."

"I agree with Calatin," Conaire said with finality. "I will not settle this by force. I will not compromise my own rule of laws."

"A most worthy choice, my King," Calatin said, throwing a small, victorious smile at Conal.

"All right," Conal agreed, giving the druid a glare in return, "but at least protect yourself. At least take your champions to escort you."

Mor looked from him to Calatin, then to his wife, still watching him fixedly. "All right," he conceded. "Call them."

Calatin's smile transformed to a glower. "You risk a great deal, taking warriors with you on a mission of peace," he told Mor. "Be it on your head, my King. I will not be countered by your . . ." he gave Conal a baleful look, "your warrior again. If you'll not heed my counsel in this, I'll say no more." With that, he turned and stalked out.

"Well then, there is at least one good thing in this," Conal said bitingly. "I'll go and call the champions now, my King."

As he went out, Mor went to a chest, opened it, and took out his traveling bag. He pulled out a plain wool cloak and began to fold it.

"So you'll go, and with no care for me," Fionualla said with sorrow. "Is the love you had for me so completely gone now?"

He didn't answer, stuffing the folded cloak into the bag.

"The true Conaire is gone then, too," she went on. "Lost, I think, that day you walked away from us at the river, vowing to come back. But you lied then. The one who left never came back to me."

He turned to her, expression grave, words coming slowly, as if burdened with an immense weariness. "When I brought you to Tara, when I asked you to be my wife, I told you what I would have to do. I told you then what you must do as well. I wanted you beside me, to help and understand and keep me going. You said then that you would. But that was before the real challenge came. If you can't accept what I am now, and stay by me, then you're released from the bond you made. But if you've any love for me, you must see that I have to do this, or there is no Conaire Mor. Anything that remains of the man you knew will then be truly lost."

He moved away from her to where his shield hung upon the wall, lifting it down from its peg.

"Until this is fixed and I've made amends for my mistakes, there is nothing else for me," he said. Then, in a pointed gesture, he hung the shield back upon its peg. He looked around again to her, his face now drawn into a taut, determined look. "Nothing!" he fiercely repeated.

Chapter Forty

Warnings

"I've sensed a great unrest in the world," Meave said, pacing the floor in agitation. "I know that Conaire Mor is in danger."

She was in the sunroom above the hall of Cruchane. Morning sun slanted through the east windows, throwing long, brilliant wedges of light across the floor that lit all the room.

"How do you know this?" Aileel asked, clearly bewildered by her strange proclamation and her uneasy state.

He sat within one of the wedges of light to bask in its warmth, bundled in a heavy cloak of wool to further ward off the morning's chill. Its heavy folds made the wolf of Connacht look more like an ancient, withered cat, squinting out at her with half-blind eyes. Nearby, Lewy MacNeesh stood, also puzzled by Meave's behavior and by the urgent summons that had brought him rushing here.

"It came to me last night," she said, still pacing the long room. "A feeling, a vision, a dream—I can't say what."

"It could be a mistake," Lewy suggested.

"No," she said with force, stopping to face him. "I felt it too deeply. It was as if nature itself had been thrown into chaos, the earth shaking, the air convulsed as with a sound like all the thunder of a great storm combined." She shook her head in frustration. "I can't describe it to you. I only know what it told me. It's the Sidhe speaking in me, I'm certain. It's their alarm I felt. Their warning. And when I understood what it meant, I remembered the words of Calatin as well."

"Calatin?" asked Aileel.

"A druid of Tara. He came to me some while ago. He told me he had foreseen a jeopardy for my nephew."

"Then you must warn him," Aileel said simply. He was even more puzzled now. "I'm surprised it wasn't done earlier."

"Calatin told me that I must keep out of it," she said. "If I were to interfere, I might put myself in danger too."

"You? But why would your warning Conaire bring danger upon you?"

"Because . . ." She hesitated, considering the admission she would have to make. But there was nothing else to do now. If she was to have their help, they must know all of it. "Because he told me that if Mor were to be destroyed, it might be myself who would take his place."

"You?" said Aileel, astonished, and Lewy looked surprised as well.

"He said that I more than any other had proven my strength and had shown myself fit to carry on his peace."

"You have done that," Aileel agreed. "And I've no doubt you could rule Ireland well, if things came to such a pass."

"But, do you understand my quandary?" she asked in anguish. "It's been a terrible confusion in my mind. When it was only the druid's foreseeing, well, I could think of it as only a distant dream, not taken seriously. But now that I've had the sense of it myself and know its truth, I don't know what to do. I've paced through half the night."

"I don't see what confusion there is at all," said Aileel. "It's clear to me you've only one thing to do. No matter what your part may be in this, or what you'd gain, or what your jeopardy is, your loyalty *must* be to the high-king. You must warn him, help him if you can."

"Wait now," said Lewy, more cautiously. "If this is in the hands of fate, then Meave's own help might come to nothing. She'd put herself in danger to no end, and lose her own chance at this great thing."

"The Sidhe may have some powers, but they've no control of fate," Aileel said with some of his old force. "And I don't believe any man's destiny is sealed. Meave must act."

"I'm sorry, but this isn't helping me," she said with some frustration. "I'm as confused now as before."

There was no question of her feelings. She knew, as if it had happened before her eyes, that Mor would soon be in mortal danger. She could act to warn him, but he might die anyway. And there was that other feeling, that longing that she ashamedly tried to push away. But it came nagging back.

"You must act," Aileel said, more urgently now, levering himself to his feet "Even beyond loyalty, there is the fact that he was your friend. He took you in. He gave you comfort. He sent you here to begin a new life. You owe too much to him."

She hesitated, feeling powerful emotions tugging at her: loyalty and greed and fate and desire all at once. She recalled Calatin's cajoling words; she heard Mor telling her that she truly wanted power. Mostly she saw the sneering face of brutal Conchobar. These things held a great sway over her.

"But, Aileel, think!" she appealed to him, stepping toward him. "To rule all Ireland! For us! For Connacht!"

But the promise of such gain had no power over the stalwart king. He drew himself up, the thinned form taking on its past valiant stance of authority once again.

"At what price, Meave?" he sternly demanded. "Has this dream of rule so entranced you that you'd sacrifice your loyalty, your honor, even the life of your own nephew? I want nothing gained by that, nor does Connacht. It would be for yourself, alone, that you'd be doing this. Could you?"

She searched her feelings critically. Was the need to prove herself and her hatred of Conchobar so strong that she would stand aside and let Mor die if it meant her gaining the throne?

"No," she said at last. "I can't. I must try to warn him, if it's not already too late."

"You must fly to Tara," Aileel said. "You'll have our best chariot, our fastest horses."

"What about a driver and an escort?" asked Lewy. "I will go."

"No," she said. "You must stay to . . . help." She looked pointedly at Aileel. "And other chariots would only slow me down."

"Then you must ask Fardia," Lewy said, though clearly not pleased at having to suggest his rival. "He's as fine a driver as he is a warrior. For you, I'm certain he'd eagerly go."

"A fine idea," she said. "Find him, will you? And see to a good chariot. I'll prepare."

As he went down from the sunroom and across the hall below, Meave watched, her face drawn in a frown.

Aileel moved up behind her and put a hand upon her shoulder. "You've made the right choice, Meave," he said earnestly.

"Of course," she agreed, but with the faintest tinge of a question coloring her words.

Sentanta paced the rampart walk of Dun Dalgan alone. His father had retreated again, a fearful tortoise pulled into the shell of his shuttered quarters.

Coming home had been a mistake, he thought. None of his questions had been answered. His confusion had only increased. He had no idea now what he was at all. Worse, he felt even more isolated, more bereft of help.

He stopped and gazed out to sea, a softly gleaming field of slate beneath the gray-clouded sky. That childhood longing to drift out on its waves came back to him again. Maybe there was a home there, an enfolding comfort, an oblivion.

He heard his name being called. It was very soft, little more than a whisper of sea breeze, but the word was unmistakable: "Sentanta."

It had drifted up to him from below, and he leaned out over the wall, peering down.

Far below him at the cliff's base was the sheltered patch of beach he had loved and frequented as a boy. And there a small figure waited, one arm raised, beckoning to him.

He left the fortress at once, making his way down the old, familiar path to the beach. There, at the edge of the surf, stood the girl he had met there once, so long ago. The girl named Faythleen.

She stood waiting for him, the slenderness of her figure accentuated by the breeze blowing her light gown against her as it fluttered her long, gold hair.

He approached, amazed. Though the years that had passed since their last meeting had brought great changes to him, she looked still the same as he remembered: a young girl, but with that strange light of eternity glowing in her eyes.

She smiled. "I hoped you would come. I called your name."

"I heard you," he said, smiling in return. For all the great strangeness in this, it seemed quite natural, as if she were an old friend, and he felt no uneasiness.

"I know why you have come back here," she said in the

melodic voice he so vividly remembered. "I feel the great anguish in your mind."

She came closer, put up a slender hand to gently caress his forehead.

He had no inclination to stop her, and the sensation it brought was a welcome one. It seemed to send a wave of warmth through him that filled him with comfort. And the fragrance of her—fresh as the sea's, sweet as the spring's—soothed his agony.

"It doesn't seem to bring me such pain now," he said.

Her hand dropped down to take his. "Come then," she softly urged. "Walk with me."

He made no argument, allowing her to lead him up the beach, she walking close along the water's edge. At times the pulsing surf welled up higher to engulf her bare feet with the chill sea, but she seemed not to mind.

"I understand what's brought such trouble to your thoughts," she told him. "Many things have come so quickly."

"They have," he agreed. "And it was here that they began. You were the one who told me first that I had a destiny."

"You're far from alone in having that," she told him. "When your mortals first came to this land, they called it Inisfail—Isle of Destiny. And so it was for them and many after. Your own still awaits you."

"Are you so certain now?" he asked. "After all that's happened . . ."

"It will work out," she assured him. "You must believe me. You cannot abandon Conaire Mor. He is a good man meaning good for Ireland. There are many who wish that, both among the mortals and the Others."

"Others?" he repeated. "Do you mean the Sidhe?"

"There are those of them who would help," she explained. "They have done so in the past and are trying to do so now. Conaire Mor was set upon his task by them, even as you were."

"As I was," he said. "Do you mean by you?"

"Among others."

He stopped and looked at her, meeting that silver gaze. "You're of them, then? Of the Sidhe?" The revelation held so little surprise for him. It was as if he'd always known it.

"It's of no matter what I am," she said. "It only matters that you keep faith and help Conaire Mor."

He shook his head and they started along the shore again.

"What you're asking me is hard," he said unhappily. "It seems as if Mor feels a hatred for me now. The trust he had is gone, and my own admiration for what he's tried to do has faded. I meant to be the great champion for him, but what I did turned him against me."

"Many things were done in the welter of conflicting loyalties," she said. "Perhaps Mor has made errors in his judgments. Perhaps you did the same in honor's name. Still, what he meant to do for those of Ireland has succeeded. And it can continue to succeed. But there are forces—forces which might challenge even the Sidhe's great might—which would destroy him. You can help to save him. It's what you were meant to do."

She released his hand and stopped, letting him go on. "And the time for it is now," she said.

"Now?" he asked.

There was no answer.

He turned, but she was gone. There was only the surf washing in, sweeping away the last trace of her footprints in the sand.

"Sentanta!" called another voice from above. He turned, looking up toward the cliff's top.

Cathbad stood on the brink, waving down at him.

Chapter Forty-one

Pursuit

The spear slammed down into the holder beside four of its fellows. Cormac Conlingas took one more from his driver and shot it home with the rest, then jumped down from his car.

All about him in Tara's yard, Conal Carna and two dozen other of the high-king's champions made weapons ready while drivers wrestled with chariots, teams, and gear. And around them, forming a solid ring, a large crowd of other inhabitants of the fortress stood looking on.

"I wish that Sentanta were back," Cormac remarked to Conal

Carna, who was overseeing the preparations. "This all seems the greatest madness to me."

"Then why wish to involve him in it?" Conal asked in a logical way. "Think instead that at least he's well out of it."

"But he's one more good sword if this goes wrong. And he's a friend to talk to."

"You have me," Conal said brusquely. "Now get on with your preparing."

"Well, and with your great warmth, how could I wish for more?" Cormac replied sarcastically.

He was turning back to his chariot when a stirring in the crowd above brought his gaze up toward the great hall. "Look there," he said. "The high-king's coming."

Conal's gaze followed Cormac's up to the hall's main doors, where Conaire Mor had just appeared, closely accompanied by Calatin.

"Aye," the older champion said darkly, "and the cursed druid as well. Like some growth he is, sprouting from Conaire's side."

The two walked across the causeway from the hall and down the slope into the main yard, then made their way through the crowd toward the grouped chariots.

"So I leave the overseeing of things in your care, Calatin," Mor was telling the ard-druid. He looked across the yard to where the rest of the learned men stood aloofly huddled outside their sanctuary, the Star of the Bards. "I trust none of the rest of that lot to do what's best for Ireland. Only you understand."

"Thank you, my King," Calatin told him with his most charming smile. "I'll surely do my best."

"This tuath of the warring chiefs is no great distance from here," Mor said. "I look to be returning soon, if everything goes well."

He looked up to where Fionualla watched from the window of her *granian*. There were no tearful partings now, only her dry-eyed stare, her drawn face, her rigid stance.

"And see that my wife's needs are attended to," he added in a toneless, detached way. "Since she's hidden herself away up there and seldom leaves, the servants may not do what they should for her."

"I will," the druid promised. "She will have the finest care."

"Excuse me then," Mor told him. "I must see if the others are ready."

He moved away to consult with Conal Carna as to how preparations were proceeding. While he did, Calatin stood by with the others in the crowd. A small smile of satisfaction played across his lips as he watched the high-king and those hated champions of his about to ride out into the chaos he'd planned for them.

But then a hand plucked at his sleeve, and he turned to see the cadaverous white face of one of his sons peering out at him from the depths of a masking hood.

"What are you doing here?" the druid sharply demanded, glancing around to see if anyone was paying note. "I told you not to show yourself in the dun. You're to wait in the grove."

"We meant to," the being rasped, "but we had to tell you: King Conchobar is here!"

"What?" Calatin said, nearly exclaiming loudly in his surprise. "Where?"

"In this very yard, Father. Over there! The tall one in the brown cloak."

Calatin's eyes scanned the crowd opposite, finally spotting the tall figure, closely wrapped in a bulky cloak, hood up to conceal the face. But still he was able to catch a quick glimpse of glittering dark eyes.

"Are you certain it's he?" he asked the son.

"We are. We saw him nosing about the visitor's dun where he had stayed before, then coming here on foot. We followed. He acted strangely enough, slipping in unknown and mixing in the crowd. Very cautious in doing it he was."

"But why come here that way?" said Calatin. "Is he mad?"

"We got close to him, Father. He's asking about if anyone's seen an old warrior in black."

"Ah, so that's it," Calatin said with realization. "Something must have happened! And for him to be taking such an enormous chance, it must be of great urgency."

He grabbed his son's arm, pulling him closer to whisper, "Quick, then, you must act. We can't have Mor seeing him, or questions will be raised. Go get him. Tell him you know where the old warrior is. Get him down to the woods below the southern duns and have someone stay with him. Tell the others I'll come to the sacred grove as soon as possible. Have everything made ready there. You know what must be done."

The son went off at once. Calatin watched him approach the

cloaked man, whisper to him, then guide him off. The druid gave an inward sigh of relief as the two went out the fortress gates.

His gaze went back to the high-king. But Mor, absorbed in the preparations, had noted nothing.

"Very well, then," he was saying to Conal. "We are ready." He lifted his voice to call out to the others, "Into your chariots, my champions. We will ride now."

As the men mounted into their cars, he moved to his own vehicle and prepared to climb aboard. But Conal called after him in surprise, "Wait, my King, you've not readied yourself! You've no shield, no spears in the car."

"And I don't mean to have," Mor answered. "I'll take nothing that seems a sign of threat or war save my own sword, and that only as a symbol of my kingship."

"Well, I'll take mine," Conal said. "It's a fool enough risk without going out unarmed."

"It's the only way," Mor answered stubbornly.

They all mounted. Mor cast a final look up to his wife, then ordered his company ahead. They rode out through the gates and down the dun's slope.

Calatin watched, walking out the gates and seeing them well away. Then he departed too, striding down toward the sacred grove.

The cut of the sword hacked a large chunk from the tree trunk.

Conchobar strode impatiently within the boundary of the woods. Each time he passed the hapless young oak he took another irritated swing at it with his blade, and its nearness to toppling gave evidence of how long he'd been at this pastime.

Not far away, one of Calatin's spindly sons sat on a log and silently watched him, only the eerie glistening of the eyes showing him to be other than a withered corpse propped there.

"My King," said a voice as Conchobar was about to strike out again.

He stopped in midswing and turned to see the dark man standing not far away. "You come quietly enough," he said, surprised at his sudden appearance.

"An old skill," the old warrior said carelessly as he came forward.

"It's a fine thing, your making me wait," Conchobar growled, hefting the sword.

"There was no choice. I couldn't chance coming here with Mor still about."

"He's gone then? And is this peace mission he's set out on a part of your plot?"

"Most perceptive, my King," the warrior told him with a little bow. "Yes. Conaire Mor has begun the journey to his doom. But," he admonished, "your coming here this way might have endangered it. What's happened to make you take such risks?"

"Cathbad," the king said simply. "I couldn't keep him in Ulster. He's had some cursed vision. He knows Mor's in jeopardy, as you feared, and means to help him. He's no more than a day behind me."

"Too late to stop Mor," the warrior said.

"Not too late to chase him down. I know that druid. Tenacious as a hound on the scent."

"Yes," the other said thoughtfully, nodding. "Yes, I believe you're right."

"And he's dangerous," Conchobar added. "If he joins Mor, your little scheme could well be ruined."

"I agree with that too. He has great skills. He's given me trouble before."

"So you see why I had to come here," the king finished.

"I do, my King, and I owe great thanks to you. But you've no need to take any further part. I'll see to it."

"You will?" Conchobar asked with great interest. "And what are you meaning to do?"

"I've not decided yet. I'll have to find some means of keeping him from Mor."

"Be careful in your plans. Sentanta will be riding with him."

"Will he?" said the warrior. "More danger still with the pair of them." Then he smiled cunningly. "And yet, it makes things simpler, too. With that meddling boy along, I have a surer way to lead them astray."

"Could you do more?" Conchobar asked.

"More?" the warrior repeated, eyeing the other searchingly. "What do you mean?"

"Kill them," the king said bluntly.

"What? Your nephew and your own ard-druid?"

"I've my reasons," Conchobar said in a harsh tone. "Both are a plague to me. Together they may be a threat to my rule. I've helped you. You help me."

The old man's mouth lifted in a delighted grin. "You and I

are even more alike than I had guessed. I applaud your ruthlessness."

"Never mind that," Conchobar said sharply. "Will you do it?"

"I've no love for either. They've troubled me as well." He gave another little bow. "It will be my pleasure." He looked around him then, and his manner grew brisk. "But now, my King, you had better get away. It's still very risky for you to be here. Go back to Ulster. Prepare to hear the sad news and put on proper mourning for your fallen high-king."

Conchobar started out of the woods, but just within its edge he stopped and turned back. "This plan for Mor," he said. "What will you do?"

"There will be an ambush," the warrior said simply. "A trap he cannot escape."

"And all the champions who ride with him?"

"I meant that he should go alone," the warrior said with some irritation. "It was Conal Carna convinced him otherwise."

"And will they die?"

The warrior shrugged. "That I can't say. Much of their survival will be their own choice. If they fight for Mor, then likely they will die. The numbers will be greatly against them."

"My son is with them," Conchobar told him grimly.

"I know. And will he choose to go to his death?"

"I don't know," the king replied truthfully. "He's practical enough, and with a selfish streak, but he has a strong loyalty once his bond is given."

"A quality from his mother, I take it," the old man said sardonically.

Conchobar glowered at that.

"Do you have a doubt, now that your own son is involved?" the warrior asked.

Conchobar considered, then shook his head. "No. He takes his chances, as does every warrior. It is a risk worth taking to destroy Mor."

The warrior nodded, smiling in satisfaction. "I thought you'd say so."

Conchobar lifted his sword to point meaningfully at the man. "Just you see to Sentanta and Cathbad," he growled, then turned and strode out of the woods.

The chariots of Cathbad and Sentanta rolled to the gates of Tara. They stopped as the sentries moved out to challenge them, but then only raised hands in greeting as they recognized the youth and the ard-druid.

"Welcome back!" one warrior said heartily.

"We've come to see Mor," said Cathbad. "It's most urgent."

"You're too late for that," the man replied. "He's ridden off on a mission of peace with his champions. They left yesterday morning."

Sentanta exchanged a meaningful glance with Cathbad.

"Where did they go?" the druid demanded.

"Tuath Mumain. Two chiefs are warring there. But he expects to return in a few days' time."

"Well, Cathbad?" the boy asked. "Is this the danger you foresaw?"

"I can't be certain," he replied, shaking his head. "It was too vague, too muddled. I saw battle, blood, smoke. But I saw Mor by the sea, too, not in the middle of Ireland."

"This might have nothing to do with your fear then," Sentanta said. "Shall we wait here for his return or try chasing him about the countryside?"

"My feeling is that we should follow him."

But Sentanta wasn't listening. Something had suddenly taken his attention. "Look!" he said urgently, pointing down the slope behind them.

From the sacred grove below a chariot had appeared. It carried a large, dark-cloaked warrior. As they watched, it headed east, skirting Tara's hill at its fullest speed.

"That was the man!" Sentanta said. "The strange old warrior I saw with the raiders! I must follow him." He touched his driver on the shoulder. "Laeg, go after—"

"Wait!" cried Cathbad, holding out a staying hand. "What about Mor?"

"Don't you see?" Sentanta said anxiously, looking after the rapidly departing chariot. "I'm certain it was that man who led Maine Morgor and the others in their raiding. I think he may even have had them in his thrall somehow. If so, it's that man who's caused all Mor's troubles. He may be behind the very danger you say is threatening Mor now!"

Cathbad stared after the figure. Something about it made him feel a wave of cold, like a sudden gust of winter wind, sweep through him. He sensed an aura, as of some energy, given off by it. And he had sensed an aura like it once before.

"Yes, yes!" he said. "I feel it too. It may well be that he's the source of the dark sorcery we've met with through all of this."

"Mor has Conal Carna and Cormac to protect him now," said Sentanta. "I think the real danger is here. We must find out about this man."

"You're right," Cathbad agreed. "I'll go with you."

"Join us, then," Laeg advised. "Even with two riders, we can follow more quickly leaving your car behind."

So Cathbad quickly climbed into the other car and they were off, following after the dark warrior at full speed.

Other than the two guards, no one at Tara noted the brief coming and going of the Ulstermen save a lone figure in the high *granian* of the Royal Seat.

There sat Fionualla, as before, still staring out over the countryside. She had watched in puzzlement as Sentanta and Cathbad rolled up to the gates of Tara, only to turn and hurriedly depart again in that distant chariot's wake. And she was still watching sometime later when yet another chariot charged at full speed up the slope to Tara's walls.

She recognized its passenger as Queen Meave, and this time, drawn by curiosity and foreboding, she went down from her sanctuary into the yard.

Meave's chariot had by then shot past the startled guards and Fardia was pulling it up before the hall.

"Fionualla," Meave said, seeing Mor's wife moving out toward her. "I must see Conaire at once!"

"He's gone."

"Gone?" Meave said, her face drawn with concern. "Quickly, tell me where!"

"To Tuath Mumain to settle a feud between two chieftains there."

"Thank you, Fionualla. I must go now! Fardia, quickly!"

But Fionualla was not to be denied. As Fardia lifted the reins to turn the team around, she ran forward, grabbing the harness of one horse, hauling its head down to stop them as she cried out, "No, Meave. You can't leave now! You must tell me what's happening."

Meave looked down at her, seeing the great anxiety in the younger woman's face. She knew she couldn't hold back the truth. "Conaire may be in great danger. I think it's coming on him very soon. I must warn him, for there are great forces in it."

"Could that be what drew Cathbad and Sentanta here too?" At Meave's puzzled look, Fionualla hastened to explain, "They came not long ago, then rode away in a great rush, following some other. But it wasn't toward Tuath Mumain they went—they headed northeast."

"I don't understand why," said Meave, "but I know that Cathbad's magic could be of great help to Conaire. It may be the only thing that can save him. Someone must go after him. Tell him!"

"I'll go, Meave," Fionualla said.

"No—it's too dangerous!"

"I *will* go," the younger woman said with force. "Conaire's in danger. I'll find Cathbad and send him after you. But go now!" She released the team. "You must warn Conaire!"

Fardia urged the team around, and in an instant they were speeding back across the yard.

"Good luck to you!" Meave called out as she was carried through the gates.

"To us both," Fionualla murmured to herself.

Then she was off too, running up the great hall's mound and through its doors.

"Loman!" she shouted to the aging chief steward, "get me the best driver in Tara. And have our fastest team harnessed as well."

"What?" he said, nonplussed by the sudden explosion of energy from this woman who had hidden away so long.

"Don't be gawking at me!" she cried. "Move now, or my husband's life will be on your own head!"

He hesitated no longer, bustling off.

"My husband. Oh, my husband," she cried in anguish. "What terrible thing are you going into now?"

Chapter Forty-two

The Tower

The whole countryside seemed to be afire.

Conaire Mor and his champions rolled cautiously ahead through hills over which a heavy pall of smoke seemed constantly to hang, darkening the sky. All around them, just beyond the rim of the hills, the sky glowed red, casting the gentle swells in ominous outline, as if lurid flames licked high there.

The air itself, tormented by strange, sharp, coiling gusts, seemed filled with the most dire sounds of great and savage warfare: the clattering of untold arms, the shrill screams of countless wounded, the wailing keen from vast hosts in mourning.

So intense a sense of battle, so heavy a dread did this create for the champions of Tara, that the hardened warriors rode at first with hands tightly gripping weapons, casting looks of apprehension about them at the eerie scene.

But after a time their concern began to give way to puzzlement.

"This is most strange," the practical Conal Carna remarked. "The land seems always all ablaze just ahead, but we never reach it."

"I've seen no fighting," said another, broad-shouldered warrior of graying hair but black, flaring mustache and eyebrows. "All the sounds of war, but not one sign has come before our eye."

"Aye, MacCecht," said a third man with short, red-brown hair. "This seems more like a nightmare."

"Listen to what Muinremar says, my King," Conal said to Conaire. "There's something unnatural working here. I feel it."

"I do as well," the king assured him. "But we've no choice except to go on."

Finally, upon a rounded hill ahead there showed the outline of a small fortress's palisade.

They rode up before it, stopping across the causeway below the outer wall, looking up to the closed gates. The gray billows of smoke rolling in the sky were tinted a ruddy hue by the fiery lights, like low dawn clouds struck crimson by the sun's first rays. No sign of life showed about the fortress, no heads thrust above the palisade, and the place seemed untouched by flames or war.

Conal directed his driver to pull the car up beside a bronze gong suspended on a post by the causeway. He drew his sword and leaned out to smack its flat sharply against the battered metal circle.

The single note rang out clearly, echoing across the hills, fading into the clouds. They waited. After a long moment, the impatient Conal lifted his sword to strike again.

"Wait," said Conaire. "There is someone."

A head had been thrust cautiously above the wooden wall. Fearful eyes peered down at them.

"Are you the foes come to strike us at last, then?" said a timorous voice.

"I am Conaire Mor, high-king of all Ireland, come to end the war in this tuath," he called back.

"Are you?" The voice was skeptical. An arm lifted to beckon. "Come forward then, where we can see you."

"I will," he agreed. He signaled his driver forward and the car pulled up to the causeway beside that of Conal.

"I don't like this, my King," said Conal.

"There's no other way, it seems," Mor replied. "They've good cause to be wary."

"I'll be beside you then."

"No. I told you, we'll do nothing to alarm them."

So a frustrated Conal remained behind, watching tensely, hand on one of his racked spears, as the high-king rode across the narrow causeway to the gates.

There was ample reason for the champion's disquiet. Mor was most vulnerable there, with the deep fosse on either side, the walls above, and no room to turn the car.

"Be careful in your moves, now," the voice from the head above him cautioned, "or it's like a hedgehog you'll be looking from our spears."

In proof of the truth of this, a dozen other heads appeared on the wall at either side of the gates. Arms lifted, and spear points glinted scarlet from the sky's bloody light. Behind them nervous, fear-filled eyes peered down.

"I'll do nothing," Mor assured them. "I've come to help."

"Help with what? How do we know you've not come to attack?"

"I've come here from Tara. The word was brought there that it was two of your own chiefs—the two Carbres—who warred. It was said that only I could end the quarrel."

"We know nothing of that here," the man said. "Nine days ago, the sky grew darker, as if a storm were coming on us. Then the lands around filled with red light. It seemed as if the fields surrounding us were all ablaze at once. After that came the winds and the sounds of great fighting. We thought the whole of Ireland must have broken out in war to raise such a terrible noise, and everything would surely be destroyed in it."

"We shut ourselves in here to wait for an attack," said another man. "Day after day the sounds and fires raged on all about, and we growing more afraid with the waiting. Our families are cowering in their houses now," he went on, his voice growing higher, more intense, the spear shaking in his hand, "knowing some great force must be coming to engulf us, afraid of peering out into the burning countryside, stopping ears to the constant sound till we've gone nearly mad!"

"Be easy, Tomaltach," a man beside him soothed, putting a comforting hand to the other's quivering shoulder.

"Like a sickness it is," the first man explained to Mor, "draining the strength and courage from all of us. Our children cry out with fear nearly all the time."

"It's a terrible thing," Mor said in sympathy. "But you've seen no signs of warriors, had no message of the war?"

"We've seen no one at all in these nine long days, save for yourself."

"This is most strange," Mor said in puzzlement.

"And are you really the high-king?" the first man asked.

"He is," said another. "I saw him at Tara at the Tailteen Fair."

"Then, do you really mean to stop this?" asked the shaken man, a note of new hope entering his quavering voice.

"I mean to try," Mor promised. "I must find the ones at war and speak to them."

"The chief fortress of Tuath Mumain is on to the south," the first man said. "And may the gods go with you, Conaire Mor, for it's the torture of ourselves and our children you'll be ending if you succeed."

Mor's driver urged his horses to walk backward, and the car rolled back slowly from the gates and down the causeway.

"Did you hear that?" Mor asked the champions.

"I did," said Conal. "And I say we turn back."

"What?" Mor said with surprise. "But it was you told me to come."

"To settle a dispute, not ride about in this madness. It's too great a risk. Go out of it until we can find out what's happening here."

"I agree with Conal," said the one called MacCecht. "There's something very dangerous at work in this."

"We can't just ride away," Mor told them sternly, "no matter what the risk. You heard that man. These people are in fear.

I have to help them, help their poor children. I have to stop this somehow, and I mean to ride on."

Reluctantly, Conal and the other champions agreed. They went south, moving even more cautiously now. But before they reached the tuath's main fortress, they saw shapes moving in the haze ahead. They pulled up, peering warily into the red-hued clouds. Soon the vague shadows resolved into a party of men in chariots, some twoscore, feeling their way forward as cautiously as the men of Tara had.

They drew up when they came within clear view of the other party. Their gazes were openly suspicious, even hostile. Some held weapons ready in their hands.

"Don't attack," Mor called to them. "We don't mean to fight you. We are from Tara. I am Conaire Mor."

"I know you are," said a young man of flowing gold hair and blue-checked cloak. "I am Carbre of the Fearghals."

"Carbre!" Mor said with relief. "It's you I meant to see. What's happened?"

The young man shook his head. "You could likely tell me as easily. Things have been the same as this for days now. My clansmen and I stayed shut up in our dun until I grew angry with the waiting and finally convinced these few men to go out with me. We've ridden the countryside all about but we've found nothing except more of our people cowering in their duns and lisses."

"But word came to me that it was yourself at war with the other Carbre."

"What, O'Beirne?" the man said with astonishment. "No, not ourselves. Oh, we had a rivalry, I'll not deny it. But we've lived at peace since we both gave our bonds to you. We've been at his dun, just this night past. He's as bewildered as we, his people near to panic."

"If there's no war, then there's nothing real about any of this," said Mor. "All of it must be some magic."

"Magic?" said Carbre, looking up into the blood-tinted overcast. "What power could create a thing so great as this? Is it the Others?"

"I don't know," Mor said, "but I mean to discover it. Carbre, go back to your people. Tell them this is a sham, a trick, and nothing to be fearing. Tell them the high-king of Ireland will see it stopped."

"I will then," the young chieftain said, "and I pray Danu you are right."

Mor turned to his champions. "We must return to Tara," he said. "If this is magic, the druids must be consulted, and quickly."

"Not too soon for me," said Conal. "Let's be riding out of this at our best speed! I smell an evil here!"

"What an evil-looking place," said Sentanta.

His chariot was pulled up below the half-fallen tower upon the cliff edge while he, Cathbad, and Laeg looked up at it.

"There's no question that he's gone there?" asked the druid.

"His track leads us here," said the young warrior. "There's nowhere else he could have gone."

"You're right," Cathbad agreed, staring fixedly at the sinister pile. "I can feel him there. It's a strong aura he sends out, foul and heavy, like a rotting corpse's scent."

"We'll be going in there, then," Sentanta said.

"Now, why is it I knew you'd be saying that?" said Laeg, adding hopefully, "Or do you really mean for all of us to go?"

"You and myself, of course," said Sentanta. He looked at the druid. "But, Cathbad . . ."

"Oh, no," the druid said firmly. "You'll not leave me behind. If what I'm feeling is the truth, it's powerful magic you'll face in this man. You'll likely need my help."

Sentanta knew he couldn't argue when Cathbad's mind was set. He ordered Laeg ahead.

The chariot rolled up, through the broken openings in the outer curves of wall, into the littered yard of the old fortress. Warrior and druid climbed from the car there and gazed toward the tower.

"I think Laeg should go with us as well," Cathbad suggested. "Who knows what we'll face in there. We might need his help too."

"What, go inside with you?" said Laeg. "But what about the car?"

"It will be as all right as it would be with you here protecting it alone," was the reply.

Laeg looked about at the eerie desolation of the place, then jumped from the car and hitched the team's reins to a stub of rock.

Together the three approached the ominous tower. There were no sounds, no movements from beyond the ragged black hole of the doorway. Only a stench of decay and disuse welled out to them.

Sentanta drew his sword and went in advance, Cathbad behind, Laeg bringing up the rear. As they moved down a shadowed corridor into deeper gloom, the driver looked back at the dwindling patch of daylight with some regret.

"Is this the better choice?" he wondered aloud.

"Quiet!" whispered Cathbad. For Sentanta had just reached an inner doorway and was peering cautiously through into the room beyond.

It was the large, circular, central chamber of the tower he carefully scrutinized now. The fire in the wide pit was very low, casting a shifting, irregular red glow about the space. As far as he could see, the room was empty.

He signaled to the others to follow and slipped quietly into the room. The others moved up close behind him.

"Do you see any sign of him?" Sentanta softly asked the druid as they edged forward.

Cathbad peered about him into the shadows. "It's hard to say." His eyes traveled across the table with its strange and gruesome collection of objects, ending on a skull with its top removed. "But this is surely the lair of a sorcerer. I smell the stink of old spells in this awful place."

"We'd best divide ourselves," Sentanta suggested as they reached the fire pit. "Search the whole room. There may be other doors."

"No need for that," came a rumbling but genial voice from behind them.

They turned to see the dark-cloaked old warrior standing by the door they had just come through. He was smiling, clearly greatly pleased. In his hand he held a naked sword.

Sentanta moved his hand to his own sword hilt, but Cathbad laid a restraining hand upon it.

"No. Too dangerous," he warned. "We've no notion of the powers here."

"Most wise," the warrior said. "I am glad to see you accept my invitation to this humble abode." He made a little bow. "Welcome."

"Invitation," said Cathbad, stepping toward the man. "You mean you knew we were following?"

"I meant you to follow," he replied, still smiling in a smug way. "It was necessary that you be kept from following after Mor."

"He is in danger then," the shrewd Cathbad guessed, "and you've some part in it."

"I am all of it, if I may speak so immodestly," the old warrior acknowledged. "At this moment, your high-king and his champions are riding into a chaos like none they could imagine, contrived by my powers to bring about his end."

"But why?" Sentanta asked. "What will you gain from this?"

"Ireland," was the simple answer.

"How can killing Conaire Mor do that for you?" asked Cathbad.

"Because when he is gone, it's my own ruler who will take control of Ireland, but only in my name. And then, finally, the brutal reign of mindless warriors like our fierce lad here will end."

Unobserved behind Sentanta and Cathbad, Laeg began to sidle back slowly, silently, into the room's shadows.

"But you're a warrior yourself," said Sentanta. "You led Ferogain and the others in defying Mor's peace."

"I led them," he agreed, "but only to their destruction."

Hidden now in the shadows, Laeg began to creep around the room's periphery, keeping to the pools of deepest black, moving closer to the old warrior.

"So you meant that from the start," Cathbad said. "Most clever, old man. To gather those most likely to disturb the new peace and have Mor do away with them at once. It must have been difficult."

"It was too easy," the other said carelessly. "The young fools were easily led, as are all their kind."

"But one thing went wrong," Cathbad corrected. "You meant them to die."

This irritated the dark man. "Mor was the cause of that," he growled. "I thought he meant to follow my will. He failed me. And now he'll be the one to die for his mistake."

"How will he die? When?" Cathbad demanded.

The man smiled again and shook his head. "Enough," he said. "I've spent too long with you already. I've other things to do. I only wanted to face you once and have you know why you would die."

Apparently unnoticed by the rest, Laeg had now reached a point near the warrior.

"What do you mean to do to us?" asked Cathbad.

"I kept you from following Mor because I have some respect for your magic powers," said the old man. "Had I time, I would be tempted to try my own against them. It might have been a mildly interesting contest. But now, regretfully, I can't take the risk that you might counteract my spells. Fortunately, there is another, simple way."

Laeg crouched to spring.

"What way?"

"Not to use one. Goodbye!"

He stepped back toward the door.

"Sentanta! Get him now!" Laeg cried out, leaping boldly toward the man.

But the old warrior moved with amazing speed. A fist came up to connect unerringly with Laeg's jaw as he came in, slamming him back. As Sentanta drew his sword to charge in, the man cast his own blade, point first, at the youth, then turned and leaped through the open door.

Sentanta knocked aside the thrown blade with his and ran forward, but too late. He collided with a massive portal that was thrown shut in his face.

The final clang of an iron bolt echoed in the tower. A jeering voice came faintly but clearly to them through the door.

"The ancient owners of this tower built it to last as long as their clan. A joke on them, but most helpful to me. This door is made of iron. The wall and floor of that room are sheathed in iron as well. Beneath it is a celler now quite filled with good oak wood and a few swine carcasses to fuel the start of a hot fire. The whole of it is being ignited now. You see, my friend Cathbad, I'll waste no more magic on you. You're going to roast alive!"

"Sentanta, break it down!" Cathbad said.

Sentanta threw himself against it, with no effect. He hacked at the rough, black surface with his sword. The keen blade creased the metal, but no more, the clang of metal against metal nearly deafening them.

"Strike at the hinges!" cried Laeg.

But the hinges were outside, the door fitted with such skill that only a faint crack showed about it.

"Could we climb up?" Cathbad suggested, gazing toward the roof hole three stories above.

Sentanta made a circuit of the room, examining the walls. While he did, a new, dreadful reek began to pervade the room.

"What's that?" Cathbad asked, sniffing the air.

"Roasting pork," said Laeg.

"The walls are too high, too smooth," Sentanta said in frustration as he joined them again. "There are no handholds."

"Look!" cried Laeg, pointing to the floor beside the fire pit. Through a crack between two of the massive plates that joined there, a trickle of white smoke was issuing.

He moved to it, dropped to his knees, and leaned forward to examine it. But as his hands came down upon the iron floor, he exclaimed in surprise, jerking them away. "It's hot!" he cried.

Sentanta leaned down and put a hand cautiously to it. Then he cast a grim look up at the druid. "It is that," he confirmed. "And getting hotter fast."

Outside, the dark warrior was climbing into his chariot. Other of the wasted sons of Calatin were moving about, busily loading the last of baskets, chests, and sacks into carts and chariots. As they were finishing, two more of the beings crawled from an opening in the tower's base. From behind them, within the blackness, there came a rising sound of crackling, and smoke began to well outward.

"Goodbye, then, foolish druid," the old warrior said as the sons climbed into the vehicles. "Now on to Ath Cliath."

They rode away, out of the yard, along the cliffs toward the south. Behind them, the smoke now poured from the opening in rapidly swelling waves that began to billow upward.

Inside the tower room, the heat was building. Already the three captives could feel it through the thick leather of their soles as they made another painstaking examination of the room.

"Any openings at all?" Cathbad called.

"None," Sentanta replied, kicking angrily at a pile of rubbish, then turning to the druid in desperate appeal. "Haven't you some magic you can use?"

"Against spells, surely. Not against a trap of iron."

"Not much use carrying a druid around if they're no more help than that," complained Laeg.

Sentanta cast a despairing look around the room. "What will we do?"

Cathbad shrugged.

"*I'll* tell you what we're going to do," Laeg supplied. "This time we're going to die!"

Chapter Forty-three

Trapped

The floor was rapidly becoming too hot to stand upon.

"Onto the table!" said Sentanta.

He swept the litter from it with his sword, the skull clattering away across the floor. The charioteer and driver climbed up onto it.

"Little good this will do us!" complained Laeg.

"It will protect you for a time," said Sentanta. "Stay there. I'll see what I can do."

He moved back to the door, set himself, and began to strike at its surface with his sword. He gave it several heavy blows, none making more than a thin and shallow dent in the hard surface. The iron door was clearly softer than the sword's metal, but of great thickness.

"You'll be eternity trying to cut through that way," Laeg called.

"And have we another choice?" Sentanta returned, swinging up his sword to strike again.

Fionualla and her driver watched from the land below the clifftop tower as the train of vehicles rolled away toward the south.

"There, that's the man they followed," she said, pointing to the dark warrior who headed the train.

"But where are the two you're seeking, my Queen?"

"They must be still in that old fortress."

"In that haunted place?" he said with repugnance. "I've heard some tales. It's terrible ones who lived there."

"Look!" she said, pointing again. A plume of smoke was now visible rising from within the walls. "Something's wrong. We must go see. "Drive on!" she ordered. "Hurry!"

He reluctantly obeyed, urging the horses up through the gateways and into the yard. There the chariot and team of the

Ulstermen still sat. "They are here, my Queen," said her driver. "I know the chariot of Laeg well enough."

Smoke was billowing from the tower now.

"There's surely a great fire within there," she said, climbing from the car. As she stepped toward the tower, she heard a slow, rhythmic clanging sound issuing from the gaping entrance. "Someone *is* in there," she said, moving closer to the doorway. "I'm going in. You stay here and watch the team."

As the driver watched apprehensively, Fionualla entered the tower. The heat was already high in the hall leading in, and smoke was beginning to fill the passageway. Her eyes streamed from its sting, and she coughed as she felt her way along, drawn by the continued clanging sound. The heat increased swiftly as she pressed forward. Her face and arms shone with perspiration. Her breathing grew more labored.

Then ahead of her there appeared a door. The clanging sound was coming from behind it. She put out a hand to it but drew it back. The metal was almost searing.

"Hello!" she called out. "Is someone in there?"

Inside, Sentanta stopped. He was in only his tunic now, the garment soaked by sweat and clinging to his streaming body. His cloak lay on the floor beneath his feet to keep them from broiling on the heated iron. So far his valiant attempts to cut through had yielded only a shallow groove in the door.

He turned to the others on the table. Laeg was now clutching the slumped figure of a panting Cathbad. The older man's strength had been more quickly drained by the punishing heat and smoke.

"Did you hear?" Sentanta asked.

The voice from outside came again.

"It's a woman!" he said, and then shouted back, "I hear you! It's Sentanta MacSualtim here with Cathbad, druid of Ulster."

"And their famous driver Laeg, son of Laegaire," the driver proudly added.

"Sentanta!" she cried. "It's Fionualla. I'll try to get you out!"

"The queen?" he said in astonishment. "No! It's too dangerous. Get away!"

"This is no time for nobility," said Laeg. "For Danu's sake, let her try!"

Fionualla had already chosen to ignore the warning. She grasped the locking bar and tried to lift it. But it was jammed tight and too hot to hold for long.

"I can't pull the bolt," she cried. "I'll get help." She turned and ran back along the passageway.

"I hope she's not too long," said Laeg, wiping the dripping sweat from his eyebrows.

There came a low rumbling from the depths of the tower. The walls seemed to shake around them and a shower of fine debris fell from above.

"What was that?" asked Sentanta, looking around.

"The fire is breaking down the tower's supports," Cathbad gasped out. "It's beginning to crumble."

"Oh, grand!" announced Laeg. "Then, with good fortune, *that* will kill us before the fire or smoke. Shall we make wagers on just how we'll die?"

Outside, Fionualla had emerged from the tower and was running toward the chariot. "Cead!" she called.

But the driver was not there.

"Cead!" she called again, beginning a circuit of the rubbish-littered yard in frantic search for him.

She came around the corner of a half-fallen shed and saw him sitting propped against a boulder at the cliff's brink, looking out over the sea.

She rushed up behind him. "Cead!" she said angrily, grabbing his shoulder.

He fell back. Dead eyes looked up to her and he grinned, not with his mouth but with a gaping cut that opened his throat and drenched his chest in blood.

She started back from him in horror. But a hand shot out from behind the stone, clamping around her wrist. It jerked her forward as a white, cadaverous face lifted like a corpse rising from its grave, followed by a bony hand holding a dagger whose slender curved blade flashed out at her throat.

She struck out with her other hand in a fist, putting all her strength behind it. The blow connected solidly on the man's jaw, snapping his head sideways. He staggered and fell back, dropping the knife, but hanging on to her wrist. He dragged her with him, and both toppled over the cliff edge, falling from view.

In the tower's cellar, the fire had reached its height now, the stacks of hard wood all ablaze, creating a fireball, a whirling cyclone of intense heat that sucked the air from all about to further feed its life.

So hot was it that the ancient stonework cracked and, expanded from centuries of moisture trapped within it, exploded.

The walls shuddered. The iron floors above, twisted by the shifting and warped by the heat, began to buckle.

Cracks in the plates of the floor began to open beneath the prisoners. They could barely breathe now in the heat and whirling smoke. And more poured up by the instant.

Sentanta had abandoned the door to join his comrades, helping Laeg to support a nearly unconscious Cathbad.

"Do you think she'll come back?" Sentanta coughed out. As the building trembled again, this time bringing down larger bits of stone that thudded about them, he asked desperately, "What happened to her?"

As he spoke, Fionualla was clinging to the edge of the cliff that dropped away raggedly to the sea far below, her feet on narrow projections in the rough stone. Just below her, the son of Calatin also clung on with one hand, feet feeling for a foothold, other hand grasping upward to get a grip on one of her ankles.

A glinting caught her eye as she fought to pull herself up, and she realized that the knife now lay just above her. She stretched out a hand to it.

His grasping hand caught her ankle, jerking her down. She slid backward, but caught herself, grimly hanging on. He used his hold on her as a lever to haul himself farther up.

She could not let him win, she told herself fiercely. It was the lives of Sentanta, Cathbad, and her own husband that she fought for now. With a strength fired by her intense need to survive, she pulled herself upward, arms straining against the drag of her weight plus that of the man below. Slowly, agonizingly, she gained. One foot found a hold, then the other.

But he rose too. He got one foot into a small ledge, then the other. He pushed up, supporting himself on the ledges, freeing his other arm. With one hand still gripping her ankle, the other lifted to grab her arm and yank her from the rocks.

Her fingertips touched the knife. She clawed at it, pulling it closer. His hand gripped her elbow. His lipless mouth split in a ghastly smile. She grasped the knife handle and, in a single move, swung backward, slashing him across the face.

He screamed out and fell back, releasing her arm. His other hand was torn lose from her ankle by his falling weight, but the jerk of it pulled her from her own precarious hold.

She dangled again above the sea, holding on by her fingertips while the body fell, fell, fell into the crashing waves.

Inside the tower, the three were nearly dead. Flames were now coming up through the wide rents in the buckled floor. The table legs were smoking, the thick atmosphere nearly strangling. Cathbad had fainted, and Laeg was sagging, close to giving in. Sentanta, fighting for consciousness, held them both on the table, but it was only moments more until his own strength gave out.

The room shuddered, creaked, rocked from the forces battling to destroy it. A section of metal plate bulged up, and the skull rolled clattering down the slope, dropping through a crack into the inferno beneath.

Then something thumped loudly against the door, and thumped again.

Fionualla, tattered and scraped but still very much alive, bashed upward at the bolt with a chunk of the fallen stone. The desperate energy that had saved her still gave her a great strength.

The tower was trembling constantly now. Pieces of rock rained around her. Behind her in the corridor a timber crashed down in flames. She paused to brush the glowing sparks from her clothes and then stubbornly hammered on.

Her efforts were succeeding: the bolt was jolting loose. One more bash with all her power and the bolt lifted from its holder. She pulled off her cloak to mitten her hands and grabbed it, pulling open the door.

A wave of heat and smoke, almost a solid wall, rolled out upon her, driving her back. But through the haze were visible the captives, already off the table, Sentanta and Laeg staggering forward carrying Cathbad.

The two rushed the druid across the floor as the room teetered about them. As they reached the doorway, the remainder of the roof crashed in behind them, smashing down on the table. The section of the floor beneath it caved into a storm of fire that belched up, tongues licking after them as they ran along the corridor.

They made their way, stones falling around them, out the crumbling doorway into the yard. There came a last great explosion deep beneath the tower, and the ravaged structure collapsed, sending a geyser of sparks and flame and smoke shooting high. It settled back upon a pile of rubble as they, safely distant, collapsed onto the stony earth of the yard and gasped for fresh, cool air.

But Fionualla lay only a moment before she was up again,

kneeling at Sentanta's side, shaking the youth's shoulder urgently.

"Sentanta, you must get up. My husband is in danger."

"We know," he said, sitting up.

He looked at the others. Laeg was sitting up too, surveying his body. He, like the others, was badly singed, limbs scorched and spotted from falling sparks, their flesh a painful red. But Cathbad seemed the worst, lying still, eyes closed, lungs pumping as he gasped for air.

"Cathbad!" Sentanta said in concern, leaning over him. "Cathbad!"

He roused, looking up at the boy. "My . . . chest!" he wheezed. "Bring it!"

Laeg limped to fetch it from the car and dragged it back to them.

With Sentanta's help, the druid managed to sit up and open it. He pulled out a jar filled with a shiny gray paste. "Here, put this on the burns," he said, handing it to the youth.

Sentanta took a scoop of it on his fingertips and passed it to Fionualla, who did the same, then passed it to Laeg. He took out a fingerful of the strange, greasy stuff and eyed it with distaste.

"Rub it on!" his young friend told him, already applying it to his badly scorched arms. "It's truly magical."

Laeg tried experimentally, then looked up in wonder. "It does help!" he said, rubbing with greater energy. "Why, the pain just vanishes!"

In moments the ointment had been applied to most of the wounded portions of all parties, its magic healing their burns and invigorating them as well.

"What are you doing here, my Queen?" Sentanta asked as he dabbed the last of the gray paste onto his legs.

"I came to fetch you," she said. "You have to go after Conaire, to help him."

"It was to help him that we came here," Sentanta explained. "We followed a man who is behind this threat to the high-king."

"The dark-cloaked warrior?" she said. "I saw him. One of his . . . his creatures tried to kill me. But we can't delay any longer. You must go after Conaire. Meave knew about the danger too. She's already gone on to find him. She sent me after you. She thought Cathbad's magic might be needed to help him."

"I know it will now," the druid said. He forced himself to his feet, groaning with the effort, but stoically drawing himself erect. "Come on, Sentanta, Laeg, we must go."

"I'm going too," Fionualla announced.

"That you are not," Sentanta firmly replied. "It is too dangerous."

"No more than this was," she returned stubbornly. "He is my husband, and I mean to be with him."

"She has a right to it, Sentanta," said Cathbad. "Let her come."

"All right then," he conceded reluctantly. "I'll drive her car. Cathbad, go with Laeg."

They moved swiftly to the chariots. Above them the smoke from the ruins billowed up, filling the sky, fanning out in a great umbrella to cover the sun.

The clouds of haze that had filled the countryside around Mor's party grew constantly thicker as they pressed ahead.

The red light of the false fires that had glowed about them had now faded, leaving them in a shrouding gray gloom like that of a heavy fog, but without the scent or feel of a real fog's dampness.

As the party made its best speed back toward Tara, this strange, shrouding gray grew thicker and thicker, until even the champions' view of each other was hazy, the engulfing clouds swallowing the sounds of harness and creaking wheels and thudding hooves, leaving them to glide along like the wraiths of warriors abroad in a Samhain night.

Soon they could see nothing of the countryside and were all but feeling their way ahead, uncertain of the path right before their horses' hooves.

"I've no idea where we are anymore," Cormac Conlingas said disgustedly. "There's not a landmark visible."

"I can't even tell if we're still moving east," said the brown-haired Muinremar. He peered upward. "The sun's faintest glow is completely hidden."

"Maybe we should stop, wait for it to clear," suggested MacCecht.

"We must get to Tara," said Mor. "It's too urgent."

"Not much good rushing toward it if we're really rushing away," the logical Conal Carna pointed out.

"Let's push on a bit farther," said Mor. "We must come to something soon that'll tell our way."

So they moved on, rolling through the unknown, silent, ghostly countryside, until Conal, at their head, suddenly ordered his driver to pull up.

"Wait!" he called out, peering ahead, putting hand to spear. "Something moved out there."

The others pulled up behind him. All stared tensely, fixedly ahead into the swirling gray. There were some vague shadows moving there, and coming closer.

The warriors waited, ready for anything. Then they relaxed in relief as the figures resolved into clear view.

It was three old people who had appeared from the strange fog: three old men, shuffling along the trail afoot. All were bent, scrawny, and most decrepit of look. The bony arms and legs thrusting from their ragged clothes were knobby as the limbs of some ancient tree. Their faces were a craggy, barren landscape, their high-domed heads bald but for a few stray wisps. So frail were they that it seemed a hard gust of the autumn wind would sweep them up as if they were dried leaves.

"Warriors!" the old man said in a dry, faint whisper, his withered face lighting with great joy. "Ah, thank the blessed Danu for answering our prayers. We have sought just such as you. We've a great need of your help."

"Our help?" said Mor. "Why?"

"It's only simple herdsmen we are," the man quaveringly explained. "Our village is being plagued by terrible beasts. For many years they ravaged our poor herds, taking half our cows as their own ransom for leaving us alone. But when Conaire Mor, good Danu bless his name, came to the rule, a great peace came on them. They went away into their hill and left us alone. For that time we prospered. Then, with the summer, they suddenly returned, more savage than before. Our herds have been all but slaughtered. Our young men tried to fight, but they were killed. Now we cannot fight them. The women and children cower in the huts and starve, growing weaker every day. Only these two and I still had strength to seek help."

"Do you know the way to Tara?" asked Conal.

"We do," said the old man.

"It's most important that we go there at once," the champion explained. "Show us the way, and we'll send help back to you."

"That we will not!" Mor said, looking in surprise at his comrade. "How can you be so callous to them?"

"It's yourself who are my first concern," the practical man said flatly. "I want you back within the safety of Tara's walls."

"I'll go nowhere until these people have been helped," Mor answered. "We go now."

"But it was you who wanted to go back," Conal protested. "Remember the trouble on Tuath Mumain."

"Those people are plagued by some illusion, but not a deadly one. The people of these men are dying. Their need comes first. They can show us the way to Tara after we help."

"Ah, great warrior, it's fine words you're saying now," the old man wheezed, he and his companions beaming with new hope.

"Climb in with us, then," Mor said, "and show us the way."

The old men were helped into chariots, and the party moved on, turning off the track onto another, and then another.

"The Dagda knows where they're taking us now," Conal grumbled to Cormac. "I feel almost as if we're heading back the way we came."

Soon, rounded forms appeared in the fog ahead, becoming visible as a collection of small, thatched huts as they approached. The chariots pulled up in their midst, the warriors looking about with pitying eyes.

It was indeed a wretched village. The untended structures were in poor repair, some half-fallen. Within the shadows of the doors, the faint, frightened glitter of eyes shone, but none of the inhabitants showed themselves.

"I'm sorry there are no others greeting you," the first old man said. "The poor women will come out for nothing now, instead staying huddled inside protecting their babes."

"I understand," said Mor. "But where are these creatures?"

"Above," he said, sweeping a bony hand up to point.

Beyond the village, they could just glimpse the rocky foot of a hill that rose steeply to vanish into the thick veil of gray clouds.

"They live up in the caves there," the man went on, "coming down to hunt when they like. Three of the beasts . . . I think."

"Just what are these beasts like?" asked Conal.

The old man shook his head. "That's the most terrible part of it. No one knows. None alive has ever seen the beasts. It's like Other creatures they are, too clever to be caught by mortals. But they're most savage, I can tell that to you."

As if in confirmation of this, a deep roaring, like the rumble of distant thunder, came rolling down to them from above. The men all looked up to it, held by the ominous sound.

"Well, if that's one of them," said Cormac, "then they're surely creatures of fair size!"

"I'll go against them," Conal announced.

"And I'll go as well," MacCecht put in.

"No," said Conaire. "I mean to go alone. Cormac, lend me a spear."

"You *can't* mean that!" said Conal in surprise as Cormac pulled one of his spears from its rack. "Let us all go with you and finish these creatures quickly, without risk."

"You heard this man's tale," Mor told him, taking the spear Cormac offered to him. "What's happened here is of my doing, as in Tuath Mumain. I'm sure of it. My own weakness has caused some breakdown of the peace the Sidhe promised to me. It may have been the Sidhe themselves who brought me here. I have to make amends."

"By getting yourself killed?" Conal asked.

"I will risk no one else for my mistakes," Mor fired back angrily. "By the order of the high-king of all Ireland, you will all stay here!"

He glared about him at the champions, then strode away into the coiling gray.

Mor quickly reached the base of the rocky hill and started up, clambering through a field of sharply edged boulders. He climbed for some while, with no way to tell how high he was reaching in the fog.

He heard the deep-throated roar once more above, and moved toward it, coming at last onto a level place where scattered lumps of stone made dim, unpleasant shapes in the shifting clouds.

He waited, motionless, listening. After a time there came sounds of movement, seemingly from all around him, impossible to pinpoint in the gray void. Faint, skittering sounds they were, as of a spear tip flicking over stone.

One of the dim shapes ahead of him began to move. It stayed low to the ground, seeming to slink or crawl as it came slowly nearer.

He crouched, the spear up, ready for a throw. His eyes strained forward to get a first, clear view of the thing closing with him.

A faint *swish* of moving air came suddenly from his right,

warning him. He turned and raised his eyes as a second form shot upward to loom over him and a massive paw swung out to rake him with the glinting curved daggers of its claws.

Chapter Forty-four

Signs

Mor brought up the spear sideways to slam against the paw as it swept in. He managed to deflect the blow, but the force of it sent him staggering.

He recovered and set himself. Facing him was a catlike beast with a coat of sleek and glowing black, a massive head, and lithe, muscled body larger than a man's. Farther away on either side of it, forming a triangle, were two more of the creatures, crouched and ready to attack.

They gave Mor little time to consider a plan of defense, springing forward again, jaws wide, snarling savagely.

With the spear clasped in both hands, he swung upward, bringing the thick bole up beneath the closest attacker's chin. Its jaws snapped closed and it fell sideways, momentarily stunned. A second cat leaped for him, and he dropped down to roll beneath it, letting it sail on over his head. But the third, which had leaped for him also, was now descending directly upon him.

He came up into a crouch, grounding the spear, its barbed head thrusting up at a sharp angle toward the cat. It fell upon the point, its own weight driving the weapon through its chest. Mor jerked the spear upward. The bole bent, then splintered under the strain, but he managed to throw the beast on over his head. It crashed down behind him, impaled on the weapon, thrashing and snarling in its death throes, the foam that boiled from its mouth red-tinted by the blood of a split heart.

Mor rose to his feet to find that the beast he had stunned had now recovered and was standing with the other surviving creature, watching him. He raised his sword, expecting their attack. But they, seeming to decide that this direct assault was too dangerous, turned to sprint away, each in different directions, disappearing up into the rocks.

Mor moved forward, peering up after them. The gray hillside above blended with the gray mist, making even more treacherous the vast maze of rocks where they might lurk unseen. A most dangerous territory to be entered by a single man hunting two such cunning beasts.

But Mor was undaunted by the danger of the task. It seemed only to make him the more determined as he strode across the level place and began to climb again.

So began a strange hunt in the unnatural fog as Mor searched cautiously through the jumble of rocks. Every boulder, every cave was a possible hiding place. He looked for any movement above, below, around, as the tension grew in him.

He kept as silent as he could in the deadening muffler of the fog, listening for any telltale sound. He breathed slowly through his mouth, feeling his throat go dry. He heard a faint drumming sound as of a distant *tiompan*, then realized it was his own beating heart.

Then there was a faint skittering just beyond a rock ahead. He edged toward it, sword out before him, tensed to act.

But it was from the rocks above, not from ahead, that one of the cats sprang suddenly upon him with a growl of rage. It crashed full onto him, bearing him back, its claws sinking into his shoulders. He dropped his sword and went down heavily. The head of the cat thrust down, its tearing fangs aiming for his neck. His hands went to its throat to push the head away. He locked his legs about its waist and rolled sideways. They went over, the cat slamming to the hard ground. He tightened his grip, squeezing his hands tighter, throttling it.

From beyond the rock, the beast which he had heard now cautiously appeared. It peered out at the embattled pair. It crouched, tail switching, mouth stretching in what seemed a grin. Then it slunk forward.

Mor was winning his fight, determination giving him a near superhuman strength. A look of quite human surprise came into the beast's eyes as it realized he was overcoming its sinewy might. It struggled harder, not to come at him now, but to tear away. But Mor hung grimly on.

Behind him, the other beast drew closer, stealthily, slowly, so as not to alarm him. Now within a short jump of the combatants, it crouched again, muscles tensing for the spring.

The two others stayed locked in a death embrace, Mor oblivious to danger in his concentration. The second cat sprang.

A javelin shot toward it, tearing through the muscles of its shoulder. The cat roared in pain and jerked its legs in, crashing down upon Mor and its fellow.

It rolled away, leaping up, wounded but not sorely so, shaking the spear loose. Its landing had broken the others apart, and its half-throttled mate rose, as Mor did.

Mor's sword lay too far away to reach. He had no defense as both cats charged at once. But Conal and Cormac suddenly leaped past him, one on either side, confronting the two beasts. Conal met the wounded one's charge with shield and sword, while Cormac attacked with a thrusting spear the one Mor had battled.

The rest of the fight was brief but savage. Conal severed the paw of his opponent, then finished the creature with a blow that split its skull. Cormac drove his spear home in the other's breast, and while it struggled furiously to pull free, Mor recovered his sword, severing its head with two hard chops.

Both creatures, even then, proved astonishingly reluctant to die, thrashing like beheaded snakes, striking out with paws, jaws working madly as if trying to bite. But finally the struggles lessened, the beasts growing quiet.

Then, as the three men watched in amazement, a strange transformation came on the dead cats. A dark haze lifted from the ground to envelop them and they dissolved, like creatures made of sand, leaving only an outline of themselves in fine, black dust to mark their place.

"What were they?" Cormac asked.

Mor shook his head. "Who knows? Perhaps more magic."

"Not more illusion?" asked Conal.

"No," Mor said ruefully, putting a hand to the deep claw wounds in his shoulders. "Not entirely." He looked at the two, his expression a stern one. "And I suppose I should thank you for disobeying me?"

"We did save you," Conal observed.

"Conal was the only one willing to go against your order," Cormac supplied.

"And you?" asked Mor.

"Oh. Well, I was the only one he could order to go with him," he said with a sheepish smile.

"And do you feel better now?" asked Conal, a trace of sarcasm in his tone. "You nearly lost your life playing the great champion of Ireland alone."

"At least one of these plagues is settled," Mor responded brusquely. "So, come on then. Let's be getting on to Tara."

Back down in the village, the other champions were relieved to see that their high-king had survived. The three old men were overjoyed.

"We're sorry the others still won't come out from hiding," one old man told Mor. "But they will come forth once they know it truly is safe again."

"I understand," Mor said. "You can tell them that we'll send food here from Tara soon. Enough to see them fed until you can rebuild your herds."

"You are a most gracious king, Conaire Mor," the old man said, tears in his eyes.

"The king appreciates it," Conal said sharply, impatient with this further delay. "But now will you show us the way, old man?"

"I will that," he said eagerly. "I'll show you to the right road for Tara."

"Best ride with me, then," Mor offered, as the champions climbed into their chariots. And as he helped the frail figure mount into his car, a realization came to him.

"Say, I've not even asked you who it is we're helping," he said to his passenger. "What place is this?"

"Cerna," creaked the man. "It's called Cerna."

"I have heard the name before," Mor said.

"Of our humble place?" The old man gave a wheezing laugh. "I doubt that. Few but those who live and die here ever know of it."

"Cerna," Mor said again thoughtfully, looking at the sad, gloomy huts huddled in the fog. Then he shrugged. "Ah well, no matter. We must be getting on." He signaled the chariots ahead and they rolled away from the village.

As they did, a puzzled Cormac leaned across toward Conal's car to ask, "How did the old man know it was Conaire Mor who helped them?"

Conal shrugged. "One of the others told him while we fought the cats, I suppose. What matter?"

"Yes. What matter?" Cormac repeated, but without conviction.

Unable to shake off a nagging uneasiness, he looked back at

the village they had just left. But it had already faded into concealing billows of the peculiar fog.

"And you say that Mor was here?" Meave asked.

"He was," said the young chieftain named Carbre, "but he headed back toward Tara."

"Strange," she said. "I saw no sign of him as I was coming here."

They were speaking in the yard of the chief fortress of Tuath Mumain, she still in her car beside Fardia, the chieftain overseeing the unhitching of teams from his own warriors' chariots.

"More strange yet is the change that's taken place," he said. "Directly after the high-king left, the clouds began to fade away. Now, look."

Above the dun was only the brilliant blue vault of a clear sky.

"I was making my way around the other duns and raths to spread the word of what Mor had promised to do, when I saw what was happening," he went on. A wave indicated his chariots and their worn teams. "We've just returned here ourselves. So, there was no need for Mor to be rushing back to Tara. There was no need for him to come here at all."

"Yet, it was supposed to be you who called him," Meave said with a musing frown.

"I know," he responded, clearly puzzled too. "Called to end a feud that was as false as the flames and lamentings brought with this false storm. He said himself it was something unnatural."

"More unnatural than even he could know," she said. "I'm certain now it was contrived against him."

"By whom?"

"I don't know, but great powers are at work. I feel it very strongly here. Mor must be warned. But if he did go back to Tara, what's happened to him?"

"It was a great fog that he was riding into," Carbre said. "Perhaps he lost his way in it."

"Then he could be anywhere," Meave said despairingly.

"I can find him, my Queen," Fardia put in. "No boasting now. My people have learned to track a kid across the hard slate of a rocky cliff. If Mor's chariots rolled upon the earth, I can follow him."

"Then I'll show you the way they were going when I last saw them," said Carbre. He called out to one of his charioteers

who was in the midst of unhitching horses from a car, "Hold
on there. Get that team harnessed again. I'll be taking it out."

While the driver, muttering something under his breath,
obeyed, Meave watched, face drawn in lines of deep anxiety.

"You see great danger for him then, Meave?" asked the
discerning Fardia, noting her look.

"Like none he has ever faced before." She shook her head.
"He'll need great help, I'm certain. I wish Cathbad would catch
up to us."

"This is not right," Cathbad said unhappily. "Please stop."

He was riding in the chariot of Sentanta, with Laeg at its
reins, speeding across the countryside away from the fallen
tower. Behind them rolled Fionualla's chariot, Sentanta now
guiding its team and struggling with fair success to match the
skill of his driver. He was managing with great effort just to
keep up.

Laeg, though not understanding the druid's sudden order,
still pulled his team to a halt. A surprised Sentanta reined his
team up next to them.

"What's wrong?" he asked the druid.

"Another feeling, but a strong one. It's foolish for us to try
to follow after Conaire. He's far ahead of us, and no saying
where by now. So, we must find out where he's headed and
try to meet him there," Cathbad said. "That man in black said
that Mor was riding into some sort of trap."

"The man in black?" Fionualla said. "I saw him leave the
tower. He was headed south, along the coast."

"That must be it!" said Cathbad excitedly.

"We don't know for certain that this man is going himself
to destroy the high-king," Sentanta said. "Mor and his champions went west, inland from Tara."

"I know. But when I foresaw the danger to him, he was by
the sea. I feel that this dark sorcerer is directing him there
somehow, and we must go there too. We might reach Mor in
time to give him help."

"Not by trying to chase that dark man south," Sentanta said
doubtfully. "I've no skill myself in following a trail." He looked
to his driver, "What about you, Laeg?"

"It's a charioteer I am," was the proud reply, "not a tracking
hound."

"And we can't be searching every point and cove and beach
along the coast," added Sentanta.

"You're right," the druid agreed. "We must know the exact place."

"Can you call up your foreseeing powers again?" the boy asked. "Maybe you can find out more now."

The druid shook his head uncertainly. "It's not an easy thing to do, even with a score of druids helping." He looked at the desperate, hope-filled faces of Sentanta and Fionualla, and then shrugged. "But we can try. What other choice have we?"

He got down from the car, pulling out his invaluable little chest. He set the three young people to gathering wood, and they formed a pile of twigs which they painstakingly gleaned from an almost treeless countryside.

Cathbad kindled a fire, took a small pot from the chest along with several vials, mixed his ingredients carefully, and set the potion down in the center of the flames. Soon a trail of gray-white smoke was coiling up from it.

"All right," he said to them, "sit here with me. You must help."

They sat down cross-legged about the fire, though Laeg did so reluctantly.

"Now, we must all concentrate," Cathbad instructed. "Fix your minds solely on Conaire Mor. Stare into the smoke. And hum."

"I'll do no humming," said Laeg.

"You must," the druid told him. "It helps to set the spell and aids in the concentrating. Hum. Like this!"

He set a low, steady tone. Fionualla quickly picked it up.

Sentanta began as well, but he noted that Laeg remained silent, a stubborn expression on his face. He tapped his driver on the knee. "*Hum,*" he ordered.

Laeg sighed, but then he hummed, the four voices joining in a single note.

They all concentrated, faces drawn in frowns. Cathbad's body grew tense, seeming almost to vibrate with the strain of his mental effort to grasp something, any faint suggestion, from beyond.

After moments that seemed an agonizing eternity to the participants, Laeg broke off his humming and shook his head angrily. "This magic humbuggery is a bloody great waste of time," he said in disgust.

The others stopped, and Cathbad shot him an impatient look. "The Seer's ritual is generally performed with sympa-

thetic druids," he scathingly returned, "not with skeptical young
fools. It's certain you're giving me no help."

"But I feel nothing's happening too," Fionualla said in despair.

"Well, it just may be that we'll get no help from the Others
now," said the druid.

"But we must!" Sentanta said with force. Then he lifted his
gaze to the sky, calling out both imploringly and with some
irritation, "Great Sidhe, you tell me I have a task, as does
Conaire Mor. But the powers against us now are too great.
We can't do this alone. If you stand aloof and refuse all aid to
us, what happens will be upon your heads, not our own. Faythleen, if you really mean to act for Ireland's good, then please
give us some sign!"

"You'll get nothing from the Hidden Ones but their anger
for such bold talk as that," Laeg said.

"No!" said Fionualla excitedly. "Look!"

A enormous white swanlike bird speckled in gold had suddenly appeared. It wheeled majestically above them, swooping
again and again through the plume of smoke.

"I've seen no bird like it before," Fionualla said with awe.

"I think I have," said Sentanta, recalling faint images from
a dream.

"It is your sign, my lad. I know it!" said Cathbad, rising.

As if in confirmation, the bird swept down low over their
heads, then rose again, flapping away toward the south.

"Quickly!" said the druid, using the hem of his robe as a
mitten to grab his little caldron from the fire. "We must follow.
It's showing us the way!"

Chapter Forty-five

Da Derga's Inn

One after another the score of long, slender boats grounded
on the isolated strip of beach.

From the craft some two hundred men, pirates and exiles, climbed out onto the sand and began to unload weapons, the rattling of the iron echoing loudly around the little cove.

"Keep it quiet there," Ingcel warned. "And everyone stay close to the boats until I've looked about a bit. Oisic," he said to a tall, brawnily built Lochlanner with a long name of white-blond hair, "you come with me. And, Ferogain," he called to the young exile, "why don't you come as well."

The blond man lifted an immense, crescent-bladed ax from his boat and started toward the captain. Ferogain moved after him.

"Wait!" Maine Morgor shouted as his boat grounded. "I'm coming as well."

He grabbed his shield and leaped from the prow onto the sand, trotting after the rest. Ingcel shot him an irritated look, but apparently decided against another confrontation and said nothing.

The four moved up from the beach onto a steep, grass-covered slope behind it, climbing to its brink.

"Careful now," Ingcel warned, directing an especially hard look at Morgor. "We want no one to see us and be spreading an alarm."

So it was with great caution that they peered above the edge of the slope.

To the west, the ground rose higher yet, sweeping up more gently to another ridge. There sat the high-walled, six-sided bruidhean on the meeting of the roads. To the south, the land fell away sharply again, into the wide half-bowl of Ath Cliath's great harbor, sparkling in the clear sun of a bright fall day. Below, they could see the buildings of the port clustered between the water and the inland hills.

There were no trading ships of other lands at the quays now. With fall came the beginning of the harsh winter winds that scoured the strip of sea between Ireland and Alban, and none but the most hardy seafarers would risk their frail ships there.

"Not many people about," commented Ferogain.

"That old man has chosen his time perfectly," Ingcel said with a certain respect. "The town and the inn will be all but empty now. No one to interfere. I hope the rest of his planning works as well."

"And just what is that plan?" Morgor asked. "You've not seen fit to impart any of it to us before."

"Only to keep you from talking its merits over with my men and confusing them," Ingcel said.

"To keep me from taking the leading of this raid from you, more like," Morgor returned.

"Enough," said Ferogain sharply. "Your private feud will have to wait, Morgor." He looked to the captain, clearly anxious. "Tell us, Ingcel, what do we have to do?"

"Only to wait, according to your man. He said that Mor would soon be coming to that bruidhean. Everything was set, he said. It couldn't fail. He's supposed to meet us here before we attack."

"And just what will we be facing?" Morgor asked. "What kind of escort rides with the king?"

"He didn't know for certain. But he hoped to have Mor all but alone." He looked to Ferogain searchingly. "Well, what about it, boy? Are you ready to take your revenge?"

"*I* am," said Morgor gratingly, gripping his sword hilt. "I've waited with great longing for this time."

"No more than I," said Ingcel. "You can return here to stay and be out of my life."

"I don't know," Morgor said, smiling musingly. "Ireland seems quite tame to me now. I may continue in this seafaring way."

"Not with my company you won't," Ingcel told him with finality.

"That'll be up to your men, I think," Morgor tauntingly replied. Then he looked back to the bruidhean, his smile replaced by a scowl of hate. "But first, I want Mor's head!"

Ferogain's gaze followed his to the inn, so isolated and vulnerable on its high point of land. His expression was clearly one of consternation at the reality of what was finally to come.

Mor's party now found itself plunged into the depths of a forest.

Though the fog had thinned, allowing a hazy sunlight through, the trees had closed in thickly on either side of the faint road, hemming the men in so that they could see only ahead or behind along the narrow channel slashed through the dense wood.

The immense, ancient, gnarled trees crowded the frail strip of roadway like creatures creeping in to devour helpless prey. The long, bony fingers of their roots had already crawled out to seize it at many points, closing around it as if to choke it off. The upthrusting knobs of them often forced the chariots to slow down, bouncing over them.

The air was unseasonably chill, tinged with that clear, peculiar tang which seems a harbinger of winter snows. The trees were already browning, the sharp breeze rustling in their tops, shaking loose the upper leaves so that the top limbs thrust up blackly, intertwining to form a weblike curtain high about. The dry leaves fell to carpet the roadway and hide the treacherous exposed roots, making the drivers all the more cautious.

Save for the falling leaves and keening wind, the woods were most strangely quiet and empty. No bird calls, no crashing of startled deer, no flutter of squirrel's tail or flash of wings. The only sounds were the rattles and creaks of the chariots and the crackling steps of the horses' broad hooves on the dead leaves.

The men too were quiet, subdued by the melancholy atmosphere. They peered about into the shadowy woods, feeling the weight of silence, tugging cloaks tighter about them against the probing chill, hands resting always on weapons.

Then, ahead, a larger opening appeared. They came into a clearing from which a half-dozen narrow tracks diverged—like wheel spokes from a hub—into the woods. Here they pulled up.

"Well, where do we go now?" asked MacCecht.

"It doesn't seem to matter," said Cormac, peering down road after road, each one a narrow track hemmed by trees, all the same, running away with seeming endlessness into the eternity of the woods.

"Well, I've surely seen nothing familiar so far," said MacCecht irritably.

"Strange," Mor said musingly. "I've a feeling as if we're really nowhere, that this journey is some dream of us forever riding on, and the time not passing."

"It could be so," growled MacCecht. "Can't see the sun enough to know if it's moved at all."

"And we do seem to have been riding for days through this," added Cormac.

"The fact remains, we can't just sit here," the practical Conal pointed out. "Which way should we go?"

"To say the truth, I've no idea at all anymore," admitted Mor.

"I think north," MacCecht said with some determination.

"Oh yes?" said Cormac. "And just which way is north?"

The graying warrior peered fiercely up into the hazy sky in his frustration.

"There's surely no sign of other travelers to give us any clue," said Conal, looking down at the undisturbed leaves on the trails before them. "It doesn't seem as if anyone's used these ancient paths for years."

"Do you suppose that old man sent us Astray?" asked Cormac.

"Well, whatever happened, we're not going to reach Tara tonight, that's clear," Conal pronounced, looking to Mor. "Shall we camp?"

"It is Samhain coming on us in a few days' time," said one who, though clearly a tough, graying veteran of many wars, was yet made uneasy by thoughts of the supernatural. "I don't like being out after dark."

"Don't be foolish, Sencha," said Muinremar. "I've been abroad often at this time and never yet seen a one of the Other folk to speak of."

"Look at that being," said an amazed Cormac, pointing up the road, "and I might believe the Sidhe creatures are abroad!"

For coming toward them was a most strange man, short, greasy-haired and craggy-featured, with one eye covered by a leather patch, and only one hand, and limping on a wooden stump that served him for one foot. In his hand he carried a forked pole of black iron, and resting across his broad, humped shoulder was a great, bristled, black pig impaled on its tines but squealing nevertheless. Just behind him walked a scrawny, crooked crone with raven-sharp features and a wide, sagging mouth.

This pair strode up before the king's company and stopped. The woman grinned, showing the black stumps of the half-dozen teeth left to her. The man smiled too, squinting up to them with his one, tiny, glittering eye.

"Well met this night, my good master Conaire," he said graciously, giving a little bow. "And a welcome to you."

The crone still stood smiling inanely, but he wacked her with the stump of his free arm and she gave a curtsey.

"And just how is it that you know of the king's coming?" Conal demanded suspiciously.

"Ah, but don't the whole land about know of the journey of great Conaire Mor?" he said, grinned more broadly yet. "And his brave acts to help the people of Tuath Mumain and Cerna?

Oh yes, it's long I've known of your comin'. For the trees' rustlin's do speak of it, and the birds' singin', and what's only pretty sounds to other men is like fine speech to me."

"Who are you to be giving me welcome?" Mor asked.

"Fer Coille, the Man of the Wood I'm called," he answered promptly. He shook the spit, making the stuck pig squeal more shrilly yet. "And his black pig with him that you may not be fastin' tonight, for you are the best king that ever came into the world."

"Is he meaning the creature on his spit, or the one beside him?" Cormac murmured to MacCecht.

"It's not food we're needing this night," Conal said, "but fit lodgings for the king."

"Ah, is that the truth?" the man said. "Well, it might be that I can show the very same to you, and not far from here, if you'd be honorin' me afterward by sharing some of my finest loin of pork there."

Mor gave the squirming animal a dubious look but nodded, saying as jovially as he could, "Of course I will do that, Fer Coille. And welcome."

"*If* these lodgings are suitable," qualified Conal, giving the man a meaningful lookover.

The man grasped the implication and grinned again. "Ah, it's not my own poor place we're going to, my good champion. No. It's a fine bruidhean, so it is. Hard by to Ath Cliath."

"Ath Cliath?" said MacCecht. "We *have* gone far afield then. We've gone right past Tara in the fog, nearly to the sea."

"Well, my King?" Conal said to Mor. "What do you think?"

"I think that we've a long way to go to Tara, and we may as well stay the night at this bruidhean." He waved to the strange woodsman. "Lead on, my good man, and you can surely dine with us at the most honored spot beside me."

So they set out again, following the man and woman, who chose to plod ahead on foot, turning onto another of the roads radiating from the spot. They moved on through the eerily silent wood that seemed never to change. But the last of the haze slowly dissipated, finally revealing a sun that now clearly seemed to move. It began dropping lower, and afternoon shadows spilled into the woods about them, bringing a sort of early twilight to the road beneath the canopy of branches.

"Look there," said MacCecht after a time. "Others on the road."

Ahead, three riders had appeared, not in chariots but on

horseback. They were riding on matching rust-colored mounts, each cloaked in crimson, bright red devices painted on the dark leather of the shields slung at their backs, clutching spears banded in red-gold. Long hair whose glowing color was the rich scarlet of fall maple leaves streamed out behind them as they sped along.

"Where did they come from?" wondered Cormac.

"Out of the woods?" said Conal. "Or from a side road?"

"I surely didn't see them," he replied, watching them uneasily.

"Riders!" Mor called after them. "Stay back and wait for us. We'll ride together for fellowship."

But the three went on, their horses staying always the same distance ahead.

"A strange thing that is," said Mor.

"Maybe they can't hear us," Conal suggested. "Cormac, ride forward and ask them to hold back and wait for us."

"Me?" he said, clearly without enthusiasm.

"Why not?" asked Conal.

"Because there's something about them I don't like."

"Just be after them, boy," the champion brusquely ordered.

Cormac sighed. "I wish Sentanta were here," he said again.

He tapped his driver and the man shook the reins. The team stretched out, drawing the young Ulsterman farther forward, away from the rest, nearer to the three. But as he began to close, they suddenly pulled ahead of him again. He had the driver put on more speed, but they did as well, keeping always the same distance between them.

"Stranger yet," he said unhappily. "Slow down."

The driver did, but so did they. And when Cormac again had the driver speed up, they did it again as well. So once more he had his team slowed.

"I most surely do not like this at all," he said glumly.

The others were nearly out of sight behind him now, and he was all but alone with the three riders on the eerie road.

"Conal ordered us," the driver reminded him.

"Always me," Cormac said with a sigh. "My Sentanta, where are you when I need your company!" He shrugged resignedly. "Well, all right, driver. Once more."

This time the riders did not speed up but let the chariot draw nearer.

Cormac called out to them, "Wait, riders! The high-king of Ireland asks you to hold back and ride in his company!"

At this, one of the men turned his head, and Cormac received a shock.

The rider's face was gaunt and very white, like that of one long dead. Against this paleness, his blood-red lips were shockingly bright. The deep-sunk eyes seemed also to glow with a ruby light as they fixed on him.

The red lips parted, and from them issued a harsh, rattling voice, chill and forlorn as the fall wind in the leafless branches.

"There is great news before us, my son; whetting of swords, destroying of life, shields with broken bosses, after the fall of night. Our horses are tired. We are riding the horses of the Sidhe. Although we are alive, we are dead."

And with that their horses vaulted forward, speeding on ahead as if Cormac's chariot were stopped in the road, vanishing away.

He ordered the driver to turn at once and rode back to the others.

"You didn't catch them?" Conal asked scoldingly as he reached them.

"It's not my fault," said Cormac defensively, and he told what had happened, repeating the words of the rider.

"Horses of the Sidhe," said Mor thoughtfully, frowning. "And a foretelling of great battle."

"It is a warning to us," said Conal. "This is a bad road."

"Ah no. Fine road! Fine road!" the Man of the Wood assured him cheerily. "Goes right to the door of the bruidhean, so it does. Not far ahead now."

"We'll not be turned by this strange sign," Mor said decisively. "It's only another part of the unnatural things that have plagued us all along. I'm weary with their constant tormenting. I mean to follow out our path, find our way home, and see this trickery stopped!"

The word of Fer Coille proved good. They had not gone on much farther when the forest rather abruptly stopped, and they found themselves riding down through swelling uplands toward the distant sparkle of the sea.

They followed the road as afternoon now gave way to spreading night.

"Ah, we'll just beat darkness to the inn," the skittish champion called Sencha said with relief.

"Aye, there it is," said MacCecht.

Ahead, the six-sided building had come into view, already brightly lit against the coming night, squares of warm, welcoming gold light beaming out from its windows and open doors in all directions.

"There's a most friendly sight," said Cormac with relief. "The first since we left Tara."

But Conaire Mor stared down at it with a puzzled frown, searching his mind for something he'd forgotten.

Soon afterward they were pulling up before the doors of the great bruidhean, the warriors dismounting, giving the chariots into the care of drivers and stable grooms, then following Conaire Mor inside.

Unlike the time of the young exiles' first visit there, the vast room was nearly deserted. A dozen men drowsed or talked over their ale. A handful of serving folk waited about or cooked a meager supply of food at the central fire. And in one corner, aloof and staring, showed the white faces of the three riders from the road.

"Well, there are those three," said Cormac, pointing. "Look, Conaire."

Mor glanced toward them, but then his attention was drawn to the ruddy-faced bruighaid who bustled forward eagerly when he saw them come in.

"A good day to you, my fine warriors," he greeted them cheerily. "You're most welcome to Da Derga's Hostel."

"Da Derga," Mor repeated. "Red. The House of Red."

And then the realization came to him, jolted into his memory by those words. The shock of it nearly staggered him as a real blow.

"Nemglan!" he said. "Cerna!" His gaze swept to the three sepulchral warriors of crimson cloak. "Three Reds!"

He wheeled around. The Man of the Wood and his crone were just coming into the doorway.

"No!" Mor cried. Stop them! Don't let them in!"

The champions before them, surprised and bewildered by their king's sudden order, still hastened to obey, blocking the doorway with their bodies.

The old man looked past them to Conaire, his face going dark with outrage. "How dare you keep us out?" he said. "Let us pass!"

"What does this mean?" Conal asked Mor. "They did help us. It's most poor manners to do this."

"It's my *gessas*, Conal!" Mor told him urgently, gripping his arm. "My bonds! They are all but gone. We must stop them."

"This is a great insult!" Fer Coille stormed, his pig squealing shrilly in accompaniment. "And if the hospitality of the king is gone from him, and if he's no room in this great house for one poor man and woman to be fed and lodged, then I will go and get them from some better man."

"No, you must understand," Mor said, moving toward them, his voice appealing. "I've no wish to be impolite to you. It's my *gessas*. The Sidhe put them upon me when I chose to be king: never to hunt the evil beasts of Cerna, never to let three Reds go before me to the house of Red, never to enter a lighted building after dark, and never to let a man and woman come in after me. It must be this! They meant those signs to warn me of this!"

"We'll go then," the man said, but he and the woman fixed hard, cold, glittering gazes on Mor. "But may nothing of your skin or of your flesh escape from the place you are in, except what the birds bring away in their claws."

And with that curse, he and the hag shuffled away into the dark, the squealing of the pig dying away after them.

Mor turned from the door to see Conal and the rest of his champions staring at him in shock.

"What does it mean, my King?" Conal Carna asked.

"The Sidhe must have foreseen. The *gessas* were meant to warn me. But I was so blinded, so caught up in what's happened . . . Now I've only this one bond left to keep."

"And if it's broken?" asked his champion.

"Then," Conaire answered heavily, "it's the end of my rule."

Chapter Forty-six

The Final Gessa

Meave peered through the late afternoon's gathering dusk at the battered little village. There was no evidence of life there.

"There are signs of a battle up above," came the voice of Fardia MacDaman.

She turned to see him descending the last rocky slope of the craggy hill that loomed above the town. "A battle?" she repeated. "With whom?"

"With *what* would be more like it." He shrugged. "There's little more about it I can say. There were three . . . somethings there, I think. But there's nothing at all left of them now. It's very strange."

"No stranger than this place," she said, looking about again. "It seems long abandoned. You're certain Mor's party came here?"

"I am that," he said with conviction. "And not very long ago. We're getting closer to them."

"But why come here?" she said musingly. "It's far off the track to Tara. And what would bring them to stop?"

She moved away from the chariot to one of the sad, sagging huts, peering through its door. The interior was nearly filled with swelling shadows and festoons of cobwebs.

She passed on to another of the forlorn bothies. It seemed to have been abandoned more recently. Some remnants of furniture were visible, and the coating of dust and mold less thick. She stepped inside, her eyes searching through the deepening pool of shadow. But there was no sign of recent inhabitants.

She turned to go, and found her eyes met by the black sockets of a fleshless skull.

She started in surprise, then recovered, moving forward. The skeleton sat huddled in a corner beside the remnant of a tiny fire. It was bundled in a tattered woman's gown and swathed in an assortment of filthy rags, as if every shred of cloth obtainable was used in a desperate search for warmth. Another, smaller pile of rags lay on the floor beside it, and a yet smaller bundle was clutched in the bony arms.

Morbidly curious, Meave bent down to the pile beside the skeleton, pulling at the clothes. She exposed the smaller skull of a young child who had died there, lying pressed against its mother for warmth. She gently plucked at the wrappings of the bundle the dead woman clasped to her breast, revealing the tiny skull of an infant, its bony thumb still held for a final comfort in its lipless mouth.

"Dead some years," commented Fardia from the doorway. He pointed to an empty bowl beside them. "Starved, I'd guess. She sat down with her babes to keep them from freezing in a final winter's cold, and they died together. It must be the little ones went first." He shook his head in sorrow. "Ah, I know the look of it, all right. I've seen enough of the like amongst my own people."

"But this is a herdsmen's village," she said. "And there's no sign of war about here. What happened to their herds? Where were their men?"

"You can guess at that as well as I. Unless it has to do with whatever happened up on that hill. Mor's party stopped. Three of them went up to fight, and from the signs, what they fought was very large and very savage."

"But why fight at all?" she wondered. "To help this village?" She looked at the three skeletons. "These people are long past it."

"Maybe there were others here," he suggested. "I found signs of some I don't think were of Mor's group. Come, I'll show you."

They went out. The last gray evening light was fading quickly, but he was able to show her some faint traces in the earth.

"See here. Three others, I'd say. Two went off still on foot toward the southeast. The third seems to have gone in the chariots. Maybe to show them the way?"

"Where did they go?"

"There," he said, pointing along a faint track that led away from the village.

"But Tara is due north. Why east?"

"Either their guide was confused," said Fardia, "or . . ."

"Or they were purposely misled," she finished grimly. "Yes, that's what I'm fearing too." She looked around at the desolate place. "This is some part of a trap for Conaire, I can feel it. Another part of a trap of awful size. And it's closing on him soon."

She looked up at the swiftly darkening sky. "The dread is building about me, Fardia. I can feel the weight of it. Almost see it as I can see that growing black."

Abruptly she turned to him, her voice taking on an urgent tone. "Fardia, we must go quickly now. You must drive us at your fastest speed. I've suddenly the most terrible certainty that it's with the night the real danger will come."

Down on the beach below the bruidhean, the pirates were sitting huddled by their boats as they had been through a long afternoon of inactivity. They had been allowed no fires that might give warning, and with the night had come a chilling breeze off the sea. Now they were bored and cold and grumbling among themselves about the delay.

None grumbled more than the hostile Maine Morgor. He paced the beach just below the slope, complaining loudly despite the warnings of those seated about him to keep still.

"How long must we wait?" said Morgor for the dozenth time.

"The old man said he'd come and join us before the attack," Fergel said impatiently. "How often have I told you that now?"

"We don't need him," Morgor sharply declared.

"You've said that before," Lomna Druth reminded him. "It wasn't true."

"Besides," said Ferogain, "Ingcel said Mor was to be alone. Instead he had others with him. We can't take chances until we know more."

"A few men," said Morgor, giving a dismissing shrug. "We have tenscore against them."

"Look here, Morgor, Ingcel's gone up to see what it's about," said the hulking Oisic. "Could you just give us all a treat and leave off till he comes back? I can't stand your whining anymore."

"Is that the truth, lout?" Morgor said angrily. "Maybe you'd like to try quieting me yourself. I'd—"

"Be quiet, you!" came the voice of Ingcel. He came into view from the dark, scrambling down the last stretch of bank and dropping onto the beach. "Fool! I can hear your arguing all the way to the top. You'll be warning everyone in the whole province that we're here!"

Morgor glowered but fell silent.

"Did you see the house, Ingcel?" asked Ferogain.

"I did. And the first thing I saw was a bright light shining out from it through the spokes of the wheels of chariots. Big war cars they were."

"Warriors," Fergel said unhappily.

"Aye, but only a score of them."

"Did you see inside?" Lomna Druth asked.

"I made my way to a window and peered in. There were men inside, but I saw no sign of high royalty or vast treasure. The old man promised us great spoils here in return for helping you."

"Ah, you've had treasure enough from *our* help already,"

said Morgor. "Many times what you and your lot would have plundered without us."

"Keep out of this now, Morgor," Fergel warned. And, to Ingcel: "You'll get your treasure from it, if the old man promised."

"I'll get nothing if this king of yours isn't even there," the captain pointed out.

"Describe them, then," said Fergel.

"Well, there was one quite grandly dressed. A young man, slim and tall, with pale gold hair like flax, fresh open looks, and no beard. The shield beside him had five gold circles on it."

"That's Cormac Conlingas, son of Conchobar," said Fergel. "Few finer fighters behind a shield there are in all Ireland."

"He's right," put in Ferogain. "And I swear by the gods my people swear by, he'd be making no small slaughter before the inn if we attack tonight."

"It's a pity for him that will be making that attack," added Lomna Druth gloomily, "if only for that one man. Maybe we're making our mistake in this."

"He's still only one," Morgor said in a disparaging tone. "Who else was there?"

"I saw another having a golden bush of hair the size of a reaping basket. He had a red shield speckled with rivets of white bronze between plates of gold."

"That man is known to all of Ireland," said Ferogain. "He's one of her greatest champions. Conal Carna, the man Conaire thinks most of in the world. That shield in his hands is called the Lamtapaid."

"A most deadly warrior he is," added Fergel. "There are six doorways into that inn, and if we attack, he'll be at every one of them."

"So, it is the king's champions there," said Morgor, eyes bright with bloodlust. "But what about Mor himself? Tell on, Ingcel."

"There was a big man with short brown hair and a red speckled cloak and a black shield with clasps of gold; and there was another, in his first grayness, with a sword of black iron hilt."

"The brown man is Muinremar, son of Geirgind," said Fergel. "The other is MacCecht, another faithful champion of the king."

"Was there one who looked a boy?" asked Morgor. "A fair-haired youth with pretty looks and the scarlet cloak of the Red Branch clan?"

"There was not," Ingcel replied.

"Then Sentanta's not with them?" Morgor said with disappointment. "Too bad. Next to the king, it was that whelp's head I most wanted to have."

"There was another very young in look, but rough in dress, with dark gold hair. He had no shield, and his cloak was a dark purple wool, not very fine. Some common warrior, I judged."

But Ferogain's eyes had filled with great sorrow at these words. "You are wrong," he said. "For it's Conaire Mor himself you saw there, in his modest dress."

"He seems a simple man," added Fergel, "and not serious. But when his anger is awakened, not all the champions in your Alban could win a battle against him."

"True," put in Lomna Druth in a gloomier tone yet. "Unless drink or the like fails him, that man alone could hold the inn till help gathered to him from the corners of Ireland."

"You exaggerate," said Morgor irritably, sweeping the sons of Donn Dessa with a disdainful gaze. "Are you all losing your nerve now? Or is it some late and misplaced welling of sweet brotherhood?"

"I've no fear of saying it," said Lomna Druth frankly. "If I had my way, the attack would not be made, but for the sake of that man alone, his strength and his goodness both."

"You truly are The Fool," Morgor said scornfully. "You are no good as a fighter. It's not love that moves you. It's clouds of weakness coming on you." He drew up, adding proudly, "But no man, whether old man or storyteller, will say that *I* drew back in this fight."

"Well enough for you to say, Morgor," The Fool returned bitterly. "You mean to be taking Conaire's head. But I know that it's my own head that will be tossed to and fro tonight."

"You will not hinder us," Morgor said threateningly, leaning down over the rotund man. "Or *I'll* take your bloated pig's head now!"

"Be careful there," Fergel warned.

"Why? Have you more courage than he?" Morgor challenged. "Will you dare to fight?"

Fergel exchanged glances with his brothers. Then he nodded. "Yes. I'll fight. We all will."

"And you, pirate?" Morgor asked, turning to Ingcel. "Have you less stomach for this than we?"

"I've said I'd fight," Ingcel sharply returned. "And if you're truly burning to begin this attack, then we'll wait no longer for that old man. Come with me. We'll go now to the beach and each man take a stone and make our cairn, to know how many are left after the fight. But," he added warningly to the exiles, "there had better be rich spoils."

The young warriors rose and started off, down toward the boats and the rest of the company, but Ingcel hesitated, seeing Ferogain still sitting staring up the hill. He leaned down over him, touching his shoulder.

"Ferogain?"

Ferogain looked up to him and he saw the glistening of tears in the boy's eyes.

"Lad? What is it?" he asked. "Are you afraid?"

"No," the boy replied honestly. "I feel no fear like Lomna Druth. My pain is in what I've been brought to do. I feel anger for Conaire, but I still feel love as well. The finest friend, the most honorable man." He shook his head violently, striking the sand with his clenched fist. "I hate what has happened. I hate what we have done. Ingcel, I tell you truly, I would be glad if he were not here tonight, for I'd wish he could escape the harm coming on him, and the shortening of his life, for he is a good man."

"Don't go," the pirate said simply.

"There's no help for me in that," the young warrior said despairingly, climbing to his feet. "It's too late now to back away. The others are going, so I must go as well." He started away, shoulders sagging in his despondency.

Ingcel looked after him. "The most awful trap is the one you've set for yourself, my poor lad," he said pityingly.

"At least Ireland had its peace for a little while," Conaire Mor said. "It wasn't all for nothing, was it, Conal?"

The two sat at a table of the inn, talking softly over their ale and plates of food. The other champions sat about them, most eating, some speaking in subdued tones, a few drowsing near the fire.

"You sound as if it's ended already," said the Ulster champion.

"I feel it," Conaire said, "as you feel the end of the living season with the first frosty breath of fall. Its chill is in my blood."

"Ah, it's foolishness you're speaking now," Conal said with a dismissing wave. "It's only the gloom of the autumn night and all these strange events that's put your mind onto such dark things. Your peace still lives, and so do you. There's nothing to keep you or it from going on."

"But, the *gessas* . . ." Mor began.

"You don't mean you hold to a belief in those?" Conal interrupted. "I know what the druids teach us about their power, but it's madness to let your life be ruled by them. *Chance* says who will live and who will die. And there's no fate so strong as a good sword in a skilled hand."

"So you've no belief in the Sidhe or in their power," said Conaire, and nodded toward the three Reds. "What about them?"

The three sat as before, not eating or drinking, staring motionless toward the fire. Cormac, sitting nearby, had been examining them curiously for some time. But now, at the king's words, he rose and went over to join Conal and Mor.

"Like graven things they are," he said. "Just sitting there, not even seeming to breathe. And a cold comes off them, like the chill breeze off the winter sea." He shivered at the thought. "Most unsettling they are."

"It's like having dead men among us," put in Muinremar, casting a hostile gaze toward them.

"I could chuck them out into the night," MacCecht volunteered. He had been indulging heavily in the ale and it had put him in an aggressive mood.

"No, don't bother them," said the one named Sencha. "If they are of the Others, you'd only be bringing trouble on us."

"I've heard a tale of such," said Da Derga as he set another flagon of ale before the king. "Three such were champions of the Sidhe, condemned for doing falsehood and deceit among their folk. It was to pay for their crime that they were to work out their own punishment three times."

"How?" asked Cormac.

"By taking part in some destruction, I think it was."

"Destruction?" said MacCecht in a loud, drink-slurred voice. "Well, there'll be no destruction here unless they mean to start a fight." He gave the three a belligerant look. "And then I'll see to them!"

"You will leave them alone," said Mor sharply, then looked around at the others. "You will all leave them alone."

They fell into a silence, the mood of gloom now a heavy pall that lay upon the whole company. It was Cormac who was first to speak again.

"I wish Sentanta were here," he remarked in a desultory way, as he had several times before.

"Yes, Cormac," said Mor. "I think I do as well." He shook his head, his voice taking on a morose, self-deprecating tone. "And it was myself that caused his leaving, as I was the cause for all that's happened. I drove Sentanta away as I drove my own wife to hide from me." He sighed, adding wistfully, "Ah, if I could have her beside me once again."

"You can't blame yourself for everything," said Conal.

"Can't I?" asked Mor. He looked away to stare into the flames of the central fire intently, as if images from his memory showed there. His tone became more musing. "You know, Fionualla told me that I'd made my choice when I left her at the River Life and started for Tara. But it wasn't then. It was when I came, naked and afoot, onto that road and turned north to Tara. I could have turned back home, but I went on, and brought the curse of this kingship upon myself. *I* did that. Not they or anyone else."

"But it was the Sidhe brought you to it," Sencha reasoned. "They chose you. They meant you to bring the peace."

"Did they? Or did I choose to go too far? In my hatred of bullying men like Conchobar and my need to make up for my own father's weakness, maybe I brought Ireland more harm than good. Oh yes, there's violence in her spirit, but there's beauty and strength and honor too. In seeking to end all the brutality, I've brought good men to abandon those other things as well: Sentanta, all those sons of our noblest chiefs, my own brothers," he turned his gaze back to Conal, "even you, my most faithful champion."

Conal opened his mouth to protest that, but then realized he could not. He had to acknowledge a great deal of truth in what his high-king had said. Instead he tried another argument: "But what about the prosperity your peace brought Ireland?"

"Did my peace bring it, or some power of the Sidhe?" Mor countered. "We can't know."

"No matter," Conal stubbornly replied. "It still worked."

"For how long, Conal? At what cost? You told me yourself

that the kind of peace I sought couldn't come quickly. I think you were right. I think maybe it will come one day, not with magic or laws or force, but with the minds of all changing slowly with the world. Still," he added regretfully, "I would like to have enjoyed it for just a little while, with my friends and my family and my wife beside me."

"Enough of this," Conal said impatiently. "I say again, it's only the night and the strangeness of our journey here that's put your mind to dwelling on such melancholy things." He put a hand to the king's shoulder, saying in a more hearty, cheering tone, "Throw off your black mood, Conaire. I know your feeling will change with a new sun. Tomorrow we'll go back to Tara. You'll find the answers there."

"Tara," Mor repeated. "The Beautiful Ridge. It's a fit name the old ones gave it, Cormac. To see it is always to feel a surge of new life." He smiled, and with an effort tried to rouse himself from his fatalistic thoughts. "Yes, maybe I am too melancholy, my friend." He stood up, calling out to the brughaid, "Da Derga, find us a harper. Bring a bard. Fill up this inn with music. We'll sing! Dance! Ah, what I would give for a chance at a good hurley game."

"And Sentanta to play against," Cormac said nostalgically. "I'd even put up with a bit of thumping from him."

There was a rattling from outside the inn. All knew the sounds as those of a chariot drawing up. The men turned toward the door, curious to see who traveled in the night.

Two figures moved from the darkness beyond the door at a run, charging across the threshold into the light. The man was a stranger to the company. But the woman they all knew.

"Meave!" said Conaire Mor, astonished.

"By Danu, the last *gessa*," breathed Conal.

"Conaire, there's a great danger!" Meave cried, moving forward. "You must be ready. You must get away from here. . . ."

Another figure appeared from the night. One of the bruidhean's grooms stumbled through the doorway, shouldering past Fardia, then pitching forward onto his face before the startled gathering.

The quivering shaft of a casting spear protruded from his back.

Chapter Forty-seven

First Assault

"There are fighting men all around the house!" cried Muinremar, peering out.

"There are fighting men here to meet them," Conal replied.

"They'll surely be wanted tonight," said Cormac, drawing his sword as he looked out a doorway toward the scores swarming up at them.

The others were taking up weapons as well.

"Quickly, cover all the doors," ordered Conaire Mor.

The warriors divided, several rushing to each of the six doors around the inn. The raiders had expected to catch the champions by surprise. But, thanks to Meave's warning, Mor and his comrades were armed and ready at the doorways as the first wave of the attackers came against the house.

The outlaws' first assault was a savage one, with all their force hurled upon the bruidhean from all sides, intending simply to sweep away their tiny opposition. But with surprise gone, they found themselves up against a most lethal defensive wall.

The champions, with only two to defend each doorway, needed no other help. Outlaws loomed up from the darkness into the wedges of light from the doorways, pressing forward. The defenders stood side by side in the openings, slashing them down as they came. They inflicted a massive slaughter on the attackers, piling up their bodies before the thresholds—as Ferogain had predicted—further hampering the efforts of their fellows to come at the doors.

The battle was furious and confused in the darkness. To the attackers, the champions who cut them down loomed large, black, and menacing against the bright light flaring out around them from within the bruidhean. To the defenders holding the doors against the onslaught from all sides, it seemed an enormous and most wild host that swept against them out of the night.

"Who are they?" cried Conal.

"Pirates," said Cormac, for in the melee the colorful garb of the young exiles made them look as one with the sea raiders, and no one recognized them.

Suddenly a wedge of attackers managed to poke through. One of the champions guarding a doorway was staggered as a hefty outlaw drove into him head-first, like a ram, slamming him back. The defensive barrier was breached. The attacker charged by him, followed by others who flooded into the room, threatening to engulf, to drown the champions.

Cormac Conlingas, leaping toward them from his own doorway, threw himself against them. As the leader of the intruders lifted up his sword in defense, the swifter Cormac swung out, taking the man's head from him in a single, hard, well-aimed blow. The body, for an instant still horribly alive, ran on another step before crashing down onto a table and rolling heavily to the floor.

Cormac paid no more attention to it as he helped his fellow champions at that door drive back the other outlaws. As the survivors were forced to retreat out the doorway, Conal grabbed up the head by its long hair and flung it out after them.

But someone outside caught it, tossing it back as if it were the playing ball in some grotesque hurley game. It sailed in, thudding to the floor, rolling across to fetch up by Cormac's feet. He looked down at it and found himself gazing into the round face and uprolled, staring eyes of Lomna Druth.

"The exiles!" Cormac said in shock. He scanned the faces of the attackers at the doors more carefully, now recognizing other of the young outlawed noblemen disguised beneath the pirates' garish trappings.

Conal, fighting nearby him, heard this. Quickly he moved to the young man's side, snatching up The Fool's head by its hair. "Quiet!" he warned, gesturing across the room toward where Conaire battled ferociously at another door. "See there? It's the most spirit I've seen in him since the exiling. He can't know of this now!" And he flung the head out through the door again, over the attackers, into the darkness.

"We can't stand here and hold these doors against them all the night," Mor now called boldly, moving into the center of the room. "We must go out against them!"

His face was bright with battle glow. There truly was a renewed energy in him, a spirit like his old exuberance newly fired by the battle's heat. His audacious decision was met by a cheer from the valiant champions.

"All right then. Two of you stay at each door. The rest with me!"

"You must take a shield, my King," said Conal, moving toward him. "Take my own."

"No," Mor said forcefully. "It was my choice to go without it. My sword will be enough."

So Mor, Conal, Cormac, Meave, Fardia, and ten others formed together. They drove out the doorway where the number of outlaws seemed smallest, taking its attackers by surprise. Mor was brilliant with only his sword, sweeping the blade two-handed about him to clear a way, leading his comrades into the press with a recklessness that made him all the more deadly.

They slashed savagely out through the press of men and then turned, working their way around the building toward the next door, where a larger mass of enemies swarmed.

This fierce company coming upon the outlaws from the side threw the closely packed attackers into panic. In the crowd and darkness, it seemed a much greater force that had come so suddenly upon them.

"More warriors!" came the alarmed cries. "A new host! Where did they come from?" And the panic spread rapidly through the whole company.

"There are more here than you said!" cried a pirate to Ingcel. "Another host comes against us. A hundred men!"

"We must pull back!" cried Morgor.

The young exiles around him made no argument, beginning to retreat, and he turned to join them.

But the hand of the pirate captain fell on his shoulder, jerking him back around. "Where is your bravery now?" Ingcel said scornfully to him.

"Look to your own brave men," Morgor spat back as he turned again to follow his comrades, for the pirates too were leaving the fight in droves, pelting away into the night. Seeing the inevitable, Ingcel joined them.

Mor and his company found themselves abruptly alone before the inn.

Mor stood gazing about with a triumphant look, his face still alight with the bright battle glow. "Sea-raiding scum," he said. "They'll not take Ireland's blood without payment of their own."

"A good fight, my King," said Conal, smiling. "I've seen no fighting spirit like that in you since your last hurley game."

"It *has* given me a sense of elation," Mor agreed with some surprise, looking down at the bloody sword in his hand. "Strange."

"Well, that lot of creatures won't have the iron to come back, I'll wager," said MacCecht.

"I'd not be wagering on it yet," said Conal cautiously. "I think we'd best get inside and keep up our watch."

"After the slaughter we did on them?" said Mor, looking around at the piled dead. "Why . . ."

But he stopped, his gaze fixed on a fallen man. He went to him, rolled him back, his face clearly revealed in the light flooding from the inn.

"But, I know this boy," he said.

His exuberant look was instantly replaced by one of consternation. He began to search about among the other fallen as Cormac and Conal exchanged looks.

"And here," Mor announced, bending over another body. "Son of a chieftain of Meath." He moved on, searching with a greater urgency.

"My King, no!" Conal said quickly, moving after him. "You're mistaken. They only seem . . ."

But Mor had stopped again, staring down in a stricken way at a severed head that lay before him. Conal stopped too, knowing it was too late.

Mor crouched, lifting the head. The poor, battered visage of The Fool, blood-streaked, its long hair matted across it, stared back.

"Lomna Druth," he said. He pulled the stray hair away from the face with a great gentleness, looking into the dead eyes. His face was drawn in sorrow. "My poor Fool. Is this what it's finally come to then?"

He sat staring into the face as Conal moved up beside him, putting a hand atop his shoulder comfortingly. "I'm sorry, my King," he said.

"So it is the exiles in this," Mor said heavily. "They've come back to have revenge on me."

"They are outlaws, Conaire," the champion harshly replied. "They've become savage like the pirates they've brought here with them."

"You knew, didn't you?" Mor asked, looking up at him.

"I did," Conal admitted, "but I didn't want you to. I feared that you would react this way."

"How else should I react?"

"They are outlaws, Conaire!"

"They are my brothers!" Mor replied in despair. "They were my friends! Now I am killing them."

"You've no more choice in that," Conal replied. "They mean to kill you. And they won't stop, now that they've come here. They'll have no better chance at revenge than this."

"And would that matter?" said Mor. "Maybe that's only as it was meant to be . . . as I caused it to be."

He stood, still clutching The Fool's head, and walked slowly, wearily back into the inn.

"What's wrong with him?" asked Cormac, coming up beside Conal to look after the king.

"Mortality," the champion answered simply.

The chariots carrying the three Ulstermen and the high-king's wife sped through the night.

They followed the strange bird with no difficulty, for its body glowed silver under the light of a near-full moon.

It flew on always to the south, pausing to swoop back when the ground slowed those it led. But for the most part it seemed to choose the best route for the chariots, and they moved swiftly.

But then another form appeared suddenly from the darkness. It was another bird—massive, sleek, shining blue-black, with a great span of wings—that swooped upon theirs from above with no warning. Its claws raked across the white bird's back. The white bird cried out, stricken, then banked and wheeled away. The other bird pursued until both were lost in the night.

"A hawk?" said Sentanta.

"A raven, I think," said Cathbad darkly.

"What, so huge?"

The druid gave him a meaningful look but made no reply.

"Now what can we do?" Fionualla asked.

"We've not much choice but to just keep on as we were pointed," the druid replied. "The sea's not far ahead. I can smell it."

"And I smell something else," Sentanta added. "Death."

The head of Lomna Druth sat upon the stones of the inn's hearth.

Conaire Mor sat dejectedly upon a bench nearby, head propped on his hands, staring fixedly into the dead eyes.

"Conaire, you can't simply give up now," Conal pleaded urgently. He and Meave sat near their friend, both trying desperately to draw the king from this new, intense, paralyzing despair.

"This is what the *gessas* were meant to warn me of," Conaire bleakly replied. "They were true foretellings, but I paid no heed to them. Now it's the end."

"Even if the Sidhe did foresee this," Conal grudgingly conceded, "that doesn't mean you must accept it, just sit there and wait to die."

Mor looked up at the champion. His face sagged with sorrow and defeat. "I'm tired, Conal," he said slowly, heavily. "I don't want to fight. I just want a quick end."

"A quick end is it?" Conal repeated, looking searchingly into the king's eyes, then nodding with a sudden understanding. "But that's what you've wanted all along, isn't it? Ever since we left Tara. It isn't this that's beaten you. You'd given up long before. Your rule was a curse, a bond you couldn't break with honor, but in one way: by death."

"No!" Mor protested. "I never meant to die. I went out to keep the peace. To help all those who trusted me . . ."

"You say so. But you rode out without a shield or spears. You risked yourself in Tuath Mumain, fighting the beasts of Cerna, and again here tonight. You left Tara meaning never to return there."

Mor looked at him in astonishment. Could what he said be true? He had told himself that he had to keep the bond, not be the failure that his father had been. But had some part of him sought death as the only escape from a life that had become intolerable?

"Conaire, listen to Conal," Meave now said earnestly, putting a hand to his shoulder, fixing her intense, blue-gray gaze on his. "Think of that boar hunt we went on together a lifetime ago. I know what's in you now, just as you knew what was in me that day. It was you telling me then that the spirit of life was still in me. And it's still in you as well. The battle fire I saw lighted in your eyes by the fight here proved that to me."

"No spirit of life, no battle fire can help me," he dismally returned. "My fate's come upon me."

"Fate?" she said. "And just what does that mean? I said then that death comes when it comes, and we've only to accept.

But I was wrong, Conaire. I was wrong! You can never cease to fight! It's only the fighting that gives a value to this mortal world. Even if we lose, we can make the choice to fight! And no powers, no fates, no gods can take that choice from us."

Fardia now came into the inn from the darkness. He carried two shields with him as he crossed the floor to where the high-king and his companions sat.

"Where have you been?" asked Conal.

"I've been out seeing what our attackers are about," he said offhandedly.

"A dangerous mission that is, my lad," the champion said disapprovingly.

"Not for Fardia," Meave told him with a little smile.

"They number some twelvescore yet," the Firbolg reported. "They've built a ring of fires about the inn, so that none can slip by them. They're embroiled in some great argument now, but I couldn't hear about what. A dark, weasely one seemed to be leading it."

"Morgor," Conal grated. "There's one that should have been put to death long since."

"We can't let them win," said Meave, "or we'll have the likes of that brutal creature ruling Ireland."

"My King," Fardia said solemnly to a still-brooding Mor, "I wanted to say to you that I feel a great honor in being here with you. I do not say that easily. I never thought to so freely offer my service to any Milesian, but I've seen few warriors so skilled in the fighting as yourself."

Mor looked up to the stalwart young warrior. He gave a short, rueful laugh. "I thank you for your loyalty, chieftain. But I wonder if you know what irony I feel at your seeing me as a warrior."

"There are many lesser things to be," Fardia said with gravity, "but for a warrior of honor, there are few greater."

These words from the proud young Firbolg seemed to rouse the king more than the arguments of Conal and Meave. "It may be you are right," he replied with more conviction in his tone.

"I found another good shield among the dead," Fardia said, holding up a stout, brass-bound one. He held out a simple but sturdy iron-bound one in his other hand. "I would feel most honored if you would use my own."

A sudden commotion arose outside the bruidhean.

"What is it?" Conal cried.

"They're attacking again!" a champion at the doors called back. "And they have torches! They mean to fire the inn!"

Mor took the shield from Fardia, standing up. His expression was now one of determination.

"All right, my friends," he called to the others, "If they mean to fire the inn, we will stop them!"

Chapter Forty-eight

The Last Spell

"I will not send my men in attacks on the inn again. It's too costly," Ingcel told Morgor with force.

The two were arguing by one of the watch fires surrounding the inn. It was some while later, another assault just ended. There was clear evidence of its dismal result in the battered look of the pirates and exiles seated about the fire with them, binding their wounds.

"They can't keep up that defense through all the night," countered Morgor.

"And why do you say that?" the captain asked. "They don't seem to have lost any vigor yet. I've had near a quarter of my men killed or wounded. So have you. We've not done more than wound a few of them. I've never come against fighting men so skilled."

"We told you," said Fergel, "they are the finest in all Ireland."

"Yes," added Ferogain glumly. "And until Conaire himself is dead, all the fighting men in Ireland and Alban won't be taking that house."

"You vowed to help us," Morgor reminded Ingcel.

"Not to be slaughtered," Ingcel sharply replied. "No more attacks."

"You fools!" came a voice, and they turned to see the old warrior coming out of the night. Behind him moved the thin, hooded figure of his driver. "What are you about?"

"So you finally came," the captain said. "We are so pleased that you're joining us after we've been so well bloodied."

"I was on business urgent to our success," he returned, glaring at the man. "And why did you go ahead with your attack when I told you to wait?"

"Mor had only a score of men with him," said Ingcel. "Morgor convinced us it would be easy. It has been far from that."

"Morgor," the old warrior growled, shooting that warrior a hard look. "Of course. Still trying to lead. Still failing."

"You failed us too, old man," said Ingcel. "I see no great treasure here, as you promised."

"You'll have it, once the king is dead."

"Will I?" the captain said skeptically. "Well, I won't lose any more men for it. It can't be great enough to make us all willing to die for it. We've already done too much."

"And just what have you done?" the old warrior asked.

"After our first assault met little success, we tried to burn the house," said Morgor. "But this too failed." He eyed the men around him scornfully. "The bravery of our fighting men wasn't up to it. Mor's champions came out, drove off our attack, doused the few fires we'd managed to begin. And, see there?" He pointed to the inn. "Now they're soaking down the thatch. They must have used nearly all the water in the place by now."

The warrior stepped away from the glare of the fire and peered up toward the bruidhean. He could see the dark figures of men upon its roof, hauling up the massive barrels of the inn's water stores through the smoke hole and pouring them out over the roof, the sparkling water sluicing down through the rows of thatch.

"I see," he said thoughtfully. Then a cunning light came into his eye. He turned to the pirate captain. "Tell me, Ingcel, will you stay in this if you don't have to attack again?"

"What do you mean?"

"I mean that you would only have to wait. I have a way to make them come out to you."

Ingcel considered, then nodded. "If you have such, we will wait. But only until daylight."

"Long enough," the dark man said, then turned to the hooded being with him.

"Go to the others," he commanded. "Take them all out to . . ." he looked around, then pointed toward the ridge between the bruidhean and the sea, "to that place there. Find the highest point. Build a great fire and prepare for me."

As the being scuttled away into the night, Morgor looked quizzically at the man. "Just what are you planning to do now?"

"Playing a trick, boy," the warrior answered. "That's all. Just playing a trick. I've no magic to kill Mor, but I can make him and his champions feel enough suffering to drive them from that place." He looked toward the inn, smiling grimly. "And then it's short that Mor's time will surely be."

The old warrior quickly joined the gathering of Calatin's weird sons.

They had already clustered on the ridge above the cove where the pirates had landed. Upon the weather-blunted tip of a spine of rock that thrust up starkly from the ridge, they had already built a fire.

"I was a fool to think men like those could handle this themselves," he complained as he strode through his sons to the rock. "I had hoped to avoid using my powers here. To do so means to risk revealing myself and my part in this. Now I've no other choice. But at least, this way, my risk is small."

He paused at the base of the rock, turning to admonish the sons, "Now all of you be watchful. Close your ring here and raise the spell, but keep some gazes turned toward that inn. Make certain no one comes too close."

The dark-cloaked man then clambered up the rock to stand beside the blaze.

One of the sons who waited there handed him the druid's rod, its black, polished length and silver tip glowing red in the firelight. Then the spindly being climbed down to join the other sons encircling the rock's base.

The dark man stared into the tongues of flame that licked high into the night. He lifted his arms, raising the stick in both hands before him. An aura of white light appeared around him, enveloping him with its translucent glow.

Then the glow dropped away from around him. The black cloak about his shoulders fell away as well, and with it the likeness of the old warrior—all shimmering down together to crumple upon the ground like a serpent's shed skin, then fading away.

The coarse, swarthy visage of Calatin was revealed, clad in his iridescent striped robe of druidry.

Now he gestured with his rod toward the ring of sons below. Once more their eerie, wailing chant lifted, filling the night.

His chest sat beside the fire, already opened. He crouched

before it, selecting his potions and powders carefully. He mixed them gently in a small crystal bowl, then stood and sprinkled the contents across the fire.

It blazed up yet higher, the flames crackling and scintillating now with streaks of blue and white and green among the reds.

"I use the elements of the earth to call upon their powers," he said. "I draw from the most arid places the spirits of their heat, their dryness. I charge them to put on those in the inn the sense of intense thirst. Enwrap that place below in your entrancing spell, invade it with your heat, your cloying smell, bring on those trapped within a sensation so real that they will feel the moisture being sucked from them, their blood turning to sand. But leave before their minds the visions of the relief they cannot have."

He pointed the silver-shod tip of the rod toward the brui-dhean, commanding, "Rise now, from the belly of the earth, my spell, and form about the inn!"

There began a rumbling, low at first, and faint, but quickly increasing in its intensity until the whole land about the bruidhean seemed to be shuddering. Within the building, the men heard and felt it, and looked at one another wonderingly.

"Thunder?" asked Cormac.

"The air is clear," said Conal, peering through a doorway up to the night sky.

Outside the inn, the surrounding band of outlaws also wondered at the strange vibration.

"What's happening?" asked Morgor.

"Look there!" said Ferogain, pointing toward the inn.

Around the building, the ground had begun to glow faintly with a greenish yellow light. As the amazed outlaws stared on, it slowly lifted, like another, curved wall rising around the wall of the inn. It was not a solid barrier, however, but a thin screen of light, so diaphanous that it only slightly blurred the outlines of the inn, as would a heat haze rising from a sun-baked strand. It also radiated a faint warmth into the night.

It rose swiftly, steadily, curving in from all sides as it lifted above the roof peak, forming into a dome there as its oculus closed above, sealing the bruidhean totally within.

The men inside were unaware of it. To them, looking out, the night seemed as before; the faint distortion, so close before their eyes, was invisible against the black.

But they soon became aware of something else.

"What is that strange odor?" said Muinremar, sniffing the air. "Like . . . burning! Like hot iron, or baking clay . . ."

"Have they set us ablaze again?" asked Cormac.

"They can't have," said Fardia. "None of them has come near the inn since our last fight, and it's well soaked now."

"It is a dry smell," said MacCecht. "I can think of nothing suddenly but parched fields of rock and sand beneath the summer's blazing sun. It makes me dry. Bruighaid," he called to Da Derga, "bring me water!"

"There is little more than a cupful left for each of us," the rotund host told him. "We've poured the rest of it on the thatch."

"A cupful then," the champion ordered impatiently. "Quickly."

And after him, others began to demand it also, until Mor, becoming aware of the strangeness of this sudden, intense thirst, ordered it to stop.

"You can't drink all we have left now," he said. "We have to make it last at least through the night. Have no more than half a cup each, if you must have any."

Many of the champions eagerly accepted this offer, gulping down the small ration of water as the bruighaid and his stewards doled it sparingly out. But as MacCecht drank, he grimaced.

"That taste of water does nothing to help," he grumbled. "It makes my thirst worse. Like dry dust clogging my mouth it is now."

"The air is too warm," the one called Sencha complained. "Bruighaid, the fire is stoked too high!"

"The fire is almost burned out, my champion," Da Derga replied. "See for yourself."

Still, the faint but irritating warmth continued, and with it the peculiar burning odor. For the trapped men, the sense of parched mouths, dry lips, and feverish bodies grew stronger constantly. And in their minds appeared visions of cooling rains, of clear pools, tormenting by their unobtainability, like beckoning mirages flickering on hot desert sands. Even the stoutest of the warriors was soon affected, many clamoring for more water, though all knew how little there was left.

"There is something unnatural in this thirst," said Mor. "It's surely some enchantment put on us."

"A deadly one then," said MacCecht, "meant to suck us dry and leave us crumbling bones."

"No spell could have such power," Mor argued in return. "If it did, these outlaws would have seen us dead long since."

"But I can feel my throat closing from the thirst," MacCecht said, not convinced. "I *know* my flesh is withering."

"We are all dying," gasped out another. "We must do something."

"There is no power can more quickly turn the most stalwart fighting man to a crying babe than thirst or hunger," Fardia murmured to Meave. "I've seen it often enough."

"But we dare not try to break out of here before daylight," Conal reasoned to the men. "So long as we stay here, we can withstand attacks. But out there, in the darkness, we'd likely be overwhelmed."

"We'll all be dead by morning for certain if we stay here without relief," MacCecht returned. "Perhaps one man . . ." he looked pointedly at Fardia, "one *clever* man might sneak out, find a way through their circle, fetch more water back."

Meave moved to Mor, leaning close to speak in a confidential tone. "Conaire, this talk of death is bringing more weakness on them than the thirst. Something could be done to give them hope, and it would quiet your most strident complainer as well, if you understand my meaning."

"I do, Meave," he said gravely, then looked back to his graying champion. "Very well, MacCecht, I will agree to what you say. It was your notion, and you seem to have the greatest need. So you will go."

"Me, my King?" MacCecht said in surprise. He turned to Fardia. "But, I thought he might . . ."

"I feel no thirst that I can't tolerate," the young Firbolg told him stoically. "I mean to stay with the king and see to his protecting."

"But it's for myself to do that too," said MacCecht. He looked to the bruighaid and his huddled men. "Why not send the stewards?"

"Why must untrained men risk themselves in this for us?" Mor asked. "No, you go."

"What about others?" the champion said. He looked around him hopefully. "There must be one willing to go?"

"So now your need for water is suddenly not so great?" said Conal harshly. "Or is it that your fear outweighs your thirst? You were chosen, MacCecht. You must go, and leave the inn's defense to us."

This suggestion of cowardice wounded the older man. He drew proudly erect, fixing Conal with a fierce glare. "I will go then," he said, "if I must battle through a thousand to fetch water here!" He looked at Da Derga. "Bruighaid, get me something to carry it in."

The host quickly fetched two large water bags of stitched hide and gave the champion directions to the nearest well.

MacCecht slung the empty bags across one shoulder. Without another word, only pausing to shoot one more glowering look at Conal, he slipped out into the night.

The nebulous wall of light was no hindrance, and he passed through without even being aware of it. Then he was away into the night.

"Will he make it out?" Cormac asked the Firbolg chieftain.

"A single man, taking them by surprise?" Fardia replied. "He should be through their ring before they even know. But I'll tell you another thing."

"Something I likely won't find cheering, is it?" Cormac guessed.

"If he does break through," Fardia said grimly, "he's the last man from this inn who'll do it so easily."

The chariots carrying Laeg, Sentanta, and their passengers rolled over a final inland swell of hills and the bruidhean of Da Derga came into view ahead.

The two drivers pulled up their chariots at once, and they all gazed down upon the scene.

"What is that faint shimmering that arches over the inn?" asked Sentanta.

"I'm not sure," said Cathbad, staring intently at it. "Nothing to our good, though. Of that I am certain."

"And look at that ring of fires about the inn's yard, too," the boy warrior added. "There are many men moving there." He jumped from the car. "Wait here. I'll go closer and see."

"Please, be very careful," Fionualla warned.

"I mean to," he answered, drawing his sword.

They waited tensely, but his circuit of the inn was swift, and he returned in a short time.

"There are men all about the inn," he reported. "Twenty dozens I'd guess, all watching the inn most warily, as if something were about to happen. Strangers to Ireland they look to be from their dress. But I also saw the chariots of Tara's champions drawn up in the inn's yard."

"Then Mor is inside there," Cathbad said with certainty. "It is the place that I foresaw."

"I must join them," said Sentanta.

"No," the druid said. "That would only mean your death to no good end. There are too many, and I'm certain that it's some kind of spell that lies around the inn. It must be broken."

"I could feel a faint warmth from it when I got closer," the boy told him. "It seemed to bring a dryness to my throat."

"I feared as much," Cathbad said, shaking his head. "A spell to bring thirst upon them. I've heard of such."

"Thirst?" said Fionualla in alarm. "Can it kill them?"

"It would take vast powers for that. Druid magic is mostly illusion, my Queen, playing on the deepest beliefs and fears of men. Little of it can do a man real harm, and then only when the victim is within the sorcerer's sight. But it surely can be used to trick a man into great jeopardy. If this spell is as I've heard, it could make them certain they are so sorely parched that they are dying. So real is the effect that it could bring a madness on them."

"What is its source?" asked Fionualla.

"Not from that lot," said Sentanta, pointing at the ring of outlaws. "I saw nothing but fighting men. No signs of any sorcery."

"Maybe from there," said Laeg, pointing beyond the inn. "I saw the glimmer of another fire, farther away."

"Let's look closer at it," said the druid.

They drove on around the inn, keeping well away from it. Once able to see past the interfering glow of the many fires there, the large cone of light upon the point of rock became clearly visible. They could see the bright-robed figure beside it and the sparkling streamers of varicolored flame shooting up into the night.

"A druid fire," said Cathbad. "Surely it is there that our dark sorcerer is raising his spell."

"There are other figures moving below him, circling that crag's base," Laeg pointed out.

"Yes," said Fionualla. "He had a company of others with him. Strange, withered beings they looked, but still, the one I met was very strong." She rubbed at the bruises on her wrist in remembrance.

"I'll stop him," Sentanta said determinedly. "He has no walls of iron protecting him this time."

"He's still far too dangerous," Cathbad warned. "You heard the queen: he has too many with him. And remember, he also has great powers."

"But we must do something," Fionualla said urgently. "My husband could be dying as we're talking here!"

"I must try to counter the spell," said Calatin. "I think I have some magic that will work."

He looked around, then led them to the closest high point, a rugged knoll. A few struggling pines grew there from the rocky ground, and they quickly gathered enough dry wood for his fire.

Like his sinister counterpart, Cathbad selected vials and jars from his invaluable chest. Into a bowl of bronze he measured and poured from them, then gently mixed, but with his hands, forming them into not a powder but an elastic mass, which he painstakingly molded into a single ball.

Laeg and Sentanta had by this time kindled his fire, stoking it to hearty, crackling life. Cathbad sat down cross-legged before it. He lifted his head to the sky, murmuring softly, then cast the ball into the flames.

There was a *whoosh* and a puff of smoke rolled upward into the night.

"Little enough can come of so little as that!" the skeptical Laeg muttered to his young master.

But he was wrong. In moments, the simple charm was causing a most dramatic effect. Far out on the sea's rim, a bank of clouds suddenly appeared, rolling in toward them, the smooth, rounded billows of its vanguard struck to lustrous silver by the moon; and a deep rumbling, as of a vast *tiompan*, reverberated across between sea and sky to them.

"It may be I can't call up beasts of the air," the druid shot toward Laeg with a touch of indignation, "nor any monstrous torturing spells of thirst. But my skills *are* enough to call up a simple storm."

He stared into the fire then, drawing himself up rigidly, and began chanting, tolling out a complex litany of sacred names that sounded only mumbled gibberish to the listening three. But the powers this incantation invoked clearly were responding helpfully, for the clouds were surging toward them with astonishing speed, soon drawing like a black curtain across the moon, abruptly shutting off its light.

Chapter Forty-nine

Duel

Calatin, concentrating on his own fire and spell, was drawn by the sudden change to finally notice what was happening. He looked around toward the coming storm with astonishment.

"What is this?" he said. "This is some magical doing."

He turned his gaze back to scan the countryside about, now spotting the other, smaller fire winking on the knoll nearly opposite the inn.

"Quickly," he shouted to the sons below, "one of you go over to that fire!" He pointed. "See what it is."

As one of them darted away, the swiftly advancing clouds drew overhead, the rumblings of thunder and flickers of lightning within their dark folds rapidly increasing in intensity.

"This is surely some druid's work," he muttered darkly. "What is it for?"

As if in answer, there was a stronger crash of thunder from just above. The clouds bunched, slowing to a stop like a vast, stampeding cattle herd coming suddenly against an obstruction. They began instead to turn and move in a circle, forming a vortex right above the inn, each coil of its spinning whorl sharply, separately illuminated by constant explosions of lightning within the mass.

The center of this vast eddy of clouds dropped down toward the inn, as if it meant to suck the building up into the maw of the whirlwind. Instead, it stopped its descent close above the dome of light. Then, from its swollen clouds a hard rain began to fall, its force localized upon the area above the inn, its droplets spattering against the curved, shimmering surface.

The meeting of the forces created by the two spells was a volatile one, the rain vaporizing as it touched the dome, fluttering back upward in ragged curtains of white steam. The rain threw the dome's upper curve into more distinct relief, and its arch grew as the rain continued, creeping farther down the dome's steeply sloping sides as each moment passed.

"Amazing, Cathbad," Sentanta told the ard-druid, looking down on the inn.

The druid paused in his chant. "If I can sustain this spell," he explained, "I can break the other spell down, wash it away."

He concentrated again, taking up the chant in a now continuous, running undertone, his gaze fixed on the smoking fire.

On the opposite height, Calatin's son was just returning to the crag. "It is the druid Cathbad at that fire," he called up to his father.

"He survived, then?" Calatin said in surprise, then rapped out brutally, "Well, I can afford no interference from him now. Take some others and kill him!"

"But he has that boy warrior with him," was the son's reply. "It might be . . . difficult."

"What? Ah, the Morrigan curse it!" Calatin swore angrily. "Now I'll *have* to use my powers. Like it or not, I'll have my chance to test myself against him after all."

He looked up at the whirling clouds, seeing the constant, intense flares of lightning within the coils of black.

"At least he's provided me with a means to strike at him."

He lifted up his rod, pointing the silver tip toward the center of the cloud whirlpool. "Come to me, you powers wasted in the storm!" he called.

Like a hound obediently answering its master's call, a line of the lightning slanted down from the clouds toward him. It seemed as if the jagged spear of energy would strike the man. Instead it struck the rod's tip and rolled into a single ball there, its glow rising to near-blinding intensity.

He lowered the rod, jabbing out toward the other hill with the charged tip. "Go and destroy!" he commanded, and the pooled energy shot away again in a stream of blue-white light.

It came so swiftly that Cathbad and his friends had no warning of the attack. The projectile of light exploded just below their knoll, shattering into sapphire tendrils that drew a crackling web of electricity across the little hill. Sentanta, Laeg, and Fionualla flinched back from it, feeling only a faint tingling from its energy. But Cathbad, fully enmeshed by it, was knocked backward, and lay for an instant stunned.

The magical lights flickered, then quickly died away. Sentanta and the others moved toward him, but he pushed himself up, holding out a staying hand, calling emphatically, "No! Keep away!"

For he'd seen another jet of light already shooting toward him from Calatin's fire.

This time Cathbad was prepared for it, stiffening himself to withstand the impact.

Once more the light burst just before the knoll, the fingers of blue-white rippling across him again, then fading. But, though Cathbad managed to remain upright through it, afterward he sagged, panting, clearly drained by the effort.

"We must help you!" cried Fionualla.

"No!" he shouted back. "There's nothing you can do. That sorcerer is expending great powers to strike at me and keep up his other spell. He can't continue to do both for long—I hope. I must stay here, hold out against him, and keep that rain upon his arch of light!"

"Look out!" cried Sentanta.

Another bolt of light shot from the night, this time bursting just before the druid's fire. The network of energy was more concentrated this time, spreading only over the knoll's top, as if Calatin was finding his opponent's exact range. The more intense power played over Cathbad, its shock jarring him back again. Then it fluttered out.

He lay still a moment, breathing in great ragged gasps. Then he shuddered and forced himself back up, doggedly concentrating on the fire again, taking up his chant. But the attack of Calatin had had its effect. The rainfall upon the dome was already lessening.

About the inn, the outlaws watched the strange storm and the spectacular play of lights on the hills around them with growing disquiet.

"Just what is going on about us?" Ingcel asked. "It's as if the gods themselves have all come here to war."

"It must be some part of the old man's trickery," Fergel replied.

"I don't like it," the captain admitted.

"You don't have to," Morgor brusquely told him, "if it works."

Within the bruidhean, the trapped company was also aware of the rumbling and the flickers of lightning, but Cathbad's rain had given them no relief.

The spell of thirst had brought them near the height of suffering now. The hapless patrons and stewards of the inn had already succumbed to it. Unlike the warriors, they had tried, futilely, to alleviate the spell's effect with vast quantities of ale. Now they lay unconscious beneath the tables or sat hunched, helpless, moaning piteously.

The champions of Mor all still remained upon their feet, but were holding back the madness only by a great effort of will, and that will was near to breaking.

Another ominous roll of thunder was heard. Cormac listened, hearing the faint hiss of the rain being boiled away so close over their heads.

"I'm certain I hear rain!" he said.

"It's the thirst making you think so," Sencha replied, looking out a door. "There's not a drop of it falling about this inn!"

"Well, if something doesn't bring us relief soon," another said, "it'll be our end."

"MacCecht will not return!" one of the champions suddenly cried out in panic. "I must have water!"

The thirst had seized his mind completely, driving him the last step into madness. Blind to all else, he bolted from the inn, rushing out into the deadly night.

The breakdown of his control was all that was needed to plunge others into the same depths of insanity. With wild shrieks of agony, two more champions followed him in his desperate flight.

Conal Carna looked around, seeing the light of final desperation now kindled in yet other eyes. A man nearby began a low, animal whimpering and started toward a door, but Conal caught him by a shoulder, pulling him back.

"Wait!" Conal said. "You can't go out. Your only chance lies here!"

Consumed by his torturing thirst, the man neither saw nor heard. He tore away from Conal's grip and plunged through the doorway.

The panic had become infectious now, spreading rapidly to others. Several more started moving toward the doors at once.

"Stop!" Conal cried, moving to intercept a pair of them. "You are abandoning your king! Cowards! Traitors!"

The men ignored him, one pushing by. He lifted his sword to block the other. The man, not to be deterred by anything in his overwhelming need, struck out. Conal parried, forcing the man back, slamming him against a table in rage, raising his blade to strike. . . .

"No, Conal!" Mor said.

The champion stayed his hand, looking at Mor in surprise.

The other used his hesitation as a chance to slip by and run for a doorway.

"But, my King . . ." Conal said in frustration as the man escaped into the night.

"You can't stop them," said Mor. "They are possessed. Let them go out. Maybe they will survive."

"They'll die!" Conal returned angrily. "And they'll condemn us with them!"

Outside, Morgor saw the first champion break from the inn and rush headlong toward them, followed quickly by two others.

"Look!" he cried in elation. "The old man did it! Come on! Come on! We'll kill them now!"

On the hill above, Sentanta also saw the first champions come out of the bruidhean.

"There are warriors trying to leave the inn!" he called to his companions.

Fionualla and Laeg watched with him as the outlaw host swarmed up to meet first the lone man and then the pair of warriors who charged down into them. They looked on with expressions of growing disbelief and shock as the three champions were surrounded, overwhelmed, savagely cut down.

"Oh, no!" cried Fionualla, turning away in horror.

Two more champions came out. Like those before, they charged without hesitation into the waiting horde.

"They're rushing to their deaths," said Sentanta in dismay. "Why?"

"The spell!" Fionualla guessed. "It must be reaching them."

Behind them, another bolt of the blue-white energy struck Cathbad, bringing their attention back to him.

The stream of power was more sustained this time, and much closer. He stood up against it valiantly, but his resistance was all but drained by the effort. When the light faded, he fell back, white, trembling, lungs laboring. The rain upon the dome lessened still further, almost stopping now.

Below, three more champions burst from the inn, like bulls goaded to blind rage, stampeding out into the waiting circle of enemies.

"I can't stay here!" Sentanta said in agony. "I've got to help."

Before the others could protest, he ran to his car, grabbed up his shield, and started at a run down toward the inn.

More of the champions were bursting from the inn doors now, in ones, twos, threes, made irrational by the thirst, driven to desperate, headlong flight into an almost certain death to escape the torment. Some did manage to cut through—their need for drink giving them a berserker's savagery that nothing could stop—fleeing away into the night. But more died.

Within the bruidhean, Mor's company was swiftly reduced to Conal, Cormac, Meave, Fardia, and Muinremar.

"There are not enough of us to hold the doors," said Conal, looking around at those left.

"Then there is no choice," said Mor. "You must try to break out too, my friends, while they are still spread out about the inn. There is still some chance if you go quickly."

"And you?" asked Meave.

"I will stay and wait to give an audience to them here," he told her with a grim smile, hefting his sword.

"You'll just wait here to die?" Conal said, the implication clear.

"I'm not seeking a quick end now," Mor assured him. "Believe me, I don't even wish it anymore. But I am the king. If I abandon my honor, they truly have defeated me. You know it's what I must do."

"Then I must do it too, Conaire," Meave said.

"No," he told her with force. "Not you."

"But you don't understand," she said urgently. "I owe this to you. I might have warned you. . . ."

He held up a staying hand. "Enough have suffered in this for the foolish judgments they've made," he told her. "Say nothing more of it. That you are here now speaks well enough for you."

"That it does not," she stubbornly replied. "I will not leave. I have to do this for myself as well as for you."

"Think of Ireland instead," he reasoned. "You have no other choice. You said it yourself: if we all die here, it'll be men like Morgor and Conchobar holding sway in Ireland."

"I promised I would never run from men like them again," she told him fiercely. "We will stop them, Conaire, I can feel that. And we will face them here, together!"

He saw her adamant expression and the keen glint in her blue-gray eyes. He sighed and looked to the young warrior with her.

"Fardia, can you say nothing to help me convince your queen that she must save herself?"

"I would say nothing to turn another warrior from the fight," he answered, "and I don't mean to do so myself." He drew himself up proudly. "No Firbolg has ever run before an enemy. And I'll be bringing no disgrace upon my people now."

"I see," said Mor resignedly. He turned to Conal.

"You know my answer already, Conaire," that stolid warrior told him.

Mor smiled and put a hand to the man's shoulder. "Of course, my most loyal champion. I wasn't even thinking to ask you."

He looked at Cormac and Muinremar. "But you two, you must go. No arguments. It's my command now."

A gasping Muinremar, clearly nearing the end of his resistance to the spell, made no argument. But an uncertain Cormac looked to the older Ulster champion and asked, "Conal, what should I do?"

"There's no point to your dying here," he answered. "You're young. You've done all that you could. And you've proven you've a nobility in your blood your father will never have or understand. Go now, while there's still time!"

Reluctantly, Cormac turned and, with the other warrior, went out into the night.

"We'd best prepare," Conal said briskly, turning to the rest. "They won't take long realizing we're so few left."

"Yes," agreed Mor. "We can't think to hold the doors. We must pull back. Form barricades with the tables closer about the fire. Meave, you and Fardia can take one side, Conal and I the other. Hurry now!"

And they quickly began to shift the tables into a defensive ring.

Sentanta had by this time reached the level ground about the bruidhean.

There were several fights in progress around the inn as the last of the fleeing champions tried to battle through the outlaws that swarmed upon them like flies drawn to raw flesh.

Nearby he saw someone greatly beleaguered, fighting within a tight knot of a score of outlaws, just managing to hold them at bay. Without hesitation, the now enraged youth leaped into the fray.

His blood fury was fully upon him, the savage instincts that lay within him totally released. His handsome face was contorted into a ferocious mask aglow with battle light. With vast and savage power he fell upon the outlaws, laying about in great strokes with his sword, ripping through the close-packed men.

The force of his attack was overwhelming. As he had once

devastated his attackers in a long-ago hurley match, he now wreaked havoc on this hapless band. In moments, all still able were scrambling away to safety.

The warrior who had been the object of their attack was suddenly revealed.

"Cormac!" cried Sentanta, his battle lust giving way to joy at seeing his comrade.

"I should have known it was you," said Cormac, beaming in response. "The gods heard my prayers at last." He was bloodied by many wounds, panting heavily from the desperate fight.

Sentanta moved to him. "Are you badly hurt?"

"No. But Muinremar . . ." He crouched to the form of a warrior who lay by his feet. He examined the man, then looked up at his young friend, shaking his head in sorrow. "Dead. He fought well, but . . ."

"We can't help him," Sentanta said brusquely. "Let's try to save what others we still can!"

And together they headed boldly toward another seething knot of struggling men and flailing weapons.

Around the inn, Ingcel moved up to Morgor as he was taking off the head of a defeated champion. "Where is Mor?" the pirate demanded.

"I don't know," said Morgor curtly, lifting up his prize by its hair. "He must be still inside."

"Your old man said that he'd come out!" Ingcel persisted.

"They *are* coming out, fool!" spat Morgor, holding the dripping head up before the other's eyes and shaking it. "Look here! We're killing them!"

"And losing five for every one of theirs. We must have Mor!"

"He'll have to come out soon," Morgor assured him.

Above, another burst of lightning crackled past the inn from hilltop to hilltop.

Calatin's aim had now been properly homed in. The bolt of energy burst upon Cathbad's fire, scattering its burning wood in a great explosion. It knocked the druid back flat upon the ground. The rippling tendrils of blue lights played over him, enwrapping him tightly. Their sparks danced in his hair, flared in his eyes. His body was held rigid, strained so taut it seemed that it must snap, twitching with the energy coursing through his limbs.

At last it faded, releasing him. He lay unmoving save for his heaving chest. The faint drizzle of rain upon the dome ceased.

"Cathbad!" Fionualla cried, moving up toward him.

"Stay away!" he managed to gasp out. "Laeg, keep her away!"

The charioteer caught her arm, pulling her back. She struggled, but he held on.

With an immense and agonizing effort, Cathbad pulled himself up. The scattered remnants of the fire were burning out about him. He crawled to his open chest, brushed glowing debris from it, and began to rummage in its depths. On the opposite height, Calatin was showing some signs of fatigue, shoulders sagging, breathing more heavily after his last attack.

"Father, you can't keep up both spells!" a worried son called up to him. "Your strength is being drained. Stop now. The rain is ended. Cathbad's spell is broken."

"No!" he bellowed in return. He took one more deep breath and drew himself erect again. "Another strike will finish it!" he said fiercely. "This time I will make certain he never plagues me again!"

He lifted the druid rod once more to point into the clouds and once more the lightning obeyed his will, a bolt slanting down to strike the tip and gather there, forming another brilliant globe of flaring energy.

Calatin grinned with a malevolent satisfaction. He jabbed out with the rod. The light shot away, stretching into a shimmering, sapphire serpent's tongue of destructive power, licking out toward Cathbad.

On the little knoll, Cathbad continued to search desperately within the chest. Finally he grasped a small gold box. He looked across toward Calatin.

Chapter Fifty

Retributions

Concentrating his final strength, Cathbad rose suddenly, pulling the lid from the little box. His arm swept over his head in a curve, flinging out the contents. It was a fine, sparkling dust that flew up in a great cloud of shimmering silver above him, drifting in the night, spreading, forming into a shining gossamer screen of light, the glittering particles seeming to grow, to fuse, creating for a brief instant a single gleaming surface like polished glass.

That instant was enough. The surface acted as a mirror, reflecting the stream of light, sending it shooting back along the course on which it had come, back to its source.

Calatin saw it, but too late, standing aghast for a paralyzed second of realization before it struck the crag.

The whole peak of the spine of stone exploded beneath Calatin's feet. The sons below scattered before the force of the blast. The druid himself was hurled backward amid a shower of rock and fire, falling from sight beyond the rim of the high, steep ridge. The last flaming debris of the druid blaze showered down onto the blasted crag, flickering out.

The explosion, more spectacular and violent than any before, drew the attention of the outlaws to the ridge.

"By Llyr and Manannan!" cried a pirate. "Did you see that!"

And, in that same instant, the dome of light vanished.

"So much for your old warrior's magic and his promises," Ingcel told Morgor. He lifted his voice to call out, "Come on, my men, that's the end for us! We'll be getting nothing here for our pains but more quick death. Pass on the word to leave this place. Back to the sea!"

"Wait!" cried Fergel in dismay. "You can't abandon us."

"Can we not?" said Ingcel. "Then look."

The pirates, bloodied and decimated by this seemingly endless fight, were obeying with no argument, already withdrawing with great alacrity.

"But there can't be many left with Mor now," Fergel reasoned. "We can go in after him."

"So *you* say," Ingcel returned. "But there've been too many of us died already in this, and for no wealth I can see. Kill him yourselves."

"We don't need them," Morgor said to the exiles around him, looking with scorn upon the fleeing men. "There are enough of us to finish him."

The pirates' captain looked to Ferogain. "You can come with us, boy," he offered. "Or do you mean to stay with these madmen?"

"I will stay," the boy said in a tone of grim acceptance. "I must see it out with them."

"Then I am sorry," Ingcel told him with sincerity, clapping a hand to his shoulder, "for you never should have been here."

And with that he turned and followed after his retreating men, leaving the young Irishmen to look after them, some with expressions of regret.

"It doesn't matter!" Morgor shouted in a rallying way, calling their attention to him. "My fellow exiles, Mor is ours! To the inn!"

Cormac and Sentanta, now joined by one of the other champions they had rescued, were just finishing a skirmish to save the one called Sencha when they heard Ingcel's shout. They saw many of the company of outlaws suddenly quitting the fight, pelting away into the darkness.

"They're leaving!" Cormac said with elation.

But then they heard Morgor's rallying call and saw the fighters left behind turn and converge on the bruidhean.

"Not all," said Sentanta. "The rest are storming the inn."

"Mor is still in there," Cormac told him, "with only three others now."

"Then we must help him," his young comrade replied. "Come on!"

The two Ulstermen and the rescued champions rushed across the yard after the attacking exiles.

They came through a doorway into the bruidhean to see a wild melee already in progress before them. The four warriors wasted no time in diving into the fight. Falling upon the surprised attackers, they inflicted a terrible slaughter, slashing through the crowd of men like flails threshing pathways through a field of grain. Sentanta and Cormac fought with their usual great skill and strength augmented by their battle rage. The two other champions, as if getting revenge for their shame in having been forced to run, fought with an equal power and savagery, cutting down man after man.

Sentanta slammed one attacker back with his shield, hacked a second from his way with a single cut, and saw another before him lifting a sword to strike. He dived in. There was a hard, furious exchange, then they locked hilts. Sentanta was amazed to find that his opponent, though very slight, had great power. Then he looked into the grim, blood-spattered face so close before him.

Astonished, he suddenly stepped back, lowering his sword. But his opponent prepared to strike again.

"Meave!" he cried. "Wait!"

Confused by this, she hesitated, looking at this tall, muscled, hard-visaged warrior. But then her eyes met his, and there was the shock of recognition.

"Sentanta!" she said in amazement, lowering her sword.

"Where is Mor?" he asked urgently.

"The other side!"

His companions and Fardia were more than a match for the few exiles left around them now. He turned and started across the floor, fighting his way toward where Mor and Conal battled against much greater numbers.

Those two had been separated, each moving back to the hearth to keep their enemies at their front, each holding more than a half-dozen men at bay. Mor and Conal were streaked with the blood of countless minor wounds, but they had piled up the dead around them. The floor was washed with a thick flow of sticky blood, and the gore of their attackers stained their arms shoulder-high. Conal fought with all the savage cunning of an old warrior, and Mor battled with the fierce tenacity of a man who would never cease to fight while he still breathed.

But so occupied was the king by the row of attackers close before him that he wasn't aware of Morgor and his two brothers slinking back steadily behind them, peering past the straining bodies and flashing blades for a chance to strike at him. And farther back, watching the fight, stood Ferogain, his face a mask of confusion, his sword hanging in his hand.

Then Conal struck out at an attacker, and the man staggered away, a deep, lethal wound streaming at his throat. As he fell, Mor glimpsed his face, recognizing Fergel, his eldest foster-brother, and the tremor of dismay this sent through him caused the slightest hesitation, the most fractional lowering of his guard.

But the sharp eye of Morgor saw this momentary opening. With his ferret-quick reflexes he lunged in, beneath another's arm, his sword sinking deep into the high-king's side.

Mor yanked himself back off the blade, his eyes turning in surprise to meet Morgor's. Then his strength failed him and he fell, sliding down the hearth to the floor.

"He's mine!" cried Morgor. He grabbed his brothers, pushing them through the other men, jerking them around to face their fellow exiles. "See they all keep back," he ordered the two. "I'll finish him."

But Sentanta had finally reached them, and he charged into

the exiles grouped near Mor. They turned from the fallen king to face this new adversary and throw up a desperate defense as the whirlwind of his sweeping blade descended upon them.

Oblivious to this fight, obsessively fixed only on a single purpose now, Morgor stooped over the high-king. Mor, conscious but too sorely hurt to move, looked up to him.

"Finally, 'my King,'" Morgor said gloatingly. "Finally I'll have the prize I really want!"

He dropped his shield, then coiled his freed hand in Mor's long hair, pulling the helpless man's head up, exposing the length of neck. He smiled in triumph as his sword lifted.

"No!" shouted Ferogain, leaping in to stop him.

"Enough of you!" snarled Morgor, and shot his blade forward instead, striking through the boy's chest.

At the force of the thrust, the boy stumbled backward and crashed down, already dead. But his sacrifice gave Sentanta the time to act. Pushing past the last of his opponents, he drove in at Morgor. One of the other Maines tried to stop him, but a single, hard blow flung the man aside with a split skull.

As Morgor lifted his sword again and swept it down at the king's neck, he found another blade swinging in to knock it away.

He looked up into Sentanta's eyes.

"So, Ulster whelp, you came after all," he said with satisfaction. "Now we can finish the fight we started at the fair so long ago!"

And in a swift move he released Mor's hair, grabbed up his shield, and leaped toward Sentanta, lunging with his sword.

Sentanta's own reflexes were a match for his opponent's. He parried the thrust and struck back. Then ensued a flurry of exchanged blows, both weapons sweeping continuously with a speed that made them blurs of light.

When Morgor realized he could gain no advantage there, he abruptly leaped atop the hearth, striking down at Sentanta from the higher point. One massive, downward cut sank deep into the iron of the boy warrior's shield boss, sticking there, and Morgor yanked back, tearing the shield from Sentanta's arm. It came loose as his blade rose, flying away, clattering to the floor beyond a row of tables.

With sword alone now, Sentanta fended off blows from both Morgor's sword and shield. Then he saw a chance, catching Morgor's descending blade against his own, sweeping out with the other hand to catch Morgor's ankle, jerking the foot up.

Taken by surprise, Morgor lost his balance, toppling backward atop the fire. It had burned down to only glowing embers now, and he swiftly rolled out. His back was smoldering in a dozen spots, but in his mad thirst for the Ulster youth's blood he seemed oblivious to any pain, leaping over the hearth to come at Sentanta again.

It was Sentanta who took the offensive now, however, wielding his sword two-handed to drive Morgor back with blow after blow, so massive they began to buckle his opponent's shield.

"Mathra!" Morgor called desperately to his remaining brother. "At him!

Mathra came in beside his brother, lunging out at Sentanta. The boy parried and thrust out in return. Morgor moved forward, slamming his shield into his brother's back, knocking him forward.

The astonished Mathra was thrown directly onto Sentanta's blade. It cracked through his breastbone, sinking deep. His forward momentum sent him on, thudding into Sentanta, slamming him back while driving the blade on through to erupt from his back. Then Mathra toppled aside as Sentanta went down, yanking the embedded sword from the boy's hand.

Sentanta thudded to the ground unarmed. Morgor instantly leaped toward him, swinging down at him. The boy rolled sideways as the blade bit into the floor, kept on rolling as Morgor lifted his sword to strike again, and got under the shelter of a table just as the blade slashed deep into its planks.

He came up on the table's other side. Not far before him lay his shield. He grabbed for it as Morgor vaulted onto the tabletop.

He turned to see Morgor above him, bending forward to swing down at his head. In a desperate move Sentanta hurled the shield upward.

It caught Morgor in the stomach, the force of impact doubling him up, hurling him backward. He crashed down from the table to the floor.

Sentanta rose and moved around the table. Morgor lay on the blood-sprayed floor, stunned, panting for breath. Sentanta yanked his sword from the dead brother and stepped to Morgor. He kicked the sword from the fallen man's hand and lifted his own.

Morgor's eyes widened in terror. "No!" he gasped out. "You can't kill me. I'm beaten. I claim mercy! Mercy!"

The boy was stone-faced. He lifted his sword higher.

"No!" came the voice of Meave. "Don't be sullying your blade or your honor with his foul blood. It's for me to pronounce his death in Aileel's name."

She looked down at the whimpering man. "He is truly a traitor to Ireland, to Connacht, to the name of warrior. There should be no honest fighting man's end for him."

She leaned down, drawing the ornate dagger from his belt. "You body will be left to rot and feed the crows, Maine Morgor," she told him icily. "Now die like the scavenger that you are."

He screamed as she plunged the blade straight down into his heart. Then he jerked once, the cry cut off as death rattled in his throat, and sank back, stilled for good.

The two looked around from him to see the rest of the battle all but ended. Fardia, Cormac, and the others had come from the room's far side to deal out more carnage among the remaining exiles, and the few survivors still able were now running from the room.

"The high-king!" said Sentanta, moving to Mor.

He knelt and gently lifted the man, cradling his head. The others came in around them, Meave kneeling at Mor's other side. She gently pulled away the bloodstained cloth of his ripped tunic, examining the wound where the crimson flow pulsed, pulsed with the king's heartbeat. She looked up to Sentanta. He saw the truth in her eyes.

Mor saw it too. "A final wound, isn't it," he said with a strange calm. "I felt as much when the blade ran into me."

"My King," Sentanta began, but stopped, knowing there was no point in denying it.

"You came back, my loyal friend." said Mor, smiling at him. "I hoped you would."

"I could not do otherwise."

Mor lifted his head with an effort, looking across to where Ferogain lay crumpled against an overturned table.

"Ferogain," he said with sorrow. "He meant to save me at the last. I believe now that he never really meant to do me harm. What a sad, sad waste."

Exhausted by the effort, his head fell back and his eyes closed.

Fionualla, followed by Laeg and a scorched, ragged Cathbad, now came into the bruidhean. The two men helped her make her way through tables and fallen men to Conaire's side. Meave stood to make room for her, and she knelt down. Her face was drawn with her anguish, but she held back her tears as she put out a hand to stroke his face.

"Conaire," she said softly.

He had been sinking, but her touch and her voice roused him. He looked up at her, his wan face lighting with joy.

"My wife! My love! So you've come too!"

"She risked herself to bring us here, to save you," Cathbad told him.

"And I will not leave your side again," she promised, taking one of his hands and gripping it hard in both of hers.

"Then the gods haven't been unkind to me," he said. "I have what I've wished most to have—my wife and my friends with me."

"And your peace for Ireland, Conaire," added Meave. "I give my vow to you, I will not let it die."

"No, Meave!" he protested, but weakly now, his strength ebbing again. "No. Let it go. A dream it is, and should stay, for it's brought the end of many good men who might have lived as friends. Let it go, Meave, or it'll destroy you too."

MacCecht came through a door of the bruidhean, stopping to stare about at the devastation. Across his shoulders were slung two leather bags, swelled and dripping with their load of water. He saw the group around Mor and moved toward it, face filling with consternation as he realized that it was his high-king who lay there.

The others, seeing him, moved aside as he approached, allowing Mor's gaze to fall on him.

The king smiled at the stricken man. "Ah, faithful Mac-Cecht," he said in a fading voice. "So you brought it. Let me have a drink now, for I'd not die with this cursed thirst still on me."

The champion knelt, tears welling in his eyes. He put out the spout of the water bag. But before the cool, fresh water touched the lips of Conaire Mor, the high-king of Ireland slumped back, letting out his final breath in a long, low sigh.

Epilogue

The face of Conaire Mor looked up to the blue sky of a clear, autumn day.

He lay, as his father had not so long before, in state upon the simple wooden bier, the high burial mound with its glowing facade of white stones looming above him. But, unlike the wretched Eterscel, Mor's youthful face was relaxed, smooth, peaceful in its death. And around him clustered many scores of mourning chiefs, learned men, and common people, along with the large gathering of druids.

As Tara's high-druids went through the final portions of the funeral rites, the chieftains and champions of the various provinces eyed one another warily. Especially did they watch Conchobar MacNessa, who glared steadily across the bier to Meave, though her own sorrowful gaze was fixed on the face of her nephew.

Separate from all the province contingents stood the few surviving champions of the late high-king, Conal at their front. With them also stood Mor's widow, Fionualla, the druid Cathbad and Sentanta close at either side for support.

The lengthy rite at last came to its close. The gray-haired

chief ard-druid took up a brand from the nearby fire, made his last prayer to the watching gods, and thrust the flaming wood into the tinder of the bier. As the fire caught, crackling up through the bundles of dry sticks to envelop Mor, the mourners began to disperse.

"Are you all right?" Cathbad asked Fionualla.

She was pale, red-eyed, but she had stood up stoutly and unflinchingly through the funeral's long ordeal.

"Yes," she assured him. "In a way, I feel he is content now as he might never have been as king. I have our time together, short as it was. It will be enough."

"What will you do now?" Sentanta asked.

"Go back to my father's people. It was there I always belonged—where we belonged together. I can remember him more clearly there."

"Then it would be my honor to see a woman of such loyalty and courage to her home," Cathbad told her, and he escorted her to the waiting chariots.

As they rode off, back toward Tara, Sentanta turned to see Meave approaching him.

"Sentanta, it's sorry I am to have so brief a meeting after so many years," she said regretfully. "But I must get home. There are great duties waiting for me there. Even greater ones now."

"I am sorry it was such a sad event that brought us together," he replied.

"He did much for me," she said, looking toward the bier.

"And for me," he added. "I thought he was my whole life. Now . . . it's over."

She looked searchingly into his eyes. "No," she said emphatically. "No, it's just begun for you. I feel it. Something in me, some voice of the Others tells me that your destiny is far from completed here."

"And do your Sidhe feelings tell you if we will meet again?" he asked.

"I think we will." She shot a look at Conchobar, who was now pushing past the other warriors toward them, his look stormy. "I hope it will be as friends."

"There will never be friendship between Ulster and Connacht," the Ulster king raged, stepping up before her. "Not so long as *you* rule there! Any bond we had is ended with his death." He pointed to the bier where the fire now licked up around Mor's body. "With that foolish boy high-king went this foolish dream of peace, and you will never take his place."

"As you intend to do?" she hotly accused.

"I've no need to rule all Ireland," he told her haughtily. "Ulster is already her greatest power, as it has always been."

"That we will see," she said in an ominous tone.

He wheeled away from her and stalked to the chariots, followed by his chieftains and warriors, but Sentanta and Conal tarried behind.

"Goodbye," the young Ulsterman said to Meave. "We'll be returning to Tara now to gather our things. Then we go home. May the blessings of good Danu be on you."

"And on you, Sentanta," she said, leaning forward to brush his lips with hers.

"Goodbye, Queen Meave," Conal told her formally. Then he looked to Sentanta and the waiting Cormac. "Well, lads, it's time to go."

They went to their chariots and rode away from the high mound, across the green and glowing countryside.

Meave, now left alone with the small flock of Tara's druids, stood awhile longer, gazing at the bier as the smoke and flames fully engulfed the form of Conaire Mor. Then, finally, she too turned to start away.

A dark-cloaked man stood not far from her, framed in the black square of the tomb's entrance.

"My Queen," came a voice low, soft, and crooning. A hand pulled the hood back to reveal a broad and swarthy face.

"Calatin," she exclaimed, at first startled by his appearance. He seemed much more gaunt, more worn and battered than he had been before.

"My Queen, I ask your leave to ride back to Connacht with you," he said. "I've no more place here. I must find someplace to go."

She hesitated. Why did she feel a strange chill, as if a winter's sharp gust wafted from this man?

"My Queen, I could be a great help to you," he told her, his tone earnest, almost pleading. "Only give me a place, and I could be of great service to you, and to your king, and to Connacht. I know you wish it strong."

She glanced around to where Conchobar was still visible, riding so arrogantly away, then looked back at the waiting, hopeful druid.

She nodded. "Yes," she said in a determined way. "Yes, Calatin, you may ride with me."

*   *   *

The ruddy disk of a new dawn's sun lifted slowly through a
heavy overcast, throwing a fitful gray light upon the remnants
of a fire.

A flock of bright-robed druids picked over the fire's remains
like birds upon a carcass, gathering the ashes of a king, while
from still-smoldering embers there rose the last, faint trails of
smoke from a dead dream.

A curious raven swooped low over it, then sailed up again,
flapping away toward the southeast. Soon it peered down upon
another mournful scene: a small band of Ulstermen, slowly
making their way back toward their own land, riding away from
the curved, high fortress wall of the great dun called Tara an
Rie.

Glossary

Following are the approximate pronunciations of some of the more difficult names.

Cerna: Ker-na
Conchobar: Kon-o-var (now Conner)
Conaire Mor: Kon-a-ree More
Connacht: Kon-akt
Cruchane: Kru-hane
Dechtire: De-tra
Donnchadh: Don-a
Emain Macha: Emain Ma-ha
Eochaid: Eo-aid
Eterscel: Eter-skel
Fer Coille: Fir-Koila
Fionualla: Fin-ola
MacCecht: Mak-Kekt
Meave: Mave
Murchadh: Mur-ka
Naoise: Nay-sa

The following are terms about which the reader might appreciate having some further information.

Ard-rie: Ard means "high." Rie means "king." This designates the supreme leader in the ancient Celtic world.

Ath Cliath (Ah Kliah): Now known as Dublin, Ireland.

Brandub: Means "black raven." A popular board game involving gaming pieces and dice.

Brehon: A justice of the Celtic court who advised the rulers in the dispensing of laws.

Bruighaid: (brew-y): The official entrusted with the running of public houses of hospitality in Ireland. A most honored profession.

Bruidhean (breen): A public house of hospitality, usually set up on the junction of several roads. It was intended to serve the needs of any traveler without charge and is an excellent example of the characteristic hospitality for which the Irish are known.

Dagda: One of the greatest champions and oldest members of the Tuatha de Danann. He figured prominently in the destruction of the Fomor hold on Ireland, hundreds of years earlier, afterward refusing the kingship of his people. In later mythology, he becomes a sort of earth-father figure to the mortal races.

Danu: The queen of the magical isle known as Tir-na-nog ("Land of the Ever Young"). She aided an outcast and wandering tribe of mortals, giving them magic powers. In gratitude they took the name Tuatha de Danann ("Children of Danu"). She became the supreme goddess in the pantheon of the mortal races.

Druid: A member of a class of intellectuals with broad knowledge of both the natural and supernatural realms. Though now largely associated with a pagan religion, the druids actually functioned as political advisers and scholars. Their training was long and arduous, as was that of the bardic class with which they were interrelated. They held a high position in Celtic society, nearly equal to the kings in rank. Though they could utilize tremendous magical forces, few abused this ability as Calatin did. Most, like Cathbad, were more than content in their well-respected roles and sought wisdom rather than power.

Dun Dalgan: Now the city of Dundalk, on the northwest coast of Ireland.

Emain Macha (Emain Ma-ha): This site of Ulster's greatest dun is near presentday Armagh in Northern Ireland.

Fidchell: Another board game, somewhat like chess, utilizing two sets of men pegged into position on a board.

Filidh: Finally meaning "poet," it originally meant more of a seer. These highly specialized learned men were, like the druids, trained for years in special schools, learning to compose poetry glorifying their rulers and chronicling important historic events.

Firbolgs: An ancient race, once closely related to the Tuatha de Danann. A division of the two caused rivalry and saw the Firbolg tribes devastated at the first battle of Maugh Turiedh some fifteen hundred years before Sentanta's birth. The invading Milesians found the scattered Firbolg tribes and quickly made them a subject race.

Gessa: A concept of taboo considered most important in the Celtic society. It was the notion that some things must be done in a certain way and that others must be avoided altogether. (Fergus MacRogh, for example, had a gessa that he must not leave a feast in progress.) Violation of a gessa would inevitably lead to trouble, loss of honor, or even death.

Granian: A sunroom. From evidence in the ancient tales, this architectural feature was not uncommon in the more prestigious duns.

Lough (Lock): The Celtic word for "lake."

Lugh Lamfada (Loo Lamvada): Called "Lugh of the Long Arm" in English. It was Lugh who led the Riders of the Sidhe in the defeat of the monstrous Fomor, making the Tuatha de Danann ascendant in Ireland. Legend hints that Lugh is also the true father of Sentanta.

Milesians: Another name for the Celts (Kelts). The Clan Milith is said to have come to Ireland from Spain (Espan) about 1500 B.C. The Tuatha de Danann, recognizing them as the proper inheritors of the island, retired before them into their mounds and sacred places.

Morrigan: Chief goddess of battle, also called the Bloody Raven because she could take on the crow or raven shape at will. In altered form she appears later in literature as Morgan La Fey in the Arthurian legends. Like Meave, the Morrigan is both a good friend and a ruthless enemy, a fit representative of the dual nature of Ireland.

Ollav: The highest rank of poet. His rank was equal to that of regional kings and chieftains.

Serpent's Egg: In ancient Celtic magic, this was a strange and powerful amulet connected with the druids, said to be formed from the foam produced by sea serpents twining themselves together.

Sidhe (Shee): Meaning "People of the Hidden Places," this is another name for the Tuatha de Danann.

Slighe Midluachra (Slee Midlakra): "Slighe" meaning "road" and Midluachra meaning "northern," this is one of five great roads said to radiate from Tara, Ireland's heart, to various parts of the country.

Tailteen Fair: A great triennial fair held on the hill of Tailteen, near Tara. The hill, it is said, is named for Taillta, foster-mother to Lugh Lamfada.

Tara an Rie: Meaning "Tara of the Kings," this was the political and religious center of the Celtic period in Ireland. This beautiful site can be found not far to the northwest of presentday Dublin. The rings and mounds of the ancient fortifications are still identifiable and are well worth visiting.

Tir-na-nog: This translates as "Land of the Ever Young," although it is also known by many other names, including "The Land of Promise." Experts disagree on its exact location, but many place it somewhere in the Atlantic.

Tuatha de Danann (Too-a-ha dae Don-an): A race of beings with long lives and great magical powers. They once held sway in Ireland but withdrew to hidden, underground dwellings (Sids) after their defeat by invading Milesian tribes. They take little direct action in the affairs of mortal man, but they do watch over him with interest and sometimes help or hinder him. The belief in these beings (also called the "Sidhe," the "Hidden," or the "Other") still exists among some in Ireland today. The Banshee and the Leprechaun are the most popularly known remnants of this once proud race.

Ulster: This ancient province now makes up most of what is known as Northern Ireland. It is intriguing that even in those early days, Ulster evidenced that separateness and hardness of spirit which were to mark it through the years. And the high passions, internal struggles, and unforgiving hearts which were to be its sorrow to the present day are also a part of these ancient tales.

About the Author

Kenneth C. Flint became interested in Celtic mythology in graduate school, where he saw a great source of material in this long neglected area of Western literature. Since then he has spent much time researching (in the library and abroad in England and Ireland) those legends and incorporating them into works of fantasy that would interest modern readers.

Riders of the Sidhe, *Champions of the Sidhe*, and *Master of the Sidhe* tell of the Fomor invasion of ancient Ireland. *Challenge of the Clans*, *Storm Shield*, and *The Dark Druid* recount the saga of Irish hero Finn MacCumhal.

Mr. Flint is a graduate of the University of Nebraska with a Master's Degree in English Literature. He has taught in the Department of Humanities at the University of Nebraska at Omaha and served as Chairman of English for the Plattsmouth Community Schools. He now writes full time.

Kenneth Flint lives in Omaha with his wife Judy (whose family has roots in Ireland) and his sons Devin and Gavin.

The Darksword Trilogy

by

Margaret Weis and Tracy Hickman

Here are the adventures of the angry young Joram, born into a world where his lack of magic powers means an instant death sentence. When he meets the catalyst Saryon, they become allies and together forge a sword capable of absorbing magic: the Darksword. Joined by the young mage Mosiah and the trickster Simkin, Joram embarks on a perilous journey, rising to power he never dreamed of, and finding himself faced with the greatest challenge in his people's history.